THE
Lonely
Orphan

Cathy loves writing because it gives pleasure to others. She finds writing an extension of herself and it gives her great satisfaction. Cathy says, 'There is nothing like seeing your book in print, because so much loving care has been given to bringing that book into being' Cathy lives Cambridgeshire.

Also by Cathy Sharp

Halfpenny Street Orphans
The Orphans of Halfpenny Street
The Little Runaways
Christmas for the Halfpenny Orphans
The Boy with the Latch Key
An Orphan's Courage

Children of the Workhouse
The Girl in the Ragged Shawl
The Barefoot Child
The Winter Orphan

East End Daughters
A Daughter's Sorrow
A Daughter's Choice
A Daughter's Dream

Button Street Orphans
An Orphan's Promise
An Orphan's Sorrow
An Orphan's Dream

CATHY SHARP

THE Lonely Orphan

HarperCollins*Publishers*

HarperCollins*Publishers*
1 London Bridge Street
London SE1 9GF

www.harpercollins.co.uk

HarperCollins*Publishers*
1st Floor, Watermarque Building, Ringsend Road
Dublin 4, Ireland

Published by HarperCollins*Publishers* 2022
1

A catalogue record for this book
is available from the British Library

ISBN: 978-0-00-838770-9

This novel is entirely a work of fiction.
The names, characters and incidents portrayed in it are
the work of the author's imagination. Any resemblance to
actual persons, living or dead, events or localities is
entirely coincidental.

Typeset in Sabon LT Std by Palimpsest Book Production Ltd,
Falkirk, Stirlingshire

Printed and Bound in the UK using 100% Renewable Electricity
at CPI Group (UK) Ltd

MIX
Paper from
responsible sources
FSC™ C007454

This book is produced from independently certified FSC™ paper
to ensure responsible forest management.

For more information visit: www.harpercollins.co.uk/green

CHAPTER 1

March 1939

Luke fled into the darkness of the night, his heart thumping, panting in terror lest they should catch him. At last he'd escaped from that place and the pain of constant beatings. It was called an orphanage, was supposed to be a safe haven for orphans, but for Luke it had never been more than a dark place that held him prisoner. His torturers were the woman they called Matron, who caned his hands and legs, and the Master who groped him and tried to do more. Luke had fought him off each time and been beaten – but tonight he'd been ready, his weapon a poker he'd found when he was shut in the coalhole as a punishment.

When the Master came at him and ordered him to undress, Luke had hit him with the poker so hard that the man went down and the boy had fled through the open door. He'd known exactly where he could climb a tree and get over the high wall that surrounded his prison, scaling it in the minutes before the Master

1

came to himself and sounded the alarm. Now he was free and he was determined never to return to that terrible place. He pitied the poor children trapped there, all those who would never have the courage to fight back or escape as he had.

Luke had no idea what awaited him in the outside world, because he could remember nothing of life before he came there. Perhaps there had been a time when he lay in a soft cot and a sweet face looked down at him and smiled. Did he remember the touch of soft hands or was that merely his imagination, his longing for something other than hard faces and cold voices that scolded, sticks that beat?

Once, after a particularly hard beating, he'd been so ill that Matron had called the doctor and he'd been taken to hospital where his bed had been soft and clean, and the nurses had smiled as they washed, dressed and fed him until he was well again. He should have run then, but he'd been lulled into a sense of security by the kindness of the doctors and nurses.

The Master had told them his injuries came from falling out of a tree and the doctors had gently scolded him and said he must be more careful. He'd tried to tell them it wasn't a fall but they wouldn't listen; the Master had told them he had a vivid imagination, was always telling stories, and so they thought he'd made it up. He'd only tried once because they'd given him some medicine to make him sleep. When he woke up, he was back in his prison and although the Master ignored him for a while, the thrashings started again and he knew that even worse things happened to other boys and girls. Luke's strength had saved him from the worst of it and it was that physical and mental strength that had made him plan his escape.

Now he was free and he knew that he had to get far, far away. He had read about London, the capital city, where there were millions of people, so he had to get there where he could get lost in the streets and no one would ever be able to trace him. Matron couldn't pounce on him and drag him off to be caned because he looked at her insolently, and the Master couldn't do the unspeakable things to him that he wanted to.

He was free! He had a bread roll in his pocket that he'd stolen from breakfast the previous day and hidden. In a moment or two he would eat it, when he'd found somewhere safe to sit for a while and think. Somehow, he had to reach London – he could find work there, he knew it. He was nearly thirteen, according to Matron, although he had no idea of his true birth date because he'd never been told it, but knew he looked older because of his size and strength. Surely, he would find work among all those millions of people? He had nothing but the clothes he stood up in and no money, so from now on he would live on his wits and eat what he could earn, beg or steal . . . No! Something inside made him turn from stealing. It would be a last resort. Luke wasn't bad, despite what Matron and Master said of him and he wasn't stupid. He'd learned all he could when he had the chance, although all too often his punishment was to sit in the corridor, staring at the wall. However, he could write his name, calculate in his head and he knew many things from what he'd read in the books he'd borrowed from the shelves in the school-room and hid under his pillow. It was how he'd learned about London, the King and Queen and the Great War that had happened years before he was born.

Luke was instinctively honest. He didn't want to do anything that the woman with the soft hands and sweet smile would be ashamed of and wondered if she was his mother. He must have had parents, but no one would ever tell him what had happened to them, though once Matron had smiled as she told him he had no one.

'You're alone in the world,' she'd told him. 'This is all you've got – all you'll ever have, so behave and make things better for yourself.'

Luke hadn't believed her, even before his trip to hospital. Other children told him about their lives before the home, and after he'd seen those nurses he'd known there was another life if he could just find it. He'd planned for his escape all the time, wondering how best to get out. Luke owned nothing. He'd been given nothing but his food and clothes so he had no possessions to take with him and no real idea of the value of money having never had a penny to spend.

He knew a few of the other children received visits from aunts, uncles or grandparents and had seen the children given a book, some sweets or money, but Luke was never given anything and no one ever visited him.

There must have been money somewhere in that

place, but Luke didn't know where it was kept; in any case, that would have been stealing, so when he'd left it was with just the bread roll. It didn't bother him. Perhaps it was true that you didn't miss what you'd never had, but those few days of comparative freedom in the hospital had shown him what he was missing and he'd known what he needed to do.

A sense of elation came to him as he saw the bus shelter ahead. He went inside and sat down, out of the wind. He chewed the roll slowly, knowing that it might be a while before he got another. Although Luke had never been on a bus, he had seen them going by the orphanage. People sat in them and were taken places so he needed to get a ride on one heading somewhere – but he also knew that money was needed, and he had none.

Sighing, he turned to leave, but just as he did, he saw something silver shining in the corner of the bus stop and bent to pick it up, turning it over and over in his hand, reading the words. There was a picture of the King's head on one side, some writing and a date, and on the other an engraving and more words. Luke read them with difficulty and then realised that he was holding a half-crown – he'd learned about money in arithmetic. How far would that take him?

Luke slipped the money into his pocket and sat down again. He'd found it, so it wasn't stealing. As he debated what to do next, a bus came along the road and then stopped. Without consideration, Luke got on and went to sit down at the front. There were six other passengers in seats and none of them looked at him beyond a passing glance. When the conductor came, Luke offered the half-crown and the man asked where he wanted to go. He said Leicester, because that was where the hospital was, and the conductor nodded and gave him a smaller coin and a ticket. He looked at the coin. It said three pence on it and he pocketed it. He wasn't sure what it would buy, but perhaps a small roll or something. It didn't matter. Finding the bus fare for the first stage of his journey showed that he was meant to leave. He would live and work in Leicester for a while and then make his way to London. The hospital was too close to the orphanage for him to stay there for long . . .

CHAPTER 2

April 1939

Betty Stewart sighed as she left her work that morning. She'd been given a few hours cleaning at the Rosie Infirmary by the Matron, Miss Mary Thurston, for which she was very grateful. Since her husband Tony's sudden death two years earlier, Betty was finding life harder and harder. It wasn't the scrubbing of the wards and toilets that bothered her so much as how to manage her small wages and feed her two children adequately. Matron had been kind to her and given her a decent wage, though it was still hardly enough, and there was nothing left over at the end of the week. However, she enjoyed her work and she liked some of the nurses, especially Nurse Jenny and Nurse Lily. Sister Rose was nice, though her tongue could be sharp.

Betty sighed. She didn't really dislike the nurse or mind her ways; it was just the drab, awfulness of her life that was dragging her down. Why did Tony have to die like that? Leaving her with nothing but the debt he owed to one of the men he'd worked with on the ships?

The man with dark red hair had appeared a month after she'd used her insurance club to bury Tony, demanding the sum of fifty pounds as a down payment on a debt he said Tony owed. According to Red Jansson, Tony had lost a hundred and fifty pounds to him in a gambling game. Betty had never known that her husband gambled when he was on the ships, though he'd often spoken of other men as being fools with their hard-earned wages.

Betty had never thought he would be fool enough to do it himself and she wasn't sure whether to believe the stranger at her door. In the end she just told him that she was penniless and slammed the door in his face.

The second time he'd accosted her, she'd told him to leave her alone or she would go to the police. 'I know my Tony wouldn't do that!' she'd shouted at him and brandished her sharp carving knife at him. 'I've told the police about you and one of them lives just up the road. Come near me again and I'll have you arrested for lies and assault.'

'Proud bitch – just like that cocky bugger, but I done for him. He thought he'd got the better of me but he cheated me of my rights and I told him I'd get even – and I did!' He'd leered at her evilly. 'You wait and see. I want money or I'll do to you what I did to him.'

He lunged towards her, but Betty struck out with her knife, scoring his cheek and leaving a bloody trail. He'd jumped back and, his hand to his cheek, gave her such a look that her blood ran cold, but she'd brandished her knife again and he'd run off, and though Betty lived in fear that he might return, two years had since passed.

Nearly six months after Tony died, the purser of his last ship brought her his effects, apologising for not getting them to her sooner but he'd been stuck on board the ship suffering from influenza the last time they were in London. Inside the brown paper parcel, she'd found an envelope with her name on it and some money inside. She opened it and counted the dirty one-pound notes. There were nearly two hundred of them and a note in Tony's writing that made her heart catch with pain.

Betty love, this is for you if anything happens to me. I've never been one for the gambling, but this voyage I got drawn into it through no fault of mine and I won. Some of it from a vengeful brute. He thinks I cheated him, so I gave this to the purser and asked him to give it to you if anything happened to me. I thought there might be enough to set me up in a little shop and I'd give up the sea and look after you and the kids – but if you're reading this, forgive me for being a fool and leaving you to cope.

Always loved you, Betty, lass, and the kids.

The tears had flowed then. Betty had thought she was getting over her grief, but his letter brought it all flooding back. At first, she hadn't wanted to touch the money but, over the years, she'd used it little bit by little bit. She'd had to. If Red ever came back after it, she would have nothing left to give him.

Walking home that morning, in early April 1939, she passed Jeff Marshall at the garage. He smiled at her as she approached. She knew he liked her, but Betty couldn't bring herself to be friendly with anyone just yet. She was too walled in with her grief, too sad and angry at life for taking away the man she loved and needed.

Tony's letter had seemed to warn that he might die and she'd cursed him for being a fool; but as time passed she understood that he'd had enough of the sea and had hoped he might be able to settle at home with her, so he needed money to do that. She understood, but still wished he'd come back to her. His hard-won money had slipped through her fingers – admittedly, on bills and necessities – but she hated that she hadn't been clever enough to do anything with it. Tony had always been the clever one and without Tony she was nothing, couldn't seem to cope or face up to life as she had previously.

Young Tim, her son, was like his father. He'd got a brain and was able to think things through. Tony had had hopes for him and said he wouldn't let him go to sea. 'It's hard on a man being away from his family all the time, Betty,' he'd told his wife. 'If anything – God forbid – should happen to me, you make sure Tim stays at school and gets a proper education so that he can get a good job – do you hear me?'

'Yes, I hear you,' Betty had said. 'I'll make sure he

stays on and takes his exams.' And she was doing her best to keep her son at school and make sure that he did his homework and though he had a habit of slipping off behind her back, he'd always done the work and got good grades at school.

Jeff Marshall was busy cleaning one of the posh motors he serviced for wealthy clients. She supposed he must be good at his work since he was always busy and there were never less than three cars in his workshop anytime she passed.

'Good day, Mrs Stewart,' he said, stopping his work to look at her. His smile invited her to stand and talk but she ignored it. 'Done your work for today?'

'Yes, I've finished,' Betty said with a brisk nod. 'Good day to you, Mr Marshall. I can't stop. I have a lot to do . . .' She knew he watched her walk away and that he was shaking his head. Perhaps she was a bit rude to him sometimes, and maybe she was a fool, but she couldn't bring herself to chat to another man; it would be a betrayal to Tony.

Tim took the shillings and sixpences from his pocket and started to count them. He put three shillings into his mother's housekeeping pot and smiled. She never asked him how it got there, so perhaps she took it for granted that it was hers. She never asked what he did after school as long as he did his homework and so Tim worked as often as he could both in the evenings and on Saturdays, and even on a Sunday if he was needed, though his mother would not like that if she knew. However, his mother worked all hours to feed and clothe him and his sister Jilly and it wasn't her fault if she couldn't manage. He knew she did her very best and he loved her.

She looked so sad sometimes that his heart ached for her and he wished he was old enough to leave school and earn a proper wage rather than a shilling here for sweeping paths and sixpence there for washing people's front widows. Tim knew his parents had wanted him to stay on at school and acquire enough book-learning to earn a good wage. He was clever enough to pass all his exams at school and was in the top five in his class, found it easy to write, read and do sums in his head, but he didn't want to sit in an office all his life.

Tim had decided, when his father died at sea, that he would not go on the ships, but he still wanted an active life. He just wasn't sure what he wanted to do yet.

Hearing his mother at the door, the boy moved away from the mantelpiece and turned as she entered, smiling at her as he saw she was carrying a newspaper packet. She'd been to buy fish and chips; one portion of fish and a large portion of chips which they would all share. Mum had made pickled onions in the autumn and they still had a few remaining in the big jar, which they saved to have with their Friday-night treat.

His mother took the plates she'd left to warm in the oven by the range, setting them on the table and sharing out the fish and then the chips. She always gave Tim the biggest piece of fish, because she said he was a growing lad and needed it, but he always sneaked a bit back on her plate when she wasn't looking.

She went to her pot on the mantel and took it

down, frowning as she counted the money. 'I didn't think I had quite as much,' she remarked looking puzzled and then pleased. 'Good. I can pay the rent and still have enough to buy a bag of coal.'

'Oh, this fish is good, Mum,' Tim said and looked at his sister. 'Eat yours, Jilly. Aren't you hungry?'

'Not very,' Jilly said. 'I had strawberry jam and butter on fresh bread at Maisie's house.'

'Oh, Jilly, why did you spoil your tea?' Betty asked, looking worried. 'You know we have fish and chips on Friday.'

'I like strawberry jam better . . .' Jilly pouted.

She pushed her plate away with all her fish untouched and only a few chips eaten. Tim grinned and reached for it, scooping it onto his plate.

'Don't worry, Mum. I can eat Jilly's share,' Tim said and did so, leaving Jilly to scowl at him as she got down from the table and went to play with her rag doll.

'I'll give you a piece of cake later, before you go to bed, Jilly,' Betty said. 'It's jam Swiss roll so you'll like that.'

The little girl's frown disappeared and she smiled, singing a nursery rhyme as she settled down with her old doll. Mum looked at Tim, smiling as he cleared his plate. 'You're growing up, Tim. I'll soon have to think about a pair of long trousers for you, though I can't afford them just yet.'

She would buy them when she had enough money, which meant he had to earn more to help her. But first he had to find someone to give him a regular job.

CHAPTER 3

Nurse Jenny sighed as she entered the infirmary building. This was the last day that her sister would work here, because she was having a baby, and they were giving her a little party at the end of the day to celebrate. Lily and her husband, Chris, had been living with Jenny in the house Gran had left them but now they were moving out to the suburbs. Chris had bought a lovely house with a nice garden and double bow windows at the front. He was a captain in the army who'd been working undercover when they'd first met, and he'd wanted their child to be born in a better area. Lily was excited by the move, though she'd hugged Jenny and told her she would visit regularly.

'I'd say you could come and live with us, but it would be too far to travel for your work every day, love,' she'd told her sister. 'But you must come to me when you have the day off and we can have lunch together.'

'I'd like that. But what about your half of the house, Lily? Do you want me to pay you rent – or would you rather I moved out so that we can sell?'

'Neither,' Lily had told her firmly. 'Gran left it to both of us and just because I'm moving out doesn't mean I'll push you out or make you pay me for it.'

'I ought to pay something,' Jenny said awkwardly. 'You're entitled to your share.'

'Gran would turn in her grave if I did that, love. No – if you get married one day and you either want to buy or sell, we will, but for now I'm content for you to live there – it'll be hard enough for you to pay the bills on your own as it is.'

Jenny had nodded. That was part of her concern. She and Lily had paid everything between them and that might prove difficult on her own, because Jenny enjoyed spending her wages on clothes and having fun.

Lily had spoken of when Jenny married, but that didn't look likely at the moment. She was being courted by Michael Grey, a taxi driver who also used his own quite luxurious car for private hires. But although he kissed her with enthusiasm when they were together and took her dancing, out for nice meals, and to the pictures, he'd made no mention of wanting to get married. Jenny suspected that he enjoyed his freedom too much to settle down and for a long time that had suited her, but with Lily starting a family and moving out, Jenny was feeling left behind.

Why had she never found a man who loved her so much he couldn't live without her? Was it her own fault? Sometimes, she thought perhaps she demanded too much from others. She'd courted Lily's husband for a while and, though her sister had secretly fallen in love with him, she'd never said a word until Jenny threw him over. If Jenny had loved him the way Lily did, it would be her moving into the posh house and expecting her first baby.

'Good morning, Jenny. Why the glum face?' Sister Rose asked as she reached the children's ward and prepared for work. 'You should be full of it today – this is a big day for Lily.'

'Yes, I know,' Jenny said. 'She'll love the party we're giving her, Sister – and so shall I.' She smiled ruefully. 'I suppose I'm not looking forward to living alone. The house will seem lonely without her. Chris is often gone on army business, but Lily has always been there.'

'She'll still be there for you – on the end of a phone or a bus ride away,' Sister Rose said. 'Besides, a lovely young girl like you must have loads of friends and suitors.'

Jenny nodded, but still wasn't sure whether she was in love with Michael. He was fun and very sure of himself – Lily thought him cocky, and he was, but Jenny quite liked that. He'd done well for himself and he was teaching her to drive his car as well as taking her to the places she liked to visit. She did like him a lot – but would she really want to marry him, even if he got round to asking?

Jenny smiled inwardly. She was too contrary. Gran had always said so and she'd been very wise. She shook her head. It was time she got on with her work and stopped feeling sorry for herself. Sister Rose was right. This was a big day for Lily. She was giving up the job she loved to live in her new home and, in a few months, she would have a child to care for.

'You must be so excited,' Sister Rose said when she shared a coffee with Lily a little later that morning. 'What does Chris think of the baby coming?'

'Over the moon, of course,' Lily told her with a happy smile. 'We both are, Rose. His only concern is what is going on in Germany . . . those poor Jews! Look what happened to them last November when their houses and shops were broken into and so many of the men were beaten up and dragged off to concentration camps. Even that horrible old Kaiser who pretty well started the last war said that for the first time he was ashamed to be a German. Chris thinks it really will come to war – especially now they're talking about bringing in conscription.'

'Yes, and he is probably right,' Rose agreed. 'I hate to think of it – and it must be much worse for you, with Chris being in the army.'

'I've got used to the separation and to his being in danger,' Lily replied. 'I hope war won't happen, but if it does, Chris will be in the midst of it from the start. It is what he does best and I couldn't stop him, even if I wanted to.'

Rose nodded, reflecting that it was one thing she didn't have to worry about with her husband. Peter, a doctor, was still in a wheelchair and any thought of serving in the army was out of the question. Besides, he was dedicated to his work with the elderly and sick of the East End, working devotedly at the free clinic, talking to his patients, giving them medicines and helping in any way he could, his kindness often the only comfort they had in their lives, even though she suspected he himself was in more pain than he let on.

'Well, I shall be visiting when I can,' she told Lily with a smile, 'and you must visit us, here at the Rosie – and at my home. I want our friendship to continue, Lily.'

'Of course, it will, Rose.' Lily hugged her. 'You're a good friend – and I'll be visiting Jenny most weeks anyway. I'll probably have more time than her, at least until Baby is born.'

'Jenny isn't looking forward to living on her own, is she?'

'No.' Lily frowned. 'We've lived in that house since we were kids and it will feel really lonely for her – though perhaps she'll marry soon.'

'Is she still courting that taxi driver?'

'Yes – though I'm never sure whether she really wants him or not,' Lily admitted. 'When I fell for Chris I fell hard – but Jenny doesn't seem to take any man seriously.'

'Perhaps she hasn't found the right one,' Rose suggested. 'Once she's sure she will want to be with him day and night.'

'Yes.' A little smile touched Lily's lips. 'One of these times, she'll fall hard and it will be a big shock to her.' She laughed. 'We all need someone to love – being lonely is terrible, Rose. I wouldn't wish it on anyone.'

'No, that's what Peter says. It's one of the worst things his patients have to endure – their loneliness . . .'

CHAPTER 4

Luke looked hungrily in the window of the fish and chip shop in Leicester. On the streets, alone and friendless, he had no money in his pocket and he knew that the shop wouldn't give him a bag of crispies – the bits from the fish batter that came off in the oil – because the man had told him he could have some if he bought chips but not otherwise.

He turned away disconsolately, feeling miserable because it was harder to be alone and to find work than he'd imagined. He'd only earned a few pence in days. Hands in pockets and freezing despite the mild day, Luke almost wished himself back in the orphanage; then a picture of the master's face came to his mind and he shook himself. He would rather die than go back!

'Excuse me, young man – can you tell me the way to the bus station please?'

Luke looked at the lady who had spoken. She was elderly and looked approachable so he smiled and nodded. 'Yes, ma'am, I'll take you there – if you will follow me.'

'Will you really? How kind! I've been visiting my friend and missed the last train but understand I can get a bus if I'm in time.'

'It isn't far, missus,' Luke said and set off at a steady pace. She followed, walking with small quick steps but managing to keep up with him. He took her by the shortest route and she saw the bus she needed standing there.

'Oh, thank you! I'm just in time.' She hurried off and spoke to the driver, who motioned that she should get on, but instead she called out to Luke, 'Here, young man. Thank you!'

Luke deftly caught the coin she spun him, staring as he saw it was a florin. Just for showing her where the bus station was! Fancy that! He called out a thank you, though she was on the bus and probably didn't hear. Luke smiled as he ran back to the chip shop, went in and bought sixpence-worth of chips and some crispies with salt and a sprinkle of vinegar.

Munching happily as he walked away, Luke wondered if he should look for people who seemed to need help in future. Strangers who visited for the day might not know their way round and Luke now knew every street and alley, because he had walked them all. He had nowhere to sleep and it was better to keep moving than to sit in doorways for long. He also knew what time the buses ran and where they went, and he knew that it was cheaper to travel to London on the train than the bus – not least because it was sometimes possible to travel a short distance by using a platform ticket to get onto a platform and then hopping aboard a train. It wasn't exactly honest but he'd seen men who looked hard up do it, because he often hung about near the entrance where it was warm and, occasionally, he found things he could use there, such as discarded newspaper to put in his shoes and twice he'd found a sandwich packet with untouched food, which had tasted nice. He'd also once reminded a gentleman not to leave his umbrella and been given threepence for his trouble.

Luke smiled as he touched his change in his pocket. That little lady had been generous, so yes, he would look out for others like her and see if he could help them, because as soon as he had enough for his fare, he was going to London.

Leicester was too close to the orphanage and Luke had already had one narrow escape. He'd seen the Master getting on a train for up north and was glad the man hadn't seen him. He knew that if he was spotted, the police would hunt him down so he had to leave soon.

A few days later Luke was feeling pretty good about the way things were going. Since the elderly lady had given him that florin his luck seemed to have turned. He'd found a shilling on the floor in the gentleman's toilets at the station and he'd been given another for reminding a lady not to leave her bag on the shelf after buying a ticket. He'd directed three people who looked lost to where they wanted to go, and he now had a whole five shillings and sixpence in his pocket. It was time to begin his great adventure in London. He bought a ticket for the next stop on the line and had decided that he was going to stay on until the train emptied itself at the end of the line. He would get off, clutching a platform ticket he'd already got, then walk off near a lady who looked friendly and say in a loud voice, 'I'm glad you came to stay, Auntie . . .' as he went past the collector. If the man noticed anything odd, he would just run like hell.

Luke smiled to himself as he found a seat and sat down. He was on his way and who knew what he would find at the next place? As long as he managed to get further away from the Master and the place he hated it didn't matter when he finally reached London. He would get there one day and then his fortune would be made.

Luke soon found life was harder in a strange town. He could no longer offer to direct people, because he didn't know the way himself and there didn't seem much work in Huntingdon, the first town he'd stopped off in for a few days. It was a quiet town that came to life when it had a market and he was conscious that people stared if he stood around. So, after a week, he caught a train to Cambridge where he immediately felt more comfortable. It was lovely with all the greens and the colleges and he did manage to earn a few shillings helping one of the stallholders on the market, so he would have liked to linger for a while, but something about London called to him, telling him that he needed to be in that magical city that was now only a name to him.

He never had enough money in his pocket to buy a ticket all the way to London and he really didn't like dodging the ticket inspector; it was dishonest and

Luke was an honest boy, so he was forced to take his time and complete his journey in stages, spending a few days in each town or village that he passed through.

Once, he got work with a farmer taking cattle to market. Luke enjoyed that and Alfie fed him well, however he didn't have enough work to keep him on full-time, but the five shillings he earned bought Luke a ticket most of the way to St Albans. A few times, he used the platform ticket dodge to go an extra stop or two but he was always uncomfortable when he did and asked the lady with the soft hands, who lived only in some long-buried memory, to forgive him.

'If I've done wrong, Mum, it's 'cos I have to . . .'

Life was hard on the streets. Luke occasionally saw and spoke to others down on their luck, usually old men and women who, like him, walked the streets endlessly. Once or twice he saw a child running wild but mostly it was the old or infirm, some of them injured ex-soldiers. One, named Tom, advised him to seek out the Sally Army when he got to London. 'They'll help yer, lad,' he said. 'I've been from Land's End to John O' Groats and I always go to them when I'm sick or 'ungry.'

It was towards the middle of May when Luke finally reached his longed-for destination. The size and noise of London shocked him, making him wonder if he should have stayed in Cambridge where he'd enjoyed working on the market. Perhaps if he had, he might also have found work on the surrounding farms in the countryside. He'd really liked it there and this city seemed too big, too harsh, and too noisy.

For the first two days Luke wandered about in a

kind of daze, nervous of the traffic and disliking the strong smell of the streets, which were often dirty, the gutters littered. However, as he began to lose some of his fear of the traffic and the noise, he realised the potential. Here, there were lots of market stalls, not just in designated squares, but parked along alleyways and around the railway stations.

Luke found work on the fifth day, sweeping up in a wood yard on the docks down by the river. He'd wandered there, because he'd kept walking the whole time, never stopping in one place long, except to join a queue at the Salvation Army Hall for some soup and bread. They'd served him along with all the other men, women and a few children who joined the queue and asked no questions, though one of the men in the queue did.

'You ain't from around 'ere are yer?' he said gruffly.

'No, sir. I came from down south.' Luke lied because he couldn't tell anyone his secret. If the Master had put out a search warrant on him, someone might be looking for him even here. 'I'm looking for work – do you know where I can find it?'

The man laughed harshly. 'You tell me, youngster. Mebbe yer'll 'ave more luck than me – but try the docks. That's where most of the work is going – when there is any. Ships coming in all the time, see.'

'Thanks!' Luke would have asked where to find the docks but the man walked off to join some others and he didn't like to follow. He would find the docks if he kept walking and exploring. It was the only way to discover a new place. He'd soon found his way round Cambridge and a part of him still wondered if he should have stayed there, but something in his head kept telling him this was where he needed to be.

So, Luke kept on walking. People seemed in a hurry all the time and he tried hanging around at a railway station, but even though he reminded someone to take their umbrella they didn't give him anything, so he moved on. He thought life seemed harder here and the people he saw weren't as well off as some he'd seen elsewhere – or perhaps it was because they wore permanent frowns.

He was hungry and beginning to wonder if he would ever find work when he saw the busy wood yard. The man barking orders at his men didn't look very approachable, but just as Luke was about to turn away, he pointed a finger at him and said, 'Are yer lookin' fer a job?'

'Yes, sir, please!' Luke said eagerly. 'I'll do anything!'

'You look hungry,' the man said and suddenly grinned, which changed his face completely. 'I'm Ern and I've got a foul temper if yer get the wrong side of me, but I have jobs fer a willing lad now and then and I pay fair.'

Luke indicated his willingness and was shown a load of crates packed with straw that needed to be stacked neatly in one corner, ready to be collected and taken away. The goods had been unpacked and there was straw and sawdust all over, so Luke had to sweep it up and put it in a bin. It took him a couple of hours and made his throat dry but, at the end, Ern returned, nodded his head and looked pleased. He gave Luke a mug of water and five shillings, which he accepted gratefully.

'Satisfied?' Ern asked and Luke nodded vigorously. 'Right, come to me on Tuesday and Friday mornings and I'll give yer a similar job – all right?'

'Thank you, sir. I shall.' Satisfied? It was a fortune!

Luke ran off. He'd been making do with what he scrounged off used plates in railway stations or a cup of soup from the Sally Army but now he bought himself three crusty rolls with cheese in them and a threepenny bag of chips with a few crispies on top.

He was very hungry and he scoffed the lot in one go. Later, he had a stomach ache from eating too much and that taught him a lesson. He would use his money sparingly and eat only what he really needed in future.

Luke smiled; he was gradually learning how to live on the streets here. Sometimes, he found a shop doorway and sheltered there out of the cold night air. It wasn't too bad now in May, and in summer it would be fine, but he knew that it would be bitterly cold in winter, so before then, he had to find somewhere he could stay cheaply. He'd seen various hostels but even they were too much money for him; he couldn't afford six shillings a week just for a place to sleep and even more if he wanted food. Luke would need a regular job for that. He'd discovered that the Sally Army would give him a bed once a week for free – they rationed the accommodation because they had too many applicants for the beds they had. However, Luke didn't much like the smells and the noises in the dorms at the Sally Army. He felt safer outside.

He was an observant lad and he noticed what the other tramps did. Most had blankets and coats they carried in a pack on their backs. Some had permanent pitches under the arches and they had collected old cardboard boxes to put on the ground. Luke wondered what happened to their things if they were working, but soon realised that most of them didn't try to find jobs; instead, they sat on busy pavements and begged. That wasn't what Luke wanted to do. He was here to work and make his fortune and he wanted a good job that would enable him to have his own home. And when he found an empty, derelict house only a few streets away from the docks he knew his problem was half solved for the time being. He had somewhere free to stay and he'd found some waste cardboard at the wood yard, which Ern said he could take. It was better to sit on than the ground and, when he was given an overcoat by the Sally Army, he had something to keep him warm at night.

Luke's life was getting better. Ern was all right, though he had a real temper on him and the men who worked under him copped an earful most days, but he seemed pleased with Luke and gave him some old dry sacks, which helped make him a bed.

He looked for work every day he wasn't working for Ern and sometimes he found an hour or two here and there, so he was managing and he was allowed to use the washroom at the wood yard to give himself a quick wash after work, which helped him to keep a bit cleaner.

Then, when he'd been working in London for nearly a month, he met the nice lady. Luke was wandering along the grimy street, his eyes constantly searching for work, when he saw a rough-looking man barge into a woman and try to grab her basket. She held on desperately and Luke rushed at the man from behind, punching him in the back as hard as he could and then kicking his shins for good measure.

'You leave her alone!' he yelled, 'or I'll set my dog on you!'

Surprisingly, the man ran off. Luke didn't know if it was the threat of the dog he didn't have or just the shock of being kicked and punched from behind. The woman was looking a bit upset but she seemed to be fairly robust because she didn't seem hurt, just ruffled. She stood there, catching her breath, and then smiled at him.

'That was a brave thing you did, lad. Thank you.'

'It's all right, missus – did he hurt you?'

'No, and that's thanks to you, lad,' she said. 'I'm Ruby – will you tell me your name?'

'I'm Luke, missus,' he said, grinning at her. 'I'll be on me way then.'

'Wait a moment . . .' Ruby reached into her basket. 'I don't have money to spare, Luke – but you can 'ave these sandwiches.'

Luke hesitated and then advanced, taking her offering. 'Are yer sure, missus?'

'Yes, I am, and thank you very much for helping me, Luke.'

Luke nodded and started to move away when she called out to him. 'I'll be here next week at the same time. There will be some food for you in my basket if you want it.'

'Thanks, missus!' Luke opened the packet a little further down the street. There were four sandwiches inside made of lovely fresh bread, thick and filled with butter, ham and a bit of mustard. He hadn't tasted ham for months – the last time it had been one little bit in a roll that was stale – and he'd never had any as tasty as this. When he'd eaten two, he put the others in his pocket to save them for later.

Whistling, he set off down the road again. This was his lucky day. He was sure to find work. Perhaps it was the confidence that Missus Ruby's food had given him, but half an hour later, Luke was offered work in a greasy spoon café washing up the lunchtime things. The café owner told him his hired help had let him down and Luke earned six shillings for the next three days doing two hours of washing up a day. It wasn't his favourite job, but it was work and he was sorry when the café owner told him his regular help was back after being off sick.

'You're a good lad,' he told Luke. 'Call round sometimes and I'll find yer a job when I have one.'

Luke nodded, but his heart was set on something permanent. He would really like to learn a trade of some sort. He tried to get work on a building site but they shooed him away, said he was too young and would get in the way. He was disappointed but Ern was giving him work three days a week now – and Missus Ruby brought him sandwiches and a rock cake in his packet each week.

It wasn't the fortune Luke had hoped for, but he wasn't hungry very often now and one of these days his luck would change and he'd find a good job, something worthwhile. If he could, he'd like a job helping folk, but he wasn't sure what.

CHAPTER 5

'Well, lass, will it do?' Sid Harding asked as his wife Ruby finished looking round the house at the end of Gin Bottle Lane. It had got its name because of a warehouse that had once dealt in empty wine and beer bottles. Two streets away from where they used to live, it was in much better condition than the house they'd left in a hurry when gangsters were after them. Quashing the thought of that terrible time, nearly two years ago now, Sid grinned as he saw his wife running her hand over the top of the door and frowning at the dust on her fingers. It was a good sign because it meant she was thinking about cleaning it up. Ruby was a stickler for cleanliness and had kept their little cottage in the country and the temporary flat they were in spotless. They'd been happy enough there, but now they were back in London where they belonged. 'I know it isn't like where we've been . . .'

'I like this better,' Ruby said and smiled at him. 'Once I've had some hot water and a scrubbing brush on it, it will be fine.'

He let out a sigh of relief. It had taken ages to find anything he thought good enough for his Ruby and he hadn't been sure she would like it. 'Shall we take it then, love?'

'How much did you say it cost?' Ruby asked again. She'd asked him six times already and he knew she was struggling to come to terms with their newfound wealth. The elderly lady who had employed them in the country had died two months earlier and she'd left Ruby what seemed a fortune. Sid had almost died of shock when the lawyer told them she'd left Ruby fifteen hundred pounds plus a small garnet and gold brooch and Sid a silver watch.

'Five hundred pounds,' Sid told her. 'I reckon it is a bargain, love. It has a bit of electric installed – I know we had electric all over the cottage and we've only got a few lights here and a plug in the sitting room and kitchen, but you've got the range for cooking and heating and we could afford to do a bit to it if we wanted.'

'I like my range to cook on,' Ruby told him. 'If we need more work done, we'd still have a bit spare as you say. You're sure the walls are sound and the roof won't leak?'

'It's a good a bit of building as you'll find,' Sid told her. 'Besides, that's my proper trade. I'll be able to fix whatever goes wrong.'

'Right then.' Ruby nodded decisively. 'I can still walk to work on a good day and take a short bus ride if it's cold and wet.' She glanced outside at the back garden, which was looking bedraggled but ought to be pretty in the summer because of all the rose bushes. 'I like it, Sid. It just takes a bit of getting used to, us owning something!'

'Well, that's down to my clever wife,' Sid told her. 'When I messed things up a couple of years ago, you went out and found that place in service and look what it got us!'

'Yes.' Ruby's face lit up in a smile of content and it made his heart catch. Sid vowed he would make a success of whatever he did now they were back in London. Ruby's hard work and kindness to an elderly lady, especially in her declining weeks, had brought them a small fortune and he didn't want to let her down. 'I've been thinking, Sid. I reckon you could use the rest of the money to set up for yourself as a small builder and odd-job man. You could buy the tools you need and work for yourself. You've done every job under the sun on that old house of my lady's – you could tackle most things, charge a fair price and earn a living that way.'

'Supposing the jobs didn't come in for a while?' Sid asked, because he'd thought of the idea himself but wouldn't have asked her, because he'd thought she would want to hang on to the money.

'We'll put seven hundred pounds to your business, Sid, and I'll keep the remaining three as a nest egg.'

'If you're happy to do that, love – well, I'd enjoy working as my own boss.' He'd had a free rein while working in the country and would find it a strain to go back to bricklaying full-time, though he'd willingly do it for his Ruby.

'Yes, you do it, Sid,' Ruby told him. She gave him a nod of approval. 'The sooner we can get out of those lodgings and into our own home the better – and I'll be going round to the Rosie this afternoon to ask for my old job back.'

'You shouldn't need to work,' Sid objected but saw the answer in his wife's face. She was still fit and strong and it wouldn't suit her to sit about and do nothing. Ruby was happiest when she was working. She enjoyed a drink now and then, especially if they had friends to supper, as they had in the old days, or went to the pub with folks they knew, but she couldn't sit idle.

'What would I do with myself?' she asked. 'Julia has another two years at school and she's settled where she is – so I'll be saving for her to go on to college.'

'You're not going to bring her back to London now we're back?'

'No, not unless she asks; she is happy staying with her friend Sheila and Sheila's mother likes her. She'll come home for Christmas and then we'll talk – but Julia is different from us, Sid. She wants to get on and that grammar school is a good one – and she's safe there.' For a brief second fear flickered in Ruby's eyes. She was remembering the time when their daughter had been kidnapped because Sid had witnessed a murder. The gangsters involved were dead or imprisoned now, but the shadow still lingered in both Sid and his wife's minds.

'Perhaps you're right,' he agreed. 'Anyway, I'll see the agent about this place while you're at the infirmary and with any luck we can move in a couple of weeks. I know they want to get rid of it because the estate went to the Crown as there were no relatives.'

Ruby nodded. 'Yes, you can see from the state of the place that the last owner was an old man living alone – but I'll soon have it like a new pin.'

Sid smiled to himself. He didn't have one doubt that his wife would spruce the cottage up in next to no time – and now that he had a substantial sum of money in the bank for the first time in his life, things looked good.

'Ruby!' Mary Thurston was on her feet the moment she saw who had entered her office on the invitation to do so. 'I am delighted to see you – you look wonderful, my dear.'

'So do you, Matron.' Ruby beamed as she spoke. 'It feels lovely to be here – I've missed it and all of you here.'

'Are you back in London to live now?'

'Yes. Me and Sid are buying our own cottage. We had a legacy left us, see, and Sid has enough left over to set up as an odd-job man for himself. He's good at building, can turn his hand to anything.'

'Then perhaps he might like to do a few jobs for us?' Mary suggested. 'There are a few things that Bert can't manage alone.'

'I'm sure he would have a look and tell you if he could do it,' Ruby said and then hesitated. 'I know I let you down when I left, Matron, because my man was in a bit of trouble with some evil men – but that's all over now and I'd like to come back, if you could trust me again?'

34

'I'd love to have you back,' Mary said. 'When can you start?'

'Tomorrow if you like,' Ruby said. 'I might want a day off when we move into our new house, just to get it clean, but for the moment, I'm just sitting about doing nothing and I'd rather be working.'

'Then you shall,' Mary replied with a smile. 'I could do with your experience, Ruby – these young girls are more trouble than they're worth.'

'Young Kathy wasn't too bad when I was here.'

'She was excellent but she got married to Bert and is expecting her first child.'

'Ah, well, you leave it to me – whoever you've got here now, I'll soon have them working to my liking.'

'Good, because I simply do not have time for problems on the cleaning side.'

Mary smiled as they shook hands and Ruby left – she hadn't even asked about the pay, but Mary would give her a raise without her asking, because she was worth every penny.

As she returned to the report she was writing, a thought occurred to her. Was Ruby still hoping to foster a child? She wouldn't ask immediately, but wait until she'd settled in before raising the possibility.

CHAPTER 6

Jenny sighed as she looked round the empty kitchen when she got in from work that evening. It was so awful living here completely alone now that Lily had moved into her new home. She'd dreaded it from the moment Lily told her she was moving to a better area for the sake of her child, but she hadn't realised quite how empty it would seem without her sister. Lily had often been at work when Jenny was home, but her things were everywhere, and the scent of her talcum was always in the bathroom. Lily had always used an expensive make called Yardley, and liked the scent of Lily of the Valley, which she felt was named for her.

Sighing, Jenny made herself a cup of tea and a bit of toast. It wouldn't have been so bad if she'd been going out with Michael that evening, but he had a big job that entailed him driving some business folk up to Manchester and he would be away for three days.

She sat down with her supper, but although she drank the tea, the toast just didn't tempt her. She'd spoken to Ruby about it earlier that day when they'd bumped into each other as the friendly cleaner had left Matron's office.

Ruby had asked for Lily's address so she could send her a present for the baby. 'Your sister is a lovely girl, Jenny,' Ruby told her. 'I'm sorry I missed her leaving – but I'll make her some things for the baby and send them closer to her time.' She'd looked at Jenny's glum face. 'You'll miss her terribly at first, love. If I were you, I'd find one of the other nurses to share with you – it's better than living alone and would help with the expenses.'

'I might,' Jenny agreed, 'but it would have to be the right person. I couldn't accept just anyone in Gran's house.'

'No, be certain you get on well,' Ruby advised.

Jenny frowned. Staff Nurse Alice had hinted that she didn't much like her lodgings a few times since she'd learned Lily was leaving but Jenny didn't fancy living with her. Alice found too many faults in others for her liking – her tongue was too sharp. Jenny realised how lucky she'd been to share with Lily all those years. It was a wonder her sister hadn't married long before, but she'd had a bad experience when she was young and it had taken her a long while to get over it.

Sighing again, Jenny pushed the self-pity from her mind. Lily was so happy, and Jenny would visit her at the weekend – but for the moment she would go out and buy herself some chips. She might buy a pie or perhaps a small piece of fish to go with it for a change. It was an extravagance, but she needed something to cheer her up.

Luke saw the woman buy her chips and leave the shop. As she did so, her purse slipped from her coat pocket. He darted forward and picked it up, running after her to tug at her arm and offer it back.

'You dropped this, missus,' he said, holding out her purse. The woman looked startled and then smiled, accepting it and making sure it was in her pocket this time. She offered him her chip packet and he took one. She urged him to take a handful. 'Thanks, missus – but you want some yourself.'

'Then walk with me for a way and share them,' she invited. 'I just came out for a bit of company and fancied a few chips but I'm not very hungry.'

Luke nodded and took the bit of fish she broke off for him. He wasn't going to refuse delicious hot food like this! She smiled at him tucking in.

'I work at the Rosie,' she told him. 'I'm Nurse Jenny.'

'I thought I'd seen you leaving the infirmary,' Luke said and grinned. 'I'm Luke. I do odd jobs for folk – I'll clean windows, sweep paths, whatever you like.'

'Well, that's nice to know,' Jenny said smiling at him. 'I'll perhaps see you there one day – and if there is a job going, I'll ask if you can do it.' She stopped outside a neat terraced house. 'This is where I live, Luke. If you come round one Saturday, I might have a little job for you. I don't earn a lot myself, but I'll share food with you.'

'Fair enough,' he said and smiled at her. 'Thanks for the fish and chips. I'll see you around.'

Jenny watched the young lad walk off, feeling his loneliness tug at her heartstrings. There was no mistaking that look in his eye. Luke was one of the street kids who could be found hanging around London's streets at any time of the night and day. He probably lived in a derelict building, existing on whatever he could earn, or the Sally Army gave him. Some of the kids were crawling with lice and smelled dreadful when the police brought them in to the Rosie, apart from being close to starvation, but Luke smelled better than most and she guessed he was doing his best to keep clean.

Letting herself back into her house, she was aware of its comfort and of all the things she had collected over the years. She had so much to be thankful for and was ashamed of her feelings of self-pity earlier. Luke and boys like him had nothing and that should be a lesson to her.

Jenny switched on the wireless so the house filled with the sound of Henry Hall's music, banishing the shadows. She decided to run a nice hot bath, wash her hair and then read in bed. What would Luke and some of the other street kids give for the opportunity to live in a house like this, take a hot bath whenever they chose and sleep in a soft bed? She laughed suddenly. Perhaps living alone wouldn't be too bad. She could do whatever she chose – and she could cook a meal for Michael when he got back off his working trip – let him see that she wasn't just a good-time girl.

CHAPTER 7

Ruby inspected the kitchen and shook her head. Those ovens would never do! She'd watched the two women who had been cleaning the Rosie when she arrived for the first time last week, and now she knew who should go and who should stay. Matron had told her that she was in charge and she knew just who she wanted – she would double her hours and sack the other lazy young madam. Cheeky as she was lazy, was Tilly Watts, and Betty Stewart could do her work as well, if she chose.

Ruby checked with Betty when she arrived for work that morning, just ten minutes after Ruby herself. Her face lit up like a candle when Ruby asked if she wanted the work. The other little madam, Tilly, grinned when Ruby told her she could collect her cards and go that afternoon.

'I'll 'ave 'em now,' she retorted. 'You can stick yer rotten job in yer stinking wards. I've got a job up the jam factory!'

Ruby nodded grimly. 'Take 'em and leave,' she said, holding out the money Matron had given her. 'And don't ask for a reference neither.'

'I don't need one from an old misery like you,' Tilly said gloatingly. 'I know the guy wots over the women's section at the factory and he likes me.' She smoothed her hands over her hips suggestively, snatched her money and went.

Ruby didn't waste time watching her leave. Betty Stewart did twice as much in an hour as Tilly had and they wouldn't miss her a bit. She smiled as she dusted her hands of the girl. Good riddance! Ruby was back in her element and things were going well.

For a moment, before she started work, she allowed herself to think about the young lad who had saved her basket three weeks back. She'd thought she might not see him again, but he'd been there when she walked down that street the next week and again this morning. Ruby gave him a packet of sandwiches each time and he'd thanked her for them.

'They were the best ham sandwiches ever,' he'd told her, and he'd said the same about her rock cake each time she saw him. He really was a lovely young lad and Ruby was curious about his life. Why was he hanging about the streets? He didn't look as dirty as some of the down-and-outs she met in London's grimy East End, so he obviously washed and did his best to keep clean, though his clothes were nearly falling to bits. She'd been tempted to get him something off the nearly-new stall on the market but didn't want to offend him in case he stopped coming. You never knew how people would react if you offered them charity.

Betty Stewart, for instance, wouldn't accept anything she didn't earn, though she'd gladly accepted the extra work. At first, she hadn't taken any of the food she was offered from the kitchens of the Rosie, but Ruby had made it clear she was entitled to it as part of her wages. Since then she'd eaten a sandwich and a cake – but Ruby hadn't dared to bring Betty a nice cake from home for the kids yet, though she knew they didn't get much like that as Betty didn't earn enough for many luxuries. Ruby would love to help her children, but she knew how proud Betty was – they all did.

Sighing, she got on with her work cleaning the ovens. Life was good but there was always a problem, though not with her Sid. He was doing quite nicely. Not much work coming in yet, but he'd got everything set up and he was starting on some maintenance work for the Rosie next week.

Betty was feeling happy as she walked home that week. The fifteen shillings she would earn for doing the extra hours would make all the difference to their lives. She would be able to buy enough food to feed her children and perhaps to make them a treat sometimes. She smiled as she thought of the tin of golden syrup she'd bought from Mr Forest's shop. Tim loved treacle tart and she could make it for his tea that evening. Jilly wasn't as fond of the tart; she would prefer a pink sticky bun from the baker's at the corner shop. Hesitating outside, Betty decided to buy her daughter a bun and a large loaf of bread. They would have buttered toast with pilchards, followed by the treacle tart for her and Tim and the sugary bun for Jilly. That would make her little girl's eyes light up and it gave Betty a warm feeling inside.

As she emerged from the shop with her purchases made, Betty was so relaxed she didn't immediately see the man staring at her. Only when he grabbed her arm did the thrill of fear go through her. It was Red, the man who claimed Betty's husband had cheated him – and she could see he was out for revenge. She pulled back in fright as he hissed at her with beer-laden breath, 'Where's my money, bitch?'

'I told you before, I don't have it!' Betty squeaked in terror. His grip tightened and she felt the pull as he tried to drag her off.

'Here, you!' A man's voice spoke loudly, and Jeff Marshall came striding across the road. 'What the hell do you think you're doing? Get away from her or I'll have the cops on you!'

Red glared at him and then at Betty. 'I'll get you, bitch,' he hissed again. 'You find me at least fifty quid or I'll break your damned neck!' Then he was striding off, leaving Betty trembling and Jeff Marshall staring after him.

'We don't want that sort round here,' the friendly garage owner said. 'Good thing I'd just come down to get something for me tea, Mrs Stewart. What did he want?'

'Money,' Betty replied. 'He's from off the ships and he says my man owed him money, but I haven't got it.'

'I should think not either,' Jeff said. 'You're not responsible for it, anyway. Besides, I doubt he's telling the truth.'

'Tony gambled and won,' Betty said. 'He never gambled, but then he did – and I think that's why something happened to him.' Tears were in her eyes as she looked at Jeff. Betty wasn't sure why she'd told him anything, except he'd been there when she needed him.

'You should go to the police,' Jeff suggested but Betty shook her head.

'No, I won't, thank you, Mr Marshall – but thank you again. I must get on now.' She was distancing herself again as she always did, though she wasn't sure why. Mr Marshall would be a good father to her children if she would let him, but she just wasn't ready . . .

Jeff stood back and let her go but she knew he was watching her as she walked away. Her back was very straight as she continued home. Pride wouldn't let her accept that she needed help. All she wanted was to earn her own living and look after the kids. She'd loved once, but men were not to be trusted. If Tony hadn't gambled, he would still be alive and her life wouldn't be so difficult. Betty didn't think she would ever trust again.

Tim was standing on the doorstep and he rushed to take her basket. 'I was worried when you weren't home, Mum,' he said and she smiled and ruffled his shock of dark hair. Just like his father's.

'I'm working more hours,' she told him, smiling with affection. 'So, I'll be making a treat for our tea – treacle tart.'

'Cor! Smashing,' Tim said and threw his arms around her. 'You're the best mum in the world.'

'I wish I could be,' Betty sighed. 'I know you try to help, Tim love, but it has been hard without your dad.' How hard she could never tell him. Life was difficult enough without worrying a child about a vicious man who wanted to tear their lives apart.

CHAPTER 8

'How is Lily getting on?' Sister Rose asked Jenny as she entered the children's ward that morning. 'I think you said Michael was taking you up there to lunch this Sunday?'

'Yes, he did – and she's blooming. I took her some plants for her garden and Michael put them in for her. He liked her house a lot and said he wants something like that for himself as soon as he can afford it.'

'Ah.' Sister Rose nodded. 'He sounds rather a pleasant young man?'

'Yes, I like him . . .' Jenny wrinkled her brow. 'He can be a bit too sure of himself – I take him down a peg or two sometimes, or I try to, but he just laughs. Nothing I say dents his ego. I'm not sure Lily likes him much, though she appreciated what he did in the garden for her. Chris is busy and doesn't get much time and Michael dug a whole patch over for her so she can plant vegetables and flowers.'

Sister Rose nodded and then said it was time to get on with their work. Nurse Margaret was already washing patients and Jenny went to the other side of the ward and began the same job. Margaret James was a nice person, with a lovely Welsh lilt to her voice, but she kept to herself most of the time and Jenny couldn't get her to talk much. If she'd been more open, she would probably have asked her if she wanted to go to the flicks one night. Not that she had much time now that Michael was back in London. He took her out three nights a week and called in for a coffee or some supper a couple of times, so Jenny wasn't really spending much time alone now and he brought them fish and chips once a week so Jenny hadn't been to the fish shop, nor had she seen Luke. She'd wondered if he might come for a job but he hadn't so she hoped he was managing all right.

She forgot about her own problems and Luke as she bathed and tended her patients. Some of the children they had on the ward just now were severely ill – especially a little lad named Collin, who had been found on the streets, beaten and battered but wouldn't say who had abused him . . .

'So, I'm asking if you can fit Collin on your list,' Mary Thurston said to her friend Lady Rosalie over the phone. 'The police found him half-dead and brought him to us. He'd been beaten and starved – and his feet were covered in sores. We've got some nourishing food inside him, tended his cuts and bruises and the sores are getting better, although it will be a month or so before he's ready for fostering out to a family.'

'That's just as well,' Lady Rosalie replied. 'My list

has filled right up again and I'm looking for more foster parents, though some of my regulars are sometimes willing to take on another child.'

'Yes, you've got some really good ones on the list. Gwen Cartwright – Thompson, I should say, now she's married again – is a marvel, but she has two fostered boys already.'

'Yes, *and* a new husband so I won't ask her to take on more right now. I know she would say yes, but I feel it would be too much to ask.'

'Well, bear little Collin in mind,' Mary said. 'So, how is your son – are his exams going well?'

'He never says, so I suspect not as well as he'd hoped. He'll be home soon for a short holiday and I'll be taking him to a few places. I thought you might like to come down to the sea with us again later in the year. I did so enjoy your company last year, Mary.'

'It all depends whether I can get a senior nurse to stand in,' Mary said. 'I would love to come, Rosalie, and I'm due two weeks holiday in the summer, but I can't leave the Rosie understaffed. We do need to hire another senior nurse or sister so that there is always one present – and that is even more important when I am away.'

'So, you've had no luck yet then?'

'No. Oh, I do miss Sister Rose being full-time, but since her marriage she just does mornings. We are managing because we have some good nurses – but Lily was a big loss to me and, although I've placed advertisements all over, I haven't got the right person for the job yet.'

'Try a temporary agency,' Lady Rosalie advised. 'I

48

know you prefer full-time staff, but agency nurses are acceptable in difficult times.'

'Yes, perhaps I shall,' Matron said. She was frowning as she replaced the receiver a few minutes later. Her friend tried to be helpful but she didn't truly understand. Mary had tried agency nurses before, but she'd found they were often a bit careless and not good timekeepers. It was as if they didn't care whether they stayed or not. She sighed; she really needed to find some more good nurses. The trouble was, not many came up to the standards of Sister Jean and Sister Rose.

CHAPTER 9

Sister Rose looked at her husband as he struggled to walk a few steps unaided. They'd been married six months now and Peter's promising beginning at their wedding hadn't progressed as much as they'd hoped, even though his general health seemed much improved.

He glanced at her and she smiled but he'd seen her worried frown. 'It's all right, love,' he said. 'It's slow going yet but I feel a little steadier on my feet. I just can't make them go as I direct every time. Some days are better than others.'

'I know.' She went to him and put her arms around him. 'If you want help, darling, just ask.' She offered her support and he made it to the wheelchair and sat, a rueful expression in his eyes as she asked, 'Will you be all right at the clinic?'

'The porter usually comes out to help me get the chair from the car.' Jeff Marshall had very cleverly adapted his car so that Peter was able to drive it without using his legs. Everyone who saw what Jeff had done said he should patent it and sell the designs to a manufacturer, but Jeff said no, he would give the idea to anyone who wanted to use it if it was to help others, but he didn't want the bother of trying to sell it.

'I do all right, Sister Rose,' Jeff had told her with his friendly smile. 'I don't want to profit from something I did for a friend – and I don't want anything for doing it either.'

Rose went outside with her husband and helped him get the chair into the car boot. He would manage quite easily until he got to the clinic, but there he would need help to get it out. Hopefully, the porter would remember to come out for him, or someone would go inside and fetch him. 'Doctor Peter', as he was affectionately called, was well-known locally and normally there was someone willing to help him. Rose's friend, Beattie, had told them her husband Ted would help whenever he could, but he worked all week and so was only free at the weekends, when he sometimes took Peter to a football match with his two adopted sons, Danny and Ron. Beattie and her family were their closest friends, but it wasn't right to expect too much so Rose knew they needed a more permanent solution to Peter's problem.

She frowned as she made her way to work that morning in June, because she knew Peter must be very disappointed that his progress was so slow. A few tottery steps in the house was not what he'd hoped to achieve by now, though the specialist had told him it might be a long time before full mobility returned – and that perhaps it never would.

Refusing to let herself dwell on that possibility, Rose went inside the infirmary and on up to the children's ward. Everywhere smelled strongly of disinfectant, which hadn't happened for a while until now. She saw Ruby Harding busy cleaning and thought the hospital wards were looking so much cleaner these days since Ruby had come back.

'Good morning, Ruby,' Rose said brightly. 'How is the world treating you – is your daughter still enjoying her school?'

'She moved to another grammar school nearer home last week, after we got settled, because she wanted to come home and be with us. My Sid is as pleased as punch over it. Julia does want to go on to college when she's older but she hasn't decided yet whether she wants to be a teacher or a secretary. If she goes for teaching it will be longer before she's earning, because technical college is shorter than the teacher training, but we're not pushing her either way. Sid is starting to do all right and so am I, and we're both so proud of her.'

'That's lovely!' Rose smiled at her. 'I'm glad you're settling back in London, Ruby. We missed you – and not just because it's all cleaner with you around. We missed your smile.'

'Well, that's nice of you to say so,' Ruby said. 'How is that lovely husband of yours?'

'Oh, managing well,' Rose replied, painting her smile in place. No point in complaining about something she couldn't fix, no matter how much she helped Peter with his exercises.

Once on the ward, Rose's mind concentrated on her patients. She must look after the children in her care and she knew Peter would cope. He'd faced his injuries stoically from the beginning and if he worried at night about his future, he never gave any sign of it when he held her and kissed her in their bed. She smiled as she thought of his resourcefulness, knowing he would manage somehow, just as he managed to make love to her.

Luke stood opposite the clinic and watched as the porter came out to help Doctor Peter from his car and into his wheelchair. The first time he'd seen it he'd been on the verge of asking if he could help but then the porter had arrived. Sometimes, Luke went inside the clinic waiting room to get warm and he'd heard everyone talking about Doctor Peter and how he'd been crippled in an accident, when a gas explosion had caused an old building to collapse, and he'd rescued an old lady named Jessie. Luke had seen Jessie in the clinic and thought she was a bit rude to most folk, but when Doctor Peter came on the scene, she laughed and joked and was a different person. Luke realised what a lovely person he was when he watched the faces of *all* the doctor's patients.

The doctor was wheeling himself into the clinic now. It was just the getting from the car to the chair that he couldn't manage. If the porter hadn't come, Luke would've asked. He would like to help the doctor, he thought wistfully. A job like that would be worthwhile instead of the many odd jobs he was given these days, though he was lucky to get as much occasional work as he did plus the job with Ern. Luke knew that many full-grown men were still looking for work, though he hadn't seen as many younger men standing on street corners recently. He wondered if, knowing that many people expected war to break out with Germany sooner rather than later, they had already joined up.

Luke sometimes found discarded newspapers, which he collected; he could use them for so many things. People dropped them on the ground, in bins and left them on park benches as if they were rubbish, but to Luke they were treasure. He took them back to his home in the abandoned house he'd made his own, along with cardboard boxes, pieces of fallen wood from the trees in the park or even those growing alongside the road. If a piece of branch fell, Luke collected it in the sack he'd acquired. He read the newspapers first, because it gave him something to do with his time when he wasn't working and he was always interested in learning about what was going on in the world. Afterwards, he tightly rolled up several pages together then twisted the result into a knot. This made good kindling which helped get a little fire going and with the wood Luke found and a few pieces of coal he bought from a delivery man when he had five shillings to spare, he was able to build a little fire to heat water in a discarded saucepan he'd found to make a hot drink, or even sometimes cook an egg if he could afford to buy one or two from the grocer.

Sometimes Luke bought ready-cooked food, but that took most of what he earned each day. Once each week he went to find Mrs Ruby and she gave him a packet of sandwiches. She made him lovely food, sometimes including a bit of apple pie or little buns she'd made herself. Once or twice she'd given him sausage rolls and he loved them. Luke had never eaten food like Ruby's, even when he lived in the children's home. He shuddered at the memory of the lumpy stews and tapioca pudding but the memories were fading and Luke was growing strong and confident as he lived free and worked.

Luke didn't know much about war – he'd learned about what they called the Great War in history lessons, and knew they'd used a lot of horses and charged with swords or fired pistols, but he didn't think it would be that kind of war this time. He'd seen people digging trenches in the park and some important buildings had piles of sandbags outside to protect them because the newspapers said if an attack came it would come from the air, and the thought of that was frightening and dangerous.

Had the men who used to linger on street corners gone to be soldiers? He asked Ern about it once and got a scowl from his employer.

'Damned fools,' Ern had said. 'Anyone would think it was a bit of fun, rushing to sign up like that – what do they think we're goin' ter do when we need men on the docks?'

Luke thought perhaps Ern was annoyed because there were not so many men asking for jobs, and he noticed that those that were demanded more money. One morning he'd overheard one say, 'Think I'm going to work for a pittance? I might as well take the king's shilling!'

Luke knew that meant join the army. He'd wondered if perhaps he should join if the wages were better, but when he'd seen a sign for a recruitment centre and gone to ask, they laughed and said he wasn't old enough.

'Come back in two or three years, lad,' the sergeant said. 'I give yer credit fer askin' but we can't take yer.'

'I'm strong and I ain't afraid of the enemy,' Luke told him as the man laughed.

'I'll just bet you're not, and I'd take yer like a shot, lad, but they'd have my guts for garters.' The sergeant winked at the other men in line. 'Come on then,' he boomed at them. 'This young lad's shown yer the way . . .'

Luke had gone off whistling then, disappointed but accepting that you couldn't always get what you wanted in life. He was managing all right and it wasn't often he went hungry these days. He hadn't quite made his fortune yet, and his life wasn't easy, but it was better than being at the orphanage.

Now, he threw a backward glance at the clinic as the doctor disappeared inside. Maybe one day he would get to help him . . .

Peter wheeled himself to his car and swung himself behind the wheel, then the porter took the chair from him, nodded in a friendly manner, and placed the chair in the boot of the car before going back inside the infirmary. Looking around for the lad he'd spotted earlier that day, Peter was disappointed that he wasn't around. He'd noticed him a couple of times now and was intrigued. Something about the boy told him that he was living rough, though he looked reasonably clean, so was trying to keep himself decent. His clothes were old and almost certainly needed washing, but his face looked bright and alert and Peter was interested in discovering more.

He'd been about to call him over and ask for his help that morning when the porter came out to collect him. He thought it was a pity. Being aware that he couldn't help every homeless boy in London didn't stop Peter from trying. He helped all those who asked for it at the clinic; sometimes there was little you could do for elderly men and women who had spent their lives on the street, but he'd helped quite a few to be free of pain for a while. Some would accept help from charities if pointed in the right direction, but others liked living the way they did, like Jessie.

Peter smiled at the memory of her in his clinic that day. She'd come with a pain in her right leg and he'd given her a bottle of her favourite medicine and five shillings for a cup of tea and some sandwiches. If she used it wisely, it would last her two or three days. Knowing Jessie it would probably go on a bottle of beer, which, he supposed on reflection, was truly her favourite medicine, even if it didn't do her much good. It probably didn't do her much harm either, so it hardly mattered as long as she was happy.

He was still smiling as he approached his home and saw his lovely wife standing outside waiting for him. Rose never failed to be there when he got home and her love restored him, no matter what kind of day he'd had. Peter's one sadness was that his recovery hadn't developed as quickly as he'd hoped. He wanted to be a proper husband and look after Rose, but until his full strength returned he couldn't promise her much other than more of the same. She never asked for more, but that didn't stop Peter wanting to give her all the things she'd never had, including a child.

CHAPTER 10

'Do you want to visit your sister this weekend?' Michael asked when Jenny slipped into the car beside him that evening. 'I'll be happy to take you – she's got a nice house there. Just what I'd like when I settle down to married life.'

'Yes, it would be nice to visit her,' Jenny agreed. 'I think Chris is still away. He is attached to army headquarters here in London, but often has to travel to all parts of the country. Don't ask what he does, though, because Lily won't tell you.'

'He's in intelligence,' Michael said. 'I asked him when I met him, and he told me. There's no great secret about it, he'll be off around the ports checking on where the invasion is likely to happen – if or when we finally go to war.'

'Oh, don't!' Jenny exclaimed. 'I hate to think there might be a war – the last one was bad enough. I can't even contemplate it happening again.'

'Sorry,' he said, looking at her oddly. 'I thought you were too young to remember that.'

'I am, but I know my father died because of it and

Mum died soon after him. We went to live with Gran, and she was wonderful – but Lily hates the Germans and everything to do with them.'

'I'd agree with her,' Michael said seriously. 'Your sister has a lot of sense. Some of my family went through that lot and they were never the same. Chris knows the truth – they're spoiling for another fight out there and sooner or later it will happen.'

'I suppose . . .' Jenny said and shrugged. 'Can't we talk about something else, Michael?'

He stopped the car outside her house and looked at her. 'Why don't we talk about you and me?' he asked and her heart thudded to a halt before racing on. 'It's about time, don't you think?'

'What about us?' Jenny said warily. Was he about to dump her?

'I'm thinking about buying a house, Jenny. If you sold yours, your half would make it so we didn't owe a penny. I can get a bank loan, but together we could own it outright.'

'Move in with you?' She was a little shocked, though she'd known he expected to make love soon or he would break up with her as he was getting increasingly passionate in his kisses and caresses.

'Don't talk daft, girl!' He grinned. 'I'm asking you to wed me. I know you ain't the kind to just shack up with me.'

'M-marry you?' Jenny felt trembly inside, shocked, frightened and excited all in one go. None of her boyfriends had ever asked her to be their wife. 'Are you sure you want to?'

Michael gave a shout of laughter. 'Do you think I

go round kissing all the girls the way I do you, Jenny? I thought you knew I was mad about you?'

'I wasn't sure,' she admitted honestly. 'I know we get on well together and – and I think I'd like to be your wife . . .'

'Only think?' For the first time ever since she'd known him, he seemed a bit uncertain. 'Don't you know we're made for each other?'

Jenny looked at him for a moment longer and then she smiled. 'Yes, I do – I just didn't know if you would ask me.'

He chuckled, delighted with her answer, grabbed her and kissed her in a way that left her breathless. 'Seeing you, wanting you bad, was driving me round the bend,' he told her, a look of glee in his eyes. 'We'll get a house down the road from your Lily and then you'll be able to see her as often as you like.'

'That would be lovely,' Jenny breathed, caught up in the moment before the doubts had a chance to set in, and it was only when she lay alone in her bed, after they'd drunk half a bottle of wine, that she began to wonder.

Would Michael expect her to give up nursing immediately? Would she be able to get to the Rosie until, like Lily, she was pregnant and ready to give up? Perhaps the most worrying thought was: was she truly ready for marriage?

Jenny knew that Michael was the only man who had ever made her feel as though she desperately wanted to make love with him, and if she wanted that so badly then she must marry. It was the only way for a decent girl like her. And a part of her was thrilled that Michael had asked her to be his wife. She would enjoy the wedding and the love-making – but would she get bored when it all settled into a dull routine?

Jenny knew herself well and she understood that she bored easily. Had she been foolish to agree the first time he asked? Lots of girls said they needed time to think about it, perhaps she ought to have done that – and yet she knew that Michael wasn't the sort to beg. No matter how much he wanted or loved her, one hint that she didn't feel the same and he would leave. Jenny had a feeling that if she'd sent him away, he wouldn't have come back. Other men she'd known might, but not Michael. He was too proud. She couldn't risk that – and surely, she told herself, she was just being foolish.

Jenny didn't truly wish to spend the rest of her life dating new men and splitting up with them a few weeks later; it was fun for a while but usually went sour. Michael was the only man who made her heart race at the thought of meeting him.

Telling herself off for being a selfish little girl and to grow up, Jenny turned over and went to sleep. She was just being silly – it would all be fine. If she had a child quite soon, it might be just what she needed to make her think of other things and people beside herself.

'You've said you'll marry him?' Lily looked at her in surprise. 'Are you sure, Jenny, love? I know he takes you to nice places – but I've always thought he's a bit sure of himself . . .'

'Yes, I know he comes over that way, but underneath I'm not so sure he really is,' Jenny said and smiled. 'Anyway, he's the only one I've ever felt this way about, so I've said yes. We're going to sell the house, give you your half share and pool what we have to buy something near you.' Jenny looked at her uncertainly. 'I thought you'd like that? It means we'll see each other more.'

'Well, of course I'd like that,' Lily replied and then gave her a quick hug. 'I'm only thinking of you, Jenny. I didn't see you settling down to married life for a few years and I know you love your job – how will you manage that?'

'I'll ask Matron if I can do three days a week and, on those days, I'll get up early and catch the underground into the infirmary. I'll have plenty of time at home to take care of the house and cook – and Michael is often out all day and sometimes overnight with his more important jobs. It will work all right.'

'And if you fall for a baby?' Lily's steady gaze made Jenny blush.

'Perhaps it will do me the world of good to have someone relying on me,' she said frankly. 'I know I've often been a selfish brat in the past, Lily, so it may be what I need to steady me down.'

'True . . .' Lily nodded and then smiled brightly at the sister she loved. 'As long as you're happy, Jenny – that's all I want for you.'

'I think I am,' Jenny said and laughed. 'It's all going to be a lot of fun, selling the house, buying another that Michael likes and, of course, the wedding!'

'I'll help with that,' Lily told her. 'Mine was kept

quiet for Chris's sake but we'll make a big thing of yours, Jenny.' She gave a little gurgle of pleasure. 'When is it going to be?'

'Before Christmas,' Jenny replied and gave a little nervous shiver. 'We haven't got any further than that yet. I have to arrange for the house to be valued. Do you want to be there when the agent comes?'

'No.' Lily shook her head decisively. 'You'll get the best price possible, I know.' She looked pleased. 'Chris is very generous to me, gives me all I want – but it will be nice to have a little nest egg of my own.'

So, Lily was happy with the prospect of selling the house. Jenny hadn't been 100 per cent sure she would be. Michael had said he could get a loan from the bank but she knew it would be best to sell if they could. One of the houses in the next street had recently sold for six hundred and fifty pounds, and it hadn't been as nice as theirs, nor did it have a garden at the back, just a paved yard.

Gran had been so proud of her garden. Jenny felt a pang as she realised that she would be parting from so many memories. She could picture Gran welcoming them home, Jenny from school and Lily from nursing college – and then, as she got older, becoming frail but still smiling, still full of love for the two orphans she'd taken in when in her later years. Could Jenny really just sell and turn her back on all the memories?

The doubts crowded in on Jenny as she wondered if she should change her mind now, while she still could . . .

CHAPTER 11

'Give me a piggyback,' Jilly said as she and Tim walked home from school that evening. 'What are we doing in the summer holidays? Will Mum take us for a holiday to the sea?'

'Where would Mum get the money for that?' Tim asked, looking at her in astonishment. Jilly did come out with some strange ideas. 'It must cost lots of money to stay at a hotel or even a boarding house.'

'Minnie Smith's mum is taking her to Eastbourne for two weeks in a boarding house. She says they go most years – her dad works in a car factory and he gets two weeks holiday at the start of our school holidays so they all go.'

'Well, then, Minnie is lucky,' Tim said shaking his head over the fact that some folk had money to spend on things like that, but not envying them. 'I wonder if Mum has made treacle tart tonight?'

'I hate treacle tart.' Jilly pulled a face at her brother. 'Oh, Tim, we never do anything nice.'

'Mum took us to the circus on your birthday last year,' he pointed out, and Jilly made a rude face.

'It smelled awful and the clowns frightened me.'

'You liked the dancing dogs and the prancing horses, though.'

Jilly considered this for a moment and then nodded, conceding the point.

They were passing the garage now. Mr Marshall was talking to one of the nurses from the Rosie and didn't notice them. Tim thought the nurse was called Margaret and she looked rather nice – the sort of person who would cuddle you if she liked you. She noticed them and called a greeting and then Mr Marshall did, too, and waved his hand.

Tim waved back. He'd run an errand for Mr Marshall the previous weekend and earned a half-crown; he'd been hoping Mr Marshall might ask him to do something again but he didn't speak, so Tim swallowed his disappointment and walked on. It wasn't easy to find enough jobs that would help save a little money to buy a gift for Mum's birthday. He'd seen a pretty silk scarf he knew she would like, but it was seven shillings and sixpence and so far he had only five shillings. He needed another half-crown.

His mother was at the stove, cooking, when they got in. She turned with a bright smile and asked what sort of a day they'd had, but Tim saw how tired she looked. His heart ached for her because he knew how hard she worked and he could do little to ease her burden. A few shillings in her pot when he was lucky wasn't enough. She was coughing as she served up their dinner and didn't look at all well to Tim, but he didn't ask because she wouldn't tell him, however ill she felt.

He thought about the pretty nurse, Margaret, and how healthy *she* appeared. He reckoned Mr Marshall was a bit keen on her from the way he looked at her. He liked Mr Marshall and it would be nice if he found someone to look after him.

Margaret James walked home most nights, especially now that it was so much warmer. The children would be breaking up from school that weekend and she reflected that it would probably result in a flood of small injuries presenting at the infirmary. Children fell over climbing up dangerous buildings and railings near the river, and harassed mothers brought them in to have scratches, cuts and broken bones attended to. Sometimes, the injuries looked too severe to be caused by just falling and Matron always wanted to know if you suspected they'd been harmed by their parents.

Matron was involved with Lady Rosalie, the patron of the infirmary named after her, in a project to rescue and foster children in need, whether they had parents or not. Sometimes, children who had what looked like secure homes from the outside were found to be at risk of harm inside their home and that was what the nurses were told to look out for.

After Tim and Jilly had walked on, Jeff had told her that the Stewart children were well cared for. 'Betty Stewart struggles to make ends meet,' he'd explained, 'but she's not a bad mother and I believe she loves those kids. It's just a pity she's a widow and has to work hard to support them. I don't think they get many extras.'

'There are a lot of kids like that,' Margaret told him. 'Money is tight these days, Mr Marshall.'

'Why don't you call me Jeff?' he'd said with a smile, making Margaret blush. She liked him; she wouldn't have stopped to talk to him if she didn't, but she was still wary of getting involved with anyone. Still it was nice to have a friendly chat and he seemed all right.

Jeff stood watching the nurse walk away. He liked the way her hips swayed so naturally, it wasn't put on the way some girls did, and he liked her smile. He always looked forward to seeing her for a few minutes when she passed by at night on her way home. Actually, Jeff realised, he liked everything about Nurse Margaret. Smiling to himself, he went back to his task of polishing the car he'd worked on all day. He'd given it a service, changed the tyres and refilled the oil and cleaned it until it sparkled like new.

Mr Fredericks owned the Wolsey salon and it was a real beauty, a deep green, and it really paid for all of Jeff's hard work. Of course, Jeff didn't drive anything as posh himself; he saved his money so that he felt comfortable and could afford anything he wanted or needed. He'd always thought he would marry and have kids one day, but for one reason or another it hadn't happened. He had once thought of asking Betty Stewart if she wanted a husband and father for her children, more out of sympathy for her plight than anything, but when he'd tried to be friendly, she'd made it clear she wasn't interested. Now he was rather glad of that. He wasn't sure whether anything would come of his friendship with Margaret James. It was merely acquaintanceship now. He hadn't asked her out and she'd shown no interest in romance – and yet there was something about her that made Jeff think she would be more than just rather nice to cuddle up to on a cold night.

Not that he was particularly cold at the moment with the warm weather. Jeff drove the Wolsey back inside the garage. It was all finished and he'd worked enough for one day. All he wanted now was to go into his kitchen and make himself a brew, or maybe have a glass of beer. He'd got one cooling in the larder.

As he slid his door into place and locked it, he caught sight of the lad he'd seen around a few times; he didn't think he meant any harm, even though he was loitering. Momentarily, Jeff wondered where the lad had come from. He'd swear he wasn't local. Jeff knew all the local lads by sight and most by name, but not this one.

Shrugging, he went inside his house and poured that beer. Margaret was certainly a lovely woman and he would like to get to know her better – but would she want to know him? She was a lot younger than him, in her mid-twenties, he thought, and Jeff believed he was no catch for any woman, even though he had a few pounds in the bank. He'd been in the big war – the war to end all wars they'd called it – though look what was happening now! If things kept getting worse, the country would be at war with Germany again before they knew it. Not that Jeff would be volunteering this time. The brown scar on his left cheek was reminder enough that he'd served his time. He'd been nineteen when he joined up, twenty-two when he'd been shipped home with a Blighty wound that had dashed his hopes of happiness then.

Shaking his head, Jeff thrust his memories of a cruel, thoughtless girl from his mind. That was years ago, and he wasn't breaking his heart over Janey now. Yet knowing how much rejection could hurt, it made him hesitate to ask Margaret out. What if she said no? Better to wait, make sure she liked him and then ask when he felt she wouldn't laugh or turn away in disgust.

CHAPTER 12

Luke watched the kids playing hopscotch in the street. It looked fun and once, when they'd all gone in, he'd had a quick turn when he thought no one was looking. He knew it was silly to feel envious of their games, watching as they laughed and chased each other carelessly in the warm sunshine, and he didn't really have much time for games these days, working long hours on the docks.

Ern was getting nervous about the war and how it might affect his business. He imported and exported other people's goods and Luke thought he did quite well out of it. Ern didn't lay out any money; he just packed and unpacked stuff for others, checking it to make sure it was all as it should be so he could sign the customs forms.

'If there's a war, half this stuff won't be allowed into the country,' he'd told Luke recently. 'This crate is goin' ter Germany – and them four came from there, too.' He shook his head, obviously counting his lost profits. 'It will be the ruin of me.'

'Will you go for a soldier?' Luke asked and Ern made a face.

'I ain't that daft, lad – and you don't want ter be either. Them what rush to sign up are mad – want ter die, they do.'

Luke hadn't argued, because Ern had given him extra work that week and a small increase in money, which meant he could afford to buy sausage and mash for his tea from the shop on the corner. But he knew from the papers and the tense atmosphere on the streets that things were getting serious. The newsboys kept saying how the Prime Minister was saying that there would be peace, but other folk were saying it would be war as the street filled with soldiers in uniform.

Luke knew Ern was cross because there were few takers for his jobs now. All the fit, strong young men were in uniform and it was only the older men or boys of Luke's age looking for work and Ern didn't trust a lot of the lads that hung around. He said they were waiting until his back was turned to pinch stuff, and when Luke had warned him, he'd recently caught one trying to pinch a wireless set that had just come out of a packing case. Ern had boxed his ears and chased him off, thanking Luke for alerting him.

The kids had abandoned their game now and were being called in for their tea. This was the time of the day when Luke felt loneliest. He'd done his work for the day, eaten his supper and now he had nowhere to go except to a bed in a deserted house with no one to talk to until the morning.

Luke wished they had taken him in the army. It might be a hard life and dangerous but at least he would have a proper bed, regular meals and companions. It was the feeling of isolation that he felt the most, of being cut off from the rest of the world with no one to talk to.

The news that Britain was at war seemed to come out of the blue over that first weekend in September, beginning on the Friday when the Germans invaded Poland, and ending with the Prime Minister making the announcement on Sunday that 'This country is at war with Germany' on the radio at eleven in the morning. Luke, of course, had no radio, but he heard people talking about it in the streets later in the afternoon, and even though Ern had grumbled about it nonstop, the news still seemed shocking.

'I'll be ruined,' Ern moaned on Monday morning. 'Folk won't risk their money sending stuff on the ships if there's a chance it will get bombed.'

'The country will need lots of things,' Luke reasoned. 'Food and stuff we need to live on.'

'I don't deal in food,' he said shaking his head. 'I'm more luxury goods, see.'

Luke saw perfectly well, but if anything, Ern's trade got more hectic over the next couple of weeks, as if people were determined to get what they could while it was available. He was kept busy and Ern gave him a couple of extra shillings one night.

'You've worked well,' he said and nodded, 'but I'm closing down now for three weeks, young 'un, so I shan't need yer.'

'Are yer packin' up?' Luke asked, feeling alarmed but Ern shook his head.

'I'm takin' a bit of time off,' he said. 'I want ter visit some of me customers up north and see what they're gonna do now.'

Luke wanted to ask him what he was supposed to do for the next three weeks. He'd been working for Ern most days recently and he hadn't looked for other jobs for a while, but he would have to find work to eat and that meant tramping round the streets again to find odd jobs. A lot of the traders on the docks had also closed their doors for a few days over the previous week's bank holiday or in some cases two weeks. They were also taking stock, trying to work out what was going to happen now war was officially declared.

Apart from big headlines and a lot of army vehicles rushing around London, Luke hadn't seen anything much happening yet and he walked the streets for two days and found nothing. No one seemed to want anything done that they thought he could do; they were boarding up windows and doors and someone nailed a Keep Out notice on the derelict building he was using but he just ignored it. At night the streets were now dark, as windows had blackout curtains put up and streetlights were not lit. Luke had to manage with candles to see at night, because there were no lights from the street – though he didn't have much money left to buy them – and some nights already felt cold, so he dreaded the winter. He'd hoped to have a regular job and a home long before now.

One day towards the end of the month, another trader told him the bad news. 'Ern's given up,' he said. 'He's gone to live with his widowed sister in Margate. She runs a boarding house and he's going to help her. He's given up his space 'ere.'

Luke felt sick inside. What would he do now? Ern had been miserly and a grumbler, but he'd given Luke regular work and now Luke was back to the beginning, looking for any odd job he could find.

Luke wandered the streets as the days got colder. The only food he had was what Ruby gave him, twice a week. Then Luke found a job running errands for a newspaper shop where he earned five shillings. He bought some chips that day and went into the public toilets to have a wash. The next day he found a job washing windows and the following day he carried a lady's shopping basket from the market. She gave him sixpence and, once again, he bought chips to fill the hollow space inside him.

He knew that with winter coming on his future looked bleak and felt anxious and afraid, but all he could do was keep searching for work. Sometimes, he heard a siren go and people rushed to the air-raid shelters in case the Germans bombed them, but it didn't happen. Luke went into the shelters with the others and he found a companionship there he'd hardly known before. His existence had always been lonely, even in the orphanage, but in the air-raid shelter people laughed, sang and talked, and they would offer him a cup of cocoa from a flask and sometimes a sandwich. Luke started to hope the siren would go and on the nights it didn't he felt lonelier than before.

Now folk were calling it the phoney war because nothing much was happening. Luke knew there was fighting in France and Belgium, but on the streets of England the only panic was caused by the false alarms from the sirens. People had settled down and some of the warehouses had reopened their doors to trade. Luke found one or two jobs running errands, sweeping up and shifting piles of wood. He was eating more regularly but never missed the food Ruby brought for him. She was a kind lady and shook her head over him.

'Are yer sure you're all right, Luke?' she asked several times as the weather got colder. She brought him an old overcoat of her husband's and told him there was a couch he could sleep on in her kitchen.

'I worry about yer now the weather's colder, lad,' she told him, but Luke grinned and made out he was all right. He could manage again now that he was earning a little, but he still didn't make what Ern had paid him and he missed his grumbling. He kept looking just in case the importer decided to return, but as the days passed he began to realise the trader really had gone for good.

If Luke was to make his fortune, he must look elsewhere. He remembered the clinic where the doctor worked and decided to return there and see if he needed help, but though he waited for three mornings in a row, Doctor Peter didn't come.

'Well, I'm glad you came,' the specialist told Peter after he'd finished examining him. 'You were right to think there was movement in your back. I do think

76

something has moved – and I believe it has helped you quite a bit.'

'I'm certainly feeling much less pain,' Peter said, 'although I still can't walk more than a few steps unaided.'

'Well, I am certain something was pressing on a nerve and that's what was causing that terrible pain that started a few months ago. But the nerve will still be bruised and suffering, my friend, so don't expect things to improve drastically just yet. However, when the inflammation lessens you should see an improvement.'

'I shan't hold you to that,' Peter said, grinning wryly. 'We both thought it was going to get a lot better than it has.'

'Yes, I will admit that it has puzzled me,' Simon replied, slipping into the easy mode of long-standing friendship rather than doctor and patient. 'I thought you would be walking before this and I wondered if the lack of progress might be mental but now I'm certain it was a physical impediment. You should have told me how much pain you were in before and we could have X-rayed your back.'

'Didn't want to bother anyone,' Peter said, looking self-conscious. 'It was only when I felt something different – a kind of loosening – that I told Rose and she persuaded me to come down and see you.'

'That wife of yours is a sensible woman. I'm sure she didn't know how much pain you were in either.'

'I didn't tell her,' Peter admitted. He smiled and offered his hand. 'I'm feeling much better in my mind now, Simon. I can't thank you enough for all you've done.'

'Haven't done much at all, old chap,' Simon said. 'Get yourself home and start living. Look for an improvement in a couple of months – and if you need me, just telephone. I can come up to London rather than you coming all the way down here each time.'

'Well, today I got one of my colleagues from the clinic to bring me,' Peter said. 'He was visiting family nearby and wants to send his children down here if the bombs start falling.'

'They will,' Simon said with a frown. 'This is just the lull before the storm, Peter. It is my opinion that Hitler is gearing up ready for a major onslaught.'

'God help us all when it starts,' Peter said and frowned. 'I feel so helpless, stuck in that chair. If I were a whole man, I could do my bit.'

'I'm not stuck in a chair, but I know where I'm needed,' Simon replied. 'You're a doctor, my friend, and they'll be needing us soon – more of us than you can possibly imagine.'

'I know how bad it was last time,' Peter agreed. 'I was a schoolboy when it ended, but I saw the men coming back and it was one of the reasons I became a doctor.'

Simon nodded. 'We can do more where we belong – in hospitals – so get back to that damned clinic of yours and do what you do best. And take care of yourself and that beautiful wife. Give her my regards and tell her I look forward to seeing her next time you visit.'

Rose looked at him anxiously as he wheeled himself into their kitchen the next day. She went to him at once and kissed him, looking into his face and then nodding.

'It was good news,' she said. 'The pain is a little better at last, isn't it?'

'So, you knew then?' Peter said ruefully. 'I thought I'd hidden it well.'

'I always know when you're ill,' she said, smiled and kissed him. 'What did Simon say?'

'He sent you his love and says he wants to see you next time I visit.'

'What did he say about your back?' Rose insisted and he laughed.

'He says something has moved and he believes my movement will improve shortly. He thinks something was pressing on a nerve and that's what caused the pain and inflammation, which may be why I didn't improve as we first hoped.'

'Yes, I see that,' Rose said and looked relieved. 'So that means we can look forward to improvement soon.'

'Perhaps,' Peter said. 'I can't count my chickens yet, Rose. I thought it would happen before, but it didn't.'

'And now we know why,' she said and smiled. 'Have faith, my darling. You will get better. I know you will – and I love you. Whether you walk again or not, I want to be with you, but I'm so glad the pain is easier.'

'So am I,' he admitted and grinned suddenly. 'Sorry, Rose. I'm not trying to play down what Simon said, but I'm afraid to let myself hope for too much.'

'You must hope and pray,' she said, 'and I shall

too. It is the only way, Peter. A little more time and you'll walk properly again.'

'Yes,' he agreed. 'Perhaps I shall – and in the meantime, I shall return to the clinic tomorrow.' He frowned. 'It's odd, but I have a strange feeling I missed something important while I was away . . .'

CHAPTER 13

Jenny looked around the sitting room and sighed. It looked strange now that all the furniture had been removed, and she felt a pang of something like regret as she closed the door on it. They'd got eight hundred pounds after expenses for the house and that was a fortune to Jenny. She'd arranged to stay in a boarding house for a couple of weeks while Michael signed the last documents that made the pretty house just two streets away from Lily theirs and her wedding day was fast approaching.

Jenny hadn't seen too much of Michael recently as he'd been working away. He'd been given quite a bit of work driving for high-powered army officers recently and she thought he was down on the south coast, though he wasn't allowed to say. Michael had told her that he had flat feet and so officially was not acceptable to the forces as a fighting man. However, he'd joined a pool of civilians attached to the War Office, who were used for driving and various other jobs, and seemed happy. Jenny was relieved, because so many of her friends were losing their boyfriends and husbands to the war.

Going out, she closed the door of her home behind her for the last time. She wouldn't much like the rented accommodation she'd taken for the next two weeks but it was close to the Rosie. Most of her stuff was in Lily's spare bedroom. Jenny could have been there too, but it was easier for work if she stayed near Button Street. After the honeymoon, she would cut her working hours and she was feeling a bit uncertain over that, but thought she might like it when she got used to it. Everything had happened so much sooner than she'd expected. The house had been snapped up by a young couple but they wanted it vacated quickly and the price was so good the sisters couldn't refuse.

Walking away quickly, Jenny frowned. She would hand the key in and return to work. It was better at work, because there was no time to think about what she was doing and she was still assailed by doubts regularly. Oh, she knew she loved Michael. Their love-making had become almost frantic now, and Jenny had been tempted to go all the way – she wasn't sure why she hadn't. Michael was frustrated but she couldn't quite bring herself to do it; Gran's warnings were firmly fixed in her head.

'No matter how much you think you're in love, wait, my girl,' she'd told Jenny. 'Slip before that ring is on your finger and it could ruin your life.'

It was daft to heed the warnings now, Jenny knew, because she had nothing to fear. Michael loved her and couldn't wait for their wedding – but still she hadn't been able to give him what his feverish kisses demanded.

Shaking her head, she quickened her step. Why did she have this uneasy feeling, the prickling at the back of her neck that told her something was about to go wrong?

Jenny stared at Michael in stunned dismay. He couldn't have just said what he had – after all he'd promised and letting her sell her gran's house.

'I don't understand – you told me the army wouldn't take you because you have flat feet.'

'Yes, I do,' he said and frowned. 'I'm not officially joining up – but Chris recommended me for this mission. They need a driver they can trust to keep his mouth shut and it's overseas – and that really is all I can tell you, Jenny.'

'But what about the wedding?'

'I thought we could bring that forward to this Saturday,' Michael said, looking at her uncertainly. 'The banns have already been called, after all. It does mean we'll just have a quick wedding and we won't get the big reception we were planning – but we can have a party later instead, perhaps at Christmas when I should be home.'

'But . . .' Jenny stared at him, seeing the silent pleading in his eyes. She'd thought she would be lucky and he'd never have to go but it seemed the army had found a way to draw him into their net anyway. 'All right – but the house won't be ours, will it?'

'I've arranged it so that you can sign alone,' Michael said. 'I've done my bit and you can do the final part.

I don't like to leave you, love – but it's better we're married, isn't it?'

Jenny considered and then smiled. To cancel everything now would be awful. They could have a quiet wedding with their closest friends and then have the party they'd planned when Michael was back from this wretched trip. After all, she, Lily and Sarah's mother were doing the catering between them so they could always put it off to a more convenient time. She supposed she was lucky that he wasn't being drafted to the Front with a gun in his hands.

'Yes, it is,' she agreed. 'Because I do love you and I want to be your wife.'

As Michael's arms closed around her, Jenny knew she'd done the right thing. He loved her very much and she loved him too – so what else could she do but agree?

The day of the wedding was bright and fine, though a bit chilly. It was, of course, autumn now and the lovely days of summer had fled too fast, days when Jenny had thought she had all the time in the world to get used to the idea of marriage. Now it was all upside down and as she dressed in her pretty white dress, glad that at least she'd bought something she could wear again and not the froth of lace that had tempted her, Jenny's insides were churning.

She had no fears for her wedding night and knew that she would go happily to her husband's arms. However, two days later he would leave her to go off to goodness knew where and she would be forced to move into their new home alone. Michael had done wonders getting it all signed and sealed but it was still unfurnished and, although he'd given her money to purchase whatever she needed, it was a daunting task to set up a home alone. Even Chris had managed to be with Lily when she chose her things and then moved in.

'Stop worrying,' her sister told her when she confessed her fears. 'You would have picked what you wanted anyway, Jenny, so what's the difference?'

Jenny knew she was right, but the situation felt all wrong; it was rushed, awkward and unsettling and she wished that Lily's husband hadn't recommended Michael for this rotten job.

However, she knew better than to complain to Michael – and the way he'd kissed her the night before their wedding told her how happy he was that he would no longer have to wait for the passion they had denied themselves.

The wedding itself was lovely, even though only a few of Jenny's friends were invited to celebrate it with them at the hotel Michael had booked for a small buffet luncheon. Lily and Chris were there and Sister Rose and Nurse Sarah and her mother Gwen. The rest of her friends would be invited on Michael's return when they had a big party.

The ceremony, in a church, seemed brief, but the reception was very well done and she knew the friends who wished her well meant it sincerely. She'd been given quite a few gifts, which would be a help, because despite years of saving a few things like tablecloths and glass dishes, she had very little, though she'd bought a double bed, wardrobe and dressing table in her lunch hours, and hoped they would be delivered before she returned from her brief honeymoon.

'Be happy and don't worry,' Lily said as she hugged her before they climbed into Michael's car and he drove them away, a trail of old tin cans and flags behind them until he stopped a mile down the road and took them off. He grinned at her.

'I'm lucky they didn't paint just married all over the car. I'd have had to spend half the weekend washing it off!'

Jenny laughed and shook her head. She'd enjoyed her wedding and, for the moment, her doubts had fled. If they only had three days before Michael left for his secret mission, they might as well enjoy them.

Michael had chosen a lovely hotel in Southend. He'd apologised that it wasn't the Devon coast or, even better, the South of France, and promised that one day he would take her to all those places, but for three days Jenny didn't care. Being married was wonderful, she discovered on her wedding night. Michael was a considerate lover and he'd made sure Jenny was happy, bringing her to a state of pleasure she hadn't been sure existed, though she'd heard other nurses talk of marvellous love-making.

He'd made love to her three times during the night and in the morning, when she'd still felt sleepy, he'd held her close and whispered of his love and happiness that she was finally his. In those few moments Jenny knew she was truly happy and all her soul searching was just plain daft. Nothing in her life had ever been as good as this moment, lying close

86

together talking, feeling content with each other and the world.

Of course, they'd had fun on the pier with all the slot machines and eating whelks from a stall that were so fresh and tasty. They had fish and chips out of a bag on the sea front at lunch and went to a posh hotel that night for a dinner dance. Jenny floated through the evening and wished it could go on forever.

On the second day, Michael bought her a pair of gold earrings in the shape of hearts with a little garnet at the heart.

'That's my heart, Jenny,' he told her, 'and the garnet is my teardrop because I have to leave you so soon. I know you hate the idea and so do I, but I have to do it. I may have flat feet so I can't march long distances like other men, but I'm not a coward and I have to do my bit. All of us have to protect you and your sister and all our friends. I shan't have a gun in my hand but what I'm doing is important or I wouldn't go.'

'I know.' Jenny turned and hugged him and felt the pain of their separation. Two days just wasn't long enough! Suddenly, she knew absolutely that Michael was the only man for her and if she lost him her life would be empty. Throwing her arms around him, she hugged him, tears on her cheeks. 'I love you so much, darling. Please come back to me soon.'

'Of course, I shall,' he said and grinned, looking ridiculously pleased. 'How could I not when I have the most beautiful wife in the world?'

CHAPTER 14

It was the beginning of November and the weather was colder than it had been for ages, frost on the kitchen windows of the houses and nipping at their noses. Tim wondered what was for tea that evening. He knew it wouldn't be much. Mum wasn't well again, constantly coughing and looking weary, and she didn't earn very much these days. She'd had to cut her hours in the infirmary because she kept fainting and Ruby had said that it was too much for her and she needed to rest and get well. Tim knew that his mother was worried now more than ever because her wage was less.

'Do you think Mum will be well enough to make Christmas for us this year?' Jilly asked, looking at her brother hopefully. 'She's so tired all the time these days and we haven't had a proper dinner for ages.'

'That's nearly two months away.' Tim looked at his little sister anxiously. Jilly often complained she was hungry, cold or tired these days and he knew it upset his mum. He was often hungry too, but he tried not to say anything to worry Mum. He thought of how Christmas had been when his father was alive.

Tim remembered being put up on his father's shoulders and taken to watch the local football club, and, at Christmas, there was always a visit to the big toy shops in the West End to look in the windows. Even back then, he couldn't have the expensive things that took his eye, but he'd been given a shiny repainted secondhand trike one year and a lovely train set that his father had bought from the evening paper another. There had been a doll with a painted face for Jilly when she was three and a little porcelain tea set the next year, but then the worst had happened and the terrible news had come just two months before that Christmas.

The darkness had descended and it hadn't lightened since his father's death. Jilly would be seven a few days after Christmas and Tim was thirteen next year. How he wished that he was fourteen so that he could find a proper job and make life better for them all, though he wasn't sure whether it was the shortage of money, or his mum's tiredness from scrubbing floors – the only work she could get – that had made her so ill. Sometimes, Tim feared that it was a broken heart instead. He'd seen her pressing her hand to her chest and knew that she was in pain. Tim still felt the pain of his father's loss inside his chest and he thought his mum must feel it worse, because he'd been able to forget it now and then, when playing football with his mates on the street or finding some way to please Jilly – and, very occasionally, to make Mum smile. She seemed to get worse all the time now, constantly looking over her shoulder as if she was frightened of something, but when he asked what was wrong, she just shook her head and wouldn't tell him. If he was fourteen and grown up, she would share her worries. He thought perhaps it was just that she didn't have enough money to manage.

It hurt Tim that his mother didn't laugh any more. He knew how bad she felt and how much she missed Dad but he did too, yet he still laughed sometimes when he was feeling happy at school – or when he saw Mr Marshall in his garage on the corner of Shilling Street.

Jeff Marshall was a little bit older than Dad had been when he died – perhaps in his forties. Tim wasn't sure and it didn't matter because he was full of energy and fun, always teasing the lads who played football in the streets around the Rosie Infirmary and sometimes kicking their ball.

The nurse called Margaret had caught their football once just before it struck a window in the infirmary, and then joined in their game for a while. She walked past the garage most nights now and always had a smile for Tim if she saw him. Yeah, she was all right, Tim thought, but Jeff Marshall was great.

Jeff had known Tim's father and told Tim what a good bloke he was, how kind he'd been to those in need. 'Your dad was one of the best,' he'd told Tim once when he'd given him sixpence for sweets for him and Jilly. 'I lived over in Canning Town but then I got the chance of this garage after I came out of the army. Your dad helped me get set up in his spare time . . .' Jeff had shaken his head then sorrowfully.

'I was right sorry what happened to him, son. I tried to offer your mum help but she froze me out – still, I'm always around if you think I can do anything.'

Tim had thanked him, but he'd known Jeff was right. Mum had frozen out all the well-meaning neighbours who had offered to help her, refusing what she termed as charity, determined to manage alone.

'Well?' Jilly said, a tearful note in her voice, because Tim hadn't answered her question. 'You haven't told me – will Mum buy us presents and make us Christmas dinner this year?'

'I don't know,' Tim replied truthfully. 'She's had a few days off work, because she was ill – and she doesn't earn very much.'

Meals recently had been a plate of mashed potato and a tiny piece of corned beef or slices of bread, butter and strawberry jam. Gone were all the delicious pies, the sausages and chips and fried onions and the roast dinner on Sundays. Now, they had a glass of milk during the morning at school and a piece of bread and dripping before they went, and either something tasteless or bread and jam for tea. Jilly preferred the bread and jam and Tim felt the same. He'd earned a few pence washing windows for neighbours that Mum didn't know about and sometimes bought some chips for Jilly and himself to share on the way home from school, because they were starving. Once he'd bought six eggs from Mr Forest at the corner shop and he'd given him a penny bar of chocolate, which he and Jilly had eaten before they got home. Mum would have scolded him for taking charity and she wanted to know where the money

91

from the eggs had come from. When Tim told her he'd earned it sweeping someone's path and helping to move a pile of bricks, she'd been cross.

'Your father would have hated you doing that,' she'd said. 'He wanted you to learn the building trade as a bricklayer – he thought that was a good job and one that would last a lifetime.' Mum's mouth thinned bitterly. 'He would have done better to leave the sea and go as a labourer. Perhaps then he would still be alive.'

Tim wished his father *was* still alive. He longed to hear his voice booming up the stairs, telling him to hurry if he wanted to see the football and to see his mum smile.

'My friend Lila will have a new pram and dolly for Christmas,' Jilly said and sounded as if she were on the brink of tears. 'Last year I had an orange and a bar of chocolate!' Tears slipped down her cheeks and she looked miserable. 'And we had a sausage each with mash and carrots for dinner – Lila's mum cooked them chicken and roast potatoes.'

'Yeah, I know,' Tim said and his tummy rumbled. It made his mouth water, just to think of a Christmas dinner like that, but he knew it was impossible. Mum had done her best last year, getting them the little oranges and penny bars of chocolate, but she could never afford a doll's pram or a chicken dinner.

'Tell you what,' Tim said spurred on by his sister's obvious distress, 'I'll see if I can earn a few bob before Christmas. I shan't be able to afford all you want, Jilly, but I might earn enough to get some food.' He would try for a present for her, too, but wouldn't tell her, because he might not be able to find enough jobs. It was getting cold and the weather was dirty, which meant that folk didn't bother about getting windows washed so often. Still, he could try, couldn't he?

Thus far, Tim hadn't gone far in his search for work, staying in the lanes he knew well where folk knew him and some of them were kind enough to give him a job even if they didn't really need anything. He'd been given a rock bun for himself as well as sixpence by old Mrs Taylor at the end of the street. Mum didn't like her, because she said she was sour-faced – but Tim had seen her struggling with her shopping basket and carried it home for her. He'd refused payment for that, but she'd told him he could wash her front windows and sweep the path so he often did jobs for her now and she never failed to give him sixpence and a bun, which he shared with Jilly – but sixpence wouldn't buy a chicken for Christmas dinner and it wouldn't buy a present of any kind for his sister, let alone a doll's pram.

Tim sighed. He thought there might be jobs that paid more down on the docks, but his father hadn't cared for the men who worked there – said some of them were a rough lot and he'd long ago told Tim to set his sights higher.

Perhaps he would go round to Jeff Marshall's place and see if he knew of any jobs going. Tim would love a paper round in the mornings or after school; he didn't mind which he was offered. Yes, he would ask Jeff if he knew of any going in the district.

They were approaching the corner of the road when he saw the boy again. He'd been hanging around for a couple of weeks. He was taller than Tim and bigger, but his clothes were dirty and ragged. Tim wondered where he lived and whether he went hungry sometimes. He waved to him from a distance and the boy hesitated, and then acknowledged him, before turning away and disappearing round the corner.

Tim wondered if he should have approached the boy and asked if he wanted a bit of bread. Mum didn't have much but she would've shared what they had. He regretted not asking and made up his mind he would next time he saw the lad standing on the corner, wondering if Jeff knew anything about him. He made up his mind to mention it the next time he saw him.

Jeff always cleaned the cars for his customers as an extra service. He never charged for it, just felt it was a courtesy owed to them for choosing his garage – and when it came to a lovely old Bentley like Mr Carson's, it was a privilege to wash and polish the beautiful paintwork and leather interior.

'Good morning, Mr Marshall!' The faintly lilting sound of the young woman's voice told Jeff who had spoken before he looked up. He took a moment, controlling the sudden beat of his heart. Jeff liked the young nurse; he liked her a lot but he was forty-four and probably looked older. He smiled as he let his eyes meet hers. 'It is colder today, isn't it?'

'Yes, it is, Nurse James,' he replied. 'Have you finished for the day then?'

'No, I'm just taking my break and fetching some

milk and tea from Mr Forest's shop. It will save me stopping this afternoon when I'm off duty.'

'Ah.' He nodded wisely. 'Going somewhere nice this evening?'

'I wish,' Margaret replied with a sigh. 'No, I just like to get home quick in the evenings.'

'I could always give you a lift in my Wolsey,' Jeff offered before he could stop himself. 'It isn't as posh as this beauty, but it is comfortable and warm on a cold night.'

'Oh, how kind of you,' Margaret said. 'I might take you up on that sometime – if you really mean it?'

'Wouldn't say it if I didn't.' Jeff was warmed by the brilliance of her smile, glad he'd asked at last. It had taken months to get up the courage. 'I could take you to the pictures one night, Nurse James – unless your boyfriend would object.'

She laughed, the lilting sound more noticeable in her laughter than her speaking voice. 'I don't have one, or many close friends either – just some of the nurses from the Rosie.' Margaret checked her watch. 'I must dash but I'll ask for that lift tonight, Mr Marshall – and then we'll talk.'

Waving at him, she walked briskly down the street, her hips swaying seductively. She wasn't one of those slender lasses that thought they were so fashionable in their elegant dresses and Cuban heels. Margaret James wore sensible black lace-up shoes for her work, which was hard on the feet and legs, and a uniform that showed up her generous hips. That was all right with Jeff. He liked a woman you could get hold of and cuddle, not someone who was skin and bones and felt as if she might break. For a moment, Jeff smiled as he thought of having his arms about Nurse James, but then he shook his head. She couldn't be more than twenty-four or so, which meant there were twenty years between them. It would do him no good to dream.

'Hello, Mr Marshall . . .'

Jeff came back from his reverie to look at the young lad, who was shifting nervously from one foot to the other. He thought a lot of young Tim, knowing how he struggled to buy a few extras for himself and his sister. Betty Stewart was a fool because folk had been willing to offer help at the start, but she'd shut them out and now she was barely keeping body and soul together. Well, that was her choice, but Jeff felt sorry for the children.

'How are you today, Tim?' he asked, wondering if he had sixpence in his pocket.

'I'm good, sir,' Tim replied and shuffled his feet. At least his mother had taught her children good manners, but it was a pity she was a stiff-necked fool, Jeff thought. 'I was wonderin' if you knew of any decent jobs I could do?'

'Ah, yes, I see . . .' Jeff looked at him consideringly. Tim was tall for his age but gangly and thin because he didn't get the good food he needed. 'What kind of job did you want?'

'Anythin',' Tim told him. 'Jilly wants a proper Christmas dinner – and a doll's pram. I can't earn enough for the pram, but I might for the dinner.'

'What did you have last year?' Jeff frowned.

'Sausage, mash and fried onions,' Tim said enthusiastically. 'It was lovely – but Jilly has set her heart on roast chicken this year.'

Jeff checked the words he wanted to say, that he would gladly provide the Christmas lunch for the family, and presents too. He knew Betty Stewart wouldn't agree to any of it.

'Well . . .' Jeff pretended to deliberate. 'Would you consider helping me, after school and at the weekends?'

'Yes please!' Tim's face lit up. 'Could I do what you're doing, sir?'

'Well, not this particular car, not yet, but in time, if you're careful and thorough and take notice of all I tell you.'

'Oh yes, I'd love to do that,' Tim enthused eagerly. 'When can I start?'

'Well, I've got this to finish – and that black car standing over there needs a wash before I polish it. Want to start now? It's hard work but I'll show you – we need to put the hose over it first.'

Jeff grinned as Tim scampered off to turn on the hose and was soon hosing the councillor's car as preparation to washing it with soapy water. When the lad had finished hosing it down, Jeff had finished polishing the Bentley and together they washed the black car, then Jeff let Tim wash it down for the last time before buffing it himself to a lovely shine. He was genuinely pleased when he'd finished because the job had taken half the time.

'What else do you want me to do?' Tim asked.

'Isn't it time for your tea?'

'Mum won't care if I'm late.'

'I think she might,' Jeff said. 'Run along now and come back tomorrow. I shan't pay you today, but at the end of the week – that way it will be more and you can decide what to spend and what to save.'

'Thanks, Mr Marshall.' As he was about to leave, Tim hesitated and turned back. 'I've seen a young boy, a bit older than me – his clothes are scruffy and he looks hungry. I wondered if you'd seen him or knew who he was?'

'Afraid I don't know who he is,' Jeff said, 'although he's probably the one I've seen around here sometimes.'

'I see him at the end of the lane sometimes and I thought he might be hungry. I get a dinner at school sometimes so I'd share my tea if he didn't run off – next time I'll ask him.'

'That's a good lad,' Jeff said and smiled in approval. Tim didn't have much and if he was willing to share that, it showed what a good nature he had.

Watching the lad run off down the lane, Jeff smiled. It never hurt to do a good turn and he'd have liked to do more for the family if Betty hadn't shut him out.

Nodding to himself, Jeff went into his house, which was right next door to the garage and very convenient. He would have a wash and shave, and if Nurse James fancied a trip to the cinema or somewhere for a bite to eat, he would be ready to take her . . .

CHAPTER 15

Margaret saw Mr Marshall waiting for her as she left work. He was dressed in a dark suit, white shirt, collar and tie, and his shoes shone so you could see your face in them, as her Auntie Josie used to say. She smiled to herself, because it was a long time since a young man had got dressed up for her. Perhaps Jeff Marshall wasn't exactly a young man, but he wasn't old and she'd liked him from the first time he'd smiled at her.

'It's so kind of you to take me home,' Margaret said as he opened the passenger door for her.

'It's no trouble,' Jeff said. 'I like driving – and I don't like to see you hard-working nurses walking home at night in the cold. It's dark round here at nights and sometimes there are a few louts about – but not often,' he added quickly to reassure her.

'Thank you for the warning.'

Margaret's eyes had widened. She had a fresh natural look about her that appealed even when she wasn't trying but, of course, she was completely unaware of what the wide-eyed look could make a man feel. She was a little shy as Jeff slid into the seat beside her and put his car into gear, but then, as he turned his head and smiled, the faint unease had gone. She was certain he was a man to be trusted or she would not have entered his car – not like that other one . . . Swiftly, Margaret quashed the memory of the nightmare that had haunted her. That was all over. Everyone said she must be strong and push it from her mind, and most of the time she could do just that. Jeff was speaking so she turned her head to listen.

'I thought we'd take you home so that you can change after your hard day at the infirmary and then we might go for a meal or to the pictures?'

'I *am* hungry,' Margaret agreed. 'But what I'd truly love is a bag of fish and chips – and I've got my skirt and blouse on under my coat. So we don't need to go back to my flat.'

'Shall we have that then?' Jeff asked, a bit surprised. 'If it's what you'd really like.'

'Yes, please.' She looked at him again and gave a little giggle. 'I'd rather go to the flicks on my day off, so I'm not tired. All I feel like doing now is sitting eating fish and chips with plenty of salt and vinegar.'

'You're very easy to please.'

'Am I?' She asked the question innocently. 'I'm not used to anything fancy. I wouldn't know what to do in a posh restaurant.'

'I'm a bit like that myself,' Jeff admitted. 'I just wanted to look smart this evening for you, Nurse Margaret.'

'You don't have to call me nurse; I'm just Margaret,' she said. 'You do look very smart and I wish I felt like going somewhere to celebrate, but I don't after a busy day on the wards. I'm on the chronic ward

100

now. It's nowhere near as nice as the children's ward, but we all get moved around.'

'Yes, I expect all you young ladies would prefer to nurse the kiddies.'

'Children are lovely,' Margaret agreed. 'It's great being with them but all sick people need nursing, so we all do our bit on the chronic ward – Matron says it's the test of a nurse. She says anyone can look after the broken bones and tonsillitis cases, but the chronic illness in adults is far more demanding.'

'I'm sure it must be.' Jeff had driven to the nearest fish and chip shop and he parked the car and went off to fetch their supper. Margaret wondered if she'd been silly to reject his offers of entertainment. Perhaps he wouldn't bother to ask her again, especially after he'd been to so much trouble to get ready.

'Thanks,' she said as he handed her the wrapped packet. 'We could eat them in my flat, if you like? I've got some beer in the pantry.'

'Why not?' Jeff replied but she thought he sounded pleased. 'I got us some pickled onions, don't know if you like them?'

'Yes, I do – if you're having them. I don't want to breathe onion all over you.'

They smiled at each other in mutual agreement. Margaret's heart fluttered a little as they stopped outside the house where she had her tiny flat. It was a big Georgian house and had been divided into three flats and what was called a maisonette. Margaret didn't like having her bed in her living room, so she'd chosen a flat to rent. She found it expensive, because her wage wasn't very high, but she enjoyed living alone. For years she'd been too nervous to be alone, but gradually her fears had waned. After all, the attack on her had done no lasting damage, inflicting bruises to her flesh and her confidence, but thanks to her aunt coming out at the right moment, nothing too terrible had happened. Had her aunt ignored her screams for help, Margaret knew she might have been raped in the alley beside her home.

She suppressed the tiny shudder. That had happened three years earlier and she was over it now, after all as Aunt Josie had said, 'You got a fright, my girl, and that will teach you to choose your man friends more carefully.'

Margaret had taken several months before she found it easy to speak to any man, but the fear had receded and she now carried a penknife in her coat pocket, which she would use if ever the need arose. After her aunt's death she'd found a new job and come here – and, so far, she was happier than she'd ever been.

As she unlocked her front door, her landlady came out and looked at her oddly. 'Gentlemen callers must leave before half past nine, Miss James,' the woman said primly.

'We're just going to have a fish and chip supper, Mrs Robins,' Margaret told her firmly. 'Mr Marshall runs the local garage and he kindly gave me a lift home.'

'Yes, I know Mr Marshall.' The landlady nodded, slightly warmer as she saw who it was. 'Well, I expect that is all right then – but you know my rules.'

'Yes, Mrs Robins,' Margaret agreed. 'We're just friends and it is too cold to eat in the car.'

Her landlady nodded and went back inside her own flat, closing the door with a little snap. Jeff glanced at her as they went inside Margaret's neat flat. She had a nice-sized room with a small kitchen at one end and comfortable chairs, a fold-up table and a bookcase at the other.

'Sit down,' she invited. 'I'll soon have these on plates.'

'Is she always like that when you bring a friend back?' he inquired and she smiled.

'You're the first,' Margaret told him honestly. 'I'd like you to know everything important about me, Mr Marshall, because I think – no, I hope – we might become friends. I had an unpleasant incident with a man I thought was to be trusted around three years ago. I'm over it now but you're the first I've really trusted since – and that's because everyone says what a lovely man you are, kind to the neighbours and children alike.'

'I would've liked kiddies of my own,' Jeff admitted. 'But my face put paid to that after the war.'

'Why? What's wrong with your face?' Margaret asked, genuinely puzzled.

'This.' He gestured to the brown scarring. 'I was burned during an enemy attack in the war, but it's only a small part of my face. Some of the poor devils had far more to cope with . . .'

'Oh, I'm sorry, I didn't realise,' Margaret replied candidly. 'I thought it was just a bit of discolouration, perhaps a birthmark. So, we're both scarred. You on the outside and me inside.'

'I'm sorry for what happened to you, Margaret,'

103

he said. 'And I can promise you I'll never try anything you're not willing to offer.'

'I know that, Jeff,' she said, letting him see that she had decided to trust him. 'You wouldn't be here if I wasn't sure – the other thing happened to the silly girl I was then and I was lucky it didn't end badly. My aunt came out when she heard me scream and she had a broom. She clouted him three times over the head and he ran off.'

'I'd have broken the blighter's neck!' Jeff said and looked savage.

Margaret laughed. 'My aunt scolded me for being foolish and going out with a bloke like that in the first place – he was a bit of a spiv, I suppose, flashy suit and shiny shoes. I liked the look of him, but I didn't know what he was like underneath.'

'And you're really over it now?' Jeff gave her an earnest look.

'Yes – as I said, my aunt saved me from real harm. I was nervous for a time, but it taught me to be more careful and get to know folk before talking to them.'

Jeff's whole face lit up with a smile that came from deep down inside. 'That makes me feel very good, Margaret,' he told her. 'I'll tell you now that I appreciate your trust in me and I'll never give you cause to regret you met me.'

Margaret smiled as she brought their meal over. 'It's good to have a friend.'

Jeff's plate was a little fuller than hers. He'd bought generous portions and there was more than enough to go around, even for her large appetite, though she didn't often treat herself to fish and chips. She opened a bottle of pale ale and poured it into two tumblers, giving him one. They sat on her comfortable chairs and balanced the food on their laps. She'd thought this informality would set them both at ease.

She raised her glass of beer to him. 'I know ladies are supposed to drink sherry but my family all like a glass of pale ale and I prefer a glass of beer, especially with fish and chips.'

'I couldn't agree more,' Jeff said and grinned. 'Here's to our first date, Margaret – and I hope we'll have many more in the future; we'll definitely go to the pictures on your day off.'

'That's next Saturday,' she said and nodded. 'I'd like that a lot.'

Jeff was still feeling pleased with himself when he drove home. Margaret was a surprising young woman. He'd thought her a no-nonsense sort of girl but to find she wasn't averse to a half of beer with a fish and chip supper told him that she was the kind of woman he could get along with. He'd thought so from his brief chats with her, but this evening had been more than pleasant and he was glad he'd offered to take her home.

Jeff wasn't sure whether his budding love for Margaret was returned or if she just wanted friendship; she wasn't a girl to flirt and he liked her for that as well as so many other things – her ready laughter, her honesty, and she was real pretty, too. Jeff liked the way her clothes showed that she was all woman underneath – but he mustn't think about that, because he couldn't afford to make a wrong move. Margaret had obviously been frightened and it must have taken courage for her to let him into her home like that – though she'd said she'd heard good reports of him from her colleagues at the infirmary.

Sister Rose would certainly speak well of him because he'd fixed her husband's little car so that it was easier for him to drive after his accident, and though Doctor Peter was getting better now, he couldn't walk far as yet.

Jeff parked his car on the forecourt of his garage and got out to unlock the garage door. Just as he did so, a small dark shadow darted at him and startled him. He was about to strike out when the lad spoke.

'It's only Tim, Mr Marshall,' the boy said. 'Sorry I startled you, but I've been waiting for you to come back for ages!'

'What's wrong, lad?' Jeff asked, frowning.

'It's Ma,' Tim said. 'She went out first thing this morning and she ain't come back.'

'Does she often do that?' Jeff asked him, looking at him uncertainly.

'Never before. I think somethin' has happened to her,' Tim confessed, clearly anxious. 'Jilly was crying so I went next door and Mrs Meadows said she would feed her and put her to bed with her daughter – and I've been out lookin' for Ma.'

'Where have you tried?' Jeff asked, hesitating. 'Do you know where she was working?'

'At the Rosie, same as always.' Tim nodded vigorously. 'I went there first and asked and they said she left at half-eleven, as always – she usually goes home, does her shoppin' if she's got any money and cleans the house.'

'And when you got in from school there was no sign of her anywhere in the house or garden?'

'We looked everywhere and we went up and down the lanes, but she wasn't about, so that's when I left Jilly next door and I've been looking further ever since. I tried the police but they said she wasn't missing until at least three days had gone and so I came here. I don't know what to do . . .'

'No, I don't suppose you do,' Jeff said feeling puzzled. Where could Betty Stewart be? She wasn't the sort of woman who went drinking and fell about in the streets, nor had she been known to take up with strange men and go off with them for money – so what had happened to her?

Jeff opened his car door. 'Jump in, lad. We'll have a drive round and see if she's about or if anyone knows where she went.'

Jeff didn't hold out much hope of finding the boy's mother in the dark, but he could see Tim needed someone to take charge. It was certainly a mystery and one that sent shivers down Jeff's spine, because he couldn't see how anything good could come from it.

If Betty Stewart had had an accident or fallen in the river, these children would be orphans and then what would happen to them? He had a vague idea that Matron at the Rosie could arrange foster parents for kids without parents, but that wasn't much to look forward to, was it?

Seeing that Tim was safely in the passenger seat, Jeff prepared to spend the next couple of hours driving round; it was the least he could do.

CHAPTER 16

'Constable Jones brought them to my attention,' Mary Thurston, Matron of the Rosie, said to her ladyship a few days later. 'Their mother has disappeared and the police are baffled. Quite a few people have been out searching, stirred up by the local garage owner, but so far there is no sign of her.'

'Have they tried the hospitals?'

'I did when Constable Jones told me about them,' Mary said, frowning. 'None of them had a patient matching Betty Stewart's description, so for the moment the children are at home and some of their neighbours are rallying round to feed them. Tim, who's twelve, seems a sensible boy and Mr Marshall is making sure they're all right, but unless their mother is found soon, it means they'll need a permanent home.'

'Yes. I quite see that, Mary.' The patron of the hospital nodded her agreement. 'I'll add them to the bottom of my list, which, as usual, exceeds the number of foster parents available.'

'Yes, of course, and I fear it always will.' Mary smiled. 'As always, we do the best we can . . .'

'Yes.' Lady Rosalie pulled on her smart tan leather gloves and stood up. 'Now, you're still coming for Christmas, aren't you, Mary? I know it's several weeks away yet, but I do want you to come to us. It was so pleasant having you with us at the coast this summer. My son felt free to go off with his friends whenever he liked, knowing I wouldn't be alone, and it will be the same at Christmas.'

'Yes, of course. I shan't be able to come both days,' Mary said, 'but Christmas Eve evening and Christmas Day would be delightful.'

Mary smiled, feeling pleased her friend had repeated her invitation. She had very much enjoyed her holiday at the seaside resort. This year of 1939 had been a difficult one. Sister Rose had been through a terrible trauma after her husband Peter had his accident, and consequently she had been off work quite often. She was now back, but only part-time, which had left Mary short of senior staff, though she had a couple of promising youngsters. However, she had a new nursing sister starting soon and believed she would be a marvellous addition to their staff at the infirmary.

After her ladyship had gone, Mary began her rounds of the wards. She believed that it kept the young nurses on their toes to see her suddenly appear with no warning, so varied the times of her inspection tours. Sister Matthews was very good but she was working less hours these days because her husband William was currently unwell and she needed to spend more time at home with him. Mary thought that she would probably leave altogether after the war.

It was never comfortable having staff changes,

Mary thought. Kathy had had her baby earlier in the year, but wasn't returning to work because her husband Bert didn't want her to do too much and her mother was ill; she couldn't cope with all that and a job.

At least there was good news on that front; Kathy's mother had improved a little and was home again and she had no problems as far as the cleaning was concerned. Ruby was in complete charge of that and the kitchens and the food were now first-rate. Ruby was a marvel, worth three times what she paid her, and would be getting a good bonus for Christmas.

Sighing, Mary banished her worries to the back of her mind. She had her rounds to make and the patients always came first. It crossed her mind to wonder what had happened to Betty Stewart. Ruby said she'd been a good worker but unwell for the past few months – so what had caused the change? If only these women would go to a doctor when they were ill or ask her nurses for advice a lot of suffering could be saved – but still, it was strange that she'd disappeared without a trace.

The woman lay in a daze for a long time, not realising that time was passing or what had happened to her. When that monster had attacked her, she'd screamed for help and seen a young lad run off and hoped he'd gone to get someone – but no one came. Her body hurt all over and when she finally roused enough to get herself up from the damp ground, her head was sore. If she'd lain there any longer, she would've died of the cold.

As she began to walk away from the canal bank, the woman's mind was blank of everything but the horror she had just endured. She did not know her name, where she came from, or what she'd been doing before she was attacked. All she was aware of was a deep fear that the man would return and attack her again. She sensed that it had been revenge rather than robbery and when she put her hand into her threadbare coat pocket, she found a purse with a small amount of money inside.

She walked to a bus shelter and sat there, shivering from fear and the cold, not knowing what she wanted to do or where she was going. Then a bus came along and it said Liverpool Street Station on its front panel. The woman got on and offered the conductor a coin.

'All the way, missus?' he asked and she nodded. He looked at her curiously. 'You all right then, love?'

She ignored the question and he moved away. She didn't know if she was all right. She didn't know anything for sure – except that she'd been attacked and she had to get as far away as she could from this place. She would get on a train and let it take her wherever it was going, because if she stayed here the man would for sure kill her next time . . .

Luke felt ashamed afterwards. He'd run off to find help instead of helping that woman when she was being attacked. It had been instinctive and he *had* tried to get help for her for ages but no one had listened to him. He supposed it was because he looked scruffy but he'd told them what was happening and they'd just dismissed it as nothing. He should have stayed and done something but he wasn't sure what. The man was big and strong and though he was tall for his age, he was just a boy; but it haunted him and after a while he went back to look but there was no sign that anything had happened.

The woman had been unknown to him but he still felt guilty that he hadn't helped her. He was lonely and it had started to drizzle with rain, which made him feel miserable. All he wanted was somewhere warm and dry where he could find peace and friendship. Perhaps if he'd been brave enough to help that woman, she might have taken him home and given him a cup of tea . . . tears stung his eyes but he brushed them away impatiently.

Tears never helped and if he gave way to them, he'd get nowhere. He was sorry he hadn't helped her but she'd gone, so perhaps someone else had, or she'd fought back and her attacker had run off – either way, he knew what he'd seen would haunt him for a long time.

CHAPTER 17

'I wish Mum would come home,' Jilly grumbled as they walked home from school. 'I don't like going from one house to another for my tea.'

'At least Mrs Morris gives us a good tea,' Tim reminded her. 'She always does egg and chips on a Wednesday night.'

'I love egg and chips – but then we have to go back home and it's dark and cold!'

'Not once I get the fire going,' he said. 'I'll go on ahead and you can come home when it's warm.'

Jilly pulled a miserable face at him. 'But when is Mum coming back? It's only five weeks to Christmas and we shan't know what to do without her.'

Tim shook his head because he couldn't answer. He wasn't sure they would even be in their house by Christmas. The only reason they were there now was because Jeff Marshall had paid their rent for the past couple of weeks. He'd overheard the conversation between the garage owner and the rent collector.

'It ain't right, Mr Marshall, two kids livin' in that house alone. I'll let 'em be for a while as long as you've paid the rent – but Mr Barret wouldn't approve. If she doesn't turn up soon, I'll have to tell him and the kids will need to go.'

'It's their home – and what happens if their mother comes back and finds the house empty?' Jeff had replied.

'That ain't my concern. I'm paid to keep things right for my boss so I'll give them to the end of the month and that's it.' Their conversation had ended as the rent man went off to bang at a neighbour's door. No one liked the rent man much, because almost everyone had weeks when they couldn't pay and had to hide out of the way rather than open the door.

Tim hadn't told Mr Marshall that he'd heard and he was old enough to know that things would indeed change soon. The neighbours were taking it in turns to feed him and Jilly, and he tried to do whatever he was able to help them in return, fetching coal and stuff like that, but the council would soon turn up at their home and they would be shipped off to an orphanage. He didn't want to go any more than his sister would but while he would accept it if he had to, Jilly would cry and scream.

Where was Mum and why didn't she come home? Tim knew she hadn't been well for a long time and sometimes she despaired, but underneath he knew she still loved them and he didn't believe she would just walk away and leave them. Something must have happened to her. His blood ran cold as he thought of his mum lying somewhere in an alley, dying or dead, and his throat closed with misery. Even though she hadn't always fed them as well as she ought, he wanted his mother – but he knew wanting something didn't make it happen. He'd longed and prayed for his dad not to be dead, but *he* hadn't come home. If Mum was dead, it meant that they were on their own and Tim would have to think of what to do. His mind went round and round as he tried to work out what he could do to save them from being taken off to an orphanage, but he couldn't think of anything.

Mr Marshall was courting that nice Nurse Margaret from the infirmary so he wouldn't want to be lumbered with two children now – and Tim didn't think they had any other relatives. He'd never heard of Mum speak of a sister or brother or even an aunt, and his father had only had an old uncle but even Uncle Maurice was dead now, because Dad had gone to his funeral and been given a silver watch, which was all that was left after the funeral costs. Mum had sold it to pay part of the costs for Dad's own funeral and any jewellery that Mum had been given was sold after Dad's death to help pay the bills, so there was nothing left of any value in the house but a few sticks of furniture and their clothes – hardly enough if they needed to be sold to pay for Mum's funeral, Tim thought gloomily.

He wondered about running away but he knew there wasn't much comfort to be had on the streets. He'd seen kids in ragged clothes, bare feet and dark shadows under their eyes. Mum had been sorry for them whenever she saw them and while Dad lived she'd slipped them a sixpence or a slice of bread if she saw them in the lane, but after he'd gone, she didn't always have enough to pay for their own food.

Tim went into their house to make a fire for Jilly while she went to their neighbour's for tea. Mrs Morris was strict but kind. She would give Jilly a cup of milk and a plate of egg and chips, sometimes a piece of cake too. When Tim got there, she'd make him cocoa and his tea would be waiting in the oven by the fire.

Tim noticed that his store of kindling was almost gone. It would hardly last the two weeks they were here and he might have to spend one of his small hoard of coins to buy more. There was still a good pile of coke left, because Mum had used most of her wage to stock up for the winter just before she disappeared.

Once again, his throat tightened and the tears threatened as he built his fire and blew on it to get it going. Perhaps he should make it up enough in the mornings to keep in all day – after all, Mum had paid for the coke so they might as well use it.

Mrs Morris would be waiting for him. Tim rinsed his hands under the tap at the deep sink. The water was stone cold but in the morning it would be warm enough for them to wash and Jilly would enjoy that. His feeling of deep unhappiness eased a bit as he thought of his sister. Some kids had no one but he still had Jilly, who was all right, even though she moaned a bit. He had his friends at school, Mr Marshall was good to him and some of the neighbours were kinder than others. He would have preferred to stay here if he could, among people he knew and liked, but the council would send them off somewhere – he'd seen it happen to other kids like them and he hated the idea. There would be no jobs to earn money for Jilly in an orphanage and they might even be split up.

Tim shook his head. He couldn't let that happen, at least, not before Christmas. Jilly must have some sort of Christmas. If the council came before then, they would hide somewhere and then sneak back in when they'd gone. It was all he could think of for the moment, but it would have to do. He knew they were still better off than some kids.

Tim couldn't get the memory of the young lad he'd seen hanging around their lane a few weeks ago out of his head. Something in the way he'd stared at him and Jilly had made Tim want to speak to him and ask if he was all right, but the lad had always walked away if he moved towards him. He was sure that the boy was a bit older than him, but he'd never been to school round here because Tim would have known him. He felt sorry for him. It must be awful to live on the streets, especially if you weren't from these parts.

Luke stood across the road from the garage. He'd seen a young boy working there and wondered if he stood a chance of getting a job, but the man who ran it seemed to like polishing the cars himself and whistled as he worked. Turning away with a sigh, he made his way towards the docks. It was the only place he'd been able to find work lately, though only occasionally.

He'd begun to wonder if he should leave London and try his luck elsewhere but he didn't know where to go. Besides, he liked the busy streets and most of the men on the docks knew him and spoke to him; they just didn't have much work for him. Half of them seemed uncertain what to do since the war. Even if they were busy in their yards, they were nervous, continually glancing up at the sky and the false alarms didn't help. Luke had followed the exodus every time it happened in the beginning, but now he just found a place to sit and waited for the all clear.

He wondered if he would ever find a permanent job. Luke had washed shop windows and cars; he'd swept front yards and been given food by a kind housewife, but some slammed their doors in his face. So far, the work that paid best was dirty work on the docks. He'd cleaned filthy lorries that had carried foul-smelling bones and animal remains and, this week, he'd run errands for a man with a big warehouse, who gave him two half-crowns for his time.

'You're a bright lad, Luke,' Mr Fisher had told him. 'I might take you on as a storeman in another year or so, providing I can trust you.'

'You can trust me,' Luke promised, because his hopes of a permanent job had been raised but in the next moment dashed.

'You tell your father to come and see me,' Mr Fisher said. 'If you're old enough you can do more jobs for me – but I don't want trouble with the law.'

Luke's smile faded, because he had no father to ask, and if Mr Fisher guessed that he was a runaway he wouldn't give him any further work.

'Yes, sir. I'll do that,' Luke improvised. 'He can't get about much since his accident but he'll come when he can.'

Mr Fisher nodded his understanding and then had asked a couple of times how Luke's father was, making him squirm with embarrassment. Looking at the sky now, Luke saw it was beginning to get dark and might soon rain. He'd found somewhere new to shelter at nights, though quite often he went down the underground, looking for company – and he couldn't put the attack on that woman out of his mind. He should have done more and if it happened again, he would. A few bruises would be better than this lingering regret that he'd not managed to help her.

One way or another, Luke was managing, but working in the rain was cold and uncomfortable and if he got soaked, he had nowhere to dry off and no clean clothes to put on. Pulling his thin jacket collar up around his neck, he pushed the regrets from his mind and began to run to get himself warm.

'I can tell you I'm worried about those kids,' Jeff said as he sat in Matron's office at the Rosie. He'd called to see her because he wasn't sure what to do for the best and everyone said the Rosie was the best place to go if you knew about kids in trouble. 'Their neighbours have all rallied round and we've done what we can but the landlord wants them out, even though I've paid their rent. I hate to think of them being carted off to an orphanage, alone and frightened, away from all they know . . .' He hesitated, then, 'I know you looked after that lad Charlie and his sister Maisie for a while. I was wondering if you might do the same for Tim and Jilly? Just until after Christmas?'

Matron looked concerned but uncertain. 'Maisie was ill, that's why we kept her here as long as we did. We're not really suitable for children to stay over Christmas unless they're ill.' She frowned. 'I'll speak to Lady Rosalie and see if she has anyone on her list that would take them in for a while, at least, as you say, over Christmas.'

Jeff frowned, because he'd hoped she might be willing to have the children there. 'Well, I'd like to see them properly settled before then. I would take them in myself – and I will if I have to – but I'm an old bachelor, Matron, and I don't think I'm right for taking care of a little girl. I'd be all right with the boy, but the girl needs a woman's care. If I was married, I'd have had them afore now.'

'I'd like to help, Mr Marshall, and I will speak to Lady Rosalie. We'll see if we can get them fixed up for Christmas, but it may have to be an orphanage.' She sighed. 'There always seem to be more children needing help at this time of year; I have no idea why.'

Walking home, Jeff felt annoyed and upset and then a solid determination came to his mind. No way would he let those children be shipped off to an orphanage before Christmas. He would have another go at their landlord's agent about letting them stay in the house a bit longer and he'd fix Christmas for them himself somehow.

If he'd got a wife, it would be so easy – and it would be nice to be married, Jeff thought. If the children's mother had let him look after them none of this need ever have happened. Glancing up, he saw what looked like a youth running off and frowned. Some of the lads round here would nick the shirt off your back if you gave them the chance.

Tim pocketed the four shillings and sixpence Mr Marshall paid him that Saturday with a feeling of satisfaction. He knew he'd earned his wages sweeping up and cleaning paintwork and he was pleased with himself. He had managed to save nearly thirty shillings over the past few weeks – enough, Tim believed, to buy them both a nice dinner at Christmas with all the trimmings. He didn't think it would buy Jilly a doll's pram, though his money might run to a cot that rocked by the time Christmas got here. Surely that would do? He'd seen a pretty one in a junk shop down one of the lanes, priced at twelve shillings, which he might just be able to afford.

Tim wasn't sure what girls put in to cover their dolls, but he thought Mum might have some old bits of curtains or things if he looked in her chest of drawers. He could fold a bit of material up and make something to finish the cot off and he could still buy all the food to make his sister's Christmas one she would remember as there had been few enough of those.

He went to the top of the stairs and hesitated outside his mother's bedroom. Tim didn't like to intrude and had only looked inside once since she'd disappeared, just to make sure she wasn't lying on the floor, but he wanted to find something that would go in Jilly's cot.

The bedcovers looked faded and worn and were in any case too big. Tim wouldn't dare to cut them up in case his mother returned and needed them. He approached the chest of drawers warily, but then took a deep breath and opened the top one. It contained papers, old letters, the ink long faded, and some sepia photographs. The second drawer had another set of equally faded bed linen and the bottom one had his mother's underclothes and two much-washed cardigans.

Feeling like a peeping Tom, he resisted the urge to flee from the room. Even he and Jilly had more clothes than their mother; he hadn't understood how much she had gone without to try and look after her children. It felt like a lead weight in his chest as he approached the wardrobe and he had to force himself to look inside. Two worn cotton dresses and an old tweed skirt hung there. Mum had been wearing her brown skirt and a fawn jumper when she went missing. Her black shoes were at the bottom of the wardrobe and that was it. Of course, she must have been wearing her coat and hat when she went to work that morning.

Oh, Mum, where are you? The question tore at Tim's heart and he'd started to close the wardrobe when he saw the brown paper parcel right in the corner at the back. Immediately, he knew it was something special. He reached for it with a hand that trembled, drawing it out.

It was tied up with string so Tim sat on the edge of his mother's bed and undid the knots carefully. As the paper fell open, he saw the most beautiful piece of lace that he'd ever seen in in his young life and with it was a sort of coronet of wax flowers and pearls. Suddenly, he remembered one of the photos in the drawer. Surely a young woman had been wearing it?

Could that happy young woman ever have been his mum? Tim's mind flashed back to the past, when their house had been a happy one. Mum had laughed a lot back then – but that was when Dad was alive.

This must be her wedding veil and would mean so much to her. Tim wrapped it carefully and replaced it in the wardrobe. It was much too good to give Jilly for a doll's cot. He would look in the junk shop or on the market for a cheap bit of lace or something pretty. He couldn't take the one thing Mum had to remind her of her happiness. It was far too precious. No, he might pick up a remnant for sixpence or a shilling if he was lucky and he still had two weeks to go until Christmas. Anything could happen by then – Mum might come home . . .

Tim crossed his fingers. *If you're out there, Mum*, he thought sending his love and prayers towards her for all he was worth, *please come back to us, we love you and need you so much.*

Glancing out of the bedroom window, Tim noticed the thin, lanky youth hanging around on the street corner again. He lifted his hand in salute because he thought he looked lonely and for a moment he hesitated. Should he go down and tell him he could come in for a cup of tea and a bit of toast? Yet it was hard enough to manage as it was and Mum might be cross if she came back and found a stranger in the house.

Luke saw the young boy staring down at him. He was sure he was the one called Tim, who worked at the garage on the corner – he had the job Luke had hoped for, cleaning those wonderful cars. For a moment he felt a pang of envy, because Tim must have a mother and he would sleep in a warm bed that night; he thought he had a sister too but he wasn't sure. Out of sheer loneliness he'd followed Tim earlier and watched him enter the house.

Sighing, Luke turned away. He would only get frozen standing out here in the bitter cold. In his hideaway he had a bit of wood he'd taken from a derelict building down near the docks. It would make a fire for a short time, perhaps long enough to boil some water to make a drink. He still had a little cocoa left in the tin he'd bought when he was working several days a week; he'd been saving it for the right moment and tonight he could feel the cold and the despair eating away at him. Yes, tonight, he would use the last of his cocoa and hope that tomorrow he would find work so that he could buy the food he so desperately needed. His stomach rumbled at the memory of Ruby's sandwiches. He hadn't eaten anything since yesterday evening and unless he found work tomorrow, he wouldn't eat then either . . .

The woman was asleep in the corner of the train carriage when the hand shook her awake. She stared at him in terror for a moment, bewildered and frightened.

'It's the end of the line, missus,' he told her. 'Everyone has to get off the train here.'

Feeling sick with fear and disorientated, the woman stumbled to her feet and left the empty train. The sign on the platform said Ely in big black letters. She had no idea where that was or how or why she'd come there. She walked in a daze from the railway station and stood there shivering in the cold. Now where did she go?

She had no idea what had happened to her. Even though the trauma of her attack had gone now, she still felt terror but did not quite know why.

'Are you all right, love?' a woman's voice asked and she blinked at the elderly woman and then shook her head.

'I don't know,' she admitted. 'I don't remember anything. I don't know my name . . .' A feeling of panic started. 'I can't remember . . .'

'I thought you looked poorly,' the stranger said to her. 'My name is Jane – and I'll call you Sally until you remember your name. Is that all right?'

'Yes,' the newly named Sally said and stared at her as she held out a hand. 'What . . .?'

'I'm taking you home with me, Sally,' Jane told her and smiled. 'I've been alone since my daughter died of pneumonia a few years ago after catching a chill. Her things will fit you and I've food enough for the two of us. I'll ask my doctor to take a look at you tomorrow.'

'No, I can't.' Sally shook her head. 'You don't know me – and I've no money.'

'You don't need any. I don't have much either but what I've got I'll share. I don't think you'll murder me in my bed – besides, what will you do if you don't come with me?'

Sally looked at her properly and saw she was elderly and fragile. She probably needed someone to look after her and Sally could do that – at least, she felt she could.

'Are you sure?' she faltered. 'I have nothing to give you . . .'

'Your company will be reward enough,' Jane said. 'I don't live far away – just down by the river. It's a short walk and you can let me lean on your arm.'

Sally gave her an arm and she leaned heavily on her. It gave Sally a feeling of warmth and of being needed, of being right. She decided to go with Jane, because she had nowhere else to go and no one to care for her – or did she? She searched her mind desperately, trying to remember her life before she was attacked, but there was nothing but blankness and fear – a fear that Jane was helping to quell.

Shutting down the awful fear, she decided to let Jane take her where she would. Otherwise, she might as well lie down at the side of the road and die.

CHAPTER 18

'Jenny – are you there?' Lily's voice calling to her made Jenny jump. She'd been lost in thought as she polished the oval mahogany table she'd had delivered that afternoon. 'Oh, that looks lovely, Jenny. I'm envious. Where did you find it?'

'In a secondhand shop just off King's Road,' Jenny said and smiled, satisfied with her purchase now that her sister had praised it. 'Both Michael and I like old stuff. The man said it belongs to the Regency period and it goes well with the chairs I kept that were Great-Grandma's.'

'Yes, it does,' Lily agreed. 'It makes me wonder if I did right in buying modern. We went to the West End and bought that oak dinning set but I think I like yours better.'

'I hope Michael will like it when he gets back,' Jenny sighed as she led the way into the kitchen. 'I'll put the kettle on, Lily. I've been working all day, getting things round. I keep finding bits and pieces in the junk shop that I like but they all want cleaning – though that's why they're cheap. That silver-plated kettle on a stand was filthy; it took me two hours to get it clean.'

'Yes, but it looks really posh now,' Lily said. 'I think I shall have to start mooching around in junk shops. I never knew there were so many nice things to find.' Her eyes moved to the tall brass candlesticks that Jenny had started to clean and left on the sink drainer. 'It must be hard work polishing those up? I bought some porcelain ones for our sitting room – they go with the clean lines of the furniture.'

'Yes, but there's something nice about brass, it's warm when there's a fire,' Jenny said and Lily shook her head.

'I never thought I'd see you so domesticated, Jenny.'

'I like making things nice, ready for when Michael comes back.' She looked directly at Lily. 'Chris hasn't seen him? He doesn't know where he is or when he'll be back?'

'No, I'm sorry, love. He hasn't mentioned Michael at all – but he wouldn't. It's work, and you know he doesn't talk about work much.'

'I know – but it's more than five weeks now. Michael said he would be back well before Christmas.'

'There's plenty of time yet, weeks,' Lily said to reassure her. 'Are you thinking of your party?'

'No, I was thinking of him . . . that I miss him and—' Jenny shook her head. She wasn't even certain herself yet, and wouldn't dream of telling her sister before her husband, that she was pregnant.

'I know it's horrid when they're away,' Lily said sympathetically. 'Let's have that cup of tea and one of those fairy cakes you've made. Worrying won't bring him back sooner, love – and I'm always here if you get lonely and need a chat.'

Jenny looked at her sister's slim figure. Her little girl had been born a week after Jenny's wedding and she'd been with her so much for the first few weeks that she hadn't noticed she was lonely, but she was beginning to now.

'Where is Marguerite?' she asked her.

'Mrs Johnson next door took her for a little while, just to give me an hour or so to myself. Otherwise I'd never get time to shop or do anything but look after her.'

'Yes, you don't get time to fret or feel lonely much with that one around,' Jenny said and smiled. 'She is gorgeous but always needing your time.'

'That's what babies are,' Lily said. 'Now, I wanted to show you this dress pattern I've bought, Jenny. If I buy some material, will you help me cut it out and fit it on me?'

'Of course I will,' Jenny said, pleased. 'You know I like cutting out the patterns and I've got a steadier hand than you. What colour are you thinking of buying?'

It was nice being close to Lily, Jenny thought as she went to bed that evening. The wind was whistling outside and she'd put a hot water bottle in to warm the sheets earlier, because it felt cold with no one to cuddle up to. Her hands went to her still flat tummy and stroked it over the nightgown. Was there a baby growing in there? Jenny knew she was late with her period but it was very quick after they'd made love to fall for a baby. Some women had to wait years, but she had a feeling that the passionate love-making of their honeymoon might have given her a child. She smiled in the darkness, because the thought that she might have Michaels's child in her womb made her feel that she wasn't so alone.

Jenny wasn't frightened to be alone in the house at night. She'd quite often slept in an empty house but she missed Michael by her side, missed the smell and the solid bulk of him. It was daft to be this way when she'd only known that companionship for a few days, but she still felt it – longed for him to be there and hold her and it amazed her that she'd ever hesitated over marrying him. Those few nights and days had been the best of her life and she couldn't wait for him to come back – didn't know what she would do if he didn't. A cold chill touched the nape of her neck and she turned sharply, burying her face in the pillow. No! She wouldn't let herself think of such a possibility, not for one minute. Michael wasn't in danger and this awful feeling of fear was just her own silly mind inventing problems, just as she so often had in the past.

'Oh, Chris!' Lily stared at her husband in dismay. 'You can't mean it – their plane just simply disappeared over the sea? How could it? Surely, they would have radioed in if they were in trouble? There would be wreckage in the water if it went down.'

'I can't answer any of that,' Chris said, looking upset. 'That's the official line, they disappeared over the sea – but it may have been over enemy territory. Even if I knew where they were or what they were doing, I couldn't tell you, love, but I don't. It was so secret that even I didn't know – the boss just wanted a good fast driver who could keep his mouth shut. I knew Michael was feeling bad over his flat feet – but I should've kept my mouth shut.'

'He could have said no if he didn't want to do it,' Lily reasoned but Chris shook his head.

'No, he would never do that – too proud. Besides, he thought he was lucky and nothing would happen to him.'

'Oh, Chris – what am I going to tell Jenny? This will devastate her and I think . . .' She bit her lip. 'I think she's pregnant!'

'God, that's all she needs!' Chris said. 'If I were you, I'd just say he was returning from a mission overseas and his plane went missing – if you don't tell her she'll open that damned telegram and the shock could harm the baby if she *is* carrying.'

Lily nodded and breathed deeply. Her husband was right. Lily had to tell her sister the worrying news. Michael, the general he'd been driving, and all his aides had simply vanished from the face of the earth, but Lily would just say they were missing. Missing wasn't dead, even though the powers that be had decided to presume it in the case of their important officers – but there was no reason Jenny shouldn't keep some hope alive. In time, if they knew for certain, Jenny could let go and grieve, but for now she must still have hope . . .

Jenny stared at her sister in disbelief. She was so stunned that she couldn't take in what Lily was telling

131

her – her sister couldn't have just said that a plane carrying Michael, a general, and aides had gone missing somewhere. She just couldn't! It could not be true.

'No,' she said faintly and sat down hard. 'It isn't possible. I won't believe it!'

'Missing isn't dead,' Lily said firmly and moved towards her as she swayed. 'Don't give up hope, Jenny. They don't know anything for sure – just that the plane disappeared.'

Jenny was silent for a moment. 'Chris told you, didn't he? What does he know about where they were or what happened to it? Was it shot down – or did it just simply disappear?'

'He doesn't know any more than I've just told you. Honestly, Jenny, he would tell us if he did; all he's been told is that the plane set off to return to England and got lost somewhere between here and where it took off.'

'And where was that? France? Did they go down over the sea? When did it happen?' Jenny's head teemed with questions but she knew, even as she asked, that Lily couldn't answer them. Michael had gone – just as surely as if he'd been on a battlefield and been killed. Perhaps then someone could have told her where he was and what had happened – but this was just like a blank wall. Just missing, nothing more. 'Why can't they tell us what happened?'

'I asked Chris that but he says he hasn't been told. I know he works with some high-powered officials, Jenny, but even he isn't told everything. Whatever Michael was doing was important.'

'Yes, he told me so,' Jenny agreed. 'No more, just that it was important and he needed to do it – I doubt if he really knew it was so dangerous that he could lose his life, could leave me, that—'

'We don't know that he has,' Lily reminded her. 'If the plane crashed in the sea, survivors may have been picked up by foreign ships – even enemy ships. They could all be prisoners of war . . .'

Seeing the flash of pain in Jenny's eyes, Lily hesitated, as if wondering if she'd said the wrong thing, but Jenny's head came up sharply. 'Yes,' she said and her eyes sparkled with unshed tears. 'He isn't dead, Lily. I would know. I would feel it inside. I knew the other night that something bad had happened, but Michael is still alive. I know he is!'

'Well, you just keep thinking like that, if not for your own sake, for the sake of the baby.'

Jenny's eyes widened. 'How did you know? I've only just been to the doctor this morning – and even he says he's not certain, but he thinks my instincts are right.'

'I'm a nurse with quite a bit of experience as a midwife,' Lily said. 'I wouldn't mind betting you're carrying Michael's child . . . so he'll *always* be with you, love. You have to look out for yourself for the sake of your child.'

CHAPTER 19

Constable Steve Jones was first on the scene when some boatmen found the body in the canal. It was caught at the side of the lock in among some reeds and by the looks of it had been there some time. The woman wore an old, mud-coloured jumper but nothing else. If she'd been wearing more when she went into the canal, no one could know for sure. The decomposition was not as bad as it might have been had the weather not been as icy these past weeks, but Steve was pretty certain she'd been in the water for a while.

He tried not to jump to conclusions too fast. The missing mother, Betty Stewart, had been on his mind for weeks and he'd always felt that she must have met with an accident or been murdered. From the wounds he'd seen on the body in the water, it looked like a brutal attack, though Steve would have to wait for the specialists to tell him for sure, but he would just give a hint of the possibility to Jeff Marshall, because he knew the friendly garage owner was looking out for the woman's children. Steve was aware of the informal arrangements for the two orphans, but he'd turned a blind eye. If he'd followed procedure, the council would have taken the poor little blighters to some orphanage; his Sarah always said he had a soft heart for kids, and it was true.

Steve couldn't imagine what it would be like for kids to lose their mother and then be taken off to a place they didn't know full of strangers. If he told Sarah, her mother would want to take them in but Gwen already had two and she was not long married. No doubt her new husband would let her have more orphans to foster in the future but Steve thought she had enough to do for the moment so he hadn't said anything. No, he would talk to Jeff and hear what he had to say and only if they couldn't work something out between them would he approach the children's welfare people or talk to Matron at the Rosie. That Lady Rosalie might find them a home, though he knew she had a long list of children needing homes already.

'Do yer reckon it's that woman we've been searching for?' Constable Smith asked him as they watched the body being taken away to the morgue.

'Hard to tell,' Steve said grimly. 'But I don't reckon that body got there of its own accord. This area had been searched – right at the beginning. It was one of the first places we looked.'

'So, dumped later somewhere upstream?'

'I think it was placed here. I don't think it drifted,' Steve replied with conviction. 'I think she was attacked, killed, perhaps raped – then hidden for a while and dumped a couple of weeks back.'

Constable Smith looked shocked and then angry.

'Deliberate, do you think? I've been told she was a decent lady, kept herself to herself and wasn't interested in men.'

'That may be what infuriated the killer,' Steve replied with a frown. 'It's impossible to tell fully from first glance, but it looked like a violent attack to me.'

'Poor woman.' Constable Smith looked over his shoulder uneasily. 'It means we've got a nasty bugger on our patch.'

'Yes, it does,' Steve agreed. 'If murder or assault is confirmed we shall have to get posters up, warning folk. If it *is* Betty Stewart, and I reckon it will be, she was a decent woman, poor but respectable. Our wives aren't safe with someone like that around.'

'No, I agree with you,' his companion said, looking upset. 'I'll have to tell Violet.' He went a bit pink in the face. 'She's my girlfriend – we're thinking of getting engaged at Christmas.'

'Congratulations.' Steve smiled. 'You warn her to be careful, Bob. If this is Mrs Stewart, she went missing after her morning shift at the Rosie so whatever happened was in broad daylight. And if she'd screamed someone would have heard at that time in the morning. She must have been on her way home or perhaps went shopping.'

'Unless she fancied a walk by the canal?' Constable Smith suggested. 'It's not always busy down here, early mornings.'

'Well, I suppose she might – though she ought to have been safe!' He felt a surge of anger. 'If a decent woman can't even take a stroll by the canal—'

Steve ground his teeth in frustration. He might

136

never know how the woman in the canal had met her unfortunate end, but he knew in his bones that someone had done her an injustice and that made it his business. He would do everything he could to find out the truth of this poor wretch's death, and in his mind he was convinced that it was Mrs Stewart, even though she wasn't wearing a wedding ring. Poor Betty. She'd lost her husband, struggled to bring up those kids as best she could and now she'd been murdered.

He might be jumping to conclusions, but he didn't think so.

Jeff was shocked and furious when Steve told him his suspicions. He bunched his fists at his sides and looked fit to murder someone himself.

'I wish I knew who it was!' he said, his face red with indignation. 'I'd kill the bugger – or at least thrash him until he couldn't stand.'

'You and me both,' Steve admitted. 'I'm the law so I'd probably just use sufficient force to take him in, but I feel the same as you – he deserves to hang, whoever he is.'

'We've got plenty of criminal types in this city,' Jeff said, 'but a lot of them would never do anything like this – they'll rough someone up for not paying up what they owe; they'll steal, fight on pay night and break into your house or shop, but rape and murder? Nah, not the ones I know round here – it has to be a stranger.' He frowned. 'If I were you, I'd look for someone off a ship.'

Steve frowned. 'What makes you say that?'

'Most folk round here respected Betty. Some of the

137

men without a woman would have wed her if she'd looked at them – but they wouldn't rape her. Why would they, when there are plenty of girls willing to sell it for a few bob down the docks?'

Steve's frown cleared. What Jeff was saying made sense. Some foreign sailors would be rough, especially if they were just off a ship and desperate for a woman – and drunk, as they often were while in dock. A stranger wouldn't know Betty, wouldn't know she was a respectable woman. But what had happened to her ring? Surely, she hadn't been desperate enough to sell it? The last thing most women would sell was their wedding ring.

'Yes, you could be right,' he agreed. 'I'll make a few inquiries down the docks. It is a while back, of course, but someone might remember an incident that could help.'

Steve was pleased as he walked home later that day. It had been a good idea to share his thoughts with Jeff Marshall. Not only had it alerted Jeff to the possibility the dead woman was the children's mother, it had given him some fresh ideas about who might have killed her.

His smile reappeared as he reached his home and saw his mother-in-law leaving. He liked Gwen and was pleased she'd been visiting his wife, Sarah. He suspected that Sarah missed her nursing although she hadn't said anything and he knew she adored their son, but he liked her to have company as he sometimes worked long hours.

'How are you, Gwen?' he asked as she stopped to have a word. Gwen always had time for everyone.

'I'm on top of the world,' she said, beaming at him. 'My grandson just called me G'anny Gwen for the first time. His speech is really coming on.'

'It is,' Steve agreed, proudly.

'I've asked Sarah to bring you all for Sunday lunch, if you can manage it?'

'I'm not working this weekend at all.' He beamed at her. 'We would love to, Gwen.'

The dark cloud that had been hanging over him since he'd been called to the canal began to lift. Work was work and he would do it to the best of his ability but for the moment he was home and his family came first – although he would certainly warn Sarah not to walk alone by the canal.

Margaret looked at Jeff in horror as he finished telling her what he'd been told in confidence. 'No, I promise I won't say a word,' she lilted in the way that he was fast learning to love. 'All I can think of is those poor little kiddies, Jeff – it's only a couple of weeks until Christmas – you can't tell them yet.'

'No, I can't and I shan't . . .' He hesitated, then, 'What are you doing for Christmas, Margaret? Do you have to work?'

'I've been given two whole days off . . .' she said, her expressive eyes looking at him expectantly.

'I was thinking we might have the kids here for Christmas,' he said tentatively and to his relief she smiled and looked pleased.

'I'd love that,' she said. 'We can do the cooking together if you like.'

'Do you enjoy cooking?' he asked. 'I learned the

basics while I was in the army and I taught myself the rest of it later. I didn't want to live on tins or fish and chips so it was a question of learn or starve.'

'I was taught to cook from an early age, but I don't get much chance in my little place.' Margaret looked a bit wistful and his heart lurched. He was much too old for her, of course he was; she was only in her twenties, after all, but if she longed for a home of her own, he could provide that – if she would take him. He wasn't much of a catch, but he'd be a good husband given the chance.

Jeff nodded to himself. He would take those two children in for Christmas and see how it worked with them all together – and then he would speak his mind to Margaret. Perhaps she would turn him down flat, but he could only hope she wouldn't.

CHAPTER 20

It was Saturday morning and Jilly was still in bed when someone rang the front doorbell. She looked down and watched from behind the drawn curtains as they rang twice, impatiently. It was two women and she didn't like the look of them so she wasn't going to answer. Tim had gone to work and he'd told her not to answer the door to *anyone*.

'You don't know who they might be so you keep the door shut,' he'd warned her.

Jilly hopped back in bed and let them go on ringing and knocking until, at last, they got fed up and went off. She didn't care. Today was Saturday and Tim had promised her they could have sausage and chips bought from the shop instead of going to a neighbour for their meal.

'We can manage at home on our own for once,' Tim had told her. 'But you must remember not to answer the door, and don't let anyone see you. Mrs Brown told me the welfare people came round the other day and said they would come back on Saturday.'

'What do they want?' Jilly asked curiously.

'Nothing good,' Tim had replied without looking at her. 'Remember what I say, Jilly; it's dangerous to open up to someone you don't know.'

Jilly snuggled down in bed. It was warm under the quilt and it was an adventure to have someone at the door and not answer it; she felt a bit naughty but her brother had told her what to do and she trusted him.

She knew that the rent man had banged at the door for an hour two nights ago and then he'd put a letter through the door. Jilly couldn't read all the words but Tim could and it said they had to leave by Monday night at the latest.

Jilly didn't want to go anywhere. Tim made the kitchen warm for her and it would be cosy when she went downstairs, but he'd said people they didn't know would make them leave, because Mum wasn't around. Mr Marshall had offered to pay the rent until after Christmas but the rent man said no; they had to leave.

Jilly's feeling of content disappeared and she decided to go down and see if there were any biscuits left. Tim had bought some for them with sweet icing on top and they were lovely.

She pulled on the clothes she'd worn the day before and scampered down the stairs without bothering to wash her hands or face. Tim made her do it every school morning and Mum had given her a strip wash once a week but there was no one here to make her, so she didn't.

It was lovely and warm in the kitchen and Jilly found some milk in the pantry. She hunted for the biscuits and couldn't find them on the shelves. Tim had bought a pot of her favourite jam and he'd said he would bring a fresh loaf home at lunchtime but Jilly was hungry now and there wasn't anything she could see that she could eat. Then she saw the biscuit tin on the top shelf. She grinned and fetched a stool to stand on, edging the tin until it fell into her hands. Why had Tim put their biscuits all the way up there?

Taking it to the table Mum used to cook on, she opened it and stared in surprise. It was full of shillings and sixpences and there were two ten-shilling notes. Mum must have left it there and they didn't know!

Jilly thought of all the things she could buy with her windfall. She would take the notes and go to the shop – not Mr Forest's shop, but the one near the school. She would buy biscuits, cakes, chocolates and sweets and surprise Tim when he came home. Oh, he would be so surprised and pleased!

Jilly saw the three boys as she approached the school and hesitated. She'd seen them before in the school playground and they were bullies. They pulled her hair, called her names and one of them had threatened her with his fist. The back of her neck prickled with fear as the tallest one approached her.

'Where yer goin?' he demanded, eyes narrowing. 'If yer've got pocket money to spare you can share it wiv us.'

'No!' Jilly shrank back, afraid that they would take all her money and leave her with nothing. 'I shan't give you anything.'

'Get her lads!' the boy said and one of them grabbed Jilly and pulled her hair. 'Give us yer money or we'll make yer sorry, yer little brat.'

Jilly's tears started and she was on the verge of handing over one of the ten-shilling notes when another lad loomed up and yanked the one who had hold of Jilly away, shoving him to his knees.

'Clear off,' a voice said. 'If I see you hanging around her again, I'll break your necks – all of you!'

Jilly didn't think they would go but then she saw the three of them slinking away. The lad who had saved her was much bigger and taller than they were, but he was dirty and he smelled a bit.

'Dirty tramp!' the leader of the gang jeered from a safe distance but when Jilly's saviour turned to look at them, they ran off.

'Are you hurt?' the stranger asked Jilly. She shook her head and smiled at him. He grinned back and she thought how nice he looked. 'If you're goin' in the shop I'll hang around and make sure they don't come back.'

'I've got some pocket money,' Jilly confided. 'I'll give you something to eat when I come back . . .' She ran into the shop and looked excitedly at the shelves. Jilly had never had much money to herself, but she would make sure she bought some things that Tim liked too – and she would give that boy outside the shop something nice. Perhaps two of those lovely sticky buns with icing on top?

Luke was glad he'd been able to help the young girl. She was a nice little thing and he hated bullying of any kind. He'd hung around after she promised him something to eat when she came back from the shop and she'd given him a bag with two iced buns inside.

'Thanks,' Luke had said gruffly. She'd smiled, told him her name was Jilly and then ran off, munching an iced bun of her own. He'd watched her thoughtfully and reckoned she was the sister of the lad that worked for Jeff Marshall at the garage.

Luke listened to gossip. Most folks hardly noticed him hanging around these days and he knew that a woman had been found murdered in the canal. He didn't know if it was the woman he'd seen attacked or not and he wondered what he ought to do about it. Should he tell the police what he'd seen? Would they listen to him – or would they simply ignore what he told them and return him to the orphanage? He couldn't risk it – he didn't want to go back there.

He was managing, finding work some days and just about getting enough to eat. He'd worked that morning at a wood yard and if he could just find a regular job again, he would be fine. No, he didn't want to go back to that awful place. Despite his hunger and his longing for companionship, he would rather be on the streets.

Jilly had bought a lot of food and Luke wondered where she'd got so much money – perhaps her mother had given it to her? Although he wasn't sure he'd seen a woman going into the house she'd come from. So how had a young girl got hold of the money to buy all that food?

Tim pocketed the money he'd earned that week and left the garage. Mr Marshall had told him that he and Jilly could stay with him for a few days at Christmas.

'In fact, you can bring her here as soon as they tell you you've got to move out, lad. It won't be forever, because I couldn't manage two children on me own – but we'll clear your mum's things out, sell them for what we can get and then we'll see what happens. The matron of the Rosie says they might find you a new home with a foster mother – that would mean if your mum turned up, she could have you back if she asked.'

Tim had thought Jeff looked a bit strange, but he'd been too excited over the thought of Christmas. It meant his savings would go further and he was beginning to think that he would have to find somewhere he could take Jilly after Christmas – a deserted house of some kind. He knew there were houses like that about, but he'd never investigated, because he didn't want to leave his home in case Mum came back – and surely, she would?

Tim made his way to the market stalls that set up on a Saturday a couple of streets from his home. They would be thinking of closing for the day and he might buy a bargain. Now that his Christmas money was safely stored in the old biscuit tin, he could afford to buy a little more food, so he would buy fresh bread and some apples, and the sausage and chips from the shop on the corner by the market. It was run by Mr and Mrs Lands and their chips were lovely.

He purchased the fresh bread, apples and a tiny piece of farm butter his mum had liked when she could afford it, and then went to the hot food shop and bought their meal. Jilly would really love this and so would he.

'I'm home,' he announced to the empty kitchen and then frowned as he realised Jilly must still be in bed. Putting his shop on the table he ran upstairs, prepared to pull his sister from her bed, but when he saw she wasn't there, the first spurt of fear set in. Jilly couldn't be missing too! He'd told her she mustn't go out alone – and she hadn't even locked the door. The landlord could have walked in and moved out all their stuff. Did she never listen?

Tim was debating what to do when he caught sight of her red skirt through the window and saw that she'd gone out without her coat and was loaded with bags and parcels. Where had she got all that stuff? What had she paid with? A sinking feeling in the pit of his stomach told him as he went into the pantry and saw his tin there; both the ten-shilling notes had gone, though there was just over twelve shillings left in coins.

Anger mounted inside him as he returned to the kitchen and saw what she'd bought as she triumphantly unloaded everything onto the kitchen table – all her favourite sweets, chocolate biscuits and packets of cakes. Nothing that was good for them and all the money gone. He knew roughly what they'd cost and realised she'd spent every penny.

'What have you done, you stupid little girl?' he demanded furiously.

Jilly's face went white. 'I found Mum's money in the tin so I thought I'd buy us some treats . . .' She faltered as she saw his anger. Tears welled in her eyes.

'It wasn't Mum's money, it was mine!' Tim said bitterly. 'I worked all those hours for our Christmas money and you've wasted it!' Even as he spoke, he realised that it wasn't quite as important now that Mr Marshall had invited them for Christmas, but it was too late. Jilly whirled round and went running out again. He knew that she was crying and that he should follow her, but for a few moments, he couldn't make his feet move. So he was a bit behind as he reached the middle of the lane, watching as Jilly shot round the corner; he had no idea where she was going and he doubted she did either.

He called to her desperately, 'Come back, Jilly! It doesn't matter. I'm sorry I was cross!'

Jilly didn't look back. She just kept on running. Tim was faster and stronger and he'd almost caught up with her when the truck came round the bend. Tim's instincts made him jump up on the pavement but Jilly didn't move and though the driver swerved, he caught her a glancing blow, which sent her face down on the road.

Within seconds the driver was out of the cab and bending over her. He looked anguished, though it hadn't been his fault.

'She came at me so suddenly. I wasn't going fast!' he said to Tim and the crowd that was beginning to gather. Jilly gave a little groan and everyone's concentration honed in on her again, but she didn't open her eyes. The driver's worried look intensified. 'I'll take her to the Rosie . . .'

'Don't touch her until I look at her,' a commanding voice said and a young woman came to Jilly and knelt beside her, gently feeling over her body and then around her head. She looked up at Tim. 'I'm a nurse – Nurse Sarah. Is she your sister?'

'Yes. I was cross with her and she ran off. She wouldn't listen or stop,' Tim said, looking anxiously at his sister's prone form. 'Will she be all right?'

'Well, I think she may have a broken arm and she *is* unconscious, so we need to get her to the Rosie.' Her eyes went to the truck driver. 'I saw it all and it definitely wasn't your fault. You did well not to hit her full on. Will you please go to the Rosie and tell them what has happened? They'll send someone to pick her up properly.'

'Thanks,' he said and took off his overcoat, putting it over Jilly to keep her warm. 'I'm glad you saw it all.' Then he was off at a run to fetch help from the Rosie.

Nurse Sarah knelt down by the little girl's side and touched her with gentle, careful hands. As she did so, Jilly stirred once more and her eyelids flickered. She whimpered and cried out as Sarah touched her arm.

The lorry driver was back within minutes with Nurse Margaret James and Bert Rush, the caretaker from the Rosie.

'I think her arm is broken,' Sarah told them. 'Be careful how you lift her, Bert. Make sure you support her neck and head.'

'I'll support her head while Bert carries her,' Nurse Margaret said and smiled at Sarah. 'It was a good thing you were nearby.'

Sarah smiled and nodded. 'I was visiting my mother,

who lives just over there.' She pointed across the street. 'I'll pop in and see this young lady another time.' She looked kindly at Tim. 'Do you want to go with them to the Rosie?'

'I left the back door open,' Tim said. 'I'll go home and lock it up and then I'll follow – where will Jilly be?'

'On the children's ward,' Nurse Margaret said and smiled at him. 'Just ask for Nurse Margaret and I'll let you go and see her for a few minutes if I can.'

Tim nodded, knowing that he would not normally be allowed to visit because he was too young, but he was Jilly's only relative – perhaps they would make an exception for him and let him visit his sister while she was in the hospital. Sister Rose had let him visit his mum three times when she was really ill after his dad died, even though he shouldn't have, because he'd been even younger then than he was now.

He ran home as fast as he could, praying that no one had been in and taken what little they had, but fortunately nothing had been touched. Jilly's contributions to their larder lay where she'd dropped them on the table, reproaching him for his anger. He'd known how sensitive and upset she was so he shouldn't have grumbled at her, spoiling her pleasure. She'd thought she had found Mum's money and spent some of it as she liked – and perhaps to please him; he saw some ginger crunch biscuits, and tears started in his eyes. They were his favourites and his sister knew it! He deeply regretted being cross over the money and wished he'd accepted what she'd done with good humour; it had just been such a disappointment after all his hard work.

If Jilly died . . . No! Tim wasn't going to let himself even think it. Making sure the kitchen door was safely locked this time, he set off at a run. He had to see Jilly settled in the hospital where he knew she would be safe and then he would visit Mr Marshall and tell him what had happened.

'She looked so pale and ill,' Tim said when he was sitting in Mr Marshall's comfortable parlour later that day. 'And it's all my fault.'

'Nonsense, lad,' Jeff said firmly. 'It isn't your fault that she ran off into the road like that and you had a right to be a bit cross after you'd worked so hard for that money. What Jilly did was thoughtless and wrong. Even if it had been your mother's money, she still had no right to take it and spend it. She ought to have shown it to you and asked if she could have some for sweets.'

'I suppose it is a long time since she had any money for herself,' Tim said thoughtfully. 'And I agree, she ought not to have spent what she thought was Mum's money, but she's not truly old enough to understand things like that unless I tell her.' He frowned. 'I was still wrong to be cross with her – it was just that I knew I couldn't buy her the present I'd planned.'

'What were you planning to get?' Jeff asked. 'A new dress?'

'She wanted a doll's pram but I could only afford a secondhand cot I'd seen in a junk shop, and now I can't buy even that.'

'Supposing I have a look round and see what I can find?' Jeff suggested. 'I go further afield than you and I might find something cheap we could do up a bit.'

Tim nodded halfheartedly. He didn't see how he could buy Jilly anything much now, because she'd wasted so much on the sweets and biscuits . . .

CHAPTER 21

Luke watched as they carried the little girl into the infirmary. She looked pale and ill and he was upset, wondering what had happened to her. If it was the boys he'd seen taunting her who were responsible, he would half kill them, but when he asked the nurse what was wrong she told him Jilly had been knocked down by a lorry.

He frowned as he wondered what her mother was doing letting her run out like that on her own. Perhaps she hadn't got a mother, he thought, feeling sorry for her. It was awful not having a mother – though she'd had a lot of money to spend on sweets, mind you. Luke had wondered about that, because it had seemed an awful lot to spend on such things – perhaps her mother had been cross because she spent the money and that was why she'd gone running off like that.

Luke made his way along the street. His job carting wood at the yard just a couple of streets away had been a bit of luck and for once he had a few shillings in his pocket. Perhaps the job would last until Christmas, only a few days off now, and he'd seen some of the shops making an effort to dress their windows for the festive season, though they couldn't have all the bright lights they normally had.

Some of the places that had shut when the war started were open again. Luke kept hoping Ern would return but his lock-up remined dark and closed. He walked past the clinic where the doctor in the wheelchair worked but saw no sign of him, though his car was parked a little way further down the road. He must be coming in earlier to work so perhaps he was feeling better. Luke hoped so. He looked nice and he would have liked to help with his chair but hadn't seen him for ages.

Shrugging, he walked off whistling. He'd been told to come back to the wood yard this afternoon and help with the piles of kindling the boss was selling round the streets from his van. It didn't matter to Luke what he did as long as he got paid and could eat once a day. He seldom had more, except for when Mrs Ruby gave him a packet of sandwiches; they would last him all day and sometimes to the next morning. She was a nice lady and he often wondered if he dared go to her house and ask for a meal. She'd told him to but he didn't like to be a nuisance.

'I give him some food once a week,' Ruby was explaining to Sid that morning as she packed her lunch and his. 'I've told him to come round if he's hungry, so don't send him off with a flea in his ear, Sid.'

'I shan't.' He looked at her thoughtfully. 'We've lost a lot of likely lads to the war. It might be that

I could find a job for him, something that would pay a small but regular wage. What do yer think to that, girl?'

'It would be good for Luke,' Ruby said and smiled at him gratefully. 'You're a good man, Sid, and I'm glad we're together. You wouldn't mind if I offered Luke a bed here sometimes – would you?'

'It's your home, too, love,' he told her. 'I'd best get off – got a lot to do today. If yer see the lad, tell him I'll set him on labourin' if he wants.'

Ruby's face lit up. It was what she'd hoped for when she spoke of Luke to her husband but she'd thought he might scoff at her idea – he probably would have, once upon a time, but Sid had changed after all that trouble with those gangsters. He was softer towards her and Julia but stronger inside, sure of himself – and he never got drunk. Occasionally, he had a drink with other men but always came home after a pint of his favourite beer. Ruby liked the new Sid much better than the old one and felt very satisfied with life. Julia was at her grammar school all day and came home at night and studied some more; she was growing up now and seemed to live in a world of her own. They were both proud of their clever daughter, even though she did seem to have left them behind.

In the long summer holidays, Julia had asked to go and stay with a friend. 'She lives in a nice house out in Hampstead, Mum,' she'd explained. 'I can't ask Shirley to come here – but I'd love to stay with her.'

'You can go for a while,' Ruby had agreed, but

she'd made up her mind that Julia was going to stay home for Christmas. Sometimes, she was guilty of wishing her daughter wasn't so clever and hadn't won that scholarship to the grammar school. Perhaps if she'd gone to an ordinary school, she wouldn't have grown away from them. Ruby missed the chats she felt she ought to be having with her daughter and thought wistfully of fostering a child but, so far, she hadn't been asked on to Lady Rosalie's list and wondered why. She could give a decent home to a child in need – so why hadn't Lady Rosalie contacted her? She'd put her name down ages ago . . .

'I was wondering,' Lady Rosalie said as she and Mary Thurston sat talking in Mary's office at the Rosie, 'whether Mrs Harding would come into my office to see me? I know she's been on my list for a few weeks, but I need to interview her so that I can see what sort of child she would be most suitable to care for – or whether she would like to have a brother and sister. I know you said Mr Marshall had taken in the Stewart children for Christmas, but will he keep them?'

'He seemed most concerned for their welfare,' Mary said. 'He asked me if we could have them here, but I didn't think it was suitable so he took them on himself. I'll get one of my nurses to pay him a visit and ask him to come and discuss it with me.'

'If you would, Mary. I do have a little boy on my list that I haven't found a place for yet.' She sighed and shook her head. 'I have many, of course, but little Jimmy is more difficult than most to place, you see. We think he had polio at some time, though there is no record of it, and his right leg is much weaker than the left and we've had to have irons fitted, poor little love. He has a sweet nature but he wets his bed and cries a lot and it will take a very special person to look after him.'

'I think you will find our Ruby *is* rather special,' Mary told her with a smile. 'I'll ask her to make an appointment, Rosalie. I think she might be just the person you're looking for.'

'Good.' Her ladyship beamed. 'Well, I must get on – but do ask Mrs Harding to come and see me. I should like to get little Jimmy settled before Christmas.'

CHAPTER 22

Jenny sat down to write her Christmas cards alone. She bit her bottom lip as she wrote 'from Jenny and Michael', thinking how strange it was to add her husband's name when he was not there to share the fun – and she wasn't sure that he ever would be. No! She would not give way to negative thinking. Lily had told her not to give up hope, though she knew that Chris was doubtful any of the passengers could have survived. He thought that something would have been heard or seen by now, but Jenny felt certain inside that Michael was still alive.

She placed her hands to her still-flat tummy and smiled. How surprised and delighted Michael would be when he returned home and discovered that Jenny was pregnant – if he got back before the baby was born. It was possible, even probable, that her husband was a prisoner of war. Had the plane crashed over friendly territory, they would surely have heard something, which meant it either went into the sea or over Germany.

She wasn't sure why her thoughts always settled

on that last alternative. Michael was in Germany somewhere, Jenny felt it instinctively. Sometimes, when she lay in bed alone, not quite able to sleep, she thought he was sending her messages, telling her not to forget him and that he would come home to her. Jenny knew that most people would shake their head at her and think she was living on false hope, but the flame of belief was strong inside her and it kept her going.

She hadn't decreased her hours at the Rosie as she'd planned. It took her over an hour to get home at night on the train but that hardly mattered. There was nothing to come back for, other than to keep her lovely house clean and tidy, ready for when Michael returned, but she didn't bother much about shopping or cooking meals. Often, she went to the fish and chip shop near where she worked and ate them sitting on the train.

She'd bumped into the young lad she'd seen months ago. He looked a little cleaner these days, as if he was prospering more, and she'd spoken to him several times, just to pass a few minutes before she caught her train home to her empty house. Luke always had a cheerful smile and, seeing him enter at the same time as her a couple of nights previously, she'd bought him a packet of fish and chips, which had made his lean face light up like a beacon.

'Do you keep well, Luke?' she'd asked him. 'Got plenty of work and enough to eat?' She'd smiled as they left the shop together, tucking into their supper as they walked.

'I'm lucky, nurse,' Luke told her. 'I've got a few

friends now and they give me food sometimes – but I like to work for my keep. If you've got a job I can do, just ask.'

'I live too far out,' Jenny said, 'but if ever I need a helping hand, I'll think of you.'

Luke had grinned at her and walked off eating his fish and chips as if there was no tomorrow. Jenny had caught her train, wiping greasy fingers on her hanky and smiling. The young lad cheered her up and made her think there was some good in carrying on, no matter what.

Sighing, she finished writing her cards, put stamps on those she had to post; the rest for her sister, Michael's family and her colleagues at work would be hand-delivered with the presents she'd bought and wrapped. She'd managed to buy some lovely lace handkerchiefs in a box for Lily, as well as a little bottle of lavender water. For Sister Rose, she'd bought chocolates and most of the nurses were getting boxes of perfumed soap. The shopkeeper had told her they weren't sure whether they could replace the soaps next year and so she'd bought one or two extra as birthday gifts or just for her own use. The effects of the war hadn't started to bite yet, but it would as the months passed and more merchant ships were torpedoed by the German U-boats.

War was so futile! Jenny sighed. She was certain the ordinary German people didn't want this any more than the British man in the street; it was Hitler and his Nazis and they ought to be exterminated like the pack of mad dogs they were. If only someone over there would do it now, hundreds of thousands of lives might be saved, because if you believed the reports in the papers, that was how many would be lost in the years of conflict to come.

Shaking her head at her gloomy thoughts, Jenny went up to bed. One of the nurses had given her a new Agatha Christie to read but she wanted it back by the end of the week, because it had been borrowed from the library and if she didn't get it back by then she would have to pay a tuppence fine.

The only person she still had to find a gift for was Nurse Margaret. Jenny could give her a box of the soaps she'd bought as spares, but she would rather like to get her something nicer. Margaret had been lovely to her recently, as if sensing her sadness but never speaking of it or intruding, just going out of her way to be pleasant and offering to get her tea from the kitchen or bringing an iced bun in as a treat.

Remembering the little silver bangle she'd seen in a junk shop, Jenny nodded. She'd liked it but hadn't bought it. She would go back and buy it for Margaret. It was two pounds and that was expensive, but Jenny thought she was one of the nicest of her colleagues and deserved something special.

'Matron asked me to pop in and see you,' Margaret said that evening when she got to Jeff's house. 'I didn't tell her we were going out; it isn't her business.'

Jeff smiled at her. 'I suppose she wanted to know how Tim was doing here. He's settling down nicely, as I'd expect of that lad – he's resilient. Very like his father – such a pity he was lost at sea.'

'And their mother is missing and Jilly is in hospital,'

Margaret said sympathetically. 'Poor lad. Yet fortunate too, Jeff. Not everyone would have done what you have – but will you be able to cope with them both?'

'It won't be easy looking after the girl,' Jeff admitted but smiled. 'I'll ask some of the neighbours to give me a hand.'

'You know I'll help all I can,' Margaret said and was rewarded with a smile that made her heart leap. Jeff wasn't one of those flashy, good-looking charmers you saw at the flicks, but he had a nice face, a square chin, a generous mouth and eyes that looked straight at you, but sometimes when he smiled it transformed his features and she thought he looked truly handsome.

'Well, that's lovely of you,' he said. 'I'll be glad of all the time you can spare, Margaret, especially when Jilly gets out of hospital.'

'That won't be for another day or so yet,' Margaret told him gravely. 'Her arm wasn't badly damaged but the accident shook her a great deal and she needs feeding up before we can let her come home. She was seriously undernourished.'

'Yes, I imagine that's been going on for some time,' Jeff agreed. 'I daresay Betty Stewart did her best, but the child wasn't given the food she needed half the time. Tim says she likes a piece of bread and strawberry jam more than anything, so that's what Betty would give her because she refused anything else.'

'That's all right sometimes, but she needs stews and soups with something good in them. She isn't keen, but I make her eat her meal before she has her afters.'

Jeff nodded. 'It is what her mother should've done, of course, but Betty was probably feeling too tired and unwell to make her eat properly.'

'What do you think has happened to the children's mother? Was she the woman whose body was taken from the canal?'

'I wish I knew,' Jeff said. 'Tim doesn't say anything but I know he's fretting underneath.' He sighed and frowned. 'The woman was definitely murdered, but if it was Betty, her wedding ring was missing and without it and the inscription inside, the dead woman can't be formally identified.' Like Constable Jones, Jeff thought it must be Betty Stewart, because otherwise, why didn't she come home to her children?

CHAPTER 23

'You're so good to me,' Jane said as Sally brought her a hot cup of cocoa and a plate of homemade biscuits. 'Where did you learn to cook so well?'

'Do I?' Sally asked looking puzzled. 'I think I like to cook – and you always have full shelves in the pantry. It's easy to make good meals if you have the proper ingredients.'

They'd shared a delicious cottage pie, made with good minced beef, celery, onions, carrots and mashed potatoes, browned in the oven with butter on top, for their lunch that day. Jane had a large sack of potatoes in her scullery, together with a slightly smaller sack of carrots and another of onions and the celery had been given to them by the milkman, Terry. The middle bit was lovely with cheese sandwiches for tea, but Sally had used the outside to flavour the pie, which gave it a lovely taste. Jane had eaten every scrap of her lunch and declared she hadn't eaten as well for months.

'And I'm feeling better,' Sally declared. 'That medicine your doctor gave me has made me feel less tired

164

and weak – and the food we eat has probably done the rest.'

'Yes, you clearly hadn't been eating properly for a while,' Jane agreed. 'I think the country air suits you more than where you were living – from your speech and your pallor when you arrived, I'd say you lived in London and it was the London train you came in on.'

'I've no memory of that journey – or of my life before you helped me,' Sally admitted. 'I know Dr Darby said my memory would probably come back just like that,' she clicked her fingers, 'but so far there's nothing.'

'You don't feel you had a home or family back in London?' Jane asked as Sally shook her head. 'Well, try not to worry, Sally love. It's obvious something bad happened to you and you need to forget for a while. You're safe here with me – and I'm glad to have you. The doctor told you that worrying about it and trying to remember will just make things worse.' Jane smiled at her. 'It's not long to Christmas now and we'll have a good time, you and me – it's been years since I had company and I'm looking forward to it.'

Sally nodded and smiled. She was fond of the elderly lady and felt safe and happy living with her; the only cloud on the horizon was a faint, niggling fear that she might have a family back in London. Supposing she had children and they needed her?

Did she have children? Sally struggled to bring them to mind but nothing came and she gave up. If she had children, she would surely remember. Her *life was better now, and she knew instinctively that it had not been good for a long time. Perhaps it was the good food, the medicine the doctor had given her or, as Jane said, the country air but she did feel well. She thought she would like to stay here with Jane always – she just wished she could remember what had happened to her, her real name – and if there was someone she loved or who loved her.*

Tim looked at his small store of money. He had a pound, now, despite what Jilly had squandered, and he was going to spend it for Christmas, he decided. He would get a small gift for Jeff and Margaret and the rest would go on his sister. He might earn a little more before her birthday, which was in the first days of January, and he knew what he was giving her for that – a trip to the pictures and some sweets and ice cream.

If he was sensible, he would keep the money in case he had to buy food when Christmas was over. He didn't know how long Jeff would keep them but he'd definitely made up his mind that if he was told they must go to an orphanage he and Jilly would find a derelict building to stay in. He would leave school and find permanent work although he wasn't truly old enough yet; but he looked older than he was and if he had a pair of long trousers he could pass for fourteen – it was better than letting them put Jilly and him in the orphanage, where they might be split up. Plenty of children lived on London's streets, like the boy he'd seen around here. Tim decided he really would go after him next time he saw him and ask how *he* lived. He couldn't let the authorities split him and Jilly up, because Mum would never forgive him.

Was his mum still alive? Tim couldn't decide. It didn't seem to him that she would just go off and leave them. His mother had struggled, but it wasn't her fault Dad had died and left her with no money. She couldn't help being ill either, so it made him think she must have been hurt in an accident and perhaps died in hospital with no one knowing who she was. What other explanation was there? Mum wouldn't just go off without a word unless she had no choice, so it meant she must be dead and that left a hollow feeling inside him and a burning behind his eyes. He would have cried, but men didn't cry, and he had to be a man so that he could look after Jilly.

CHAPTER 24

Margaret was feeling pleased with herself that evening as she got dressed up in her best blue suit with a white blouse and a pair of navy leather shoes. Jeff was taking her to the pictures and she was really looking forward to it. Hearing his car outside, she picked up her bag and coat and ran down the stairs to the front door, opening it to him with a look of anticipation.

'You look amazing and you smell gorgeous,' Jeff told her with a smile that embraced her. Aware of a chill in the air and the heavy smell of woodsmoke as she stepped outside, Margaret shivered suddenly. 'I hope you don't mind, Margaret, but I've brought young Tim with me. As you know, he's moved in with me until after Christmas. Rather than leave him on his own, I thought he might like to see the film – we could go to the James Cagney gangster picture instead of the musical we'd planned – if you didn't mind?'

'No, of course I don't,' she said cheerfully, swallowing her disappointment. She'd been looking forward to the musical extravaganza, *The Ice Follies of 1939* with James Stewart and Joan Crawford, but what could she say? If she made a fuss about the change of plan, Jeff might think she was mean and bad-tempered and then he wouldn't ask her out again – and Margaret had started to really look forward to their evenings together. She decided to make the best of things. 'I quite like James Cagney,' she said cheerfully.

'Tim is very excited; he has never been to the pictures, though he's planning to take his sister for her birthday.' Margaret immediately felt selfish for resenting the boy's presence on her date. As a child, she'd been taken to the pictures occasionally for birthdays.

'He will really enjoy James Cagney then,' she offered and smiled at the lad in the back as she slid into the front passenger seat. 'Hello, Tim,' she said cheerfully. 'Jilly was awake when I came off duty. She's still feeling a bit sore but doesn't seem too bad – she was so lucky there were no internal injuries.'

Tim's face lit up. 'She isn't going to die then?'

'No, most certainly not,' Margaret told him. 'She was asking for you, and I told her I would tell you to visit her in the morning. Sister Rose will be on duty, so she is sure to let you visit – just a quick one mind.'

Sister Rose was so easy-going these days. Margaret had heard that her husband was feeling a little better recently, getting over that nasty accident he'd had the previous year at last. That was probably the reason for the smile she'd seen on the senior nurse's face.

*

The film was good and they all enjoyed it, Tim most of all. When she thought about it afterwards, Margaret realised that half her enjoyment had come from the boy's obvious excitement. He'd been to a pantomime once as a birthday treat when his father was alive, but he'd never experienced the magic of the big screen, or if he had, he didn't remember it. His father might have taken him when he was too young to know, because his dad had taken him places when he wasn't at sea, but that was long ago, so he told them afterwards. He was very aware that night and took in all of it, relishing every second. They showed a trailer of Walt Disney's *Snow White and the Seven Dwarfs* which they were going to be showing again soon and Tim said how much he thought his sister would enjoy it. He told them that's what he was going to take her to see for her birthday in January, and buy an ice cream for her as a treat as well.

'We could go in the cheap seats,' he said and grinned, looking so happy that Margaret felt much better and it made her appreciate what Jeff was doing for the children even more. He'd paid for the better seats and he'd treated them all to an ice cream from the girl who came round in the interval and a fish and chip supper at his place afterwards.

When Jeff told the boy it was time to go to bed, he went but not before thanking his friend again for one of the best nights of his life. And then kissed Margaret on the cheek. 'You're nice,' he told her. 'I'm glad Jeff has you as his girlfriend.'

'What a lovely lad,' Margaret said after he'd left

the room. 'Most of the boys round here wouldn't behave like that.'

'His mother certainly taught him good manners,' Jeff replied, frowning.

Margaret nodded. 'Have you told Tim yet that his mother might be dead?'

'No, I didn't want to spoil his Christmas. But I'm going to pay for a proper funeral for the woman – Betty is the only local woman who's been reported missing for months, so the police are pretty certain it's her. After Christmas I'll take him to visit the grave and lay some flowers. There will be plenty of time for him to face up to it in future, so why ruin Christmas?'

She nodded, understanding once again. 'What will happen to them?' Margaret asked after a moment's thought. 'I know you've taken them in for Christmas – but would the authorities let you keep them permanently? Could you cope?' She'd asked him the question before, on behalf of the Matron, but he hadn't been definite then.

'I'm still not sure of the answer to either of those questions, if I'm honest,' Jeff said. 'It's probably no. Alone, I could manage Tim but his sister is another matter. A little girl needs a mother. She'll need things I can't supply.' He sighed and ran his hand through short dark blond hair that was now sprinkled with silver. Jeff was in his early forties, not a young man, although still fit, healthy and strong. But Margaret knew that what he said was right. On his own he couldn't give a little girl a proper home, but if he had a wife— Her thoughts stopped abruptly. The thought of him having a wife aroused feelings she knew were jealousy – unless that wife was her.

Margaret knew she liked Jeff a lot. She had, from the first moment of meeting him; he was honest, kind, considerate and he seemed to see her for what she was, an intelligent nurse, slightly too plump, nice-looking but not pretty. Most men saw her either as an object of pity or as someone they could take advantage of and use. Three men she'd been out with had all demanded intimate relations with her after a first or second outing and, when she'd refused, they'd dropped her. The third had been verbally insulting, physically abusive and his attempt to force himself on her had made her wary of accepting offers to go anywhere for a long time.

'Why do you think any man asks you out?' he'd jeered. 'For f---ng, that's why. No one would want a fat lump like you for a wife. He'd be laughed at by all his mates.'

Even in her own mind, Margaret couldn't say the filthy word he'd used. It was just the f-word to her and she had felt hot and shamed, hiding away in her room after work for weeks. She'd turned away every time a man smiled at her, believing those cruel words. Men only wanted her because they thought she would be desperate and let them use her for sex.

Margaret knew some other nurses who were over-weight like her, perhaps even more so, and she'd discovered that two of them had affairs all the time. Their boyfriends only wanted sex and it seemed they didn't care; they got presents, trips out to pubs and dances, and when Margaret asked a nurse named April why she put up with it, she just shrugged.

'It's either go along with it or be alone. What does it matter? It is just sex. I'm not beautiful. Men don't fall violently in love with me and ask me to marry them but they like a good time and so do I!'

'What if you have a child?'

'I'll face that if it comes to it,' April said. 'I reckon that at least I wouldn't be alone then. My nan would look after it while I work – she had the same thing happen to her.'

Margaret hadn't been able to accept that kind of behaviour. She didn't want to sleep with lots of men, even if they took her out and bought her things. So, she'd refused all offers, buried herself in work and come to London. Jeff was the first man who'd smiled at her and said hello. At first, she'd just smiled back, unable to resist because he was so friendly and natural, unlike others who looked as if they were stripping her naked. Gradually, she'd realised how much she looked forward to their brief chats and she'd made a habit of walking past his garage on her way home at night, though it was the longer route – and then, to her delight, he'd asked her out. She'd trusted him enough to take him back to her home and although he'd given her a little kiss or two, mostly on the cheek and one brief kiss on the lips since then, he'd done nothing suggestive or unpleasant. Margaret had wondered if he would put his arms around her and hold her close, and in one way she'd wanted him to, but she was enjoying what she saw as courtship. She had wondered if he would ask her to marry him but dared not hope for it. Now, she held her breath and waited but he just nodded and got up to take the dirty plates into the kitchen.

'Shall I wash?' she asked.

'We'll just leave them to soak and I'll run you home, love.'

'Will Tim be all right?'

'Yes, I told him earlier that I would – I'll lock the front door but he can get out the back if there should be an emergency. Tim is used to an empty house; he's sensible.'

'Yes, of course,' she replied. 'It was a lovely evening, Jeff. Thank you.'

'I'm sorry you didn't get to see the film you wanted to see,' he said as he escorted her to the car. He held the door for her and she smiled, loving his manners, as she was beginning to love everything about him. The trouble was, he didn't seem to love her that way . . . Then he said, 'I'll take you another night. Tim can come if he wants or go to a friend's for the evening. I'm thinking of enrolling him in that boy's club Steve Jones runs. He'd learn self-defence and have an interest – make more friends.'

Margaret nodded and smiled. Jeff was a good man, concerned about others and kind. She was pretty sure now that what she felt for him was love – but could he ever feel the same way? It was no use thinking that if she slimmed down he might fall in love with her; she would still be the same Margaret she'd always been.

After he'd dropped Margaret off and seen her safely inside her home, Jeff drove back to his house. As he unlocked the front door, he had a strong sense of being watched and strained to see into the dark corners of the road. Then, at the edge of the light from the streetlamp, he saw a figure move fractionally. It looked like a young boy, a bit older than Tim and of an unkempt appearance. Jeff wondered if it was the youth Tim had mentioned and called out. Vaguely, he half-recalled seeing him standing there a few weeks back but then he'd disappeared for a time.

'Hello – did you want me? Come here so I can see you.'

The shadow moved swiftly away into the darkness.

'Don't be afraid. I just want to help you.'

There was no answer and, after waiting for another few seconds, Jeff went into his house and closed the door, locking it after him. What did the stranger want? Was he looking for help or the chance to steal?

In the sitting room, Jeff could still smell a faint whiff of his guest's lavender perfume, which he liked. It was light and refreshing – like Margaret herself. She was a country girl, born in Wales but brought up in Hampshire after her father had been killed in a mining accident, so she'd told him, and even though she'd settled in London and seemed happy here, she reminded him of a yellow buttercup, luscious, cheerful and there to light up his life whenever he saw her. She thrived like a buttercup and Jeff could imagine her spreading through his house like they did through wild meadows, filling it with her golden glow and bringing fun and laughter into their lives – and therein lay the problem, because Jeff knew he was thinking of adopting the Stewart children.

There, he'd admitted it to himself at last. He'd been mulling it over for weeks. He would have married their mother for the children's sake, but luckily she wouldn't let him in – because now he'd found a woman he could love.

Jeff could hardly believe it had happened at last. He'd thought himself past all that – at forty-four, he'd settled for a life alone. He had mates down the pub and his customers. His work took up most of his day and he knew everyone in the streets and lanes hereabout and they all stopped to chat. He was never lonely – but now, after Margaret left, it was as if the light went with her.

Of course, he was too old for her. Deep down inside, he knew that, knew it wouldn't be fair to ask a young woman – she must be twenty-four or so – to be tied to a man nearly twice her age. How could he do it? Being Margaret, she wouldn't laugh at him; she would try to let him down lightly, but that might hurt even more. He didn't want sympathy from her. Sometimes, he ached to hold her and make love to her, but he'd tried a light kiss on the mouth and thought he felt resistance. He hadn't dared to try more because he was afraid of losing her friendship.

Preoccupied with his own thoughts and hopes, he forgot the figure in the shadows. He was more than a match for any thief that broke into his home or business. His thoughts went back to the decision he must make soon.

If he took on the two children, that would be asking even more of Margaret. It just wouldn't be right. Jeff sighed deeply. He was torn two ways – take the children and make them happy, and content himself with Margaret's friendship – or risk asking Margaret to marry him and then decide about the children. But if he did the second, the children might have to go to an orphanage and that would break their hearts.

It was a dilemma, and Jeff wasn't sure which way to jump. Perhaps he should wait until after Christmas to decide . . .

CHAPTER 25

Sid Harding looked uneasily over his shoulder. He'd had the feeling that he was being followed again. It had happened a few times lately, but although he glanced back, he could never see who was following him. He'd thought all his old enemies were either dead or in prison and therefore it would be safe to return to London to their new home. Ruby was so happy, back at the Rosie with the people she knew and liked, loving her new house and her job. Sid knew she'd asked Matron about fostering a child and Matron had approached Lady Rosalie on their behalf. They were due to go for an interview after Christmas; Ruby had had one and been approved but Sid needed to be vetted too and he was desperate not to upset the apple cart. He didn't want anything to upset his Ruby and he was quite looking forward to having a boy about the house, though of course they might get a girl. Sid loved his Julia and no girl could ever come up to her in his opinion – but he wouldn't mind a boy to take fishing in the canal or play a game of football with in the lane.

Sid went into the shop selling fishing tackle and stood just inside the door looking out of the glass window. Two men walked by, both in business suits; they didn't glance his way and Sid frowned, waiting even though the shopkeeper was looking at him suspiciously – and then he saw him across the street, a young lad of about thirteen. His hair was long and greasy and his clothes were too small and filthy by the looks of them. He bent and made a pretence of tying his shoelace, but watching the shop all the while.

Smiling to himself, Sid approached the counter and purchased a length of fishing line. He stuck it in his jacket pocket so that the packet showed above, made sure his money was in his inside pocket and went back outside, walking down the street. If the lad was after robbing him, he would get a little shock.

Sauntering down the street, Sid didn't glance back again; he just kept on walking at his steady pace, allowing the lad to follow and attempt his robbery if he chose. The boy was still there, his senses told him that, the prickling at his nape making him aware that he was under the lad's scrutiny. Sid ignored it and just kept on until he reached the end of his street. The scruffy boy had made no attempt to rob him and when he looked back, he'd gone. No sign of him loitering at the corner.

How strange was that? Sid couldn't work it out. He'd given the boy plenty of chance to rob him – so if he didn't want to steal, what did he want?

Shaking his head, Sid went into the house. The lad must want something so eventually, he would take a chance or approach Sid.

Of course, he might have been paid to follow Sid, to discover where he lived. A cold chill touched his nape. No! Please don't let it be the criminal element who had made it impossible for Sid to stay in London before. If his wife was threatened, they would have to move again – and he wanted to stay where he was, to be safe and comfortable. He wished to goodness he'd never seen that murder, never hidden the knife used and got involved with those evil monsters. He'd thought that was all over years ago – they were all in prison or dead, surely?

And then he suddenly remembered Ruby telling him about the lad she took sandwiches for sometimes and he realised that perhaps the lad had been trying to pluck up the courage to speak to him, perhaps ask him for a job. He smiled with relief, dismissing his fears.

As he entered the kitchen, he could smell his dinner – probably shepherd's pie from the lovely aroma – and his mouth watered. Ruby was singing and looking happy and he couldn't help smiling back.

'Something smells good.'

'It's your favourite,' Ruby told him with a loving look. 'I know what you like, Sid, and I'm making a fuss of you – shepherd's pie with beans and apple pie with custard for afters.'

'What have I done to deserve that?'

'Matron told me her ladyship says if we pass our tests – and she is certain we will – we can have a chid after Christmas! Just think, Sid. She did have a little boy she considered us for but someone asked for him and we'll get our chance after Christmas. I don't mind if it's a girl or a boy. Oh, Sid! We'll have another young one to look after. You're doing so well now, I don't have to work long hours, just the eight to twelve shift – and then I'll be home to look after everyone.'

'That's wonderful, love,' Sid said and kissed her. She gave him a big hug in return and when his wife hugged, you knew it. 'That's worth everything, that is.'

Sid whistled as he went upstairs to change out of his working things and wash his face and hands. Everything was playing out just fine.

Ruby was happy the next day as she walked to work. She was walking to save a little bit of extra money to get Sid a nice present for Christmas, a thick silver chain to go with the pocket watch that was part of the legacy they'd got from their last employer. It was a good watch, a repeater, and much better than anything Sid had ever had. If he wore it with a nice chain and his best waistcoat and suit when they went for their interview, he would be certain to pass. Sid paid for dressing; he was still a good-looking man and Ruby still fancied him like mad.

She passed the jewellers to glance in the window and then felt the touch of a hand on her arm. Looking down, she saw a slightly dirty hand on her sleeve and smiled.

'Hello, Luke,' she said. 'How are you this morning? It's cold, isn't it?'

'I ain't cold, missus,' the boy said and grinned at her, showing a gap she hadn't seen in his front teeth before. 'Just 'ungry.'

'What happened to your tooth?'

'I 'ad a bit of an accident the other day,' Luke said and shrugged. 'Fought a gang of rough types that tried to rob a young girl a time ago and I scared 'em off but they jumped out at me the other night to give me a hiding – but they look worse than I do!'

'You be careful, Luke. I don't want anything to happen to you, lad. You brighten my day,' Ruby said and meant it. She liked Luke a lot and wished he would take her offer to come to hers for food. 'My husband might have a little job for you, Luke. Why don't you come and see him?'

'I might . . .' he said.

He continued to look at her hopefully and Ruby took a greaseproof packet from her basket. It contained four egg sandwiches and a piece of Victoria sponge and she handed it to him. She'd made it for herself, because this wasn't his day as a rule, but she could get a bite to eat at work though she preferred her own food, and his need was greater. She thought he looked leaner and she worried that he wasn't getting enough food.

'Why don't you go to the Rosie and ask for Matron?' Ruby said. It wasn't the first time she'd suggested it but he shook his head. 'She might help you – and my Sid is doing a job there today.'

'Don't want to go in no orphanage,' he said. 'I can manage on the street wiv what you give me, missus. Sometimes, I get a job and then I don't beg – but you make the best food ever.'

'Why don't you come to my house then? I told you where I live.'

Luke nodded, his look speculative. 'Yer husband might not like it . . .'

Ruby shook her head. 'My Sid is a lovely man; I've told him about you and he would welcome you. So don't you go hungry, Luke – and you come and have a bit of dinner on Christmas Day. You can have a wash and I'll find you something better to wear.'

'The Sally Army will do that near Christmas,' Luke told her. 'They gave me an overcoat once and told me I could have more at Christmas.' He hesitated. 'I wouldn't mind a bit of hot dinner one day, though. I don't mind eating it in the shed.'

'You come to the kitchen door and we'll have you in,' Ruby promised. He nodded, thanked her and ran off. Ruby stood and watched him go and then went inside the jeweller's shop. She had placed a silver watch chain to one side and she paid another pound on it. That left her just ten shillings to pay next week so that she could take it home in time for Christmas.

She smiled as she left. She would buy Luke a nice warm jumper and some shoes for his Christmas. She could cut down a pair of secondhand trousers from the nearly new shop and buy a shirt from the market. Perhaps, if Luke looked right, he would get more work on the docks or Sid might give him something. Ruby smiled as she continued her walk. He seemed a decent lad, though she knew nothing about his past life, but she hoped he would come for his dinner one day. Washed, dressed better and given decent food she reckoned he could make something out of himself.

CHAPTER 26

Sarah Jones popped into the children's ward at the Rosie and smiled as she saw Sister Rose making her rounds. The senior nurse was smiling as she walked up to her. Sarah felt glad she'd decided to visit, because it felt good to be back at the Rosie, even for a short time.

'Sarah, how lovely to see you,' Sister Rose said. 'Are you on your own – no son and heir?'

Sarah laughed. 'I left him with Mum. He was a bit fractious this morning so she told me to go and visit friends and leave her to cope – so I came to see how you're all getting on. How is Doctor Peter?'

'A little better I think,' Sarah said. 'His progress is much slower than he'd hoped but he's in a lot less pain than he was so we're hoping things can only improve. But how are you managing?' she inquired of her former colleague. 'Is it difficult fitting work in around your home and husband?'

'I only work morning shifts now,' Rose told her. 'It suits me – keeps me interested and yet gives me time to enjoy being a wife.'

Sarah nodded. 'I've been wondering . . .' She hesitated and Sister Rose smiled and nodded encouragingly, finishing the question for her.

'Whether you could do part-time?'

'Yes.' Sarah laughed ruefully. 'I do miss the routine of it and seeing everyone.'

'Yes. I think I should find it boring at home all the time,' Sister Rose admitted. 'There's something special about being a nurse, isn't there?'

Sarah agreed there was and smiled. 'Well, I'll leave you to get on then. Oh – how is Jilly getting on after her accident?'

'She is doing fine, apart from some pain, which is due to bruising on her thighs and her broken arm. We kept her in to feed her up a bit rather than because she needed nursing care. However, she had a lucky escape and we must thank God that nothing worse happened to her.' Sister Rose smiled at her. 'I understand that you were one of the first on the scene and it may be due to you that her injuries were not aggravated.'

'I did very little except prevent the driver carrying her to the Rosie. Bert and Nurse Margaret did the rest between them.' Sarah glanced round the ward. 'Nurse Margaret seems to be getting on well. Is she not on this ward now?'

'Doing her stint on the critical ward,' Sister Rose replied, looking thoughtful. 'Why don't you go and visit with Jilly for a little while? I know she's feeling a bit down at the moment, wondering if she'll be home for Christmas.'

'It isn't long now, under two weeks . . . But where

will Jilly and her brother stay?' she asked, wondering if she should suggest taking the children for Christmas herself.

'Jeff Marshall from the garage has taken young Tim in with him already and is planning to have them both as soon as we release Jilly.'

'I know him – he did your husband's car up, didn't he?' Sarah said and smiled. 'He always seems friendly when I see him, but I don't think he's married – can he really cope with two children on his own?'

'That's a question only he knows the answer to,' Sister Rose replied, 'but I'm sure he will manage over Christmas, because he has invited Nurse Margaret to spend the day with him. She's going to help cook their dinner and I think she is really looking forward to it.'

'Oh, that's good,' Sarah replied feeling relieved. 'I know Mum manages her two boys very well, but I'm glad she is married. It makes life easier for them all.'

'I am sure it must,' Sister Rose said and smiled. 'Gwen invited us to tea at the weekend and I'm looking forward to it. Your mum is a lovely cook, Sarah.'

'Yes, yes she is.' Sarah laughed as she moved away to allow the senior nurse to get on with her work. She spoke to various children as she walked down the ward, asking how they were and what was wrong with them. Several of them had been in before, victims of bad chests or falls and other small ailments. When she reached Jilly's bed, she could see that she looked bored and restless. 'Hello, young lady,' she said and smiled. 'How are you feeling today, love?'

'My arm hurts,' Jilly complained but looked more fed up than tearful. 'I want ter go home.'

'I'm sure you do,' Sarah replied. 'And you'll be able to go as soon as the doctors think your arm is healed well enough.'

'When will that be?' Jilly frowned. 'Shall I be able to go to Mr Marshall's for Christmas? They'll have a goose and everything and I've never had goose. Is it nice?'

'I've only had it once,' Sarah told her with a smile. 'It was very nice, but we usually have chicken.'

'I don't remember having that either, though Tim says we did, years ago.' Tears filled the little girl's eyes, making Sarah's heart ache for her. 'I wish my mum would come . . .'

How did you tell a vulnerable child that her mother was probably never coming back? Sarah didn't know how to start. She knew that her husband believed that their mother was dead but the children didn't know and he'd said he was leaving the telling to Mr Marshall when he thought the time was right, because he was their unofficial guardian.

'If he asks to adopt them legally, I shall support his case,' Steve had told her before he left for work that morning. 'He's a good bloke and I know he thinks a lot of them – especially the boy.'

'But little girls need their mothers, Steve,' Sarah had replied. 'I'm not sure he would manage alone.'

'He says he can afford to get a housekeeper if necessary, so that would probably be enough.'

Sarah had nodded, because she wasn't sure a house-keeper would be enough, but Steve knew Mr Marshall

187

well and if he thought the garage owner would be a good father and guardian, who was she to argue?

After visiting Jilly, Sarah left the hospital, speaking to one or two friends on her way out. It was a nice bright morning and not too cold so she decided to go for a walk. Her son would be happy with his grandmother who doted on him, so she had no reason to hurry home and decided to take a short stroll down by the canal. She wanted to see if the ducks were still about. Her father had taken her to the canal often as a little girl; they'd fed ducks and sometimes swans with stale bread and Sarah was looking forward to doing something similar with her son. Steve had warned her to be careful walking on her own since they'd found the murdered woman in the canal, the woman they thought was poor Jilly's mother, but it was the middle of the day so she was sure she would be fine – who would attack her in broad daylight? Besides, hadn't the incident happened much further along the bank, and she wouldn't go too far . . .

Luke stood staring into the dirty canal water, frowning as he thought of the incident he'd witnessed some weeks back. He'd seen that woman walking there alone and then this man with red hair and a beard had suddenly appeared. They'd seemed to argue for a while and what Luke had seen then had been so shocking that it was still like a nightmare. The man had done something terrible to the woman and knowing he wasn't big and strong enough to stop him, Luke had run off to find help. Only there was hardly anyone around and when he finally saw a woman with a pram, she'd just hurried away from him. It took ages for him to find anyone he knew – a man who had employed him occasionally to scrub filthy lorries. When Luke explained what he'd seen, Mr Barret had laughed.

'It will just be a whore with one of her customers,' he'd claimed, but Luke had begged him to go and look, telling him about the screams and the way the woman had fought and in the end, he'd followed Luke to the scene of the incident – but there was nothing to see and the woman and the man with red hair had both gone.

'There you are,' Mr Barret said grumpily and slapped Luke around the ear. 'Wasting my time, you idiot – or did you make it up just to annoy me?'

'No, sir, no!' Luke said holding back the tears despite the stinging pain. 'I did see it and I don't think she was a whore or whatever.'

'Probably out for a bit of fun behind her husband's back and got more than she bargained for,' Mr Barret retorted. 'And if you waste my time again, you'll get more than a clip round the ear. You'd better come back and do a job for me – and if I catch you slacking, you'll feel my hand again but harder next time.'

Luke had gone with him to do the dirtiest jobs but, in the end, he'd been paid. Mr Barret had grudgingly agreed he'd earned his half-crown and Luke had spent one penny to get into the toilets and wash himself and then he'd bought fourpence worth of chips and Fred Giles had filled the packet up with crispies for him.

Fred Giles was a lovely man. All the kids went there for chips when they could afford it and he treated them all well. He'd given Luke a bottle of lemonade once and that had been a real treat. Luke had wondered if he should tell Mr Giles about what he'd seen, but perhaps he would just think he was making it up.

Now, as Luke watched another young woman walking on the towpath and the memories flooded back, his nerves were suddenly alert and jangling, so that when he saw the man jump out at her from behind a bush he knew he had to do something immediately, and instead of running away he picked up a good-sized stone and threw it at the man's head. To Luke's delight and surprise, it hit him on the temple. He gave a shout of pain and rage, turning to glare at Luke. That momentary lack of concentration cost him his victim. His back was turned to the young woman and she shoved hard, tipping him forward. His feet slid on the mud at the edge of the towpath and he tumbled into the water with a yell of anger and surprise.

The young woman darted at Luke, took his hand and told him to run. His instinct for self-preservation made him obey her instantly. Behind them, they could hear the yells of the man who had attacked her.

'Come on!' she urged when he looked behind. 'He'll get out and when he does, he'll come after us – he won't let us get away with that, even though he's got no worse than a soaking.'

Luke nodded but saved his breath for running until they joined the busy streets again. They both stopped then, gasping for breath, but when she'd got her breath back, she smiled and Luke smiled back, because she was so pretty and nice. He was glad he'd thrown that stone to save her!

'You saved my life,' she said, as if reading his thoughts. 'That was a splendid throw.'

'I could do better if I had a sling,' Luke said. 'I like throwing stones.'

Her eyes moved over him. 'Will you let me take you home and feed you?' she asked. 'I'd like to do something for you – but I don't even know your name.'

'I'm Luke,' he said and shook his head. 'You don't owe me anything – I wasn't going to let him do to you what he did to that other lady. She screamed and I ran for help but no one believed me . . .'

'I believe you,' the lady said. 'My name is Sarah, Sarah Jones – and someone was killed not far from where I was attacked. Did you see that happen, Luke?'

'Well, I saw him attack her,' he replied carefully because he hadn't seen the woman die. 'He was doing something bad to her and I ran for help, but no one listened for ages, so this time I threw that stone.' He looked at her uncertainly and Sarah smiled.

'I'm so glad you did, Luke. I do owe you quite a lot, even though you think not. What will you allow me to do for you?'

'Give me two bob?' he said hopefully.

Sarah smiled and nodded. 'I'll give you more than that.' She opened her purse and took out four half-crowns and handed them to him. 'This isn't enough, Luke, but I live at the police house three streets away from Button Street. If you ever want anything, just come and ask – and really, you should tell my husband about that man you saw.'

She saw the way he drew back, the look of fear that crossed his face, knew she must not push him too hard or he would never tell Steve what he'd seen.

'I believe it is important,' she said quietly. 'So please, tell me you'll think about it, Luke?'

'Yeah, all right, I will one day,' he said. 'I know your husband anyway – he gives me a shilling when he sees me. He's all right.'

'Why didn't you tell him about the other lady, Luke?'

'I didn't think he would believe me,' he said simply. 'No one else did.'

'Yes, he will believe you,' Sarah said. 'Trust me, Luke. My husband *will* believe you. I'll tell him what happened and I know he will want to ask some questions – but no one will harm you or try to make you do anything you don't want.' Sarah looked at him hesitantly. 'Are you sure you won't let me help you – give you a meal and a bath now?'

'Nah, I'm all right – thanks, though . . .'

Luke smiled as he walked off. He thought he could probably trust her and he had wondered if he should speak to the police constable who gave him a shilling now and then, but he'd hung back for fear of being told he was a liar, but this lady believed him and that made him smile. He pocketed the money she'd given him, more than he'd ever had in one go in his life. As he turned and walked off, he was whistling. At the moment life was as good as it got on the streets and he still had hopes of getting a job in that garage.

When Sarah told Steve about the incident by the canal that evening, he almost blew his top. 'I warned you not to walk by the canal!' he said, looking at her in a mixture of disbelief and fear. 'You might have been raped and murdered.'

'It's all right, Steve. I was saved by a young lad throwing stones and I pushed my attacker in the water. I'm sure he was drunk – but what I need to tell you is that the lad, Luke, saw him attacking another woman some weeks back and it sounds as if it might be the woman you fished out of the canal.'

'Thank God for that boy,' Steve said, calmer but still anxious. 'Can you describe the man who attacked you, love?'

'Yes,' she said, and described everything she could remember. Steve nodded and wrote it all down; she noticed that his hand shook slightly and realised he was still upset over what might have happened had Luke not been there. 'I'm sorry, Steve. I know you warned me but it was such a nice morning and I never dreamed anything bad could happen at that hour.'

'Nor did Betty Stewart,' he said. 'You had a lucky escape, Sarah. Please, promise me not to do it again until this man has been caught?' He nodded to himself. 'Jeff Marshall thought it might be someone off a ship and it looks as if he might be right – it sounds like a seaman, perhaps one dismissed for drunken behaviour.'

'He spoke English but with a foreign accent, not that he said much except when he was in the water swearing at us.'

'I suppose he got out?'

'Oh yes, he would get out there because there are iron rings on the wall,' Sarah said confidently. 'Once he got over the shock of the icy water, he could grab them and haul himself up.'

Steve nodded thoughtfully. 'One side of me wishes he'd drowned,' he admitted, 'but it's best that we arrest him and make him pay for what he's done.'

'Will my evidence – and Luke's if he ever gives it – be enough?'

'That would be up to the coroner to decide,' Steve admitted, 'but we'd like something more if we could get it, of course. Most women are avoiding the towpath now but he'll try again and from now on I'll be asking my sergeant to have a man patrolling there in plain clothes for part of the day.'

'Attacking in broad daylight is mad,' Sarah observed. 'Perhaps he can't help himself, Steve – the drink or his urges or something.'

'Then he's a danger to society and needs to be put away for good – or hanged.' Steve's mouth hardened. 'Scum like that deserve no sympathy, Sarah.'

'No, they don't,' she agreed and left it at that. 'I'll finish getting your supper now, love – and I'm sorry I ignored your warning. It won't happen again.'

'Make sure it doesn't, because I couldn't bear to lose you, Sarah.'

'I know – the feeling is mutual,' she said and went to take his meal out of the oven. Steve was right. She had had a lucky escape and it was all due to Luke. She wished he'd come home with her, let her give him a good meal and clean him up, but he was too independent and wary. Forcing the issue would have set him against her, she was sure. As it was, she was hopeful he would come forward and talk to Steve.

CHAPTER 27

Ruby looked for Luke on her way to work the next morning. She enjoyed talking to him and she'd packed a couple of extra sandwiches but it looked as if they might be wasted; then, just as she was about to give up hope, he approached from behind and touched her on the shoulder.

'You made me jump,' she said and smiled. 'You look bright and cheery this morning, lad.'

'I went up the Sally Army and they give me some new clothes and then I had a bath.' Luke grinned at her. 'I smell a bit better now, missus.'

'If you wanted to be clean you could come to mine whenever,' Ruby told him. 'In fact, you could live with us if yer wanted. I spoke to my Sid and he said he would give yer a job with him, at least until you found yer feet.'

Luke nodded. 'Thanks, missus. I might come on Christmas Day – if yer meant it.'

'Yes, of course I did,' Ruby said and smiled. She found the young lad's smile attractive and looked forward to their little chats of a morning. 'Here's yer sandwiches and you're welcome at my house whenever yer like.'

Luke accepted the greaseproof package and smiled. 'I like your food, missus,' he said. 'You're a nice lady. I wish you'd been my mum.'

As he walked off whistling cheerfully, Ruby felt tears sting her eyes. His saying that had made her feel on top of the world and she quickened her step, ready for the day at work. She enjoyed her work at the Rosie so much, loved the nurses and the patients, particularly the dear little kiddies, lying there in those narrow beds, looking so poorly. But my how their faces lit up with pleasure when she took them ice cream, jelly and fruit – such a treat for the poor little mites. Those who were a little better loved her egg sandwiches or ham when they had it, and a nice glass of cold milk or squash.

Ruby had quite enjoyed looking after the old lady who had given them a home and jobs for a couple of years when they'd first left London, fleeing from the gangsters. She'd been so grateful to them towards the end as she grew frail and they'd taken care of her, which was why she'd been generous to them in her will, but Ruby much preferred the wards of the Rosie.

She smiled as she greeted staff on her way to the kitchens, ready to begin work for the day. The only thing lacking in her life now was a child to love and spoil now that Julia was so grown-up in her ways.

Luke felt good as he left his friend with the packet of food tucked inside his jacket pocket. Things were looking up again of late and he was pleased with himself for stopping that attack on the copper's wife. He'd distrusted everyone when he first ran away from the orphanage, but he'd learned slowly that some folk were to be trusted and he reckoned Constable Jones was one of them. He never tried to order Luke off the streets, just stopped to ask if he needed anything and passed on a shilling for a cup of tea. It bought more than just a cup of tea. Luke could buy hot chips for fourpence, two cups of tea at the Sally Army canteen and an iced bun with a shilling, enough to keep him going for the day. The four half-crowns Mrs Jones had given him were folded safely inside a dirty rag in his inside pocket. He hadn't spent anything yet, because the Sally Army gave him a hot meal and a bath once a month.

Luke reckoned that was fair enough. He couldn't expect them to feed him properly all the time; there were too many others in a similar position and they had to ration the help they gave. And Luke preferred to work and earn a bit, but he was fed up with the dirty jobs on the docks, which was all he'd been able to find lately. He still missed Ern and wished he hadn't disappeared soon after war was declared. Luke reckoned that was all a bit of a myth anyways. Nothing much had happened, except there were more men in uniform and the occasional false alarm from the siren. However, his recent adventures and the extra food Missus Ruby had given him, had made Luke think that perhaps he could do better. First he would go to the man at the garage and ask if he wanted someone to learn the trade. It was the way to a better life and he didn't intend to live on the streets or in derelict buildings all his life. He didn't much mind what the trade was but he would start with the garage owner because he had a friendly face.

Jeff looked up from polishing the expensive car to see the youth watching him. He probably wasn't much older than Tim, but looked bigger, stronger and tougher somehow – as if he'd suffered a lot in his young life. He'd noticed him hanging around before but he always ran off if Jeff spoke to him so this time he just stood and waited.

'Hello, mister.' The boy approached tentatively. 'I've been watchin' for a bit and I know you've got a lad works for you nights and Saturdays. I wondered, though, if you'd like someone to learn the trade?' He shifted his feet nervously as Jeff was silent. 'I'd like to be an apprentice . . .'

Jeff frowned. The lad seemed polite and he was much cleaner today, better dressed. Had he not already made the decision to adopt the Stewart children and perhaps make Tim his apprentice, he might have given this lad a chance, but he'd got enough on his plate for now. He still hadn't sorted out what he was going to say to Margaret that evening when she came and his mind was preoccupied with her reaction to what he wanted to ask her. Reluctantly, he shook his head.

'Nay, lad, the position is filled. Sorry, I'd have liked to help.'

'It's OK, mister,' the lad said and started to walk away.

'Just a minute,' Jeff said quickly. 'I might know of

199

someone who is wanting a bit of help.' The lad stopped, turned and looked at him, hope dawning. 'There's a tailor's shop on Silver Street. The owner's name is Soliman Rashid but folk call him Solly. He was in here yesterday, telling me he needed a boy to tidy his shop and run errands. The pay won't be much but he'll pay you fair and square and if he likes you, he'll teach you the trade.' Jeff smiled at him. 'You tell him I sent you and he might give you a chance – I warn you, though, he likes nice manners in a boy, no cheek, and he needs you to turn up every day.'

'Thanks, mister!' The lad's face lit up.

'You're welcome – but before you go, what's your name, lad?'

'Luke, sir. I don't know the rest of it; I was always just Luke – or "you there".' He grinned at Jeff. 'I shan't be rude to him, Mr Marshall, and I won't let your friend down. I'm grateful for the chance.'

'That's right, Luke. You never get anywhere being rude. I hope you like being with Solly. He can be grumpy but he's all right really.'

'I know him,' Luke said. 'He gave me sixpence once for washing his path.'

Jeff felt better as the youth walked off whistling. With a bit of luck, if Solly was generous enough to give Luke sixpence for washing his path, he would probably take him on for deliveries and sweeping up the workroom. The lad had got some decent clothes from somewhere and looked more presentable. He was only sorry he couldn't give him that apprentice-ship, but it would take all his time and energy to look after the children he was now committed to.

He nodded thoughtfully, smiling as his thoughts became personal once more. His appointment with Matron at the Rosie had gone very well.

'If it was down to me, Mr Marshall, I would give you legal custody now,' she'd told him. 'However, that will have to come through Lady Rosalie. I'll recommend you to her, she'll interview you and then put you on her list of foster parents and you can foster them for a few months – after that, you can apply to adopt if you're still of the same mind.'

'Oh, I shan't change my mind,' Jeff told her cheerfully. 'When I set myself to do something, Matron, I do it.'

'Yes, I rather thought you might,' she agreed. 'I'm sure you'll have no trouble with young Tim – but Jilly can be a bit of a handful. She needs a woman's understanding sometimes.'

'Aye, I know it – and I'm hoping I can maybe sort that one way or another.' He'd looked at her bashfully. 'There's a lady I intend to ask to wed me – but she's considerably younger and she may say no. If she does, I'll employ a housekeeper who is right for the child.'

Matron's face had lit up. 'Would I know the young lady, Mr Marshall?'

'Aye, you would, but I'd appreciate it if you'd keep it to yourself.'

Matron had nodded and smiled. 'It is your secret, Mr Marshall. I shall not say a word.' She'd looked very pleased with herself. 'You won't mind if she continues with her work at the Rosie, I imagine, and she loves it. She can work school hours if things go as you wish.'

Jeff had frowned over that one. He didn't much want his wife working too hard, but if it was what Margaret needed and wanted, he wouldn't object.

He would pop the question to her when she came that night and keep his fingers crossed that she understood that it wasn't just for the children's sake that he was asking her to be his wife . . .

CHAPTER 28

Margaret put on a pretty green wool flared dress that evening. It was new; she'd bought it on a whim in a sale, because it had been expensive and not something she would normally be able to afford, but at half-price she'd splashed out and purchased it for four pounds, which was a shocking sum for a frock but it did look smashing on her.

She was smiling happily as she left her flat and walked to Jeff's house. She had a fluttery feeling in her tummy because she was almost sure that tonight he was going to ask her to marry him. She couldn't be certain, of course, but her instincts told her he'd been building up to it recently and she knew her answer. She was going to say yes.

Margaret knew that she cared for the cheerful garage owner in a way she'd never cared for a man before. She trusted him, felt safe and happy with him and she was sure she loved him. Not that she'd had much experience of love, because apart from being fond of her aunt, she'd never truly known love – but she had a warm squidgy feeling inside when Jeff took her arm or gave her a brief kiss and she thought that perhaps that was love – or as near to it as she would ever get. That romantic flaring of torches and scorching heat of passion she'd seen on the big screen at the movies was probably never going to be something she experienced, but she thought what she felt for Jeff was nice, warm and comfortable – and probably preferable for her.

His smile of welcome when he opened the door to her made her light up inside and when she went into his warm and cosy parlour, she knew that she could call it home and it was what she wanted.

'You look beautiful, Margaret,' Jeff told her and she felt that soft melting inside and smiled back at him. 'Really wonderful – that green suits you. Not many women can wear it, but you certainly can.'

'Back in the valleys where I was born they say it is the colour of a witch,' Margaret replied teasingly as he took her coat off to hang it up. He brought her a glass of sherry and motioned she should sit down. 'I don't believe that – do you?'

'I'm not sure,' Jeff said and his eyes teased. 'I think you've bewitched me, Margaret . . .' And then he went down on one knee in front of her as she sat on his sofa and took her hand. 'I'm not much of a man with words, Margaret, but I care for you as much as a man ever could – and I'm asking you to be my wife.'

'Oh Jeff, what a lovely proposal,' Margaret said and tears started to her eyes. 'Thank you for asking me – and yes, I would love to be your wife.'

A huge grin spread over Jeff's face and he produced a black leather ring box from his pocket. 'I saw this in an antique shop and bought it, because I thought it was just you – but if you don't like it, I can get you a new one.'

Margaret gasped, because the ring was the most beautiful thing she'd ever seen. It had a square topaz stone set on either side with baguette diamonds that sparkled in the firelight and she felt her heart catch. She'd never seen any other woman wear an engagement ring like this and it was just so right for her.

'It is the loveliest ring I've ever seen,' she said and meant it with every fibre of her being. 'I love it, Jeff – will it fit?'

Jeff slid it onto the third finger of her left hand and it looked as if it had been made for her alone. 'That was lucky,' Jeff said sounding a little breathless. 'The jeweller told me that he could size it to fit but it's just right – it must have been waiting for you.'

Margaret nodded her agreement. Her heart was full and when Jeff kissed her softly on the lips, she felt her eyes moisten with happy tears.

They drank their sherry and then Jeff took her to a small, intimate restaurant where they had a lovely meal of Dover sole, sautéed potatoes, tiny peas and thin beans, followed by a creamy lemon mousse and coffee with mints.

Margaret even enjoyed the white wine Jeff chose and she didn't normally like wine much, but that night it was all perfect. She told him so when he took her home and kissed her softly before saying goodnight.

'That was the most perfect night of my life, Jeff. You've made me so very happy.'

'Good,' he said and looked pleased. 'I feel like I've won the jackpot, Margaret. I must be the luckiest man on earth.'

After Jeff left her, Margaret gave a little scream of delight. They would have the banns called straight away and marry soon after Christmas, Jeff had said, which meant she could soon say goodbye to the lonely existence she'd known here. She would have Jeff and the two children to care for and reduced hours at the Rosie, but Jeff said she could keep her job as long as she wished.

It all seemed so perfect to Margaret that she thought she must be dreaming and pinched herself to make certain it was real – but the beautiful ring was still on her finger and she knew she wasn't dreaming. She was engaged to the man she loved and everything was wonderful. She couldn't wait to be married!

Jeff felt shell-shocked when he got in. He'd been building his courage up to ask Margaret for so long and convinced himself she would turn him down, so her obvious delight and pleasure all evening had been a delight to see. She really was his golden girl, lit up like a candle on a Christmas tree. He loved her so much that he thought he would burst. She was going to be his wife.

She hadn't actually said that she loved him but she'd been really happy. She'd loved her ring and the wine and the food and told him it was the best night of her life – surely that must mean she cared for him?

Jeff shrugged. If Margaret didn't feel quite as he

did it was only to be expected; he was twenty years older and not much of a catch, whereas she was beautiful and desirable and he adored her. He was so lucky she was willing to be his wife that he could accept it would be a marriage where he loved more than he was loved.

Margaret didn't want to take her ring off ever again but knew she had to for work so she slipped it on the chain that held the gold cross her auntie had given her. She could wear it under her uniform, close to her heart, but she was itching to show it to some of her colleagues. She hoped Sister Rose would be in a happy mood, because then she could show it to her and tell her about her engagement. She wouldn't tell Staff Nurse Alice just yet, though, because Alice had a sharp tongue and she didn't want to hear any sarcastic remarks. But she would definitely show it to Ruby, knowing she would be genuinely pleased for her.

Some of the other nurses might be a bit jealous, though they were friendlier here than in the big hospital Margaret had worked in before she came to the Rosie. She was singing inside as she walked to work, her happiness overflowing as she waved and spoke to the people she'd got to know in the lanes. When she'd first come to the East End of London, she'd known no one and had felt lost and lonely, but now she had a whole new life – and it was all due to Jeff.

She bounced into the kitchen and saw Ruby busy scrubbing the countertops, ready for the day. Ruby glanced up and smiled at her.

'You're glowing today, lass,' she said. 'What's making you so happy then?'

'I'm getting married!' Margaret said proudly and pulled out her chain with the ring securely fastened to it. 'I'm engaged to Jeff Marshall.'

'Well, that's lovely,' Ruby said, looking genuinely pleased for her. 'I shall expect an invite to the wedding – and I'll make your cake if you like.'

'Oh, thank you, Ruby!' Margaret exclaimed delightedly and caught her around the waist in a hug. 'I'm so happy.'

'So you should be,' Ruby told her. 'That Jeff Marshall is a lovely man and he's given you a beautiful ring. I'm real pleased, love – and I'll be wearing me best hat to church. Will it be church or chapel?'

'Church,' Margaret said, nodding. 'In the valley it was chapel but I left that behind when we went to live with my aunt.'

'Good. I do love a nice church wedding,' Ruby said. 'Have you thought what you'll wear – will you have a long white dress?'

'I don't think so because you can't use it again afterwards. I'll have a nice outfit of some kind with a pretty hat, something I can wear for best.'

'Very sensible, love,' Ruby said. 'It's not easy when you haven't got a family to help with the expenses.'

'Well, Mum had nothing to leave and Auntie left me all she had,' Margaret told her. 'I've got a little bit of silver and a few pounds in the bank but I don't think I'm the type for a long white dress somehow.'

'I wasn't either,' Ruby agreed. 'I had a pretty cream

208

dress, a flowery hat and smart shoes and Sid said I was the prettiest bride ever.'

'Jeff says I look beautiful . . . I don't, of course!'

'You've got a pretty face and a wonderful smile,' Ruby said. 'You're not one of those thin girls, but most men like a proper woman to get hold of – that's what Sid always tells me. You're certainly slimmer than I was when I married, Margaret. I've always been a bit on the plump side but it don't matter if you're happy.'

'No, it doesn't,' Margaret said and for the first time in her life she believed it.

CHAPTER 29

Rose looked at her husband. He still looked a bit grey in the mornings sometimes, even though his back pain had eased considerably. She hated to leave him but he'd insisted she return to work as soon as they'd returned from his treatment, and her friend Beattie came in most days to tidy up and make him a snack and a cup of tea. Rose was only working in the mornings at the moment but if Peter ever returned to full-time working himself, she might do longer hours. Currently he went into the clinic for a few hours each day and they spent the afternoons together. Beattie was happy to do the housework and anything Peter needed while he was there.

As Beattie had told her, 'Our little house takes me no time at all to do, and Ted and the boys are out most of the day, Rose, so I might as well come here and work for a couple of hours to save you. Your lovely Peter has been so generous to me and I want to repay him as much as I can.'

Beattie had two young boys she and her husband Ted had adopted, of whom Rose was fond. Perhaps one day she would either have a child of her own or adopt a little boy. It depended on whether Peter recovered completely. It still wasn't easy for him to manage more than a few steps, which made it difficult for him to get about and he needed his chair at the clinic. It wasn't easy to load it in the back of his car. One of his neighbours or even Rose could manage it for him, but he didn't like asking for help at the other end.

It was a dilemma, and Rose hadn't managed to work it out yet. Sometimes, Peter had to ask a stranger for assistance and some of them were not helpful; some just walked straight past and others made an excuse.

She sighed. There were always going to be problems until he was stronger and could either push himself to the clinic or didn't need the chair. He'd refused to let her stay home and take him everywhere and, so far, he was managing.

Leaving for work, she kissed him goodbye and received a loving smile in return. Peter wouldn't hear of her giving up her work for his sake so she just had to let him do what was right for him. Once at work in the children's ward, she was soon too busy to think of anything but her patients and it was some hours later that her thoughts went back to her problem. She found herself wondering how he was getting on and if he would find someone to help with his chair today.

Oh well, it would soon be Christmas and then she was home for three whole days and so was he. She smiled because it would be lovely. Beattie and Ted would bring the boys round and help Rose cook their lunch and the two men could chat and that would be pleasant . . . She glanced at her watch. It was eleven, now, and Beattie would've helped him get his chair in the car; she was very strong and it was easy for her. Rose would be home when he returned – but what would he do when he got to the clinic?

'Sister, could you come a minute please?'

Rose awoke from her private reverie as Nurse Margaret summoned her. The girl was looking happy today, if a little bemused, as if something had happened to her that she still didn't quite believe. Rose would ask her later why she was so happy but for the moment she must get on with her work; she had another two hours of her shift to go. Hopefully, someone at the clinic would assist Peter with his chair.

Luke had been filled with hope when he left Mr Marshall's garage the previous morning, but the tailor had shaken his head mournfully.

'You should have asked last week,' he told Luke with a long face. 'I signed an apprentice on yesterday.'

'I didn't know you needed anyone until today,' Luke had replied. 'I would've worked hard, sir.'

'I know – you're a good lad, kind,' the old man said sorrowfully.

'Thank you, sir,' Luke said and walked away, his heart sinking down to his boots. He'd tried half a dozen shops since then, asking for work, but they all said they had the help they needed and he felt his spirits drop because it meant he would have to keep on with the dirty jobs to earn his living.

As he approached the free clinic, where all the poorest folk of the London streets went for treatment, Luke saw Doctor Peter's car parking, and something made him stand there and wait. The car door opened and the doctor looked about, obviously needing something. Luke approached him, standing a short distance away.

'Can I help, sir?'

The doctor looked at him and nodded. 'Can you go inside and find a porter to lift my wheelchair out, please?'

'Yes, sir.' Luke looked in the back of the car. It looked to be very light, made of some kind of metal and canvas and it would need pushing. 'I could get that out for you, sir,' he said and did so before the doctor could tell him it was too much for him. It was heavier than he'd imagined, but the months shovelling muck on the docks had made him really strong.

He took the chair out, looked at it and pulled it so that it looked right and then wheeled it round to the doctor, who nodded, smiled and heaved himself out of the car and into it.

'You're a strong lad,' he said with a look of approval. 'Have you got the time to push me into the clinic?'

'Yes, sir, I've got all day,' Luke said and grinned. 'I know who you are and what you did – I've heard about it from the old lady you saved from that building that collapsed. She says she'd be dead if it weren't for you. Sometimes when I see her outside the clinic, she tells me to go in with her and they give us a cup of tea.'

'That's our Jessie,' Doctor Peter said and laughed. 'She's a bit of a character, walks the streets with that pram of hers, but she was an actress once and she has a real sense of fun. Wheel me inside and I'll give you half-a-crown, and if you return and wait for me to come out in two hours, I'll give you another.'

'I'll be here,' Luke promised and pushed his chair inside the clinic. Once he was inside, the nurses all ran to Peter and a rather large woman said she would be helping him that day. Doctor Peter winked at Luke.

'I'll be all right now, lad,' he said. 'Don't forget our bargain.' He tossed him a half-crown and Luke caught it neatly.

Luke left him to do his work and went back outside. He decided he would go down the road to the library for two hours, because it was too cold to stand in the street that long. He didn't need to find work that day now, because what he'd been given was sufficient for his needs.

Luke enjoyed the rare times when he could sit in the library and read rather than look for work. Glancing at the clock he calculated the time and how long it would take him to get back to the clinic; he would go a few minutes early rather than be late. He'd been reading a book about motor mechanics but now, since he'd given up that dream, he took one from the shelves about medical stuff and sat reading it. He'd thought it might be dull but found it exciting as he read what doctors do and how long they had to study to become one. His new friend must be really clever to have learned all that stuff. The time went quickly and

214

Luke was back outside the clinic when the doctor came out; he was actually a bit late but Luke didn't mind. One of the nurses had spotted him and brought out a mug of tea, which he'd soon drunk and returned the mug just inside the door.

'Good lad,' Doctor Peter said and swung himself into the car, letting Luke see to the chair. He leaned towards him, smiling. 'Get in beside me for a moment – too cold to stand around outside.' As soon as Luke was settled, Peter asked his name and then nodded. 'Luke, that's a good name. I've been thinking – how would you like to work for me all the time?'

Luke couldn't believe his luck. 'Do you really mean it, sir? What do you want me to do?'

'Well, I'll take you back to my house now and my wife will give you some tea and then I'll want you to come each morning about nine-thirty, if that suits you?' Luke nodded vigorously. He didn't know where Doctor Peter lived but he'd find somewhere nearby to sleep. 'Your job will be to come with me wherever I go and get the chair in and out of the car – and push me about, either in the clinic or round the town if I want to go shopping.' He looked at Luke expectantly. 'Would you be happy doing that?'

'Yes, please, sir, I would,' Luke said eagerly. He thought that he must have landed in Heaven. Surely, this couldn't be happening?

'I'll pay you five shillings a day and we'll feed you when my wife gets home – how's that?'

'It's too much, sir,' Luke said. 'I took the five shillings today, but a pound a week is a fair price for a lad of my age.'

'You're honest as the day is long, Luke – I suspected as much,' Doctor Peter observed. 'Tell you what, to make life easier for both of us, we'll give you a bed and your meals and a pound a week – what does that sound like?'

'It sound great, sir,' Luke replied grinning for all he was worth. Now he knew miracles *did* happen.

'That's settled then. Now, do you want to fetch your things from wherever you live first?'

'Don't have anything worth fetchin',' Luke replied honestly. 'I've only got what I'm wearing – and this.' He showed Doctor Peter the coins he had in his pocket. 'You gave me five shillings and Constable Jones' wife gave me ten for saving her from that horrible man.'

Doctor Peter wanted to know who the man was and what Luke had done and they talked about it as he drove back to his house. A lady came out of the front door but when she saw Luke she waited, watching as he fetched the chair and held the door for the doctor to slide out. He then shut the door, locked it with the key Peter gave him and pushed him towards the house.

'Hello,' the lady said smiling. 'I'm Sister Rose, Doctor Peter's wife. Have you been helping him?'

'Luke here is going to push me around in future,' Doctor Peter told her. 'I am paying him a pound a week, his bed and board – is that all right, Rose?'

'I think it is very fair,' she said and stood back for Luke to push her husband into the house.

For a moment in the hall, Luke thought it really must be Heaven. The smell was so gorgeous – a

216

mixture of lavender polish and food cooking – and he couldn't believe he was going to be living here.

'We'll have our supper first,' Sister Rose said, 'and then I'll go and make a bed up in your room – you can have the one that used to belong to Danny, my friend Beattie's son; you'll meet him when you live here. It is a very nice room and just right for a lad of your age.'

Luke was feeling a bit shy in the hallway but when they got into the big, comfortable kitchen it was so pleasant and smelled so good that he relaxed. He'd been invited here and he had what he'd dreamed of all these months – a decent job to do and a safe roof over his head. He still felt a bit shocked at how quickly it had happened but it was a lovely shock and he felt as if he were living in a dream world. Surely it was too good to be true?

Luke had never slept in a bed as soft or one that smelled so sweet. He'd gone out like a light and only woke when Mrs Peter woke him with a mug of tea.

'There's bacon and egg for breakfast,' she said. 'We're spoiling ourselves today because I wanted to celebrate my husband's independence. With you to look after him, Luke, he can do so much more than he could before and I will never have to feel guilty about leaving him alone. It is so kind of you to take on the job.'

He stared at her. Didn't she realise how wonderful it was for him? She was thanking *him* while he felt he ought to be thanking *her*. He was so grateful he could have burst into tears, but he didn't; he just grinned and made a silent vow that he would never let these good people down. Never. If ever he got the chance, he would repay them for their kindness.

Luke felt as if he were a king as he went down to the kitchen and found the doctor reading the morning paper. Something smelled good but he wasn't sure if it was the food, which looked delicious when the plate was put in front of him, or what was simmering on the stove.

'I don't know if you like proper coffee,' Sister Rose said. 'We have it as a treat – would you like to try?'

'Yes, please.' Luke spoke eagerly, ready for any new experiences in this life that seemed too good to be true. 'It smells lovely.'

His first taste of hot, sweet coffee was so good that he almost burned his tongue, drinking it as fast as he could. Sister Rose laughed, her face lighting up; her pleasure made Luke feel good and he laughed too.

'Yes, I felt like that the first time I had the real stuff,' she told him. 'Here, have some more.'

Luke drank it more slowly this time, savouring it and the bacon and eggs with fried bread and tomatoes. He'd had bacon and eggs at the Sally Army once and thought it was good but it hadn't tasted like this!

'You're a good cook,' Luke told her with an appreciative smile.

'Not as good as my friend Beattie,' Sister Rose replied. 'You wait until you've tasted her cakes – and her beef stew. She cooks us meals three times a week and leaves it in the oven.'

'If she's your friend I'll like her food,' Luke said. Was it possible that any food could taste better than the meals he'd had so far in this house? Luke didn't think it was likely. He glanced at Doctor Peter, who was listening and watching, not saying much. 'Are we going to the clinic today then?'

'Not today,' Doctor Peter said and looked pleased. 'Now that I've got you, I can do some visiting of elderly patients at home, something I haven't done since my accident.'

Luke nodded. He didn't mind what he did; he was just happy to be of use and to live as he was now. Luke couldn't believe the miracle had happened, but now he had he would hang onto it with all his strength, because these were good people and he was so very lucky to have found them.

CHAPTER 30

Jenny was feeling a bit sick. She'd got up that way and had vomited three times before eating a piece of toast and sharp marmalade. Morning sickness was unpleasant but it usually went off during the day; today, for some reason, it hadn't. Feeling the vomit rush up her throat, she made a dash for the bathroom and bent over the toilet, feeling shaky and a bit dizzy as she wiped her mouth afterwards. Jenny frowned, realising she'd probably caught one of the winter bugs going round. She gingerly made her way downstairs to make herself a hot drink of lemon, sugar and a spoonful of medicinal brandy, before returning upstairs to bed.

Having this kind of illness was always rotten, but being on her own made it worse and, once in bed, she gave way to a bout of self-pitying tears. Life could be so unfair. She needed someone to get her a hot-water bottle and a couple of aspirin rather than having to get up and fetch them herself but since she was alone there was no help for it. She drank her hot lemon and then pulled her dressing robe on tight, holding tight to the bannister rail as she struggled downstairs. Why hadn't she thought to get a hot-water bottle first? With the kettle on, Jenny searched for the strip of tablets she needed and had just discovered them at the back of the kitchen drawer when she heard the noise outside – a rattling sound and then a cough.

Her blood froze. Who could be out there? If someone was trying to get in, she was hardly fit to fight them in her condition, but she wouldn't give in without a fight, even if her head was aching like mad. There it was again! The door handle rattled and then she heard it:

'Jenny? Are you there? Are you awake? Come on and let me in!'

Jenny stared in disbelief and then shot for the door, unlocking it with shaking hands. A dark figure stumbled forward and pitched into her arms. In an instant, Jenny forgot that she was feeling sick and dizzy as she looked and saw her husband – and in such a mess. His clothes were filthy, his hair dirty and he looked white and gaunt.

'Oh my God!' she gasped. 'Michael – it is you! What happened?'

'Long story,' he muttered wearily. 'I need something to eat and drink – and to see Chris, in that order.'

'I'll get you a hot drink and a sandwich,' Jenny said, glad she'd bought some cheese and ham that day. She didn't always bother, but she'd decided to shop for once and she took fresh bread, butter, ham and mustard from the cupboard, making him a tasty sandwich while the kettle boiled. He ate it hungrily and drank two cups of tea and then looked at her.

'Can you telephone Chris for me, love? I know it must be late, but it's really important.'

'Yes, of course.' Jenny went into the hall and dialled the number.

Chris answered, sounding odd. 'Jenny – are you ill?'

'No, no – it's Michael. He's home but in a bit of a state.'

'I'm not surprised. I got word of something earlier but I couldn't tell you because I wasn't sure. I'll be round right away. I need to debrief him immediately.'

Jenny heard the receiver go down with a bang at the other end and blinked. She'd always known that Michael must have been doing something that was both dangerous and important, but she'd only thought about the danger. Returning to the kitchen, she saw that Michael was half lying across the table, his head on his arms. Should she try to wake him? He was clearly exhausted. She was inclined to leave him in peace.

Chris had no such qualms when he arrived a few minutes later. He shook Michael roughly to wake him and then hauled him off to their sitting room, half-asleep on his feet, shooting an order at Jenny to make a pot of strong coffee over his shoulder. She did as she was bid, carrying the tray through to the sitting room where the two men were seated. Michael had been telling Chris something but stopped as she entered.

'Thanks,' Chris said tersely. 'Sorry to turn you out of your own front room, Jenny, but this is top secret. You should go back to bed; you look tired to death.'

'I've got a winter bug,' Jenny said. 'I'm going to make myself another hot drink and take it upstairs – but what about Michael? I'm concerned for him.'

'I'm all right now, love,' Michael said and smiled at her. 'Chris will look after me and I'll sleep on the couch down here.'

Jenny nodded. She wasn't happy, resenting the way Chris had just taken over what was a precious home-coming for her. However, she was a sensible girl and she did feel rotten. If she hung around in the kitchen waiting, she might collapse.

She made herself hot milk with a little brandy, leaving the brandy on the table in case her husband felt in need of a little. Sighing, she took the mug upstairs, sat up in bed and drank it, wondering what was going on downstairs, before she put the light out and went to sleep. When Chris let himself out a couple of hours later, she was none the wiser.

Jenny awoke to the smell of coffee and opened her eyes to discover Michael carrying a tray with mugs of coffee and a plate of buttered toast with marmalade.

'I've rung the Rosie and told them you're having the day off,' he said as Jenny smiled at him. 'I'm sorry I barged in last night when you were so ill, love. I ought to have gone straight to Chris.'

'Did he tell you that?' Michael nodded and she frowned. 'No, he's wrong. You did right to come here, Michael. This is your home and I'm your wife – where else would you go? I was so relieved to see you. I've been so worried, Michael. Everyone thought you were dead!'

'Except you, apparently,' he said and smiled. 'I kept telling you to hang on and I'd get home to you, it seems that got through.'

'Yes.' Jenny looked at him seriously. 'It did. I wouldn't believe you had just gone, Michael. Even though my heart was breaking, I never gave up.'

He sat on the edge of the bed and reached for her hand. 'I'm sorry you were worried, love. It was just bad luck. Everything had gone well and then . . .' He shook his head. 'I'm not allowed to tell you much. Lives are at stake. You see, we were in enemy territory and I was the only one who got away. Chris told me to take a compass and I did. I've walked more miles than I care to think about, and I got to England in a fishing boat that damned near capsized more than once. The chap who took me was decent enough, but he had very little money and food was scarce – not that I could keep it down on that boat . . .'

'Oh, Michael.' Jenny reached forward and took his hands. Holding them tightly. 'You must have been so scared and hungry.'

'Yes, but I was determined to get home to you,' he said and leaned forward to kiss her on the lips. 'The thought of you kept me going, Jenny; knowing you were here in our house waiting for me gave me something to hang onto when it was tough.'

'This is lovely,' she said as she sipped her coffee. 'But I should be looking after *you*, Michael.'

'We've got the rest of our lives for that,' he told her with the smile that made her tummy flip. 'How are you now, love? I was worried last night that you hadn't been looking after yourself . . .'

'I'm better now. It was just one of those bugs that make you feel rotten and is gone in a few hours, luckily.' She smiled at him. 'I'm so glad you're back, Michael, darling.'

'So am I – and I love what you've done to the house so far. How did you know I prefer traditional to modern stuff?'

'I think you must have said at Lily's once – but I do too; it's another way we're perfect together.'

'Yes, we are perfect – *you're* perfect,' he said and reached out to touch her sleep-tousled hair. 'I love you more than you could ever know, Jenny. I know I can be a cocky so-and-so – but the first time I saw you, you floored me.'

'You took a while letting me know!'

'Yeah? Well, I reckoned if I threw myself at your feet like all those other idiots, you'd get bored.'

'With you? Never,' she said and knew it was true. Perhaps she hadn't been entirely certain before her marriage, but now, after thinking she might have lost him, she was in no doubt about the way she felt. She smiled into his eyes. 'I've got a bit of news and I'm not sure how you'll feel . . .'

'Just tell me, love.' He looked at her anxiously.

'You're going to be a daddy. I know it is quick. I couldn't believe it could happen so quickly . . .'

Michael stared at her in amazement and then reached out and grabbed her, sending the plate and the last crumbs of toast flying. 'That's the best news I've ever had!' he told her as he hugged her and then kissed her passionately. 'It's wonderful . . . as long as you're happy?' He sat back to study her face. 'Is it too soon for you?'

'No, no! I'm glad we're starting a family,' Jenny said and grabbed his hands. 'When they told me I might have lost you, I clung to the fact that I was carrying our child – at least then I would still have had a part of you.'

Michael looked hugely pleased. He rescued the plate from the floor and smiled. 'Stay in bed for a while . . .?'

Jenny nodded and drew back the covers. 'Only if you get in with me,' she said, giving him a wicked look. 'I've missed you here with me . . .'

Michael laughed and began to strip off so that he could oblige. Jenny felt the warmth spread through her. Like so many other wives in this terrible war, she didn't know what the future would bring – but her husband was here with her now and she intended to make the most of every minute they had together . . .

CHAPTER 31

Sally fetched the Christmas trimmings from the attic as Jane bade her. Jane had told her they would trim the tree a week before Christmas and the house too. She'd ordered a tree from the man on the market that Thursday and a cockerel for their Christmas dinner from the butcher on Fore Hill. Jane always used the same butcher, because he was friendly and gave her decent cuts of meat, even when she didn't have much to spend.

'Lester will see us right,' she told Sally. 'I'll have a small piece of gammon to boil and some sausage meat for sausage rolls and we'll make mince pies. I haven't bothered much with Christmas since my girl died – but this year it is like having her back.'

Sally beamed at her; Jane looked happy and content and she couldn't help feeling some of the excitement rub off on her, even though the shadow of doubt hung heavy over her head. Life was good here with Jane in her little cottage near the quayside in the city of Ely. It was pleasant to walk on the towpath even when it was cold because the view of the cathedral was nice and the sound of the river lapping against the quay, where all the punts were moored, was soothing. Children played in the open spaces, sometimes pinching the punts to go out on the river, until worried parents or angry owners ordered them back. She felt peaceful and relaxed here in this quiet little place – she sensed much happier than she had been in years – but she was haunted by the thought that there was someone she ought to remember or something she ought to do.

Sometimes, Jane asked her why she looked sad and she'd tried to explain, but Jane just told her not to try and force her memories. 'It won't help, Sally, love. The doctor said amnesia cures itself or it doesn't. Some folk never remember – but for most the memories return when they're ready – or perhaps when you are ready for them.'

Sally knew she was right, but often there was a terrible ache of longing and loneliness inside her and she felt that someone was trying to reach her. Was someone looking for her, crying for her? Was it a child, a husband? She shook her head at the last, for something told her she did not have a man who cared for her – but perhaps children . . .?

Looking at the trimmings in the old cardboard box, Sally saw they were made of glass and were beautiful. Birds in rainbow colours with long fluffy tails, Christmas angels and trumpets and delicate balls that glittered in the light. The tree would look gorgeous covered with them.

'Jilly would love these,' Sally said aloud.

'What did you say?' Jane asked, looking at her oddly. 'Who is Jilly?'

Sally stared at her and then shook her head. She searched deep inside for the owner of the name, but she couldn't find her. Something was blocking the memory – something black and horrible that she couldn't get past. For a moment her head spun and she thought she might faint.

'I don't know,' she admitted at last. 'I just said the name but I don't remember who she is or anything.'

'Pity,' Jane said and frowned. 'If you did remember you had a family – or a daughter, say – you could bring them here, Sally. This is your home for as long as you want it. You don't have to go just because you remember.'

'Thank you – you're so good to me,' Sally said as she held back tears. Jane didn't like a fuss. Sally had discovered that her friend suffered a lot of arthritic pain and she did her best to help her manage her life, keeping the coal and wood buckets filled, assisted with the shopping and carrying it home, helping to cook and wash up and keep the house clean. In return, Jane fed and clothed her and provided a warm bed to sleep in. It was fair for both of them and Sally would hate to leave the little nest she'd found for herself – but who was Jilly and why was she calling to her?

'Why are you crying, lovey?' Nurse Margaret asked Jilly as she saw the little girl sobbing her heart out. 'Is your arm hurting again?'

'No, but my heart aches,' Jilly answered mournfully. 'I want my mummy . . . when is she coming home?'

'I don't know, Jilly. I don't know why she went

away and I can't tell you when or if she will come back.' Nurse Margaret sat by her bed and reached for her hand, holding it carefully but in a firm grip. 'I can tell you that you will be staying with me and Mr Marshall over Christmas – and afterwards, if you would like. You will have a lovely Christmas dinner and presents too, if Father Christmas thinks you've been a good girl.'

'I've been bad,' Jilly said. 'I spent all Tim's money on sweets and he worked hard for it. He was so cross with me.'

'Yes, he was, but he isn't any more because he loves you and he's looking forward to Christmas too.'

Jilly nodded and smiled a small wan smile that wrenched at Margaret's heart. 'I think it will be nice to have a lovely dinner and Mummy didn't always get us a nice dinner, Tim says 'cos she has no money, but I do wish she would come and see me.'

'I am sure your mummy would come if she could,' Margaret said and held the child's hand a little tighter. 'Sometimes, things go wrong for grown-ups and they can't do what they want to. Your mummy wants to be with you, I am certain of that – but for some reason she just can't.'

'Why can't she?'

'I don't know the answer to that,' Margaret told her. 'Perhaps she might be not quite well or something.'

How did one tell a small girl that her mother might never come home? It was impossible, especially when Margaret herself didn't know the truth. No one really knew, even though the police seemed to be accepting the body in the canal was Betty Stewart.

'Shall we pretend I'm your auntie for a little while?' Margaret suggested. 'I'll be cooking your dinner at Christmas and looking after you.'

Jilly looked at her uncertainly. 'When will I be able to leave hospital?'

'Soon now – perhaps on Christmas Eve. We'll be trimming a little tree then. You'll like that, won't you? Uncle Jeff has lots of nice things to go on it – you'll see how pretty it will look when we've done it. I promise we'll wait until you're home to do it.'

Jilly nodded, smiling properly now as Nurse Margaret went to look after other children on the ward. She was getting most of what she'd longed for this Christmas – but she'd thought her mother would be there, too. A lovely Christmas dinner and presents were what she'd longed for, but they didn't make up for the empty space her mother had left.

Nurse Margaret glanced back at her, smiling, and Jilly smiled back, because Auntie Margaret was nice and there was a lot to look forward to, but it didn't stop the feeling like there was a big stone inside her chest, because her mother was gone. Tim said she must have had an accident and be in hospital somewhere, but he couldn't find the one where she was. He said Mum wouldn't leave them if she could help it and Jilly knew that was true. Mum must be ill or something. Once she'd been ill in the Rosie for some weeks – so perhaps it was like that and she was in a hospital somewhere and too ill to let them know where she was.

'I love you, Mummy,' Jilly said fervently. 'Please come home soon – we need you . . .'

231

Tim needed Mum to come home too, even though he didn't say much; he was like that – kept things to himself. Jilly knew Tim loved Mum just as much as she did and surely, their mother must know how much she was needed? She would come home when she could, Jilly was sure – but would it be before Christmas?

CHAPTER 32

Margaret couldn't believe she was to be married on the Saturday after Christmas. It all seemed like a dream she was worried she would wake up from. No, Jeff really had asked her to wed him and she'd accepted. The beautiful ring she wore on her finger whenever she wasn't at work on the ward was reminder enough if she'd needed it.

'I'm older, Margaret,' he'd told her the next time they'd met, 'and I've taken on the children – but that need not affect your nursing. I can manage most of their needs. It is just the little girl who will need your woman's instincts and your tender care, love.'

'I can manage Jilly,' Margaret replied nodding, because she understood what he was asking, 'and no, I don't mind having them around. I was part of a big family once in Wales but then we moved away and after Mum and then Auntie died . . . to be honest, it has been a bit lonely ever since.'

'You won't be lonely with the kids and me around,' Jeff told her. 'I know I'm asking a lot, love, but—'

'Don't be daft, Jeff,' she said. 'I shall love that little

girl like she was my own. I'm not quite as good with boys of Tim's age, but I'll learn.' She'd smiled at him then. 'A boy for you and a girl for me.'

'Isn't that the best way?' Jeff asked. 'Boys need the guidance of a father and girls need a mother.'

'I always wanted a daughter, Jeff. Don't worry, I can look after her fine. We've already made friends on the ward.'

Jeff had smiled and they'd spent the rest of the evening talking about the wedding, who they should invite and where to hold it. Jeff asked if she wanted a white wedding and she shook her head.

'I'll wear a white suit or dress and jacket, if I can find one,' she said, 'but I can wear that again and I couldn't a long dress. It's such a waste of money. I'd rather spend it on other things.'

She'd blushed as she thought of the pretty silk lingerie and nightgown she planned on buying for her wedding night. It hadn't occurred to her when Jeff proposed that he was marrying her simply to make a home for the children. That had happened when Matron congratulated her and said it was the best thing to do for everyone's sake, making it sound like some sort of bargain she'd made, not romantic at all.

'Not many girls in your situation get to marry so well,' Matron had said, beaming at her. 'I'm glad you've been sensible, Margaret. You don't need to be violently in love – a good home for you and the children is the best thing. Much nicer than Mr Marshall's idea of perhaps having a housekeeper to care for his foster children. I told him how much easier it would be for him to adopt if he had a wife so I'm glad he asked you and that you accepted, dear.'

Margaret's heart had sunk with every word spoken. It felt somehow demeaning that he'd discussed asking her to be his wife with Matron. Of course, she understood Jeff needed her help with the children and she was pleased to give it – but she'd thought there was more than that when he'd kissed her. She'd thought that perhaps he did love her a little, at least.

Margaret had cried herself to a restless sleep that night. But in the morning she had thought everything through and told herself that even if he didn't love her, it didn't matter. It would still be much better to be a part of his and the children's world than be alone for the rest of her life. It spoiled her happiness a little, but she was a sensible girl and knew it was the best offer she would ever get. She just had to accept that she loved more than she was loved.

Jeff was delighted when he learned that Luke was working with Doctor Peter. It was a great solution to both their problems. The doctor was a good man and would look after Luke, and he was an honest lad who would do right by his benefactor. Jeff would have gladly taken him as an apprentice if he hadn't had Tim's future in mind.

'I reckon that has worked out really well,' he told Margaret when they next met. Tim had arranged to meet a school friend at the boys' club Steve Jones ran and so he was taking her to the musical she'd wanted to see at the cinema.

'Yes, it's lovely,' she said smiling, but without

her usual bright glow. Jeff had a feeling of unease. Something wasn't quite right with his golden girl, but he couldn't be certain what it might be. 'Do you take a lot of interest in kids, Jeff?'

'Yes, I suppose I do but I'd seen Luke hanging around – and well, I couldn't help him so I'm glad he's settled. We've had enough poverty and hardship these past years, love, and I've done well. I just feel I'd like to help others.'

'And you do. You're a lovely man,' she said, hugging his arm. Suddenly her glow was back and Jeff breathed easily again. For a moment he'd thought she was regretting her promise to wed him, and it would break his heart to lose her now. He'd been sailing high all the time since she'd smiled and kissed him back, saying how happy she would be to be his wife.

Once again, he wondered if he'd asked too much of her. She was taking on not only a new husband but a couple of young children. Was he being fair in asking so much of her?

'Is everything all right, Margaret?' he asked, looking at her anxiously. 'You haven't decided you're taking on too much with me and the kids?'

'No, I'm looking forward to it,' she said firmly and that golden smile he loved was back in place. 'I'm used to caring for sick children, Jeff, so it isn't a problem for me – and I care about you a lot so I want to be your wife.' She blushed faintly, looking so delicious that he could have eaten her up. He squeezed her hand, knowing he had to exercise strict control until they were wed. Margaret would be shocked if she knew how much he hungered to make love to her. With a modest girl like Margaret, he had to be careful and not rush things – and he certainly wouldn't attempt anything until they were married. Even then he would be sure to take it slowly and make certain she was happy with their intimacy.

Jeff nodded. She cared about him . . . well, that was good. He'd been a fool to hope for romantic love at his time of life. Of course, that wasn't on the cards – but he loved her so much he thought he would burst. If he spent the rest of his life worshipping her and looking after the kids, that would be enough. He was lucky to get so much.

On his way out to the boys' club, Tim overheard Jeff and Margaret talking. She was saying she was used to looking after children and it would be no problem for her to take care of him and Jilly. He liked Margaret nearly as much as Jeff and he was glad they were getting married, even though he knew she'd said she could love Jilly, but Jeff would manage him. Tim felt a little hurt that Margaret couldn't love him, but if she was good to Jilly, he reckoned he could get by. Jeff was a lovely bloke, fun to be with, and trustworthy.

Tim didn't want to be any trouble to anyone, but he instinctively knew that his mum wasn't coming back and he couldn't look after his sister as she deserved and needed. He'd been taking the biscuits and sweets she'd bought into the hospital and visiting whenever he was allowed. Sister Rose let him in in the mornings on weekends and Margaret let him visit after school for a few minutes. Jilly knew she would come home on Christmas Eve, which was only three days away now, and was looking forward to it.

'Will Mum be back?' she'd asked once and Tim shook his head.

'I reckon she's with Dad now,' he told her and she'd frowned, not quite understanding. 'I think they're both in Heaven. Mum was lonely without him and so she went to be with him.'

Jilly nodded, settling for her brother's truth even though she wasn't sure what it meant. 'So, we shan't be with her again?'

'One day, perhaps,' Tim said. 'When we're older – but we'll be all right. Nurse Margaret is going to marry Jeff and they'll look after us. We're lucky, Jilly. If Jeff hadn't taken us in, we would've been sent to an orphanage – and I don't want to go to one of those, do you?'

She shook her head solemnly. She didn't know what an orphanage was, but if he didn't want to go, it must be bad.

'Will there be presents for Christmas?' she asked, her mind hopping to what she'd been thinking about for quite some time.

'I'll buy you a little gift and I'll take you to see a lovely film for your birthday,' Tim promised. Her dream of a doll's pram would have to wait for another year, but at least she would have a lovely Christmas dinner, and sweets and cake to look forward to and then a lovely birthday just over a week later.

Tim reckoned it wasn't too bad, all things considered. He wanted Mum to come home, but he was now certain something bad had happened to her because she would never have gone off and left them all this time if she could help it . . .

Sally sat on the edge of her bed and paused halfway through wrapping the small gift she'd bought for Jane. It wasn't much, just some bedsocks she'd knitted with wool she'd purchased from the market. Most of the money she'd had in her purse when she arrived had gone now and she'd thought she would need to look for work, but Jane told her she would give her six shillings a week for looking after the house and cooking for her.

'I'd have to pay anyone else,' she'd pointed out. 'And I'd rather you stayed here with me.'

Sally felt she was being given more than she earned if you took the bed and board into account, but Jane seemed satisfied and she certainly wasn't ready to walk away from all the kindness she'd been shown. However, she had the strangest feeling that she should be wrapping presents for other people. Sally wasn't sure who those people were, but recently she'd found she was looking at clothes for young people – children. At the back of her mind now were shadowy images of a boy and a girl but she still couldn't put a name to the shadowy figures who flitted in and out of her mind.

Who were the children she felt she ought to know? What were their names and where did they live – and perhaps more importantly, were they hers?

Sally couldn't remember and it distressed her. If she had children, she should be with them, preparing for their Christmas. How were the children faring, were they safe or in trouble? It worried Sally that she didn't know, even though the name Jilly often came to mind.

Oh, why couldn't she remember? This was a good life here in the cottage by the river, but she would leave it for her children if she could remember them. She shook her head, scolding herself for being unkind. She couldn't just desert Jane when she needed her – but sometimes Sally felt the tug of those children's voices calling her.

Or perhaps there were no children, just the call of a lonely heart . . .

CHAPTER 33

'Doctor Peter brought young Luke into the station to report what happened on the canal bank,' Steve told Sarah when he got home the day before Christmas Eve. 'An artist did a mock-up of Luke's and your descriptions and we're putting posters up all over the docks telling people to be on the lookout for him. Luke's description pretty well matched what you said – he's an observant young man.'

'Yes.' Sarah looked sombre. 'Oh, I was so lucky he was there. Otherwise, I might have been badly hurt.'

'You could have been killed,' Steve said and looked anxious. 'I shudder to think of it, Sarah.'

'I know. I'm sorry, love.' She put her arms around his waist and was enveloped in a hug that made her feel loved and safe.

'Well, anyone can make a mistake.' He looked at her thoughtfully. 'I asked Doctor Peter if he thought Luke would enjoy learning self-defence and he's going to ask him. So, I invited the lad to our Christmas party this evening at the club.'

'What a good idea,' Sarah said. 'I'm so pleased.'

She smiled at him; he was a good man, always thinking of others. She snuggled up to him as she thought of something she knew he would like to hear. 'It's our son's first real Christmas. I know he's still too young to really appreciate it this year but I've got him a lovely Noah's Ark playset.' She sighed. 'The man in the shop said I was lucky to find it; toys are selling out fast and they don't know when they'll get more stock in, because of the war.'

'Yes, I know. It's the same story everywhere. We've got to make the most of this year, Sarah, love. Buy all the food and presents you want, because next year it may not be so easy. This war isn't going away and no one knows what the future will bring.'

'I've planned and ordered it all,' she told him with a smile of content. 'I'm not going to let a little thing like war spoil our Christmas, Steve.'

'Good.' Steve smiled adoringly at her and laughed. 'That's wonderful, Sarah. And I bought him a football. And yes, I know it is too soon!'

Sarah giggled and reached up to kiss him, hugging him and laughing as he lifted her and swung her round easily. He was so strong! 'I'm glad Mum will be back from her holiday in time for Christmas with us. I know they wanted a few days away on their own to celebrate their anniversary before Christmas, but it wouldn't be the same without her.' She laughed softly. 'I've been making sure the boys are all right for food – but they don't think I'm a good cook. They will be glad to get her back for Christmas Day, just as we shall.'

'And her husband,' Steve said smiling.

'Of course. I like Theo very much,' Sarah said. 'Of course, I'll never think of him as my dad, but he's good to Mum and that's all I care about.'

'He's very good to Gwen,' Steve agreed. 'I like him, Sarah.'

'I do too.' She nodded. 'Come and eat your tea then, love. You'll want to get off to your party for the kids.'

'Yes, I mustn't be late,' Steve said and smiled. 'They're all looking forward to it.'

Luke glanced round the room. In one corner was a Christmas tree, dressed with glass balls, fairy lights and small presents. At the end of the long room, a table was laden with sausage rolls, sandwiches, cakes and little jellies. Luke wouldn't have been sure what they were, except that Rose had given him one for his tea the previous day; it was his first and he liked the fruit in it but wasn't keen on the jelly. The sausage rolls looked nice, though, and there was fruit squash.

All the club members were laughing and talking about the championships they'd entered that year and what they were going to do the next. They seemed friendly enough and Luke had been welcomed as a new member though he felt a little bit separate from it because he had no particular friends here. Waiting until the crush at the table had eased, Luke took two sausage rolls, an egg sandwich, and a piece of fruit cake, which, out of habit, he put in his pocket for another time. He was no longer lonely the way he had been, but felt a bit out of it here as he didn't know any of the other lads.

He ate his sandwich and the tasty sausage rolls, which Steve had told them his wife had made, and then looked at the table – dare he take another? There was still plenty left.

'Go on, have what you want,' a friendly voice said at his ear and he turned to look at the boy who had spoken. 'I'm Jamie. I come here most nights. It's fun and you make friends – and it teaches you how to protect yourself from bullies.'

Luke nodded. 'That's what Constable Jones told Doctor Peter. I was invited tonight to see what I thought.'

'We don't always get free food,' Jamie said. 'We have to pay sixpence if we want anything as a rule, but it is Christmas.'

'Yeah, the best one for me ever,' Luke said and grinned. 'I'm living with good people and they're having goose this year. I'm looking forward to it.'

'We're having chicken which is always good and Arch – he's my older brother – buys me presents, and other people do too. It wasn't always as good as it is now.' Jamie's gaze measured Luke's size. 'You're bigger than me but I'd like to show you how it works here. If you join, I'll help you fit in and learn everything.'

'Thanks,' Luke said, smiling. 'I think I shall after Christmas. I live with Doctor Peter and his wife Sister Rose – but I don't want to play gooseberry every evening. They don't say anything but I'm sure they were glad of a while on their own tonight – and it's better to have somewhere to come than sit in my bedroom or wander the streets.'

'Wandering the streets is no good,' Jamie told him. 'You get in with a bad crowd then and you're soon in trouble. I tried that for a bit, but I didn't like it much.'

'No, nor me,' Luke agreed. He grabbed two sausage rolls and shoved one in his pocket, eating the other in one swift gulp. 'Why don't you show me a few things now?'

'Yeah, all right,' Jamie said. 'It's never too soon to start learnin'.'

Luke left the club with Jamie after having more fun than he ever recalled having in his life, apart from his work with Doctor Peter, which he loved. The doctor was always joking and teasing everyone, and it made Luke feel happy just to be privileged to help him. However, the club was exciting and fun and before he left, he had joined.

He parted from Jamie at the end of his new friend's road and set off for Doctor Peter's house, whistling. Life had never felt so good and Luke could hardly believe how lucky he'd been finding so many friends just because he'd done a good turn.

It was when he'd reached the end of the lane that led to his new home that he felt the hands grab him from behind. One closed over his mouth, choking off his cry for help, and the second went around his neck, securing him in a hold he could not even attempt to break free of. He could scarcely breathe and clawed at his captor's hand in blind panic.

'Got yer, yer little bastard!' a guttural voice hissed in his ear. 'Think yer can throw things at me and get away with it – you'll be sorry you interfered in my business.'

Luke's heart sank as he was tossed over a shoulder like a sack of rubbish and carried away. He yelled for all he was worth, but he knew he wouldn't be heard. If people were in their homes in the warm, they wouldn't come out, because they wouldn't want to get involved. Besides, what could Doctor Peter do against a man like this?

He could feel the man's brute strength and knew that it was futile to wear himself out struggling. He'd been manhandled like this at the orphanage. Luke hadn't been as strong then, but even so this man was much stronger; if he struggled, all he would do was get himself even more of a beating. It would take two or three large police officers to tackle a bear of a man like this – and Luke needed to save his strength and wait for his chance to run. Even in his terror he realised that if the man had wanted him dead, he would already be lying on the ground, his neck snapped.

What would his friends think when he didn't return? Luke wondered if Doctor Peter would alert the police that evening – or would he just think he'd run off? Luke's heart dropped into his boots. Even if the man didn't kill him now, he might never be found. He had only one chance and that was to run when the opportunity came.

Luke knew that despite his fears of what was going to happen to him, he must wait for his opportunity to escape.

CHAPTER 34

'He wouldn't just go off,' Peter said to Rose as the clock's hands moved round to midnight. 'Obviously, something has happened to him.' He frowned and then made up his mind. 'I'll ring the police station. You go to bed love.'

'No, I'll wait up,' she said. 'I'm as worried as you are – and like you, I don't believe he would stay out this late. The party was over by nine-thirty and it would take him half an hour at most to get home, even if he stayed talking to friends for a while.' Her face was white and strained. 'It's like what happened to Danny all over again. He was taken away against his will, except we knew who had taken him and we don't know what has happened to Luke.'

Peter nodded. She'd suffered badly when Danny, the young lad she and Beattie had fostered, had been kidnapped by his brutal father. He'd escaped and been returned to them and his father was now dead. Rose had already become fond of Luke and Peter didn't like to see her upset. He felt a spurt of anger at the boy. How could he do this to them? In the next instant, his instincts told him it wasn't Luke's fault; he was too honest to just go off like that.

'He liked being here,' Peter said. 'I have a feeling for these things and my gut tells me he's in trouble. I can't search for him, so the police are the only way.' He cursed his inability to go anywhere without his chair.

'Will they look for him tonight?' Rose queried. 'They usually say wait a few days if someone is missing – but if we rang Ted he might go and have a look. He could push your chair.' Their good friend Ted had helped Peter in the past and Rose knew he would come if they asked.

'Yes, give him a call,' Peter agreed. Beattie's husband was a strong man and could be relied on in a crisis. He cursed the disability that prevented him from walking the streets to look for Luke.

He frowned, listening to Rose make her call. Ted and Beattie would probably be in bed, but they knew what it was like to have a boy go missing and would want to be involved. Rose was looking less anxious when she returned.

'Ted's on his way and Danny and Ron are coming with him. Ron will push you and their eyes are young. It can't hinder you and might help. You only need to search the lanes between here and the club; it shouldn't take long. If he isn't lying hurt there, he could be anywhere and that means you need the police, Peter.' She hesitated, then, 'I'll ring them, but they may not start a search tonight.'

Peter nodded. 'I know, but we should still alert them. Ted and I and the two boys will search tonight. In the morning, I'll put out an alert with friends of mine at the clinic. We have to find him, Rose. I *know* Luke's in trouble and I think it may be serious, because this just isn't like him.'

'Yes, I think you're right,' she agreed. 'I want to find him, love. He's a lovely lad and I was enjoying having him here – I'd bought him presents for Christmas.'

'So had I,' Peter confessed. 'I may never be able to give you a child, Rose. You know that. I thought perhaps . . .'

'Yes, I did too,' she said blinking back tears. 'I think it would be wonderful all round, my darling. I am so happy with you and I don't need anything more, but that boy needs us, Peter – and he really helps you.'

'Yes, he does, and I need to help him now.' He looked at her with grim determination. He might be stuck in that damned chair but it wouldn't stop him searching for Luke.

It didn't take Ted and the two boys long to get there in the truck Ted was allowed to use by his generous boss. They collected Peter and, armed with big torches, set out to look for Luke. Ted was full of hope when they left Rose to hold the fort in case Luke returned, but when they came home two hours later, they all wore worried frowns.

'There's no sign of him,' Ted said when Rose looked at him anxiously. 'Luke left with one of the other lads and we managed to get him out of bed. Jamie said that Luke was happy and had joined the club; they'd arranged to meet up after Christmas.'

'That means he's been abducted,' Peter said heavily.

'I can't see what else it could be. Unless he did just go off on his own . . .'

'You don't know him that well yet, but you believe he's a good lad,' Ted replied looking anxious. 'So why would he leave now without telling you?'

'He's been taken like I was,' Danny said, speaking of the ordeal he'd suffered when he'd been forcefully taken from Rose and Beattie the previous year. They all looked at him. 'I didn't want to leave Beattie and you, Sister Rose. I was dragged off by my father – someone must have taken Luke. I know he wouldn't go otherwise. When you've had a hard life and some- thing good happens, you don't run off, you hold tight with both hands.'

'Danny is right,' his adoptive brother Ron added firmly. 'I wouldn't have left Ted once I trusted him and nor would Luke leave you and Doctor Peter, Sister Rose. He knows he's lucky to have you and he wouldn't do this.'

Rose looked at her friends and then nodded slowly. 'Yes, I agree with the boys. Luke was settled and happy here. I think he was excited about Christmas, the first one he remembers in a home – a proper home. He was in an orphanage up near Leicester and hated it. That's why he ran away.'

'Could someone from there have grabbed him?' Ted asked but Doctor Peter shook his head. 'No, I'm sure they would approach the police and try to take him back legally, if they did discover he was living here.'

'Who else could have done it?' Rose asked frowning, but her husband suddenly looked at her as the answer came to him.

'The man he stopped attacking Sarah Jones!' Peter said. He nodded to the lads and then met Ted's eyes in shared anxiety. 'And whoever he is, he's clearly a nasty bit of work. He probably saw Luke walking back alone and grabbed him.'

'But why? What for?' Ted asked worried but puzzled too.

'To get revenge and make him work for him,' Danny said and once again they all looked at him; because he'd suffered abduction by a cruel bully and probably knew how men like that thought. Danny's father had dragged him away from a church fete in the middle of the afternoon just for those reasons.

'That makes more sense than anything else I can think of,' Rose admitted. 'Why else would he carry him off? If he'd just attacked him to hurt or kill him, his body would be lying in the street.'

'I'll ring the Rosie and the police,' Doctor Peter said. 'Get off now, Ted. Thank you – and you too, lads. I'm grateful for all your help tonight. I couldn't have done it alone.'

'I'm sorry we didn't find him, sir.'

'Yes, me too,' Ron agreed with Danny.

'Perhaps it at least gives us hope he is still alive,' Doctor Peter said and smiled.

He wasn't smiling after he finished making his calls, because the police didn't offer much hope and Luke hadn't been taken to the Rosie.

'I feel so helpless,' he told Rose as they went to bed at last in the early hours of the morning. 'I've let him down.'

'No, you haven't,' Rose told him. 'Beattie thought

251

the same when Danny went missing but that wasn't her fault and this isn't yours. If Danny's idea is right, and I suspect it may be, it's down to a vengeful man – and all we can do is hope that Luke either manages to escape, as Danny did, or the police find him soon.'

Luke lay on a pile of rags in a derelict house. He knew they hadn't gone far, which meant his abductor, who he'd recognised the moment the man put him down, was clearly living in the area and had made this place his base. Luke had slept in many similar buildings over the past few months, and he was missing the warm bed Doctor Peter had given him, feeling apprehensive and in fear of his safety. The red-haired man was angry because of what had happened to him that morning at the canal. All he'd done was hit Luke a couple of times but he'd been drinking heavily and when he sobered a bit, he might become more violent.

Luke had suffered worse beatings in the past and he'd just gritted his teeth and taken it; he had no choice for the moment, but he would be watching for his chance to escape. His captor, whom he called Red in his mind, had muttered a lot but Luke thought he was just drunk. It had all been about getting even and swear words that made Luke squirm. He was sure now that Red had worked on the ships and was both a bully and a brute. His anger must stem from more than the soaking he'd had, or so Luke imagined. He'd tossed Luke onto the rags, muttering all the while and sitting hunched up for an hour or so over a small fire, drinking what smelled like whisky.

Luke had smelled that before, on the breath of the master at the orphanage.

He knew that Red had used a chain and a padlock to secure the door behind him and guessed that it was an old workshop of sorts, as there were benches and discarded tools everywhere. Perhaps he'd found the padlock; Luke couldn't imagine a man like that buying it to secure the door.

Why wasn't he on the ships and what had caused this simmering fury that had caused him to attack decent women and abduct Luke? What did he hope to gain from him?

Luke would have to wait to find out. Red hadn't bothered to go through Luke's pockets so he took out the food he'd put in them at the boxing club and started to munch on it. The action soothed some of his fear and anxiety, though it didn't ease the cold in his hands and feet or stop him worrying about Doctor Peter and Rose. How would Doctor Peter manage without him and would they miss him?

CHAPTER 35

Jeff looked at Constable Jones in consternation. He'd just heard the news and it had fair taken the wind from his sails. To hear that Luke had settled with Doctor Peter and his new wife was a pleasure that was devastated by the abduction. Who would do such a terrible thing? You heard tales, of course, but Luke was big and strong and not the sort to take liberties with – so what was his abductor after?

'I know you must be searching all over for the lad. What are the chances that you'll find him?' he'd asked Constable Jones.

'Alive, you mean?' Steve frowned. 'Slim, I imagine. If it *is* the man who murdered Betty Stewart, the boy's body might turn up in the canal.'

'Surely you're organising a search party?'

'Yes. We've got dozens of officers on it and as many concerned citizens,' Steve said and frowned. 'Every derelict building will be searched but he's had him all night. Luke may already be dead for all we know.'

'Why carry him off if he just wants to kill him?'

Jeff questioned. 'Tim has gone to fetch Jilly from the hospital but I'll ask him if he's seen or heard anything when he gets back – and if you need more volunteers for the search, just ask.'

'You'll have enough looking after those two for Christmas,' Steve replied. 'My sergeant has cancelled all leave for us so I'll be working as many hours as it takes and I'll let you know when there's news.'

'That's rotten luck for you constables.'

'It goes with the job,' Steve said. 'Sarah knows I couldn't just sit at home and wait anyway. She'll save me a bit of Christmas dinner and I'll have it when I get in.'

Jeff nodded as the policeman moved off to make more inquiries. He still thought it was rotten luck to have his leave cancelled over Christmas, but it would be even worse for Luke.

'Poor little blighter,' Jeff muttered and went back inside. All his work in the garage was now finished and he had two days clear holiday, which he intended to enjoy with Margaret and the children. It was hard luck for Luke and for Doctor Peter and his wife. It was the second time in just over a year that a boy Sister Rose had cared for had gone missing. That was a rotten deal in his book and must have ruined her plans for Christmas. Jeff didn't know how he would feel if it had been his Tim . . . It was strange how quickly he'd come to think of Tim as his – more of a son than a rescue lad he'd taken in. He was really looking forward to making this Christmas special for both children and he wouldn't let this news spoil their Christmas too.

Margaret would be a little later arriving that evening because the nurses at the Rosie were having a little party.

'It is nothing much,' Margaret had told him, smiling. 'Nurse Jenny suggested it. She is going to bring in some food and we'll share it and give the children on the ward a cake and a few treats.'

'Sounds nice, love,' Jeff said. 'You stop as long as you like and enjoy it.'

'I rather like Nurse Jenny,' Margaret said. 'She is much happier now her husband is home again and I've added her to the list for our wedding. I hope you don't mind?'

'You invite as many as you like – the more the merrier. Bring this Nurse Jenny round for tea one day. If she's as nice as you say, make her your friend.'

Jenny smiled at her husband as they finished trimming their tree and placed brightly wrapped parcels beneath it. They'd left it until the last minute so that they could really settle down and enjoy Christmas together. Michael had no work for the next three days and neither did Jenny. They were having Christmas lunch with Lily and Chris, who was at home for Christmas Day, and the rest of the time they would have together.

'It looks lovely, don't you think?' Jenny asked as her husband placed a star right at the top. She'd decided she preferred the Christmas Star to a fairy and Michael agreed.

'Maybe we'll get a fairy when the little one grows up,' he said and stroked her tummy, which was still too flat for his liking. 'Are you sure he's in there?' He looked at her slim figure.

'Yes, he or she is there,' Jenny said laughing up at him. 'You wait – I'll probably get huge, just like Lily did.'

'Yes.' He nodded happily. 'She did and she's got a lovely baby.' He drew her into his arms, kissing her tenderly. 'Happy Christmas, darling. Do you want your present now – or in the morning?'

'Oh, let's keep them until the morning,' Jenny said. 'We'll open everyone's together – unless you really want to give it to me now?' she teased.

'Just one,' he said looking like a small boy on thorns. 'I've bought several little things – but there's one I can't wait to give you.'

'All right then.' Jenny closed her eyes expecting to be kissed and carried up to bed, but instead he placed a small parcel in her hands. She opened her eyes and looked at the blue velvet jeweller's box and smiled. 'What is this?'

'Open it and see,' he said and so she did. Inside was a pendant in gold set with diamonds in the shape of a heart on a fine chain. Jenny gasped as it twinkled in the light of Christmas tree candles.

'Oh, Michael, it's beautiful! I've never seen anything as lovely.' She kissed him excitedly. 'You spoil me too much.'

He grinned, looking as pleased as punch. 'You're worth spoiling,' he told her and hugged her. 'You're the key to my heart, Jenny. I've never loved anyone before, and I don't think I could ever love anyone the way I love you.'

'Me too,' she mumbled, choked by her emotions. 'I love you, Michael. I never thought I would love a man the way I love you.'

Michael kissed her and then swept her up in his arms. She giggled as he carried her upstairs, her arms around his neck, his gorgeous gift clutched in her hands. She was so lucky to have him home for Christmas. A tiny shudder went through her as she thought of what might have happened. Her husband had made his escape seem so easy, but she knew it hadn't been; she knew that he could have died and she felt her heart swell with grateful thanks that she had him home.

Jenny knew in her heart that it wasn't the end of Michael's service to the army. He'd said something about their plans to enrol him as a driver and give him the rank of sergeant.

His casual announcement told Jenny that he would be leaving her again in the future. He was useful to the army and they weren't going to let the excuse of flat feet stop him serving in some capacity. She'd struggled to accept this for a while, but then remembered that Lily had to cope with a similar situation all the time. A part of her blamed her brother-in-law Chris for getting him involved, because she knew he was why they'd taken Michael on in the Intelligence service, but that wouldn't be fair, because Michael could have said no. He wanted to do his bit and perhaps most of his work wouldn't be quite as dangerous as the last mission. She could only pray that it consisted mainly of driving generals from one end of the country to the other, but knew that Michael would do whatever they asked of him.

So, this Christmas was doubly precious to her. Like Lily, Jenny must make the most of each day that her husband was with her and just pray he would always manage to return.

She thought about all those women whose husbands were away fighting. Any of them could be killed at any time – and there were the poor little Stewart children, whose mother had gone missing and was presumed dead. No, Jenny couldn't grumble or feel hard done by. So many others had it far worse and she had her husband with her now, so she was lucky and, in the morning, they would go round to Lily's to enjoy Christmas.

On Christmas morning, Tim grinned to see his sister so happy. Jeff's house had four bedrooms, though one was quite small. He used that just as a storeroom but he'd given the other two to Jilly and Tim. Hers had pink and green curtains at the windows and Tim knew they hadn't been there a few days ago. Margaret had found them on a secondhand stall in the market and washed them and they looked fresh and lovely, just what Jilly would like. Her bedcover was a white candlewick one and his was dark green. His curtains were the ones that had been there all the time, but he didn't care. He knew he was lucky to be here and even more fortunate that Jeff was planning to adopt them both.

Jeff had shared the knowledge the previous evening when they were alone. 'I wanted to make sure you were comfortable with that before I signed the forms, lad.'

'Mum is dead, isn't she?' he'd asked looking straight at Jeff. He'd seen the answer there even before his friend spoke.

'Who told you that?' Jeff asked but didn't deny it. 'I think she might be but I wasn't going to tell you until after Christmas. I didn't want to spoil things . . .'

'You haven't because I thought it anyway. I saw the landlord had got her house back and I heard someone say it was only to be expected if she was gone.' Tim sniffed holding back his tears. 'I wish she wasn't, but I knew when she didn't come back. Mum would never leave us like that if she could help it. Things were hard but she did her best for us.'

'Yes, of course she did,' Jeff agreed. 'Your mum was a proud lady. We tried to help her but she wouldn't let us.'

Tim nodded. 'How did she die?'

Jeff hesitated, then, 'The police think she may have been attacked and killed, Tim – perhaps by the man that attacked Constable Jones' wife the other day.'

Tim went white but inclined his head. 'He must have been desperate to rob Mum. She hadn't got anything worth havin'.'

'If it's the one the police think, he's a nasty sort Tim, and sometimes they do things just because they're bad.'

Again, Tim nodded. 'Don't tell Jilly, please. I told her I thought Mum had gone to be with Dad in Heaven. She doesn't need to know the truth.'

'I shan't tell her, Tim. I paid for the lady they found

to be buried and we'll go to her grave after Christmas, you and me, together, take some flowers, but we shan't tell Jilly.' He hesitated. 'It isn't certain it *is* your mum, but we might never know for certain.'

'Mum would come back for us if she was alive.' Tim brushed away his tears. 'All right. I'm glad you told me, sir.'

'Why don't you call me Jeff – or Uncle Jeff if you like,' Jeff had said. 'Since we're to live together, I think it would be nice, don't you?'

'Yes, please, Uncle Jeff. I'll call you that so Jilly knows what to call you, otherwise she'll be too shy.'

Tim had shed a few more tears in his bed that night but he reckoned he was old enough to get on with it. Life had hard knocks; he'd learned that when his dad died. He had to look after his sister and make the most of the chances that had been given to them. They had a nice home to live in and a good friend in Uncle Jeff.

It was better than most orphans had, and Tim appreciated what he'd got. Jilly would be delighted to have his present in the morning and he knew that both Uncle Jeff and Margaret had bought her things too. It would be the best Christmas for years and crying over something that couldn't be changed was daft.

Tim had fallen on his feet when he started to work for Jeff Marshall. He was so much luckier than the lad Jeff had told him about. He'd heard from kids he knew that Luke had gone missing and that the police were making inquiries, but no one held out much hope that he was alive. Tim felt sorry that it had happened, and at Christmas too.

261

Luke would have been as well off with Doctor Peter as he and Jilly were with Uncle Jeff, so he knew for sure he'd been hurt or carried off, because he would never have run away from his home, not when he'd known how hard it was being alone. Tim reckoned that was scary. He was comfortable roaming the streets in the daytime but at night they became full of shadows with dangers lurking in dark corners and things that were evil waiting for young children; at least, that was what his mum had always said. The thought brought another bout of tears, but then he fell asleep, worn out by his emotions and fears. All he really knew was that Jilly must be protected from the truth about Mum and he wanted her to be happy for Christmas.

And on Christmas Day morning, with the cot he'd bought for her, and the shiny black pram Jeff had sprayed so it looked like new, fancy lace covers and a doll with a china face, she was as happy as he'd ever seen her. She wouldn't have had any of those lovely things if Mum had been home and yet Tim knew in his heart that Jilly would have swapped them all for a smile from their mother.

Sally opened the presents of silk stockings from Jane and a blue and white silk scarf from Terry, the friendly milkman, and blushed. He'd been smiling at her a lot recently and making remarks about how pretty she looked, but she'd been shocked when he'd left the parcel with their Christmas milk order. She didn't really know him, did she? And he could know nothing about her because she didn't even know herself what kind of person she was – or even her real name. It wasn't Sally, though she answered to it to please Jane.

At first, she hadn't wanted to open the gift from Terry, but then Jane had told her not to be daft. 'He's a widower and a decent bloke, Sally,' she'd said. 'I'm not suggesting you wed him, girl, but you can take a gift and say thank you like a sensible adult.'

When she thought about it, Sally realised she could. Terry was a nice-looking man and very gentle and considerate. He'd rescued a kitten for them from Jane's ancient oak tree, gone right up after it and brought it down inside his overalls to keep it safe and warm. She'd noticed how gently he'd handled the tiny thing, which was even now nestled in a basket by Jane's fire; it had made its home with them and Jane said they would keep it.

Tim and Jilly would love that, Sally thought, and felt an icy chill at her nape. Tim? Yes, Tim and Jilly. The names were so familiar and now she thought she saw their faces looking at her anxiously. Yet she still didn't know why they seemed to be a part of her that she sensed had existed before whatever had happened to rob her of her past.

Sally felt sick inside as she suddenly knew for certain that these two children must be hers. They had to be, because they were there in her head; she felt they were a part of her. Where were they? Were they safe and well? Who was looking after them? Why had she left them? Something dark and hateful hovered at the back of her mind and she instinctively drew back from it – no, she mustn't think of the

263

children, because the horror would return – but were they safe?

The questions raced through her mind but she still couldn't find the answers. Yet the certainty that she had children was like a hard knot in her chest, making it difficult for her to breathe.

'What's the matter, girl?' Jane asked suddenly aware that something was very wrong. 'You're as white as a ghost.'

'I've remembered – Tim and Jilly,' she said and found she was shaking. 'I know they belong to me, but I can't remember where they are or where I left them!'

'Are you sure the children are yours?' Jane looked anxious.

'Yes, I know they must be – and I've heard them calling to me in my mind.' She gave a little sob. 'Supposing they are starving or ill from neglect?'

'Someone will have taken them in – or they may be in an orphanage if folk think you're dead.' Jane looked guilty. 'I was that pleased to have you here, Sally, but I should have made inquiries long ago.'

'What could you have done?' Sally shook her head. 'It's not your fault – neither of us knows where I came from.'

'I would say London,' Jane said. 'We'll ask the local police to make inquiries about a missing woman from London, the East End I'd think.' She nodded as her thoughts travelled on. 'We'll ask Terry to help us, too. He's always saying he'll do whatever we want – well, now he can see if he can discover what your real name is, where you come from, and if you have children called Tim and Jilly. That shouldn't be too hard – the mother of a girl and boy of that name who has gone missing? We'll find your two in no time, love.'

Sally looked at her with dawning hope. 'Do you think so?' Jane made it sound so easy but surely it couldn't be.

'Yes, I do,' Jane said firmly. 'And when we do, you can fetch them here to live with us. I've always wanted grandchildren to fuss over.'

Sally felt the tears drip down her cheeks. Jane was so kind. She could never thank her enough if she lived to be a hundred, and inside she was beginning to feel a bright flame of certainty. Flashes of things were coming to her mind now. She could see Tim's smiling face. Pray God it wasn't too late to find them alive. If anything had happened to them, she would never forgive herself.

CHAPTER 36

Lying on the cold stone floor, Luke could hear the church bells chiming somewhere close by and he thought that was the church where he'd been given an iced bun and a cup of tea by the rector a few weeks back. There were church bells all over London, of course, but Luke had learned the sound of them; he knew the sounds of the bells better than the names of the buildings. Though he'd heard people say various names and he could read the signs, the only church he'd been into was a few streets away from where he lived now. If he was right, he hadn't been carried far the night he was taken.

A shudder went through Luke as he remembered Christmas Eve, the worst day of his life, at least since he'd left the orphanage. Red had woken in a foul mood and taken his temper out on him by kicking him awake. He'd been awake anyway, but hadn't responded to his instruction to get up. The big man had towered over him and was clearly suffering the effects of drink; his eyes were bloodshot, his face haggard and he was angry. Very angry and terrifying.

'So, you're awake, you little bastard,' he'd grunted savagely. 'Get up, we've got work to do.' His speech was rough, guttural, and Luke could hear the foreign accent even clearer now. He might have been a Danish seaman from his speech although they mostly had blond hair, Luke thought. He was certainly a man in a temper wherever he came from and he meant to take it out on Luke. 'You can pay for what yer did to me by begging on the streets, earn our grub.'

'I've never begged,' Luke said indignantly. 'I always work for what folk give me.' He got warily to his feet in time to earn a blow to his ear, determined not to do as this bully demanded.

However, after several heavy blows to the head and threats of what he would get if he didn't do as he was told, Luke had approached passers-by on the busy streets and asked for food. Because it was Christmas Eve, everyone seemed in a hurry and most were in a good mood, despite the gloom of the past months since the war had been declared. It was as if they'd put the thought of war away and were deter- mined to enjoy life at Christmas. Red kept right behind him and his wild thoughts of escaping had evaporated as he made the attempt, was chased, caught and cuffed again.

'Damn you, you little devil! Do as you're told or I'll kill you – and then I'll go and kill that cripple you've been working for.' The cruel gleam in Red's eyes made Luke shiver with fear. He'd never dreamed the bully's malice would extend to the people who had taken Luke in. He couldn't allow that to happen no matter what this bully did to him.

How could he run now? If he managed to get away, Red would harm Doctor Peter and Luke knew how vulnerable he was in that chair. If Red attacked him, he wouldn't stand much chance of getting away. He couldn't do that to the people who had been so kind to him, people he was beginning to care about. Tears of fear and regret ran down Luke's cheeks as he listened to the church bells ringing out their joy that Christ was born on Christmas morning.

Why did this have to happen to him? He'd been truly happy for the first time in his life and now he was the prisoner of this bear of a man, who was far faster on his feet than anyone would guess.

People had been generous when he'd begged on the streets on Christmas Eve, sliding money into his hand with a smile of sympathy. Luke had done what Red ordered him to do, pointing to the man on the ground, his feet bound up in bandages and another around his head, a crutch by his side.

'You tell 'em I'm yer father and I've been badly hurt at sea and can't work no more. Tell 'em yer starvin' – 'cos yer will be if yer don't do as yer told.'

Luke had hated telling the lies, feeling like a cheat and a thief as he accepted the half-crowns and one ten-shilling note. He knew he'd collected a lot of money when Red grinned evilly and told him it was enough. He'd taken hold of his arm and pushed him ahead of him, never letting him more than a couple of steps away.

They'd gone to a public house, which smelled of strong drink, urine and sweaty bodies, where men with loud voices were steadily getting drunk, and Red had bought a bottle of whisky and settled down in the corner to drink it. Luke had hoped he might get a chance to slip away but Red stretched his legs across in front of him, penning him in. He'd bought himself a plate of sandwiches and eaten all but half of one, which he'd shoved at Luke. The boy's stomach had revolted at the thought of eating where his captor's mouth had been, but he ate the other side, nibbling up to where it had been bitten and saw Red laugh nastily.

'It's all yer'll get in future. Yer'll learn not to be fussy or yer'll starve.'

Luke had been getting used to having a full stomach over the past weeks, first because of Mrs Ruby's sandwiches and then the lovely meals he'd been given at Doctor Peter's house. Now, he was learning what it was to go hungry again and wished he'd kept some of the cake he'd been given at the boxing club party.

Luke thought of the friends he'd started to make there. Some of them came from poor homes and he knew they wouldn't have goose for their dinner today, or Christmas cake and the other treats Rose had been making, but they would have something. Luke knew that Red must have spent most of the money he'd begged for him the previous day, because he'd brought a second bottle of whisky back to the hovel he called home and nursed it all night in his arms.

How was he going to get away from his captor? If he escaped and warned Doctor Peter, perhaps he could tell the police and they would protect him. Luke sat in the darkness as dawn slowly came into the dismal workshop, showing it as the forlorn place it was. He'd been abused and beaten at the orphanage and he'd managed to get away. Perhaps he could do it again; he was young and strong and bright and this man was a drunken fool. Gradually, hope and courage returned as he heard the bells begin again, others chiming in in the distance as they proclaimed the day.

It was Christmas Day and it should have been wonderful. Luke wondered if Doctor Peter and Rose were worried about him and decided they must be. The police would be looking for him; perhaps they would find him and catch that Red devil. Luke knew now that he'd committed murder. What he'd witnessed that day by the canal was not just a wicked act, it was a terrible sin and surely the God whose son had been born today would not let him live with so much evil in him? Luke's sense of right and wrong was strong and he grew angry at his treatment. He wasn't going to put up with this a second longer than he was forced to.

Luke moved slightly, testing whether Red was awake, and heard him snore. It was what he'd been waiting for. Time to get up and explore his prison – see if there was any other way out other than the padlocked door.

Gingerly, he stepped over Red's body and moved slowly, carefully away from the stench of his enemy. He had to be so careful because if Red woke and caught on to what Luke was doing, he would beat him until he collapsed. His heart racing, Luke began to search behind the boxes that had been abandoned and left to rot when the workshop had closed down, as so many places of work had done recently. Times had been hard everywhere but were just getting a little better. In London the shops had been filled with festive delights for Christmas and Luke had noticed that people looked happier and brighter as they hurried to do their shopping, despite the shadow of war. And the war had brought about more employment, which was a boon for those who had been suffering the hardest of times, with factories closed and queues of unemployed at shelters. Now, the factories were churning out supplies for the army and men who wanted to work could find it. And both men and women had been generous to the poor cripple and his son when he'd begged for their money.

Luke had felt ashamed of the lies and deceit, but it wasn't his doing; he'd been forced to it by Red's brutality. Left to himself, he would never do such a thing again, but he could see the future as his captor's slave and knew that Red would don his false bandages and make him beg or would force him to work some other way to earn the money for his whisky. So it was imperative that he find a way to escape!

It was difficult to see the window, covered by thick sacking, at first. Luke only found it because of a tiny hole that let a chink of light through. He cautiously lifted it at one corner and saw the glass and the catch, which had been secured by a piece of thick wood and nails to stop it opening. To get that off, Luke would need a wrench of some kind and it would make a lot of noise. He could hear Red grunting as he began to wake up and knew that his chance of escape had gone for now. He would have to wait until his tormentor was drunk and fast asleep again to see if he had enough strength to release the window and get away before he was discovered.

He decided he would go to the police first when he escaped and tell them where Red slept in the hopes that they'd catch him, because only then would his friends be safe.

For now, he must spend Christmas Day doing whatever Red decided and make the best of it, but the foolish tears he'd shed earlier had gone. Luke had a plan now, and because this workshop had many abandoned tools, he could use one to pry that wood free and escape.

Hearing Red get up, he moved away from the covered window and relieved himself in a corner. His captor would be looking for him any moment and he must not discover the window.

Red saw him as he moved nearer to him and grunted. 'What are you up to, runt?' he demanded.

'I needed a wee,' Luke replied in a small voice.

'"I needed a wee",' Red mocked. 'Why don't yer say piss like a man?'

Luke didn't answer and received a smack round the ear for his silence.

'Answer me when I speak ter yer or yer'll be sorry.'

'Yes, sir,' Luke squeaked and heard Red laugh nastily, but he said no more. Instead, Red removed his trousers and defecated in the corner, the stench of it making Luke want to vomit. This man was violent. He would kill as easily as he bullied and Luke knew his life was in danger every moment he stayed here.

'Ready to beg again?' Red muttered a few seconds later. 'You'd better be – unless you fancy a spot of burglary. It's one or the other, please yerself.' He glared at Luke. 'Let me tell you something. I've been cheated by a man I thought was a mate, thrown out of work for having a drink or two and I ain't got much to lose.' His eyes narrowed and he leaned in so that Luke caught the stink of him. 'I've killed, see. It was easy . . . See these hands?' He showed Luke his big, scarred hands. 'I've done murder! Filthy little bitch wanted money but I showed her.' His face twisted with bitterness. 'But I'm done for unless I can get away and for that I need money – so I wouldn't bat an eyelid killing you. Understand?'

Luke nodded and didn't answer, quaking inside but determined not to show his fear. He had to have the guts to stand up to this brute; he found himself pushed towards the door, which was then unlocked. He found the courage to speak at last as they emerged into the fresh air.

'I'm hungry.' Luke's stomach was rumbling loudly. He was frightened and miserable and struggling not to let his captor see it.

'Well, maybe we'll get something from the Sally Army today,' Red told him with a leer. 'The soft buggers serve anyone who turns up on Christmas Day.'

'Why do you need me?' Luke asked without knowing how he dared.

'Because I've been spat on and treated unfair and folk feel sympathy for kids more than a bloke like me.' Red surprised him by answering, though he

273

followed it up with a smack of Luke's head. Bells rang in his ears and it wasn't from the church this time. He shook his head, trying to clear it as he walked just ahead of the big man. The streets were cold and empty and Luke wondered if they would see anyone out and about, because, surely, they were all in their homes preparing dinner, so where was Red going to make him beg today?

His answer came as he saw the church ahead of him. Red planned on making his pitch when people came to worship and give thanks. He stopped Luke in his tracks, then began the ritual of applying his filthy bandages. The crutch he'd carried so easily over his shoulder was suddenly under his arm and he altered his stance to look like an injured man as they approached the church and saw the early worshippers.

Once again, Luke felt the lurch in his stomach and looked about to see if there was a chance of escape, but the folk attending early morning service were unknown to him and would probably reject any appeal for help. Red looked so convincing; he must have been doing this for a while, because the first lady who noticed him went straight up to him and slipped a coin in his outstretched hand.

'You poor man,' she exclaimed and then looked at Luke. 'Is this your son?' She pressed another coin into his hand without being asked. 'Buy yourselves a cup of tea and a sandwich.'

Luke flushed and looked down, wishing desperately he dared tell her the truth but knew he could not. He had to get clear away and inform the police, because otherwise Red would harm Doctor Peter and

Rose too if she was there. Luke couldn't let that happen. He needed to tell the police everything and make sure they got this awful man locked up so he could do no more harm.

CHAPTER 37

Afterwards, Margaret thought that she had never enjoyed Christmas as much as that morning, watching Jilly open her gifts. Jeff had managed to find her a doll's pram, which he'd repainted and polished until it looked like new. Margaret had made her some pretty covers and bought her a doll with a china head to replace the old rag doll she'd had previously. None of the gifts were brand new but they had delighted the child and that made Margaret very happy. Watching her play contentedly was a pleasure to them all. Jeff had also given her the money to buy Jilly two pretty dresses, a cardigan and a pair of shoes. The cardigan was red as were the leather shoes; one dress was red with white spots and the other navy and white with a red belt.

Jilly hadn't been able to believe her eyes at all the gifts. Tim had bought her a cot, crayons, a colouring book and some sweets, which she loved. His gifts of a penknife and a new jumper and a pair of good school shoes made him smile, but his eyes really lit up for a minute or two when he saw the bike Jeff had done up for him. Margaret had bought him a book on football, and he'd smiled and thanked her politely, but she'd sensed something wasn't right with the lad, who was normally full of life. Once the children had settled down to do a jigsaw puzzle one of Jeff's neighbours had brought round for them, she asked Jeff what was wrong as he helped her with the washing-up after lunch.

'He was delighted with his bike, but I saw him looking oddly at his sister. Do you know what might be wrong? Might he be jealous of her gifts?'

'No, I'm sure he isn't.' Jeff looked sad. 'The thing is, I told him about his mother. I think he had a cry when he went to bed last night and he's probably feeling a bit upset still. I thought it best, though, because he was asking questions and I wanted him to know they had a home here for as long as they want and need it.'

'Oh, I see.' Margaret nodded. 'That must have been hard for you both.'

'He already sensed the truth, but suspecting it and being told for certain is different,' Jeff replied and nodded. 'He's a sensible lad and I know that once he gets over the shock he'll just get on with things. He's had a rough time since his father died and I wish I'd been able to do more before this, but Betty Stewart wouldn't let anyone help her.'

Margaret nodded understandingly. Jeff had given her a beautiful topaz and diamond pendant to match her ring, and it sparkled around her throat. When she'd protested that he'd already given her a beautiful ring, he'd said, 'The ring isn't a Christmas present, it's to show our feelings for each other.'

She smiled at him now. 'I'm looking forward to moving in with you and the children, Jeff. I hope I can help to improve their lives and to make you happy.'

'You do that every time I see you,' he said and the look on his face caught at her heart. He was such a lovely man and she felt her love surge through her. 'I think Jilly is already learning to turn to you – but Tim may take longer. He trusts me, Margaret, and I know he likes me, but I'm sure he will love you when he settles down and we're all together.'

Margaret nodded her agreement. She would be happy to settle for the little girl's affection and Tim's polite respect, though it would be nice to be a close and loving family. Margaret hadn't had much of that as a child, because her mother was a hard woman and her father a drunkard who died in the mines long before his three score years and ten, followed soon after by Margaret's angry mum, leaving Margaret to the more loving care of Aunt Jeanie. So, she would do her best to provide a warm and giving home for Jeff and the children – and she hoped they would show her love and affection in return.

Sometimes Margaret was almost positive that Jeff did love her, but at other times she couldn't be certain it wasn't just the convenience of having a wife to help look after the kids.

On Boxing Day morning, Margaret spent most of her time clearing up and cooking another tasty lunch for them all. She had finalised all the arrangements for their wedding and Jeff had said he would help move her stuff into his house on Thursday. They were having a church wedding and a reception for about forty friends and then one night at a nice hotel. Jeff said the children were old enough to spend that night alone and he would get the people next door to pop round last thing and again in the morning.

'It isn't much of a honeymoon for you,' he'd told her, 'but I'll take you out to a nice hotel and to a dance and things once we're wed. Tim is a sensible lad and I can trust him to make sure Jilly is all right. In the summer we'll all go to the seaside for a couple of weeks. Where would you like to go – somewhere down south?'

'I went to Bournemouth once,' Margaret said and gave him a quick hug. 'I'd love that, and we'll all know each other better by the summer.'

Jeff had looked serious then. 'I'm not rushing you into this – am I?'

'Oh no,' she'd assured him. 'I'm looking forward to it.' And she was; it was all just a bit strange and she was nervous of getting things right, that was all. She didn't know much about what a man needed from his wife, but she was perfectly willing to give it – she just needed Jeff to show her what he wanted from her.

Margaret had got tea for them all that afternoon, and after she enjoyed hers, she rose to wash up but Tim said that he would wash up and put the things away.

'You should sit down with Uncle Jeff,' he told her. 'Let me do my share.'

'Well, if you're sure . . .' Margaret looked at Jeff

279

and he nodded so she'd left him to get on with it. Jilly came up to her and pulled at her skirt.

'Are you stopping here now?' she asked shyly.

'I shall be living here fully the week after Christmas when your Uncle Jeff and I get married,' Margaret said and patted her lap. Jilly climbed onto it, gazing up into her face.

'Will you be my real Auntie Margaret then?' she asked.

'Indeed I will be,' she said and smiled tenderly, reaching out to stroke the little girl's soft fair hair. 'But only if you would like me to be?'

'Yes, please,' Jilly said. 'And you won't disappear, will you?'

'No, I shan't do that,' Margaret said. 'I'm working at the Rosie tomorrow so I have to go home soon – but I'll be here again to put you to bed tomorrow evening and when I marry Uncle Jeff, I'll be here in the mornings too.'

Jilly nodded happily. 'I'm glad. I didn't like being alone at our house. I was frightened when people came and banged on the door. Tim said they wanted to take us away.'

'They won't take you away from us,' Jeff told her and smiled. 'You're going to live here with us until you're grown-up, Jilly – and we shall look after you, won't we, Margaret?'

'Yes, we will,' Margaret said and smiled at him over the child's head. 'I'll go to work, but I shan't do the long shifts I used to and that means I'll be here when you and Tim get home from school to make our tea. I'll look after you, darling.'

Jilly jumped off Margaret's lap and went running into the kitchen to tell her brother the wonderful news. Jeff smiled at Margaret as they heard her excited chatter.

'I told you she already likes you,' he said to Margaret. 'She'll love you as if she's always known you soon.'

'Yes.' Margaret looked at him with content. 'We'll all be one big family, Jeff.'

Later that evening, when she was alone in her cramped flat, Margaret started her packing. She didn't have much furniture of her own, because the flat had been let as furnished, though she'd added a few bits she liked, just small tables and a nice comfy chair. Jeff had told her he would borrow a truck to move her things but she could make a start with her books, records, shoes and clothes. She'd kept a few of her aunt's glass vases and china figures that were mostly still packed away, but Jeff's house had plenty of room to stand her pretty things – and she would put the little lady figures in Jilly's room, and the spare set of silver dressing table pots she hadn't wanted to sell or throw out but didn't need.

A smile touched her lips as she moved about the flat, packing a few bits and pieces. It was going to be very new and exciting too – and there was just one hurdle to get over. If Jeff loved her, it would be easy to share his bed, but if he didn't, she would feel embarrassed. How did he want her to respond – as a loving wife or simply a live-in aunt and companion? She didn't want to make a mistake by seeming too forward and have him think he'd married a wanton, but she didn't want to make him think she didn't love him either.

Sighing, Margaret shook her head. She had no experience of love and she would just have to let Jeff show her the way.

CHAPTER 38

Christmas Day for Doctor Peter and Rose was ruined. Because they'd arranged for Beattie and her family to share their Christmas dinner, the goose was cooked, served and eaten, followed by all the traditional fare. However, it was a sombre party and everyone listened for the door or the phone the whole time. It didn't ring and the lack of news weighed heavily on them all. Not even the two boys, Danny and Ron, truly felt as if it was Christmas, even though they ate all their food. Like all growing lads, they had huge appetites and so the food wasn't wasted, though they were subdued and only mumbled a thanks to Doctor Peter and Rose for the gifts they'd been given.

After dinner was eaten and cleared away, Beattie and Ted took the boys home. 'You'll be best here quiet on your own,' Ted said, 'but if there's news and you need help, give me a ring.'

Rose thanked them for coming. She'd attempted to eat some of the delicious food because it was such a waste not to, but each mouthful had been forced down and she tasted nothing.

'I never thought I'd be so affected by the fate of a street urchin,' Doctor Peter said when they were alone. 'We hardly know Luke, Rose, but I feel he belongs to us and I can't help feeling sick with worry over his disappearance.'

'I think the same,' Rose said and went to touch her husband's hand sympathetically. 'He is such a lovely lad and I know he wouldn't do this to us on purpose – that's why I'm so sure he's in trouble.' She gave a little sob. 'I'm so worried for him, Peter.'

Her husband nodded and squeezed her hand. 'There's no way Luke would go off like this,' he said quietly. 'One of the officers who was here yesterday told me to check if anything had been stolen and said street kids were often unreliable but Luke isn't like that – he was grateful for his job and a home. I know he was.'

'Yes, very much so,' Rose agreed. She took a deep breath. 'I'm afraid something has happened to him, Peter.'

'Try not to be too anxious,' he advised. 'Luke is strong and resilient. I'm quite sure that, wherever he is, whatever's been done to him, he hasn't given up hope – and I won't. I know he's capable of getting through whatever is happening. He will believe that we've got people looking for him and he will wait for his opportunity to get away if he can. He told me how he planned his escape from the orphanage where they abused other boys and beat him. Luke is clever and I know he'll be working it all out now.'

'Yes, I know he's a good clever boy,' Rose said

holding back tears. 'All we can do is wait and pray God will bring him back to us.'

Peter nodded his agreement. 'Make a cup of coffee and put some brandy in it,' he said. 'We could both do with something to calm our nerves. Sitting here fretting isn't going to cure anything, Rose. After we've had coffee, we'll put on our coats and go for a walk. Well, I'll walk, you'll push!'

Rose smiled and went to make the coffee. Peter was right. Sitting here would do no one any good.

Red had called it a day after church finished and brought Luke back to the derelict building. The brute seemed to have forgotten that he had promised to take Luke to the Sally Army hall for a free lunch and sat mooching in his corner, drinking steadily. The first old lady had been the only one to give them more than a shilling and what money they had was in Red's pocket. Luke didn't think it was enough to buy another bottle of whisky, which might be the reason his captor looked so morose. He was mumbling into his beard, not looking at Luke, who was feeling hungry, his stomach gurgling in protest.

'Aren't we going for that free food?' he ventured at last and Red looked at him, spitting on the ground.

'Ain't hungry,' he growled.

Luke knew it was no use saying he was. Red would as soon let him starve as bother with what he needed – and if Luke didn't collect more money than he had that morning, Red would soon get tired of him. What would happen then didn't bear thinking of.

'Nuisance,' he said clearly. 'Bloody runt – no good

to anyone.' The look in his eyes was so terrible then that Luke was afraid he would get up and come for him, but although he made a movement towards him, he stopped and slumped back, taking another swill of drink. Luke hoped desperately that he'd fall asleep but he just sat there, hour after hour, staring sullenly in Luke's direction and then, just as it was getting dark, he half-stood and lurched to the back of the room. Luke heard him stumbling about, clearly looking for something, and then he returned and slumped back on the ground with a grunt. In his hand was a bottle of a clear liquid. It wasn't whisky, and, as Red started to drink from it, Luke caught a strong smell that reminded him of something the builders had used at the orphanage to clean paint brushes. He thought it might be methylated spirits and shuddered. Surely that stuff wasn't fit to drink?

Red was swigging it down, and then, when it was too dark to see his captor any more, Luke heard a loud snore. Getting to his feet carefully he stepped softly to the man's side, avoiding the empty meths bottle. Red's mouth was open and he was in a drunken slumber.

Luke knew that this was his one chance of getting away from the bully who had captured him. Tomorrow, folk would be busy counting the cost of their celebrations and it was unlikely that they would collect any money. Red's temper was so uncertain that he was likely to beat Luke to death without thought. If Luke didn't leave now, he was in serious trouble.

He had planned what he would do and knew it was a risk, but if he waited for a better chance, it might be too late. He located the wrench he'd discovered the previous night and went to the window, stripping off the sacking, and then took a good look at the length of wood nailing it shut. Fortunately, it wasn't thick, just an old bit of ply, but there were several nails hammered in all the way along and it would take all Luke's strength to pry them out – he just hoped Red wouldn't wake at the first sound of wood tearing.

The first wrench sounded loud and terrifying to Luke and he hesitated, listening for sounds that would indicate Red was stirring but none came so he risked another go and then another. Fortunately, at his fourth attempt, it came free. The window opened easily then, swinging back, and he understood why it had been nailed; the hinge had rusted away and it hung loose.

Luke didn't waste any time trying to shut it. If Red hadn't woken while Luke was breaking that wood, he might sleep for a long time. Pausing to note the name of the lane, where the workshop was situated – a little alley named just that, Little Alley – Luke sped off as the dawn began to break. He would go to the police station first and pray that they would believe him and move quickly to arrest Red before he could get away.

The lights were on in the police station and Luke couldn't believe his luck when he saw Constable Jones behind the counter. He was panting for breath but before he could even gather it enough to tell his tale, Constable Jones was round to the front and had hold of his arm. He looked at him in concern.

'Take your time, Luke, and then tell me what

happened. Doctor Peter reported your disappearance and we've been searching for you for two days.'

'H-he caught me and carried me off. Red,' Luke panted when he'd recovered enough breath. 'He made me beg on the streets but he's given me nothing to eat – and he's the one that attacked your wife, sir.'

Constable Jones nodded. 'I did think it might be him, out for revenge. How did you get away, lad?'

Luke explained about Red drinking all his whisky and then a bottle of methylated spirits. Constable Jones looked concerned and then angry as Luke's story poured out in detail. When he'd finished, he wrote it all down in his notebook, asking a few questions and frowning.

'Well, I'd best take you back to Doctor Peter. I could feed you, but you'll do better at home.'

Luke hesitated. 'He threatened to kill Doctor Peter if I escaped and went back there – and Doctor Peter is vulnerable in that chair. I don't want anything to happen to him, sir, or his wife. Sister Rose is lovely to me.'

Constable Jones smiled. 'Don't you worry about Doctor Peter and Sister Rose, lad. A rather nasty individual thought he would get the better of them once before but they saw him off. You ask him about it, and tell him to show you his pistol. I can't condone him using it, but he has a licence for it and if he shoots to wound rather than kill there's not a judge in the land would find against him protecting himself. Especially against a man like Red.'

Luke looked at him uncertainly and then nodded. At least the police had been warned and if they were lucky, they would catch Red. He had a lot to answer for – attacking Constable Jones' wife, abducting Luke and forcing a horrible act on a woman who was later found dead in the canal. Luke knew that didn't prove he'd murdered her, but it was more likely than not and perhaps the courts would find him guilty and put him away for a long time.

Constable Jones set things in motion before he took Luke home and a team of six police officers was already on their way to Little Alley by the time Luke and Constable Jones left the police station. Someone had let Doctor Peter know and the door was open when they got there. Sister Rose flew out and grabbed Luke in a huge hug of relief, telling him over and over how glad she was that he was safe and promising him a lovely breakfast as soon as he was ready.

'I smell awful,' Luke told her. 'He took my new clothes and I think he sold them then made me wear these rags.'

'Never mind, I've got some new things I bought you for Christmas,' she said. 'Let's get you in the bath – unless you want to eat first?'

'Can I have a piece of cake and then breakfast when I'm clean?'

'I'll cut the Christmas cake for you. We didn't touch it because we didn't feel like eating much at all without you here. The goose was roasted because Beattie and the boys came and she did most of the cooking but only the boys ate much.'

'They were hungry,' Luke said simply accepting the fact that, like him, they would always eat what they were given. 'First, I have to tell you and Doctor Peter – that man threatened to kill you both if I came here. Are you sure you want me?'

'Of course we do!' she told him and smiled lovingly. 'You're a part of our family, Luke. Doctor Peter needs you to help him – and we've both come to love you.'

Luke looked at her and gulped back his tears, because he could see that she was crying and that she meant every word. After his ordeal at Red's hands, his homecoming was all the sweeter, because he knew it was truly his home. Doctor Peter and Rose were his family – something he'd never known before. His heart filled with an overwhelming emotion he'd never known before and he knew that he would always feel it for these good people.

'Thank you,' he whispered, but couldn't say the words he wanted to. Luke knew Rose had touched something deep inside him, but was it love? He couldn't say for certain, because he didn't know what love meant yet – but he knew these people who had taken him in were important to him and he would do anything for them.

Sister Rose seemed to understand. She gave him a brief hug and took him into the sitting room. Doctor Peter had been talking to Constable Jones and they looked very serious, but he smiled as he saw Luke.

'I'm so glad to see you back, Luke. We missed you and worried about you – and Constable Jones has told me you're anxious about my safety. Well, I know I can't walk much yet, but that's why I keep this with me.' He took out a metal object and placed it on the table. 'This pistol is mine and I'm a pretty good shot,

Luke. If that ruffian comes here, I'll make him sorry. I'll shoot to wound and if he's attacking my family I'll be exonerated. He is an evil man and should be behind bars – or, if he is a murderer, he should pay the ultimate penalty.'

Luke nodded. He approached the pistol tentatively and touched it with one finger. 'How does it work?' he asked and Peter nodded.

'Perhaps you should know – you prepare it to fire by pulling this hammer back and then pull the trigger here, but don't try, because I keep it loaded just in case.'

'Good!' Luke grinned at him, feeling happier. 'He thought he could get away with it because you're in that chair, but you'll show him if he comes.'

'Yes, I'll show him,' Peter said firmly. 'Don't you worry. Eat your cake and then have a nice long bath.'

'Yes, sir, I will – and thank you for showing me.'

Luke went off munching the Christmas cake, which tasted better than anything in the world right then. He felt much happier now he'd seen the pistol and knew how it worked. If ever Red came here and Doctor Peter somehow got knocked over or let go of the pistol, Luke wouldn't hesitate to use it.

CHAPTER 39

'Sister Rose told me she was going to have Christmas for Luke this Sunday, when she has the whole day off,' Margaret said to Jeff when she saw him the morning after Boxing Day. 'She'll buy another goose if she can, but if they're all gone, they'll have a chicken and they'll have sherry trifle afterwards.'

Jeff nodded and smiled at her. 'It's a relief to know that he got away all right – had he been hurt much?'

'Sister Rose said he had bruises all over his body and she took a photograph of his back for evidence when they arrest that awful man.'

'That's if they catch him,' Jeff said with a shake of his head. 'I've been told he'd left his hiding place when they got there – he must have known it wasn't safe for him any longer.'

'What a pity,' Margaret said looking anxiously at him. 'It means he's still at large and a danger to the public – and Luke, Rose and Doctor Peter in particular.'

'Constable Jones told me they will keep an officer on the beat close to the house at night and outside the hospital.' Jeff frowned. 'It would be better if they'd managed to get him, but that was always a long shot.'

'Well, let's hope they do soon.'

'Yes, we can all rest easier then.' Jeff looked at her pale face and then changed the subject. 'Did you bring some of your clothes in the suitcase, love? If there's anything of mine you need to throw out, just do it. I've had most of it a long time and I don't mind a change if you want to keep yours instead.'

'I like most of your stuff and I'm only keeping the things of mine I really like – which isn't much,' Margaret told him with a smile. 'I love your home, Jeff. I feel so comfortable here.' She hesitated, then, 'Where should I put my clothes?'

'The second wardrobe is empty, ready for you,' he told her. 'I never needed the two for my clothes – just the gent's single, so the double is all for you.'

'I doubt I'll fill it,' Margaret said. 'I wear uniforms for work and just have a few skirts and jumpers and about four nice dresses.'

'Well, we'll have to do something about that,' Jeff said with a loving smile. 'You'll be able to afford a few more when you're my wife, Margaret – and you'll need a nice dress for when we go dancing or to a fancy meal.'

'I've got one I like for special occasions – and my wedding outfit; that's new, of course.' She nodded happily, because it was really smart and she would be able to wear it when Jeff took her out. The sky-blue dress and jacket she'd decided on rather than a long white lace dress, or even a white suit, could be worn over and over again in the future, as could the pretty white hat decorated with pink roses. Her white gloves and court shoes would also be useful.

'You're special to me, Margaret,' Jeff said and her heart caught, because when he looked at her like that, she felt loved and that was wonderful, making her tingle with all sorts of feelings she had yet to understand. 'I think you're the nicest, sweetest person I've ever met and I can't wait for you to be my wife.'

Margaret glowed with happiness but didn't know how to answer, so she took her suitcase up and hung her clothes in the wardrobe. She'd brought most of her best ones but not the dress and jacket and the long skirt and top she'd bought for their stay at the posh hotel. The excitement was mounting now and she felt happier than she had in a long, long time.

Jeff sighed after he dropped Margaret off at her flat and drove back to his home. He couldn't wait for their wedding and for her to move in. The thought of their wedding night was a bit nerve-wracking, because it was a while since he'd made love to a woman. During the war he'd met a few girls and he'd been tempted to go to bed with them, but he'd been faithful to his sweetheart until she ditched him. After that, he'd paid for sex with prostitutes a couple of times, but he didn't find that at all to his taste. Over the years he'd had one brief fling with a young woman who had been looking for a bit of fun and excitement. It had meant nothing to either of them and Jeff had just packed in all thought of finding love after that – until his golden girl arrived and lit up his life.

He hoped his lack of expertise wouldn't spoil their wedding night. Jeff wasn't sure if he was much good as a lover. No one had ever told him otherwise, but he knew that he longed to hold his Margaret in his arms and his body tingled to feel hers close to him, to stroke the softness of her skin and be one with her. Kissing her was wonderful, though he never pushed it too far for fear of making her think it was sex he was after. Making love would be great but just having her close in his bed would be exquisite. Her fragrance, softness and warmth would fill him and give him everything that had been missing for so long and he wanted to please her in every way.

Jeff worried that he was too old for her, that he wouldn't be able to satisfy her in bed, but if it was love and affection she needed, he had more than enough for two. Margaret didn't have to love him as much as he loved her. He just wanted the chance to be with her and have her as his wife, to know that they would be company for each other for the rest of their lives.

Margaret felt happy at work the next day. Sister Rose was beaming at everyone and looked like someone who had come into a fortune – or had the child she loved restored to her, which of course she had. It was wonderful to see the happiness bubbling out of her with every smile and every word she spoke, lighting up everyone's life.

Margaret sailed through the morning and into the afternoon. Matron visited the ward at three and inspected everything and then left without speaking a word to Margaret, though she had a brief word with Sister Rose.

'Lady Rosalie is coming to see little Julie tomorrow,' Sister Rose told her after Matron had gone. 'She thinks she has a foster family for her and I was able to tell her that Julie is ready to leave once they place her.'

'She was very poorly when she came in,' Margaret said and frowned. 'I know times have been hard, Sister Rose, but she was nearly starving – what kind of parents treat their child like that?'

'I understand the father was a drunkard and the mother not much better. He beat his wife and both neglected Julie.'

'That's wicked,' Margaret said indignantly. 'Jeff is so good to those kids he's adopting.'

'Yes, but Jeff Marshall is one of the special ones,' Sister Rose replied. 'You and I are the lucky ones, Margaret, to marry husbands who have so much heart and kindness.'

'Yes, I know,' Margaret said and smiled at her. It was unusual for Sister Rose to say so much personal stuff to her, but of course she had extra reason to be thankful now that Luke had been restored to them. 'Did you manage to get that extra goose for this Sunday?'

'Yes, I did,' Rose said. 'Mr Rowe said he had a nice one left over at Christmas that he'd put away in his big fridge and he says it will still be fine for this weekend – so Luke will have a special Christmas dinner after all.'

'That's really nice,' Margaret replied. 'I'm glad things turned out so well, Sister Rose.'

'Yes, in the end,' Rose said, reverting to her brisk manner. 'We'd best get on, nurse. They will soon be bringing in the children's tea and we haven't finished those dressings.'

Margaret scurried off to fetch the trolley with the sterile dressings for young Tommy's leg. He'd fallen off a high ledge where he'd been playing, against his mother's wishes, and scraped all his legs, knees and thighs. Because the leg hadn't been cleaned properly at the time, it had become infected and he'd been brought in by his distraught widowed mother when it started to swell and he developed a fever. Good nursing and careful watching had brought Tommy through the dangerous stage, but his wounds still needed dressing and she and Sister Rose were behind with their work due to the Matron's visit.

As she worked with gentle, soothing hands, Margaret was thinking what she would do when she got home that night. She wasn't seeing Jeff because he had a meeting at the parish council and the two children were off to the pictures to see *Snow White and the Seven Dwarfs*. As promised, it was Tim's early birthday gift to his sister, and she knew Jilly was looking forward to it. Margaret wouldn't have minded going with them, but she hadn't been invited so she would simply get on with packing her things.

CHAPTER 40

Jenny saw Michael wearing his army uniform when she got home from work that afternoon. He was sitting at the kitchen table staring into his mug of tea. A little chill ran down her spine because she knew instantly that he was leaving.

'They've sent for you,' she said trying not to let her voice rise with emotion.

'Yes, Jenny love,' he said. 'Chris came round earlier – he's under orders too and I think we'll be gone for a few weeks.' He got up and moved towards her, opening his arms.

Jenny moved into his embrace, lifting her face for his kiss. She was determined not to cry or show her upset, to just let him hold her and kiss her. 'Well, I'm glad Chris will be with you this time,' she said and hugged him. 'Take care of him – and you.'

'Would I let anything happen to Lily's husband?' he said and grinned in the cocky way she loved so much. 'He'll be quite safe with me, so neither of you need worry.'

'We shan't,' Jenny said and gave him a tap on the

backside. 'Do you want something to eat – or don't you have time?'

'A sandwich. I leave in half an hour.'

Jenny nodded, turning away to take the ingredients she needed from the pantry. She would use the ham she'd bought for supper and put a little mustard on it, the way he liked. She wouldn't want much herself that evening and she could always make an omelette or visit the fish and chip shop.

She made thick doorstep sandwiches, which made Michael smile as he bit into the thick buttery bread and tasty ham. She'd sliced a large pickled onion on his plate and he shared it with her, chewing with evident pleasure.

'I'll have to suck some mints so that I don't breathe all over the others,' he said and then smiled at her. 'It was a good Christmas, wasn't it, love?'

'Wonderful,' Jenny agreed. 'Next year we'll have our son or daughter and hopefully the war will be over.'

'I wouldn't count on it, Jenny.' Michael frowned. 'Chris reckons the Germans are a lot more prepared – and a lot more powerful than we are. This could go on for years.'

Jenny shuddered. 'Don't! I hate wars and I have a bad feeling about this one sometimes.'

'Yes, I do too,' he agreed and finished the last of his sandwich. She rose as he did and they embraced. 'Whatever happens, keep strong. Remember our love and our child and get through, whatever it takes, Jenny. I'll always be with you in spirit, watching over you, and as soon as I can I'll be back with you.'

'I know,' she said and hugged him. 'We're the lucky ones, Michael. We have so much to be thankful for. Lots of people have such terrible lives but we have this lovely home and you and I both have good jobs and good friends and our family and we can't just lose that. We'll come through – whatever Hitler throws at this country.'

Michael kissed her and she laughed. 'You smell of pickled onions. You'd better have those mints!' She picked up a packet from the dresser.

He grinned at her. 'You do too, but as you're not going to be kissing anyone else it doesn't matter.'

'I'll never want to kiss anyone else again,' she said and looked into his eyes. 'That's a promise – just come back to me safe when you can.'

'Oh, I'll be back,' he said. He picked up the mints, grabbed her and kissed her again, and then he was gone.

Jenny heard the front door shut with a click and promptly burst into tears. She cried for a few minutes and then told herself not to be a fool. Michael had come back to her despite the odds last time and he would again – all she had to do was to look after herself and their child.

CHAPTER 41

In Ely, three people stood in Jane's warm kitchen. 'Of course, I'll do something,' Terry told them when Jane finished explaining what was needed. His gaze moved to the third person. 'If you'd told me your story, I'd have been on to it before this, love.' He smiled at Sally. 'I reckon I'd do anything for you.'

Sally blushed and glanced away, feeling odd inside. She liked the friendly milkman and was grateful he'd said he would help, because she hadn't a clue where to start and Jane didn't have the energy.

'I know we've no right to ask – but it worries me that those children may be in danger,' she said looking at him half in hope and half in embarrassment. 'It must sound strange to you, I know you must wonder how I could just forget my own children . . .'

'Nay, lass,' he reassured her with his open smile that made all his customers trust and like him. 'No one thinks wrong of you. I shall be off to London first thing in the morning.'

'But how can you? What about your milk round?' Sally stared at him, horrified that he would go to

301

such lengths. 'What will happen to your customers' orders?'

'I've got a boy who can take over for a few mornings,' Terry replied cheerfully. 'I've a load of holidays owed to me I never bother to take. Being on me own, I don't see the point. Rather work, I would, as a rule – but it's time I saw London and it will be an adventure for me.'

'Oh . . .' Sally was lost for words because his kindness was overwhelming and she couldn't find a way to thank him, so she just smiled and touched his hand. To her surprise, red colour swept up his neck and she realised that under his cheery manner, he was quite shy and uncertain. 'You're a lovely man and I'm so grateful.'

'Do anything for his customers,' Jane said briskly, but Sally knew this was more – Terry was taking a leap of faith into the unknown for her sake and it made her feel warm and happy. She was aware of a desire to sing, which was something she'd forgotten she liked, but after Terry had left, she started to sing a song she'd known for a long time but hadn't realised she knew.

> *'Cherry ripe, cherry ripe*
> *Ripe I cry*
> *Full and fair as my love's lips . . .'*

The merry sound made Jane stare at her and smile.

'That's right, love,' she said nodding contentedly as Sally started on the baking, singing yet another song she hadn't realised she knew. 'You sing to your heart's content. Terry will find your children and bring us news, you'll see.'

Tim enjoyed polishing the cars with Jeff. It was such satisfying work and the smell of the polish was pleasant, especially the one they used on the old leather seats. It was an antique wax and Jeff used it on the wood facia and to restore the cracking leather of interiors that had been neglected. Cars came to him looking tired and worn out but when he'd finished with them, they were a thing of beauty. Tim loved to see the transformation and being a part of it was very satisfying to him.

'There, that looks good, doesn't it?' Jeff said, sounding satisfied and proud of his work. 'Fit to take away my bride this Saturday night.'

'It's smashing – and thank you for letting me help you get it ready for Margaret, Uncle Jeff.'

'Nay, lad. Thank you for helping me,' Jeff told him. 'It took me half the time it would on my own and you've done as good a job on your sections as I've done on mine.'

He smiled at Tim and put his hand in his pocket. 'Nip to the shop and get us a piece of cod and three portions of chips. We'll share a big piece of fish between us, because Jilly won't eat much of the fish, will she?'

'Can I fry her an egg instead with her chips?'

'Of course you can, lad. Do you prefer that as well?'

'No, I'd love to share a piece of cod with you,' Tim replied and grinned at him, 'but Jilly is faddy.

Mum used to get cross sometimes, but she said we might as well let her have what she wanted – not that we could always afford eggs or fish and chips.'

'I know, lad. It was hard for you after your dad died. I wish I'd done more for you all back then . . .'

Tim nodded, accepted the florin that Jeff offered and ran off to the fish shop. In some ways, life was much better now than it had ever been but he'd still have his mum back if he had the chance. He'd been so sure she was dead, but it was very strange, because just lately he'd felt she was close. He'd turned round on the street several times looking for her, but she was never there and it just upset him.

He was being daft. He had to be a man and grow up, accept that he couldn't get his mum back. In his heart, he knew how lucky they were that Jeff had taken them on. Jilly had settled well and he sometimes thought she didn't miss Mum at all, the way she cuddled up to Margaret and seemed quite happy to sit on her lap.

Tim liked Margaret. He knew she meant well by them all and he didn't mind that she'd taken to Jilly more than him, and he liked Jeff a lot – but for him, memories of his mum and his dad were still strong. It wasn't quite the same for Jilly because she was too young to understand. He just couldn't help thinking about his mum . . .

'What you're saying is incredible.' Constable Jones looked hard at the man who had just told him the fantastic tale. 'What proof do I have that you're telling me the truth and haven't just made it up?'

'I did wonder if you might ask something like that,' Terry replied with his easy smile. 'So, I took this picture on my Box Brownie – it looks very like her and it's nice and clear. We call her Sally, because she didn't know her name, and I doubt it's her real one.'

Constable Jones took the picture and studied it for some minutes and then took another long hard look at Terry. 'The woman in this picture is called Betty Stewart and she does have two children, named Tim and Jilly.'

Terry's face broke into a grin of delight. 'That's wonderful news! So where can I find the children so I can take them home to Betty?'

'Hold hard there,' Constable Jones said and looked concerned. 'I daresay you're a decent bloke and the tale you tell may well be true – but we can't permit you to take the children like that.'

'Ah.' Terry looked at him warily. 'Want to see her in person, do you?'

'It isn't a case of Betty turning up and just taking the children,' Constable Jones told him. 'It does sound as if she may have been the innocent party – we thought she'd been murdered, but it might be that she was attacked, lost her memory and wandered off . . .' He ran his fingers through his hair, looking anxious.

'That's what I've been telling you,' Terry said. 'She still hasn't got it back completely, but she remembered the children's names – and I've come to find them and take them back to Ely, where they'll have a good home.'

'They have a good home where they are,' Constable Jones said. 'Mr Marshall is in the process of adopting the children and they're happy and well cared for.' He frowned and then nodded. 'He's getting married tomorrow and I can't pop this news on him just like that.' For a moment he was silent, then made up his mind. 'You go back to Ely and talk to this lady friend of yours. Tell her to come down next week. I'll have spoken to Jeff and my inspector by then and I'll take you both along to see him. I'm blessed if I know what to do for the best.'

Terry wanted to argue. If they were Betty's children, she surely had a right to them now and there was no right or reason for this police officer to deny her access to her children. Yet, it was reasonable to say Betty must come in person to claim them – after all, he could be anyone – so he nodded and left the station. He smiled to himself as he caught sight of his stocky figure in a shop window. Surely no one would think he was a gangster or a dealer in stolen children? The idea made him chuckle and then he frowned. No one who knew him would dream of questioning his integrity, but the London copper didn't know him from Adam – so no doubt he'd be in touch with the Ely constabulary and check he was who he said he was, which meant Jane and Sally – no, Betty – might get a visit from one of the local bobbies.

He was considering whether to get the next train home when he saw the constable leave the station and set off at a purposeful pace. Terry had hung around because he was unsure of his next move but now decided to follow Constable Jones, just in case it proved interesting.

*

'I wasn't going to tell you until after the wedding, but my sergeant said I ought to,' Steve told Jeff a few minutes later. 'I think this Terry Baker is a genuine bloke, but appearances can be deceiving. I know you're going away for a night and won't be back until late Sunday evening. Would you like me to take the kids home to Sarah? She would be delighted to have them.'

Jeff looked anxious. 'Yes, I think you should, Steve. Thanks for suggesting it because you can't be too careful. If this man is after the children for his own reasons, I'd never forgive myself for leaving them alone.'

'Right. Sarah will take them home after you two leave and we'll keep them until you fetch them.'

'That's relieved my mind,' Jeff said and smiled gratefully. His smile faded as he thought of something. 'Do you believe his story that Betty Stewart is still alive?'

'I'm not sure.' Steve looked thoughtful. 'It seemed improbable for a start but my sarge was saying he'd heard of a few cases of bad amnesia before and he seems to think it could well be the truth.'

'And what is the position with the children?' Jeff pondered aloud. 'I mean, I know she is their mother and I suppose she has the legal right to take them – but I was going to sign the fostering papers next month and then apply for permanent custody.'

'Unfortunately for you, if Betty is alive, she would have to sign the papers to release them for adoption and, knowing her, she would refuse. It would mean we'd have to have her ruled as an unfit mother.'

'Damn,' Jeff swore softly. 'I've become attached to those kids – especially the boy and Margaret loves the girl. This is very upsetting.'

'Yes, I know, and I'm sorry to spoil things for you . . .' Steve looked awkward. 'I'm not sure what difference it makes to your other plans?'

'If you mean marrying Margaret, it makes no difference. I asked her because I love her – but I'm not sure how big a part the kids played in her mind.' Jeff sighed. 'I'll keep it to myself until Betty turns up, I think. I won't even tell Margaret. This might be a hoax or an attempt to steal the kids.'

'It might,' Steve admitted. 'It was my first thought but afterwards, when I spoke to my sergeant, I realised it was likely to be genuine. It's damned unfair on you, Jeff – but Betty has the law on her side. Unless you want to try and prove her unfit?'

Jeff sighed and shook his head. 'Those kids have been through hell, but I know Tim still thinks of his mother – he would never forgive me and I couldn't do it to him. I don't mind admitting it has taken the wind out of my sails a bit – but if it is Betty, she has suffered enough.'

'I didn't think you would go to court if it was her,' Steve said and smiled. 'I apologise for putting a damper on the wedding but . . .'

'No, you couldn't do that,' Jeff replied and grinned. 'Margaret is all I could ever want so I'm a lucky man. I'm sad if we lose the kids but I still feel lucky. All I hope is that if it really is Betty and she takes them, she looks after them properly.'

'I'll be alerting the Ely constabulary to the situation,'

Steve told him grimly. 'If she neglects them, they'll be taken away from her.'

Terry saw the constable enter the garage, saw the name Jeff Marshall over the plate glass window and nodded his satisfaction. He took a photograph on his camera and waited. At three-thirty that afternoon, two children came running up the lane and went inside the garage. They were laughing and looked happy. He tried to take a picture but knew it was getting a bit too dark so it was unlikely to come out properly.

Wild thoughts of barging in there and demanding they hand over Betty's children went through his mind, but he knew that wouldn't work. He would probably be arrested for trying to steal them. No, much as he hated to return to Betty without her children, it was the proper thing to do. Betty must come with him to claim them – and if these people tried to hide them or prevent them from taking them, he would do everything it took – but they would do it legally.

At least he could tell Betty her name and the good news that her children were well and happy. Terry nodded to himself as he walked away. He would catch the 6.15 train back to Ely and visit Betty that very night to tell her the good news and the local chemist would have the photographs developed in a couple of days. He felt pleased with himself. He'd imagined it might take much longer to find the children, but he'd seen a poster soon after leaving the train at Liverpool Street station which had asked for information about a missing woman, though it had given no details except for the telephone number and the name of a police station. He'd taken a taxi there immediately and was glad he'd followed his instincts. Betty was the missing woman all right, but they'd thought she was dead because another woman had been killed nearby – which meant Betty was lucky to be alive. Terry was convinced she'd been attacked by the same monster who had killed the other woman in the same area, and he was determined to look after her in future – and her kids once they'd got them back to their mother, where they belonged.

He reflected that it had been easy to find Betty's children after he'd seen the old poster, but wished it had been as easy to bring them home.

CHAPTER 42

'Are you sure you want to go to the boxing club tonight?' Rose asked Luke that Friday evening as he pulled on the warm duffle coat she'd bought him. It was a nice camel one and it fitted Luke perfectly, making him look as if he came from a loving home, which he did. 'The police haven't picked Red up yet – though they have discovered more about him.' She frowned. 'He's well-known on the ships as a trouble-maker, has had a dozen or more jobs in the past few years and been sacked from all of them for drunken behaviour. He was banned from the docks a few months back and the harbourmaster has warned the shipping people not to give him work.'

'That must be why he is so angry at the world,' Doctor Peter said, nodding. He'd wheeled himself into the kitchen and smiled at the boy he'd taken as his own and was now in the process of adopting. 'He must know the police are searching for him. I think Luke should go; he can't just sit at home every evening because he's afraid of being attacked.'

'Me mates from the club have said they'll walk

home with me,' Luke explained. 'Jamie, Arch and Rich are all pretty handy with their fists. Rich was knifed once, so he doesn't box now but he teaches at the club and he's told me it's best to learn to defend yourself so that you can stand up to bullies.'

'That's right,' Doctor Peter encouraged. 'You stand up for yourself, Luke, and don't let anyone intimidate you. The bullies of this world usually back down when they get a taste of their own medicine.'

'Thanks, Doc,' Luke said and grinned. 'Don't worry, Aunt Rose, I shan't let him get me like that again.' He patted his pocket. 'I've got my penknife that Aunt Beattie and Uncle Ted gave me for Christmas. It wouldn't kill him, but a slash across his hand would make him let go of me – and one across the face would make him jump back.'

'I don't like you to think of using knives, even if it is only a little penknife,' Rose told him looking anxious. 'I always think violence breeds violence.'

'Let him have it if it helps him to feel safe,' Doctor Peter said. 'He won't harm anyone unless he's attacked – and the only person likely to do that deserves all he gets.' He nodded to Luke. 'You'll learn to defend yourself at the club and eventually you'll be able to throw someone twice your size, I daresay – but that takes time. So yes, keep the knife on you in case Red tries anything. I know I feel safer for having my pistol, even though I would only use it in extreme circumstances if it was one of our lives at stake; even then, I would only shoot to wound, never to kill. Remember that, Luke. It isn't for us to take life.'

'I know. It's only to defend myself if I have to.'

It was dusk when Luke set off for the boxing club. When he got there, Ron and Danny came over to him at once and, during the evening, Luke was shown the moves to defend himself, both by the instructor and several of the boys, as he learned the skills of self-defence. It was quite an art to throw someone and Luke gravitated towards the boxing ring. He watched some of the older boys and thought he liked the look of it more than the intricate ritual of jujitsu. Rich saw him watching and came up to him.

'Interested?'

'Yes, very much so,' Luke said. 'I'm not sure I can learn how to throw someone, but I'd like to learn to box.'

'That's how I felt when I was your age.' Rich looked at him with approval. 'You've got the right build for it so I reckon with some proper exercise and tuition you could be a boxer.'

'You were a champion, weren't you?'

'Only an amateur and at a lower level but I had hopes for the future until I got knifed,' Rich said with a wry look. 'Never mind, I'm still alive and I earn decent money driving my own car.' He nodded and smiled. 'Tell you what, I'll start you off tonight and take you home in my car. If you think you want to carry on, we'll start you on a regime of exercise to build you up, though I can see you're already very strong.'

He held the ropes back for Luke and told him to climb into the ring. 'I'll show you how to put your fists up and how to duck and dive.'

Luke grinned; he was really enjoying himself now and he knew he'd found something he could apply himself to, as well as look after Doctor Peter and Rose. That was his first priority, of course, but learning to box would be fun and useful. The stronger he was, the easier he would find it to stand up to bullies like Red. Constable Steve Jones had told him that though they hadn't managed to catch Red yet, they were closing in on him and that it was only a matter of time before he was behind bars.

When the club closed, Rich took Luke, Jamie and Arch home in his car and they all talked enthusiastically about boxing and martial arts.

Jamie had a championship contest soon and Arch was boxing for the club at an exhibition next month. It was a lovely time, talking excitedly with his new friends and learning what he needed to do to get fit enough to become a boxer. It was more than fun – it was exciting, and Luke looked forward to learning a new skill. His days of being very lonely were over at last and he had good friends as well as his new family. Sometimes, Luke needed to pinch himself because he was afraid he might wake up and discover it was all a dream.

Doctor Peter and Rose looked at each other when Luke told them he'd been brought home in his new friend's car, smiling and looking very pleased. 'Rich is going to help with my training,' he announced, filled with excitement. 'He says we'll go running first thing in the mornings before I start work for the day and then I'll go with Doctor Peter and help him after breakfast.'

'Well done,' Doctor Peter said and smiled in approval at him. 'We're going to have to give you a bit of schooling too, Luke. I understand you wouldn't want to go back to a regular school and I need you with me – but I'm going to teach you a bit more about the world during the evenings you don't go to your club – is that a deal?'

Luke looked at him doubtfully because he wasn't sure what sort of lessons the doctor meant. He'd learned to read and write and do sums at the orphanage and he hadn't much liked the teacher but for some reason he thought it would be different learning from his benefactor.

'I'm willing to try, sir,' he said, and Doctor Peter nodded.

'I think you'll find my lessons will be quite fun.' His expression was serious as he looked at Luke. 'What do you think you might like to do when you get older – to earn a living? You'll always have a home here, but one day you might want one of your own, a wife and family too. Have you ever thought of a career you would like?'

Luke stared at him and then at Rose. 'I'd like to help people,' he said. 'I'd like to do the sort of thing I do for you, Doctor Peter – but perhaps for sick folk who need even more help than you.' A warm glow spread inside him as he saw his friend's face light up and knew he'd pleased him enormously.

'You could study hard and become a nurse or a hospital porter,' Rose said smiling. 'You would be helping people then, Luke. Wouldn't you like that?'

'Yes,' Luke looked at Doctor Peter again. 'And, if I become good at boxing, I'd like to help train people when I'm older and know how.'

'Well, I think they are two very worthy ambitions,'

Doctor Peter replied with a warm smile. 'I think we'll give you a general education so you learn lots of things a man needs to know – is that all right with you?'

'Yes, please, sir.'

Luke went to bed after a supper of hot cocoa and a slice of plain cake, feeling very happy and content. His life seemed full to bursting point and he wasn't sure how he would fit it all in, but he knew that the lonely hours of sitting cold and miserable in a doorway with no food and nowhere to go were over for him. He was so lucky and a sudden twist of fear caught at him, because if all this was taken away from him now, he didn't think he could bear it – but no, it wouldn't happen again. He was safe with his friends and family . . .

CHAPTER 43

Matron looked at Jenny and nodded, pleased with her answer. 'It is good of you to volunteer to work over the New Year and to go on night duty. Nurse Margaret has asked to be excused from night duty and wants to work just days in future.'

'My husband is away on duty,' Jenny told her without going into further detail, 'and so I have no reason to want to go out over the New Year or in the evenings until he comes home. Rather than spend every night at home, I prefer to work. I can visit my sister during the day and we'll share a meal at each other's home.'

'Practical and sensible,' Matron said and smiled at her. 'You realise that we've had quite a few staff changes recently here at the Rosie, so this helps me with the rota for the next few weeks? I have been advertising for more nursing staff and I have found two young women I think will fit in here as nurses – as well as an excellent nursing sister. She was due to have come to us two months ago but was delayed by family problems but happily they are now resolved and she will start next month.'

Jenny congratulated her and left. Her night shifts would start the next day, and that evening she was going to spend some time with Lily who was also feeling a bit lonely in the evenings. Since she didn't care to leave her baby alone at night with a sitter, they'd decided they would just go out during the day when Marguerite could come with them.

Jenny went to buy a lovely fresh cream cake from Lavender and Lace, their favourite tea shop. She would take it as a treat for them and perhaps when they were out shopping, they might visit the tea shop for a nice plate of cakes and sandwiches. She smiled at the thought; it would be almost like old times, when they'd lived together with Gran and neither of them had been married.

Jenny had decided that she had to live her life and just get on with it. Michael would come home when he could and, as Lily said, 'We love them the way they are, Jenny, so we have to accept what they do.'

It was true and Jenny had learned to accept it, just as Lily had. At times she still lay awake worrying, but working nights would cure that because she'd be too busy to worry about what ifs – and perhaps by the time her baby was born, Michael would be home again.

Matron was content as she went about her business, checking on patients and nurses, and changing rotas to fit in with all the staff holiday requests. She'd enjoyed her Christmas break with Lady Rosalie.

318

They'd talked and laughed together, enjoyed good food and exchanged gifts, and Lady Rosalie had told her some excellent news.

'We have a young boy for your Ruby Harding,' she said as they ate their sherry trifle. 'He is eight years old and full of mischief and life. His father used to be in the building trade but he was killed in a road accident and his mother died of a severe bout of influenza. She had been struggling to cope for a while with a growing son and not much money.' She'd paused and smiled. 'Does that sound as if it will suit?'

'It sounds marvellous,' Matron had told her. 'I think Ruby is settling nicely and this will make her very happy – and the kitchen and cleaning staff have been no trouble since she took over. I was so glad when she returned.'

'Good, then I'm glad we've found such a lovely boy for her – his name is James, but his parents called him Jim.' She smiled, got up and poured a cup of tea for them both and then sat down next to matron. 'Mary – have you thought what you will do when you retire?'

'Oh, that's years away,' she replied, a little shocked by the sudden change of subject. 'I'm not too old yet.'

'Far from it,' Lady Rosalie replied and passed her a cup of tea. 'But one day you will start to think about it, Mary dear – and I want you to know that you will always have a home with me. I do not intend to marry again and I think that we would be good companions as we grow older. We share the same interests and enjoy each other's company – we are good friends, are we not?'

'Yes, we are,' she'd agreed and smiled as she touched her friend's hand. 'We both care deeply about children who are in need and I admire the work you do for those orphans. It would be a pleasure to share your life and work one day, but I'm not sure it would be right for me to live here in your home.'

'You could have your own rooms so that you are entirely independent,' her friend said. 'Think about it, my dear Mary. There is no rush for an answer.'

Making her rounds of the infirmary, which she felt was her home, Matron couldn't get the idea out of her mind. The more she thought about it the more it appealed, to share her old age with her closest friend – but what could she give Lady Rosalie in return? She could not just take. Of course, Rosalie's son was growing up fast, and one day he would leave home and go away to work and live so she, too, would be alone. What Matron could give was her support, friendship and her love. Perhaps that was enough.

CHAPTER 44

Margaret's wedding day had arrived. All her things had been taken to Jeff's house, apart from her wedding outfit and suitcase. When she closed the door on her flat today, she wouldn't be coming back. She just had to put the key back through the door and leave. Rose's husband was taking her and her suitcase to the church, and Rose would wait to see her down the aisle with her witness, Tim, before taking her seat in the church. Margaret needed someone to give her away, and she'd decided who better than Tim, whom she was beginning to like more and more.

They had several guests coming to the wedding. Rose, Doctor Peter, also Sarah Jones and her husband if he could get off work, Nurse Jenny, and three other nurses, Ruby and her husband Sid. All the rest of the guests would be people Jeff knew and had invited.

Margaret had decided to ask Tim to be her witness as well and Jilly to be her attendant. It meant the little girl could dress up in one of the new dresses she'd been given and hold Margaret's flowers, which she was very excited about. Even Tim had seemed excited about being given the job of witness and Margaret smiled as she recalled the look of pride in his eyes. There was no one else in particular that she wanted to do the job and it had been a sudden impulse that had turned out well, as the boy had been friendlier to her than ever before.

Margaret's nerves were tingling on the way to church, as she thought about her wedding night. What would Jeff expect of her – and how should she behave? Should she smile and welcome him to bed, giving him her love and her body freely or would he think her too forward and turn his back on her?

If only she knew how he really felt about her! At the start, she'd believed he loved her, but Matron had put doubt in her mind and she couldn't shift it, no matter how kind Jeff was or how much she tried.

The bells pealed out joyfully as Margaret left church on Jeff's arm. She was his wife now for good or bad and decided to stop worrying about what came next. They posed for pictures and smiled, Jeff looking as pleased as punch – and he said the words, my wife, at least ten times in as many minutes to everyone he spoke to. Quite a crowd of locals had turned out and the church was filled with people, even though they hadn't all been invited. Margaret was given ten good luck charms from strangers and with her wonderful bouquet of roses and freesias that Jeff had provided, her arms were loaded as they got into the car and a friend of his drove them to the reception.

'Happy, love?' Jeff asked and leaned in to kiss her

softly on the lips. 'You look wonderful, Margaret. That dress and little jacket look so smart.'

'So do you.' He was wearing a navy-blue pinstripe suit with a white shirt, blue tie and polished black shoes. She smiled at him shyly. 'So smart and handsome . . .'

Jeff chuckled. 'It's nice to know my wife thinks I look good.' He played with her hand, touching the wide gold band of her wedding ring, to which she had added her lovely engagement ring. It had been on a chain about her throat during the ceremony but was now where it should be, with her wedding ring.

She was Mrs Marshall and it sounded and felt wonderful. Margaret was tingling with happiness and it surrounded her with a golden glow as she received guests by Jeff's side, and accepted so many small gifts of things for their home that she wasn't sure where they would put them. Jeff thanked everyone for coming in his speech, told them all what a happy man he was, and they cut the cake together.

Afterwards, there were photographs and Jeff went round and thanked everyone. Then they were in his car, which smelled deliciously of polish. She glanced at him nervously, but he looked relaxed and happy and gradually she settled down and began to smile herself.

When they arrived at one of the most expensive hotels in the West End of London, Margaret gasped, overwhelmed and delighted. She'd never dreamed she would ever stay in the Savoy Hotel, and even though it was for one night only she felt like a princess. The porter and receptionist were so friendly as they were shown to their room, which was like a little bed-sitting room with two nice comfortable chairs and a desk and chair besides the bed, wardrobes and a little bathroom on the side.

A bottle of champagne was waiting in an ice bucket with a small box of truffles – and a dish of straw-berries. Margaret couldn't believe it. How could Jeff have got strawberries for her in the middle of winter? They must have been grown in a greenhouse and cost the earth. She felt tears well up in her eyes and looked at him in wonder.

'All this, Jeff – for me?'

'Of course,' he said. 'I adore you, Margaret, didn't you know? I would give you the moon if I could.'

'Oh, Jeff, I wasn't sure,' she said chokily. 'I love you, but I thought . . .'

'Come here,' he commanded in a masterful tone that sent her straight into his arms. He looked deep into her eyes. 'I didn't ask you for the children,' he said. 'I asked you for me – because I love and want you . . .'

Bending his head, he kissed her in a way he'd never done before and at once the most delightful sensations flooded through her and she relaxed into him, all doubts fled. She knew in that instant that Matron had been wrong, so very wrong. Jeff loved her as much as she could ever wish, and she loved him. Joy flooding through her, smiling up at him, she surren-dered her heart, mind and body as he led her towards the sumptuous hotel bed . . .

In the morning they stayed late in bed and had a delicious breakfast brought to their room before they

324

checked out at noon, rested, bathed and as content as any two people could be. Jeff told her about Betty's reappearance as they drove back through the Sunday-quiet streets to their home.

'Oh, Jeff, I'm so sorry!' she exclaimed. 'I know how fond you are of those children.'

'I enjoy their company,' Jeff said, 'but nothing can spoil what you and I have, my love. Yes, I'd have liked to train young Tim – but I can always find another lad to do what he did, and if his mother is telling the truth it would be wrong to try and stop her taking her children, don't you think?'

'Yes indeed – because if she lost her memory it wasn't her fault they were left on their own. She should be very grateful to you for what you did, Jeff – but it wasn't her fault.' She smiled at him. 'It's typical of you to see her side of things, love. As you say, you'll find another apprentice easily enough.'

'It hardly matters,' Jeff said fondly. 'I couldn't be happier and I hope you're happy too?'

'Yes, I am,' she said. 'I never thought I could be this happy, Jeff. I love you more than I can ever tell you.'

'You're my golden girl,' he told her. 'You lit up my life when you walked into it, Margaret. I was a lonely old man until you came along and now, I feel like a teenager again.'

Margaret giggled and blushed. Jeff certainly had plenty of stamina and energy if their wedding night had anything to say to it. 'I don't think anyone could call you old,' she said, a teasing lilt in her voice.

Jeff chuckled but looked pleased and Margaret felt

a kind of power she'd never experienced before knowing she had the means to make this man happy by a word, a look, or a caress. She would do all she could to keep things that way so that they grew closer over the years and perhaps . . . Margaret felt a little tingle inside as she realised the possibilities of their passionate love-making the previous night. She was young and healthy and it was entirely possible that she could give her husband a son or daughter, or perhaps, in time, one of each.

CHAPTER 45

Peter stretched and felt a sense of well-being that had been missing for a long time. He'd known it would take quite a while to get over the serious injuries he'd received while rescuing Jessie, but the shock to his spine had debilitated him to such a degree that he'd begun to think he never would feel well again. Now he walked slowly across the room and felt a surge of elation as he reached the door without falling over. So far so good . . .

'Peter?'

Hearing his wife's voice, Peter turned to smile at her. 'Rose, my love. How are you this morning?'

'I'm very well – but you look very much better! Are you in less pain?' Her eyes looked at him with tenderly love. He smiled at her, feeling his heart swell with love for this wonderful woman. His accident had robbed them of so much, but soon he might be able to be the husband she deserved.

'I feel the best I have since it happened,' he told her. 'I walked across the room unaided, Rose. It didn't hurt at all and I didn't fall.'

'That's wonderful!' She watched as he eased himself into the wheelchair. 'Has it tired you, Peter?'

'No – not at all,' he replied with a warm smile, 'but I'll let it happen gradually, Rose – besides, there's Luke to think of.'

Rose nodded, understanding what he did not put into words. Luke had come to them to help Peter with his chair so he could work. Once Peter no longer needed help – would he want to stay?

'Surely he will understand that we love him and want him with us?'

'Luke is very independent,' Peter said using that insight he'd gained as a doctor to the old, poor and sick but still independent folk of the East End. Luke wasn't London born and bred, but he had that fighting spirit Londoners showed – a spirit that was coming to the fore in these days of war. Here, at home in England, it was still talked of as the phoney war despite a few attacks from the air, mainly on docks and coastal areas, but overseas the news was often bad with stories of British and Allied troops meeting defeat; there were victories too, but overall it seemed to Peter that things were not going well for the Allies. The Germans had proved much stronger than expected and people had started to think an invasion more likely.

'Let the buggers come and we'll shoot 'em,' Jessie had told him the last time she visited the clinic. 'Give me a gun, Doc, and I'll shoot a few for yer.'

The memory made him smile. It made Rose laugh when he told her, and they were still chuckling as they went through to the kitchen for breakfast. Luke was setting the table. He'd really made himself at home since he returned from his ordeal at the hands of that monster, Red. He grinned at them, looking pleased with life.

'What are we doing today?' he asked looking at Peter with an alert eagerness that made Peter glad he hadn't told him yet that he might soon be able to manage without his chair. He would give Luke time to accept that this was his home and to understand that he was a part of their family whether his help was needed or not.

Luke had settled into a routine that he truly enjoyed. He worked with Doctor Peter every day, pushing his chair, running errands, and, as he became known and accepted in the clinic and the Rosie, doing some small jobs for the nurses and the other doctors as well. His strength was helpful for pushing trolleys and chairs for patients and the porters welcomed his help, chatting to him and telling him about how rewarding their job was and how much they liked helping the sick and needy.

'If I was smart enough, I'd do what the doc does,' a porter named Bimbo told him with a grin. 'But I ain't – so I do this. The pay ain't great but it's steady work, better than hanging about on the docks waiting for a job.'

Luke agreed that it was and smiled. He hadn't decided what he was going to do himself yet, but Doctor Peter said he had plenty of time. He'd given him books to study and Luke liked the medical encyclopaedias best. He read about all kinds of illnesses of the mind and body and thought how fascinating it was. Some of the words were hard to read but either Rose or Doctor Peter would explain if he asked. Being a porter like Bimbo would be a good life, but Luke thought he might prefer to be a nurse, though there were very few men doing general nursing.

Talking to some of the male patients, Luke knew that they would much prefer a male nurse to wash and dress them if possible. One man told him, 'Me wound ain't never cleared up since the last war, see. Took a bullet at the Somme and a bit of shrapnel when I got blown up on my second tour out there. Too old I was and should've died but you can't kill an old dog. I'd sooner fight the Hun than have a pretty nurse turn up her nose at the smell of me leg.'

Doctor Peter told him that the patient had suppurating ulcers and he often treated them himself. 'Jim is a proud soldier and he likes a man's touch.'

Luke nodded his understanding. 'Do you think I could learn to look after men like him?' he asked. 'To be a nurse like Aunt Rose?'

'I'm certain you could,' Doctor Peter said and smiled warmly. 'Do you know how much that would make me happy?' He looked hard at Luke. 'But is it what you truly want, Luke? You're not saying it just to please me?'

'No, sir.' Luke grinned at him. 'You're the easiest person in the world to please – but it's what I'd really like to do once I'm old enough, and if you don't need me all the time by then.'

'I still need you for the time being,' Doctor Peter

said, 'and I'll always want you around, Luke. I'm going to teach you all you want to know about medical things and when you're old enough you can apply for training as a nurse. However, your home is with Rose and me for the rest of your life – or until you get married and have a home of your own, but even then, we'll still want you to visit us often. You're like a son to us, Luke, and we both love you.'

'Yeah, I know,' Luke said and swallowed to hold back his emotion. 'I reckon I love both of you, too. I don't know much about love, to be honest – but if it means caring that someone is all right and looking after them, then that's how I feel.'

Doctor Peter blinked hard, as if his eyes had suddenly filled with tears but he smiled back and nodded. 'That's love all right, son – and I think you'll find that you have a big heart to fill with love; for us, for a wife one day and kids of your own – as well as all the folk you will look after in your life.'

'I reckon it was my lucky day when I asked you if you wanted a lift with your chair,' Luke said and Doctor Peter shook his head.

'No, Luke, I think it was mine,' he said. 'Come on, let's go. I want to visit a couple of patients I'm concerned about – and then we'll go and buy Rose some flowers as a surprise.'

Rose checked that the back door was locked. She'd done that half a dozen times since she got home from work at just after two that afternoon. Why, she wasn't sure, except that she'd felt she was being followed on her way home. It wasn't the first time she'd felt that, but when she'd glanced over her shoulder, she'd seen no one – no one loitering at the corner or standing in a shop doorway.

It had to be her imagination and yet she was uneasy. She couldn't imagine who would want to follow her – except that the police hadn't caught the man known as Red. Could he possibly be watching the house, waiting for his chance to attack them? He'd made no move to harm Rose, but of course he would be more interested in Luke and perhaps Peter. Her husband was vulnerable in that chair, or at least most folk would think so if they didn't know him. Rose knew how resourceful he was and was not as anxious as she would have been otherwise. He'd saved her from attack once, though he'd fallen to the ground afterwards and might have suffered serious injury had Ted not turned up.

Rose considered whether she should alert Beattie's husband Ted to the fact that they might have a dangerous man lurking outside their house, but she knew Peter wouldn't be happy for her to do that; he'd told her they must face up to Red themselves if he turned up and caused trouble.

'We don't want to ask Ted all the time,' he'd said with a little frown. 'He's been a good friend and he wouldn't object – but I'd rather tackle this brute myself, Rose. If he tries to attack any of us, I'll use my pistol. Considering that he is wanted for murder, rape and attempted rape as well as the kidnap of a young boy, I think that any court would consider that reasonable force.'

Rose remembered his words and held her nerve.

She knew Peter could shoot straight, having accompanied him to the shooting range and watched him score bull's-eye after bull's-eye. Yet she found herself watching anxiously for the return of the man she loved and the young boy she already thought of as her son.

CHAPTER 46

Sally had looked at Terry in wonder, her heart seeming to stand still as he recounted his tale of seeing her children return home and of the garage where they now lived.

'Constable Jones insists you have to come to London with me to claim them, Betty love,' he told her. 'He says the folk who are looking after them are good people – and the man looked decent enough. The children were smart and clean and looked well.'

She nodded, still bemused and shocked, because she'd hardly expected him to bring the news so quickly. She'd even wondered if she'd made the children up and thought he might be annoyed she'd sent him on a wild goose chase – but here he was and he was telling her that her children were safe and well.

'You've seen them?' she said breathlessly, unable to take more in for the moment. 'But they wouldn't let you bring them back to me . . .'

'The police officer insisted you must go and explain what happened yourself.'

'Do I have to?' she asked fearfully. 'Supposing they don't believe me?' She was trembling so much that Terry put his arms around her and held her. Her first reaction was to shrink away but then something comforting in his smell or his person stopped her and she stood quietly, letting his strength and kindness soothe her until she was breathing more easily and her fear was almost gone. She looked up at him. 'Will you come with me?'

'Of course,' he said instantly and smiled, and she felt the warmth of it fill her and chase away the darkness that lingered inside her head. 'If you want me, Betty, love, I'll always be here for you – as a friend, as a husband, as both if you want . . .'

She half-nodded, not really sure what she felt or thought, except that he made her feel safe. A small smile tugged at the corners of her mouth.

'I'd feel better if you were there.' She hesitated, then said, 'Did you say my name was Betty?'

'Betty Stewart,' Terry told her. 'Your husband Tony was killed at sea at few years back, love, and you've had it hard ever since. The police officer seemed to think you might have been attacked by a man they're searching for – a real bad type by the sound of it. He has red hair and folk call him Red because of it. He used to be a seaman and is a foreigner.'

Betty stared at him. His words meant nothing but she felt a cold tingle at the nape of her neck, a return of fear. Reaching for Terry's hand, she held it tightly. 'You won't leave me alone there?'

'No, that I shan't,' Terry said stoutly. 'If I have my way, I'll be bringing you and the kids home to Ely.

To Jane's house for a start – but perhaps one day you'll all live with me as my family . . .'

Betty nodded again. She thought what he was saying sounded right, though she couldn't think it through yet or what it might mean to her and the children she'd missed so deeply even when she couldn't remember them.

'In time, Terry,' she promised, only vaguely aware of what she was saying, 'but we must look after Jane too.'

'Aye, we'll do that,' he said. 'You can still cook and clean for her and we'll make sure she's always looked after and never lonely – but you know she has quite a few friends.'

Betty agreed. Jane knew everyone who lived near the river, and all the shopkeepers kept their best for her under the counter. The butcher halfway up Forehill always had a lovely piece of meat that just happened to be cheaper than it should be, and the grocers kept the best produce for Jane. She had the first of the new potatoes in spring from a neighbour's garden and the tender garden peas straight off the vine, so she'd told Betty.

'I get lovely little tomatoes from Fred's greenhouse before we can get them in the shops – and they smell wonderful; it's having them straight off the vine that makes them so sweet and have such a gorgeous smell.'

Jane would never be lonely, and Betty would never desert her – but perhaps there was a future with Terry. It was just too soon to be sure. All Betty knew for sure was that he made her feel safe and secure and if she got her children back it would be because of him. Without him at her side, she couldn't even have attempted the return to London to fetch them. She didn't even have enough money for her fare, let alone the children's too, to come back here.

Constable Jones looked long and hard at Betty Stewart when the couple presented themselves at the police station that January day. It was Betty right enough, he knew her instantly, but she was different. The old Betty had been tired, harassed and grieving but she'd been strong and able to fight her corner. She had stood on her own two feet, not asking or accepting help from any of the well-meaning folk who had tried to help her. This woman looked a bit lost and turned constantly to her companion, looking for reassurance and help.

Fortunately, he seemed the dependable type. If the man had been cocksure or flashy, Steve would have refused to take them round to the garage – though he had a feeling that Terry knew the way. He'd come and shown them that Betty was alive, as requested, but there was a sense of strength there – he reminded Steve a bit of Betty's husband but he was shorter, stockier and a man who wouldn't stray many miles from his home city of Ely. He had confessed that it was only the second time he'd ever been to London and, by the look in his eyes, he wasn't planning on returning unless it proved necessary.

'I'll come with you, Mrs Stewart – and you, sir. You'll come with us?'

'Yes, of course. I'm here to look after Betty's interests – to make sure she gets treated as she ought.'

'Yes, I understand that,' Steve replied. 'My colleague has alerted Jeff Marshall and he kept the children home from school today so we'll go there together and sort this business out. I daresay he'll be upset; he's fond of the kids – especially Tim.'

'Right. We can understand that,' Terry said, 'but Betty is not at fault here and I won't have her blamed. Whatever happened to her made her forget everything, but deep down she never stopped loving her children – and as soon as she remembered their names, she asked me how she could find them.'

'And you came to search for them – what seemed an impossible job made easy because you saw a poster for a missing woman at the railway station.'

Steve nodded. The poster at the station applied to the murdered woman, of whom they still had no details. Betty was lucky that she'd had good friends to take her in and help her rediscover herself – but the woman Jeff had paid to have buried, because he'd thought it was Betty, was still unnamed.

'I'll take you round now, it's not far.'

Terry nodded and Steve knew that he'd discovered where the children were for himself. Well, that proved he was a decent chap in Steve's book, because he could have just grabbed them and gone. Though if he'd done that the police would have had no option but to set a search in motion and take the children into care. This way it was legal and it could all end happily – except that it would be damned hard for Jeff and Margaret Marshall.

*

Jeff saw them coming. He shut the garage door and went through to the house, calling to the children. They came running, looking at him anxiously. He hadn't told them anything in case it was a false tale but now he knew with his own eyes that it was true enough. Betty was alive and looking better than she had for a long while – rested and decently dressed.

'There's someone to see you two,' he said and smiled, putting on a brave face for their sake. 'No need to look anxious, Tim – it's wonderful news.' He heard the rattle of his front-door knocker. 'Do you want to answer that, Tim? I think you'll find it is for you and Jilly.'

Tim glanced at him uncertainly. Jeff took Jilly's hand and went behind him, watching carefully as Tim opened the door and then just stood there staring for several seconds before turning to look at Jeff.

'It's – it's Mum . . .' he said uncertainly.

'Mummy!' Jilly screamed and rushed past him, flinging herself at her mother crying and screaming all at once, half in emotional disbelief and half in delight. Betty bent down and scooped her up, hugging her and kissing her, repeating her name over and over again as she embraced her. And then her eyes went past her to rest on the young boy.

'Jilly, my darling. How I've missed you!' Betty's tears welled over as she was reunited with the daughter she clearly remembered. 'Tim . . .?' She sounded uncertain now, anxious, as he just stared for a moment. 'Tim – I-I'm back for you . . .'

'Mum,' he said. 'Where have you been?'

'I've been ill,' she said and looked at the man with her. He nodded and held her arm reassuringly. 'Something bad happened to me and I lost my memory. It started coming back in little bits, but seeing you standing there it all came flooding back. I was attacked by a dreadful man and afterwards, when I came to myself, it was dark in my mind and I couldn't remember anything although I kept thinking about you and Jilly, only I didn't know who or where you were until just before Christmas . . .'

'You forgot us?' Tim's voice and eyes were accusing. 'I thought you loved us.'

'I did – I do,' Betty said and tears ran down her cheeks. 'You and Jilly were the first thing that came back to me, but I couldn't remember where you lived, and I wasn't sure . . . Please forgive me for leaving you. I am so sorry . . . but I couldn't help it . . .' She looked hopelessly at her companion.

'It's all right, love,' he said and looked at Jeff. 'May we come in? Betty is struggling with all this and she could do with a sit down and a cup of tea – and I'll try to explain to the lad.'

'Who are you?' Tim asked. 'Why are you here?'

'I am a friend of your mother and I'm here to look after her – and to take you and your sister back to Ely with us.'

'No!' Tim turned and walked back into Jeff's sitting room. Everyone else trooped after him. Tim stood with feet apart, looking at his mother and Terry with angry, hostile eyes. 'I'm staying here with Jeff. He's been good to us – took us in when we were near starving. I don't want to go to Ely, wherever that is.'

340

'Tim, you can't mean that!' Betty said, looking at him with hurt eyes. 'You're my son. I love you, I want you to come home with me. I know things were hard after your dad died – and before I was hurt, but they'll be better in future. I promise you. And I am truly sorry that for a while I forgot you both but my wedding ring was missing – that man must have taken it when I lay unconscious – and I didn't even know I was married. It wasn't my f—'

'You're sorry – until the next time you go off and leave us,' Tim said, his face set stubbornly. 'I'm staying here with Aunt Margaret and Uncle Jeff.'

'You can't decide things like that, Tim,' Constable Jones told him seriously. 'It's up to your mum where you live – the law says so. She really couldn't help what happened.'

'I don't care! I'm not going.'

'Well, I want to be with Mummy,' Jilly said clinging to her and glaring at her brother. 'You've got to come with us, Tim. You're my brother.'

Tim looked at them stonily. 'You go with her if you want,' he said and sat on the settee. 'If you make me go with you, I'll run away and come back here.'

'Tim, don't you love me now?' Betty asked plaintively and for a moment something flickered in Tim's eyes though he didn't speak, crossed his arms over his chest.

Jeff looked at him. 'Your mum has the right, Tim. I've loved having you, son, and I'm sorry – but she does have the right to take you and I can't stop her, even though it hurts to lose you.'

'No.' Betty's voice was firm and strong and she

looked more like the woman Jeff remembered. 'No, I shan't force him to come, Mr Marshall. Are you prepared to give him a home still?'

'Yes, of course,' Jeff said, looking at her uncertainly. She looked and sounded like her old self but she was suggesting something the old Betty would never have done. She was suggesting that she would give up her son if it was what he wanted and needed. 'Are you sure? I was going to foster him officially – with a view to adoption had you never returned, but he's your son, Betty.'

'Yes, and I want him to be happy.' She put Jilly down and went to where Tim was sitting, squashing down next to him. 'Look at me, Tim – is this what you truly want? I know you're angry with me and perhaps I deserve it, but I do love you.'

'I don't want to come with you,' Tim said. 'London is my home and I want to stay here. I want to learn to look after cars the way Uncle Jeff does and to drive them when I'm older.' He looked at her steadily and his eyes lost some of their hostility. 'It will take me a while to forgive you – I'm not like Jilly. One day me and Jeff will come and visit . . .' He looked for confirmation to Jeff, who nodded but didn't smile or say anything. 'I'll live with Uncle Jeff and maybe I'll visit sometimes but this is my home now.'

'All right, my darling,' Betty said and her voice trembled, but she didn't cry even when Terry moved towards her in protest. It was all clear in her mind now. Everything had come rushing in since the first moment she saw her children. 'No, Terry. Tim is like his dad – it's his pride. Tony didn't forgive easily. I won't compel him to come. Tim must do whatever he wants.' She looked at her son with eyes of love. 'You will always be welcome to stay with us. I'll leave my address and I'll write to you, send you things – and when you're ready, you can visit me and Jilly.'

Tim nodded, watching as she stood up.

'Give me a few minutes,' Jeff said. He went and packed a small case with Jilly's clothes then brought it down to the sitting room. Then, with one backward glance filled with meaning, they left, Tim's mother holding Jilly's hand and her companion carrying the case, Constable Jones trailing behind with a little shake of his head.

'Bye, Mum,' Tim said just before she went through the sitting room door. 'Be happy.'

'You too,' she replied and went out quickly, letting the front door shut with a little bang.

Jeff sat down next to Tim, looking at him anxiously. 'Are you certain this is what you want, Tim? Don't let pride or anger stop you going if you want – your mum won't mind.'

'I want to be here with you,' Tim said, and gave him a wobbly smile. 'I'm glad she's alive – and we will visit them sometimes, please, but I love you too – and Aunt Margaret. I want to stay here if you want me.'

'More than anything else I can think of,' Jeff said and suddenly hugged him. 'You're my boy, my Tim, and I should miss you like hell if you left.'

'Good!' Tim grinned at him. 'I know it wasn't her fault, though. I'll write and tell her another day.'

'You do that, son,' Jeff said. 'You do that when you're ready.'

'Yes, I see.' Matron nodded her understanding when Jeff told her what had happened. 'Well, that is a nuisance for you – though of course we must be pleased that Betty isn't dead.' She thought for a moment. 'I see no reason why you should not sign the papers to foster Tim, as before; all the legal bits are already in place. Adoption would be more difficult – you would have to get Betty's agreement and signature.'

'Yes, I thought it might be the case,' Jeff agreed. 'I don't think we need to worry about that for the moment. Tim wants to stay with us for now, but he might change his mind in time and decide to go to his mother. I shan't stand in his way whatever he wants. Margaret was a little upset when she got home from work and discovered Jilly had gone, but we knew it could happen – and for the moment we still have Tim.'

'Why do you think he chose to stay rather than go with her?'

'It might have been anger at her just turning up like that, or emotional turmoil at seeing her so suddenly. Perhaps she should have written and prepared him or perhaps I should have said more. I thought the surprise might make him happy, but it didn't.'

'And he hasn't said anything since?'

'Nothing much – except that it wasn't her fault and he'll visit her sometime. I think he's too upset to talk about it much.'

'Probably best to let him come out of it in his own time.' Matron looked thoughtful. 'It must have been a complete shock to him, her turning up just like that.'

'Jilly just went straight to her and clung to her. She didn't so much as glance at me, though I saw her look at Tim in a bit of a strange way. She relies on him a lot and she'll be sure to miss him.'

'Perhaps – perhaps not,' Matron said. 'Children are resilient. She clung to him because her mother had gone, but now she has her back she'll cling like a limpet to her.'

'Well, I just hope she'll be well cared for – her companion looked a solid dependable sort, so perhaps Betty has fallen on her feet at last.'

CHAPTER 47

'What a little sweetheart,' Jane said when Betty brought Jilly to her. She took her on her lap and Jilly gave her a kiss. 'That's right, kiss Nana Jane.'

Jilly obliged and promptly curled up and went to sleep on her chest. Betty looked and smiled at her friend. 'She's tired out; she fretted for Tim after we left the house, though she was excited by the train journey and Terry bought her some sweets and a colouring book and pencils at the station. She was watching everything but then she kept asking where Tim was and cried when I told her he wasn't coming yet.'

'She'd worn herself out with excitement,' Jane said. 'Where is Terry?'

'He said he would leave us to settle and come tomorrow to see how things are.'

Jane nodded. 'He's a sensible man. You could look a lot further and do a lot worse.'

'I know.' Betty bit her bottom lip. 'I remember everything now, Jane. When we got to Button Street and then Marshall's garage, it all started to fall into place. I knew I was near where I'd lived and then the minute I saw the two children in Jeff Marshall's house and my Tim called me Mum and looked at me with his dad's eyes, I knew what had happened to me. All of it came flooding back . . .'

'So, what have you done about it?' Jane asked, her shrewd eyes on Betty's face.

'On the train, I told Terry everything so he knows I was attacked, beaten, and – and raped. I remembered the face of the man who attacked me and left me for dead. Terry rang that police constable in London and told him all I remembered. Some bits are missing, I think, about what the man did to me, but most of it is clear in my mind.'

'Then the police will know who to look for.'

'They're already searching for him,' Betty said. 'Another woman was attacked and murdered and they believe it was the same man. He's called Red because of his red beard and hair and apparently a young lad saw the attack. Anyway, Red seems pretty good at avoiding the police so I'm glad I'm not still in London. I should be in fear of my life. Here, I feel safe.' She smiled at Jane. 'I'll never be able to thank you enough for taking me in the way you did . . .'

'All I want is to see you happy, lass,' Jane told her. 'I'm sorry your boy wouldn't come, Betty love, but you mustn't give up hope. He'll probably come after he's thought it over.'

'Perhaps,' Betty sighed. 'He looked just like his father when he sat down and crossed his arms. I knew there was no moving him, so I didn't try. He has the right to be happy and to live with his friends if he wants – after all, he didn't have much of a life with me the last few months or so before I disappeared. He has a new home, a new life and he was wearing long trousers – a proper grown-up he looked.'

'Perhaps he had to grow up after you disappeared, Betty. It must have been hard for him as the oldest.'

'Yes. He looked after Jilly until Jeff stepped in. Constable Jones told us that much – and I know my Tim. He earned a few shillings doing small jobs and he always put some in my housekeeping pot. That is the kind of boy he is – thoughtful and kind.'

'It wasn't kind to refuse to come with you . . .' Jane suggested, but Betty shook her head.

'That was my fault for just turning up. I should have written to him first, given him a chance to think about it, but I wasn't completely sure, Jane. I didn't know the children were really mine until the moment Jeff Marshall's door opened. Even when Terry told me that he'd found them, it was still unreal – only when I saw my Tim, did I know who I was and then, of course, I remembered it all . . .'

Tim wasn't sure why he'd been so angry with his mother. Until the moment she turned up at the door with no warning, he would've given anything to have her back. But the moment she smiled at him and said hello, he'd felt the fury rush through him and he'd wanted to punish her for leaving him. Yes, he'd heard the explanations and he knew in his heart she wasn't to blame, but it didn't take away the anger, nor did it make him feel he could trust her ever again. He'd loved her so much and when he thought her dead had grieved deeply inside, but the way she'd just turned up made him feel that she didn't care about what it had cost him and Jilly.

Jilly was too young to think things through. She'd seen Mum, rushed at her and clung to her, just glad to have her back. Tim wished he could have done that too, but he couldn't. Perhaps there was something wrong in him but he felt she didn't deserve to be forgiven just like that – even though that was a bit unfair. She hadn't asked to be attacked or to lose her memory, but why had she not gone to the police straight away? They would've known her, brought her home after a stay in hospital, and her children would never have had to endure the agony of a missing mother and eviction, hiding from the council for fear of being taken away. She'd run away and left them – and although he knew that wasn't a fair accusation, it had stayed in his mind.

Could she be trusted to look after Jilly? Tim felt a bit guilty at abandoning his sister to a mother who might not be capable of caring for her – but Jilly had wanted to be with her and he'd let her go. Afterwards, when he looked at the doll's pram she'd left behind, he'd felt the guilt.

'Jilly wanted that so much,' he'd told Jeff.

'We'll take it down for her in the car,' Jeff said, 'and the cot you gave her and the other things. I'll close one Saturday and we'll take a trip up there, stay at a hotel one night and come back on Sunday. We'll make it a day out for all of us.'

Tim nodded solemnly. 'She would like that,' he'd said, not sure whether he meant his mother or Jilly.

He hadn't changed his mind about staying in London. It was his home and he would hate to change schools and to lose the chance of becoming Jeff's apprentice. Tim liked his life and, although he was torn because his sister had gone with his mother, he did not regret his choice. The anger had cooled now but his resolution had not wavered. Much as he loved his mum and Jilly, he wanted to stay here.

'Well,' Margaret said to her husband when he told her what Matron had said, 'I think you can be sure Tim wants to stay but I agree we should take him to visit one weekend and let him see what it is like there.'

'What if he changes his mind when he sees her again?'

'Then he will,' Margaret said and smiled at him. 'We'll still have each other, love – and perhaps he will still stay with us . . .'

'Yes, you're right.' Jeff reached for her. 'I'm right fond of that boy, love – but I've got my golden girl and that's the main thing.'

Margaret smiled and hugged him. She knew he loved Tim and she was fond of the lad, too, but if he wanted to return to his mother it was his choice.

CHAPTER 48

Rose glanced over her shoulder uneasily. It was the second time she'd felt that she'd been followed, and even though nothing had happened the previous time, she still had that sense of danger. As she approached her home, she saw one of her neighbours and waved to him. He crossed the road to join her and they talked for a while about her husband and her work at the Rosie.

'Well, I'll be seeing you,' he said. 'It was nice having a chat.'

'Would you walk up to the door with me, Mr Smith?' she asked. 'I think I've been followed home – and this is the second time recently.'

'Where?' He swung round, looking, but shook his head. 'I can't see the beggar, Rose – but I'll see you inside safely anyway.' He accompanied her to the door and waited until she unlocked it. 'You should telephone the police – alert them to what's happening.'

'Yes, I shall,' Rose agreed. She smiled at him. 'Thank you so much.'

'That's all right – glad to be of help.' He went off

whistling as she closed and locked the door behind herself.

Rose decided to telephone the local station, blessing the fact that Peter had insisted they needed the telephone put in just in case he was wanted at work. It was an added protection and Rose felt better as she spoke to Sergeant Macintyre.

'I'll send one of our officers round immediately,' he said. 'If it's the man we're after we might get lucky.' He hesitated, then, 'You might like to know that we've discovered who the murdered woman was. She was one of the local prostitutes who works by the canal. Her friend saw her go with a punter – and her description matches that of the man we're looking for, so it seems we were on the right track. We just have to find him.'

Rose frowned as she replaced the receiver. The police knew who their mysterious victim was at last because a witness had come forward, but they were no nearer to finding the culprit. Red must either be good at disguising himself or have a lot of convenient hiding places.

Constable Jones came to the door fifteen minutes later. 'We've got three of us searching the area, Rose. If we don't find him, we'll put a guard outside your house all night.'

'Thank you,' she said gratefully. 'I'm sure it must be him. I'm not given to fancies and I'm certain I was followed on at least two occasions – but he hasn't approached me or tried to get in yet.'

'Perhaps there were too many people about for him to try anything in daylight. These bullies are often cowards deep down and won't take any risks

– he seems to attack women or young boys, despite his boasts of what he'll do.'

'I'll be glad when you catch him,' Rose said with a little shiver.

'You and me both,' he said and nodded grimly. 'He attacked my wife and I shan't forget that. If your Luke hadn't thrown that stone and hit him, anything might have happened.'

'Yes, you're right to worry,' Rose said. 'He is a danger to any woman while he's at large, and to others too.'

She made sure the door was locked after Constable Jones went on his way and when Peter and Luke came home, she told them. Peter frowned and went to the window.

'I thought I saw several police around so he'll be long gone for the moment – but I don't like the thought that he follows you home. I think we need to come and pick you up after work in future and bring you home.'

'That takes you away from your work,' Rose protested. 'You can't run after me all the time, Peter.'

'Who else should I run after?' he asked and raised his eyebrows. 'You're my wife and your safety means everything to me – and to Luke. We insist, don't we, Luke?'

'Yes, Doc,' Luke said and grinned at her. 'Two to one, Aunt Rose. You can't walk home alone while that beast is free. We're not having him attack you.'

Rose looked at him and then smiled. How could she resist in the face of two determined and devoted admirers?

'I give in,' she said. 'If they haven't caught him by morning, I'll let you drive me to and from work, Peter.'

Rose woke with a start. It was dark but she could see a tall, dark shape by the bedroom window and caught her breath. She could see that Peter was peering out into the garden without putting on a light.

'What is happening?' she whispered. 'Is someone out there?'

'Yes, I'm almost certain I heard a window break a few moments ago. I'm going to wake Luke and then go downstairs. I want you to stay here, Rose.'

'Can you manage?' she asked and heard his intake of breath. 'I'm sorry. I shouldn't have asked but it isn't long since you managed to walk across the room . . .' She hesitated, then, 'Let me go and ring the police.'

'And have him attack you? No, Rose. I'll take my gun with me.'

'All right.' Rose gave in, though she knew she would follow him to make certain he was managing. Her heart was racing and she felt fear gnawing inside her, because he could be in terrible danger.

Yes, he had the gun and if he fired it instantly it might save him – save them all – but if he hesitated that evil man would be on him.

Breathing deeply, she listened for Peter's steps as he went quietly down the hall, hearing the creak as he trod on the loose floorboard. If Red had managed to get into the house, he would surely hear it and be warned . . .

Getting softly from the bed, she slipped on her dressing robe and went barefoot from the bedroom. Hearing a sound behind her, she spun round and saw Luke coming down the stairs. Rose motioned for him to go back but he shook his head. She saw he was armed with the poker from his bedroom and he looked grimly determined as he went by her, preceding her along the hall. A smile touched her lips; it seemed the men of her family were determined to protect her.

She heard movement in the kitchen and followed Luke towards the noise. Neither of them had trod on the squeaky floorboard so whoever was there wouldn't know they were coming. Just as Luke opened the door, the light snapped on and Rose could see clearly into the large room. A shiver went through her as she saw the huge red-haired man facing Peter with a snarl. The thought that Peter must shoot immediately became words and she yelled, 'Shoot him!'

'Damn you, bitch! You're like all the rest, taking unfair advantage and treating me wrong – and I'll show you. I'll show all the bastards they can't treat me like dirt!' Red's face twisted with bitterness as he lunged towards her and she jerked back.

As she did, Red flung Peter sideways to the floor. Her husband grunted in pain and lay still as the gun went skittering across the kitchen floor. Afterwards, Rose was never quite sure what happened, but as Red went to clobber Peter with some kind of club, Luke flung the poker at him, making him roar in rage. Luke dropped to his knees, grabbed the gun and fired. The sound was deafening in the kitchen and the sound of Red's scream was terrifying. Rose looked and saw that because of the angle from which Luke had fired, the bullet had struck Red in his groin and the agony was written all over his face as he rolled about clutching at himself, bleeding profusely.

Peter was on his feet again and he touched Luke, who seemed frozen in shock at what he'd done. 'Give me the gun, Luke,' he said gently and took it from his trembling hand. 'It's all right. You did what you had to do.'

Turning to Rose, he said, 'Get my bag, love – and then ring the police.'

Numbly, Rose did as he asked. She watched as he took a syringe from his bag and filled it with a drug she knew would render the injured man unconscious. 'Can I help hold him?' she asked, but even as she did so, she saw that Red had stopped moving, his face a ghastly putty colour as his lifeblood drained away. Peter had the needle in his thigh before she turned away to do as he'd asked to telephone for help. She asked for the police first and spoke to the night sergeant, who promised to send men instantly, and then she rang the central London hospital and asked if they could send an ambulance. She was told they had none available but would send one in an hour or so if she thought it necessary. Biting back an angry retort, she said it was an emergency and returned to the kitchen.

She found Peter binding up the unconscious Red's wound with Luke assisting him with bandages and pads of lint. The boy was still very pale, but he was doing all he could to help Peter, his eyes wide and scared.

'He'll probably live,' Peter said and stood up, using Luke as a prop as he walked to his chair and sat heavily, clearly exhausted. 'And he has only himself to blame.' Now he was looking at Luke, serious and yet gentle, just as he was with patients who were very ill. 'Now, young man, stop blaming yourself. You did what I should have done the minute I saw him. He broke into our home with the intention of causing harm to you, Rose, and me. Had you not been so quick to act, he would have killed me and then you and Rose. So, you acted in defence of us all – and that is something you must accept and not let his pain upset you.'

'If I'd known what it would do, I might not have shot him,' Luke admitted and Peter nodded grimly.

'I hesitated for just that reason, Luke – and look what nearly happened. If he'd got the gun, he might have killed us all.'

Luke nodded, accepting his words as the truth. 'Yes, I know. It scared me when I saw what I'd done – but I had to, and he deserved it for all the wicked things he's done.'

'Yes, he did,' Peter agreed. 'I prefer to save life rather than take it, but even if this miserable wretch lives, he will certainly hang for murder. He's been identified as the killer of that prostitute and, I'm told, he may be wanted in Sweden for similar crimes.'

Luke nodded. 'Will the police arrest me for what I did?'

'You?' Peter shook his head. 'You didn't do anything, Luke. It was an accident.' He glanced at his wife. 'You saw what happened, Rose – he knocked me down and as I fell the gun went off. It was a pure accident and I'd warned him not to attack me, warned him that I would shoot. He was the aggressor not I. Besides, a man in my position is entitled to protect himself and his family.'

Luke stared. 'But—'

'But nothing, Luke. You were still upstairs where you should have been.' Peter's eyes met Rose's. 'That is just the way it happened – isn't it, love?'

'Yes, of course it is.' She went to Luke and embraced him. 'No one will blame Peter for what happened and we don't want a shadow hanging over you for the rest of your life. We three know the truth and we know what a brave and selfless thing you did to protect us. It was a lucky shot because, had you missed, Red would've killed us all.'

Luke swallowed hard. 'Are you sure it's the right thing to do, sir?' he asked, looking directly at Peter. 'I am prepared to take my punishment.'

'In a just world you'd get a medal,' Peter said, 'but I know how some police officers can be, and while Constable Jones would understand, he might feel obliged to report it. I can look anyone in the eye and tell them it was an accident, because you just got lucky. You're not a trained shooter and you didn't intend to harm him, only to protect us. So, go upstairs to bed. Rose will bring cocoa up and talk to you and I'll talk to you after the police have been – and, please, stop feeling guilty.'

Luke rushed to him and threw his arms around him.

'I just wanted to protect you!' he said, hugging him. Peter bent his head and kissed Luke's hair.

'I love you, son, and I'm grateful to you,' he said. 'You did the right thing – but it has to be our secret.'

Luke allowed Rose to take him back to bed and tuck him up. She went back down to the kitchen and made cocoa, taking Luke a cup up just as she heard the sound of the police arriving.

'Drink this and don't worry, Luke,' she told him. 'Peter knows what he's doing and it is all for the best. A lot of people would thank you if they knew.'

Luke nodded and smiled at her. She left him to settle as best he could, knowing that he'd have a few tears and move on – what he'd done had been instinctive and brave, but still shocking.

Returning to the kitchen she discovered that Constable Jones was one of the three officers who had attended. One of them was busily writing down all that Peter said.

'So, you didn't consciously fire the gun then, sir?' the young officer asked, pausing to lick his pencil.

'I threatened him with it, told him I would fire if he didn't get out of my house at once. I've only just started walking again, officer, and it was the only way I could defend myself and my family from a dangerous man.'

'So how did it happen?'

'He knocked me sideways and I fell but as I did so, my finger must have pressed the trigger – which is why I caught him in such a vulnerable spot . . .'

The officer bent his body, trying to see how it had happened, looking puzzled, but Constable Jones nodded.

'It's perfectly plain what happened here, Constable Smith. Doctor Peter and his family have been attacked before, so he was prepared to defend his family. I'd have done the same in his place – this man brought about his own fate. Also, Doctor Peter immediately tended to his injuries and saved his miserable life – which the hangman will probably end once he's been tried in a court of law.' He looked at Peter. 'You acted perfectly properly, sir. A man in your position with a family to protect has to have some sort of deterrent. This man broke into your house with intent to maim and kill, so you acted in self-defence.'

Constable Smith scribbled hastily. 'What about an ambulance, sir?' he asked.

'The London couldn't send one for an hour,' Rose told him. 'I phoned them immediately.'

'Perfectly proper, as you see,' Constable Jones said. 'We have the Black Maria here, sir. We could get him in the back of that between us and take him to the hospital for you.'

'I should be grateful,' Peter said. 'We'd like to get this place straight and have a brandy for the shock.'

'Yes, of course.' Constable Jones was clearly in charge. He had his two colleagues carry out the unconscious Red to the police vehicle and once they left the room, Constable Jones looked at Peter. 'Whatever really happened here, you acted within your rights, sir. That man is a menace to the public and, if I were in charge, I'd give you a medal.' His eyes went to Rose. 'Or you,' he added, clearly believing that it might have been Rose that fired the shot. He smiled at her. 'Given the chance, I might have done it myself . . .' As he left the kitchen, Peter looked at Rose.

'Thank goodness for Constable Jones,' he said and sighed. 'How is Luke?'

'A bit tearful,' she said and he nodded. 'I'll clean up this mess,' she glanced at the blood on the floor, 'and then I'll get us that brandy . . .'

'I can manage to get the brandy,' Peter told her. 'I think we can both do with it and the sooner that stain is gone, the sooner we can all breathe again.' He nodded at the bloodstained floor.

They drank the brandy and then Rose fetched a mop and washed the floor, using disinfectant and soap. The window that Red had broken to get in was hanging at an ungainly angle and Peter managed to tie it up so that it would hold until the morning. With Red in hospital and possibly fighting for his life, they were safe enough.

'I'll get someone to fix it in the morning,' Peter said and yawned. 'Well, we should try to get some sleep, Rose.'

'Are you all right?' she asked, going to him in concern. 'You thought about Luke's shock and mine – but it happened to you, too.'

'The only thing I feel is shame and self-annoyance because I didn't fire straight off,' Peter said. 'It was my job and my intention. I just hesitated one instant and if it hadn't been for that brave lad of ours . . .' He shook his head. 'It doesn't bear thinking of.'

'No, it doesn't,' she agreed. 'So, don't. Put this out of your mind, Peter. That man broke into our home and after what he did to Luke, I think he deserved what he got – and personally I don't care a jot if he dies, except that it would be easier for us if he lives.'

CHAPTER 49

'I want my dolly's pram,' Jilly said to her mother a few days after they had returned to Ely. 'It was my Christmas present from Uncle Jeff and it was lovely.'

'I didn't know about it,' Betty said. 'I'm sure we can get it for you, love. I'll ask Terry what's best to do when he comes later.'

Jilly nodded, then, 'When is Tim coming? I miss him.'

'So do I, darling,' Betty said, feeling a stab at her heart. 'But perhaps he will visit us soon.'

How she wished her son was here. Betty listened every day to the worsening news on the wireless. The war was not going well and the commentators talked of the possibility of invasion and that they would probably be soon bombed by the Germans.

London's East End was the powerhouse of Britain's industry, Westminster the seat of Government. If the bombing was bad in London, anything could happen to her child, and yet she knew in her heart Tim must decide for himself. His home with Jeff Marshall was a good one, and he had the chance for a good life, as long as they remained safe. She didn't have the right to demand anything from him after the way she'd left them to manage alone. Both Jane and Terry told her it wasn't her fault – but what kind of a mother would forget her children so completely? Betty felt guilt that she couldn't shift, no matter what anyone said to comfort her.

When she spoke to Terry about the pram, he said he would ring Jeff Marshall. 'I could go up and fetch it. And the boy suggested he might—'

She shook her head. 'Perhaps Jeff can send the pram,' she suggested. 'I don't want to put you to that trouble.'

Terry told her that it was no trouble, but in the event when he rang Jeff, he let him know that they would be coming to Ely the following weekend.

'Tim said Jilly would be wanting her pram so we're bringing all her stuff in the car. My wife, Margaret, will be with us and we'll stay at a hotel overnight – I've booked in with the Lamb – and if Tim wants to stay overnight with his mother, he can. It's his choice what he does.'

Terry had thanked him and Betty had indulged in a flurry of cooking and cleaning, making things her son had always enjoyed when she could afford them. Here, at Jane's, she could give him a lovely shepherd's pie and a treacle tart. They had been his favourites and she hoped it would make him smile.

Tim was excited and nervous by turn as they packed the car and set off. The journey took several hours and it was late in the afternoon when they finally arrived, after stopping for a picnic lunch Margaret had packed to give Jeff a rest from the driving.

Ely seemed such a quiet, quaint place after London. There was a magnificent church Jeff said was a famous cathedral and a lot of old buildings, and a long river that wound through the city. It was close to the river and not far from the railway station and the cottage that his mother lived in with her friend Jane.

'It would be easy for you to come by yourself as you get older,' Jeff said, pointing out how close the station was to the riverside house. 'But I'm not suggesting you have to, Tim. You'll make your own decisions – and I'll accept whatever you want.'

Tim nodded and thanked him. His stomach clenched with nerves as he approached the old-fashioned cottage. It looked centuries old, with whitewashed walls and a low, sloping thatched roof. Inside, it smelled of lavender polish and he smiled as he remembered it was the kind his mother liked when she could afford it.

Jilly threw herself at him as he went in and then at Margaret and Uncle Jeff, who hugged and kissed her. Her things were unpacked and she was all smiles. Tim was silent as he was introduced to his mother's friend Jane – or Granny Jane, as his sister called her.

'Nice to meet you, ma'am.' He returned her greeting formally. 'Thank you for having us.'

'Your mother has cooked a nice tea for you all,' Jane said and shook hands with him and then Margaret and Jeff. They were all smiling as they sat down to a lovely meal, which everyone enjoyed, including Tim. He thanked his mother for it afterwards.

'Your cooking is just as good as it always was,' he told her. 'I love your treacle tart.'

'Yes, I know,' Betty said. 'I'm glad you liked it.'

'We'll take ourselves off to the hotel,' Jeff said after they'd eaten. 'Tim will stay with you tonight and we'll be back to collect him in the morning.'

'What time?' Tim demanded instantly.

'Half past ten – it will give us plenty of time to get home, lad.'

Tim nodded. 'Thanks, Uncle Jeff. I'll be ready.' He looked at his mother when Margaret and Jeff had gone. 'I'm pleased to see you and Jilly – and to meet your friends – but I'll be going back with Uncle Jeff in the morning.'

'Yes, I understand that,' Betty replied, looking at him steadily. 'I'm not going to try and force you to stay, Tim.'

'If you did, I'd run away,' he said and it was clear that he meant it.

Betty blinked but did not cry, nor did she answer. Her son had a mind of his own and nothing she said or did would change it, she knew that.

Tim spent most of his visit playing with Jilly, helping with her puzzles, though he did have a walk by the river with Betty after breakfast the next day. Jilly had stayed in the warm with Granny Jane.

'You know you could stay if you wish?' Betty said as they walked. 'You will always be welcome here.'

'Even after you marry Terry?' Her son looked at her hard. 'You like him and I think you'll marry him one day. Dad wouldn't mind. He'd be glad you had someone to look after you – make sure nothing bad happens to you again.'

Betty's eyes stung with tears. 'How would you feel if I did marry him?'

'I don't mind – he seems all right,' Tim said and smiled at her. 'I'm not angry with you now, Mum – and I do love you, but I still don't want to live here with you. I'll visit – but my life is in London with Jeff and Margaret.'

'All right, love, if it's what you want.' Betty smothered a sigh, accepting the inevitable. 'But if the Germans start bombing London and you're scared, you could come and stay with me, all of you.'

Tim grinned at her. 'Thanks, I'll tell them – but it will take more than a few bombs from old Hitler to make us run away. Jeff was in the last war and he's not bothered so I'm not either.'

Betty nodded. 'Your father would say the same,' she said, smiling at him. 'But don't forget that you have a home here if you need it.'

Tim nodded and then went to her, putting his arms around her and giving her a quick hug. 'I'll never forget you,' he said and she felt a sting of self-reproach because she had forgotten him so completely for a time.

Margaret looked at Jeff as they settled down with a cup of tea back at home. Tim had thanked them both and gone up to bed. He said he wanted to study for a school test before he went to sleep and neither of them questioned it.

'How do you think he is?' she asked her husband. 'He didn't talk much on the way home except to say that Jilly would be happy now she has her things. Apparently, he's told her that he'll send her cards and little gifts and she was quite content to let him come away.'

'Jilly is being spoiled by her new granny, her soon-to-be stepfather and her mother. She clung to Tim because Betty was missing, but I think she'll settle soon enough.' Jeff frowned. 'Tim is different. He thinks things through and I'm pretty sure he knows exactly what he wants. When Betty disappeared like that, Tim had to be the big brother and take on too much responsibility. He learned to trust me – and I think that's why he chose to stay.'

Margaret's smooth forehead wrinkled. 'You mean he doesn't quite trust his mother?'

'He loves her, very much I imagine but, no, he doesn't trust her not to disappear. That is why he wanted to visit – to make certain that Jilly would be safe and looked after. It was his responsibility, you see.'

Margaret nodded, her puzzled frown clearing. 'So, he thinks that Jane and Terry will take care of her, even if his mother won't?'

'Yes, I believe so,' Jeff said, nodding to himself. 'He told me Terry was a good man, reminded him of his father – and he knew he would take good care of his mother and Jilly. He liked Jane, too. He says she is a nice person and he thanked her for looking after his mother when she was lost and ill.'

'He is a lovely lad,' Margaret said and smiled in content. 'I'm glad he stayed with us, Jeff.' She hesitated for a moment and then gave him a shy glance. 'You don't think he'll be upset if he has another little one to help care for in a few months?'

Jeff stared at her, clearly puzzled by her meaning and Margaret went to him, kneeling at his side where he sat and reaching for his hand. 'I hope you'll be pleased, love – but I'm pretty sure, even though it's very early days. I've always been so regular, you see, and I'm ten days overdue . . .'

Jeff's gaze narrowed and then, suddenly, the penny dropped. 'Are you sure? You think I'm going to be a father?'

'I do.' Margaret blushed then. 'Well, we have been quite enthusiastic in the bedroom . . .' she said and he gave a shout of laughter and jumped up, pulling her to her feet and hugging her.

'I never thought it would happen at my age – thought I was too old to have a child.'

'Never!' she said and laughed in delight at his triumph and pleasure. 'I can't be a 100 per cent certain, Jeff, but I've never been late before.'

'That's wonderful,' Jeff said, kissing her softly now. 'I couldn't be happier, Margaret. I thought I had everything when you married me and then Tim stayed – but this is an amazing bonus.' He smiled broadly. 'And no, Tim won't mind. I think he knows he has his place with us and nothing can change that.'

'If we're lucky we'll have a little girl,' Margaret said. 'Then we'll have one of each, though a boy would be fine.'

Jeff grinned. 'You want your little girl to dress up and take out and I've already got my boy to train and play football with in the street. We must be the luckiest pair on the planet.'

'Yes,' she said softly. 'It's what I feel too, as long as you don't feel it is too soon?'

'How could it be, love?' he said, looking at her softly. 'It's just another person for me to love and a bigger slice of happiness than before.'

CHAPTER 50

Luke had come to terms with what he'd done when he fired the gun at Red and wounded him in the groin. The hospital had brought him round and he was then charged with various crimes, to which Red had spat defiance at the police officer and vowed to get even with the bastard that shot him. He'd been formally arrested and, as soon as he was well enough, removed to a secure hospital within a prison, where he was recovering pending his trial.

Constable Jones had told them that he would be convicted of a string of crimes, including murder. 'The young woman who worked the streets with her murdered friend has identified him as being the punter she went off with, and we have the Swedish police wanting him for questioning. They say they have a cast-iron case and that he has committed a string of brutal attacks of rape plus murder over there. They want their chance to prosecute him and so he may stand trial there as he is one of their nationals.'

'As long as he doesn't get away with it,' Doctor Peter said looking grim.

'I doubt they'll let him slip through their net – and if they did, we'd demand he was sent back to us so that we could put him before our courts. He'll get what he deserves, Peter, be certain of that.'

'Good. He was a bitter man after what he considered injustice done to him and a menace to others.' Peter had frowned. 'And what of my actions against him?'

'As we thought, dismissed as necessary force in self-defence of your family. The wheels grind slowly, but you'll get an official letter to that effect soon.'

'That's it, then,' Doctor Peter told Luke when he'd got home from the club where he was learning to box and to defend himself without the use of a weapon. 'The police are closing the case as far as we're concerned – and Red may stand trial for his life in two countries.'

'It is what he deserves,' Luke said. 'I felt bad for a while, sir, for what I did, but I know that I had to do it, because otherwise he might have done terrible things to us all.'

Doctor Peter smiled. 'Yes, Luke. That is exactly right. So, we're all going to put it behind us and move on.'

Luke nodded and then looked at him anxiously. 'You can walk now, sir, far more than just a few steps. Will you still need me?'

'More than ever,' Doctor Peter told him. 'You know that the Germans will probably start to bomb us, don't you?'

'Yes – it'll be like the newsreels we've seen of the bombs falling in Warsaw when the Germans invaded

Poland, won't it? It looked as if the city was on fire . . .' Luke frowned. 'I know a lot of folk were hurt.'

'Yes, they were, Luke.'

'What if you're caught in an air raid?'

'Well, I can walk slowly but, in a crush, I'd never manage to reach the air-raid shelters and negotiate the steps without your help. Also, we're going to have a lot of sick people to treat, Luke. The docks will be an obvious target for the Luftwaffe and all those old houses and factories there will catch fire. I'm sure a lot of our patients will be caught on the streets with nowhere to shelter. We'll have casualties and sick people at the clinic. I'm going to be busy and that means you will be too.' Peter smiled at him. 'You will learn on the job. I'll teach you to treat burns and cuts so that by the time you train officially you will know more than any other student in your class. We'll study for other things sometimes so that the gaps in your education are filled, but by the time this war is over, you'll be nearly as good a doctor as I am.'

'Doctor?' Luke stared at him. 'Do you really think I'd make a doctor? I hoped to be a nurse at best.'

'And that's a good job and takes a lot of studying too,' Peter told him, 'but if you're half as bright as I believe, you'll make a damned fine doctor. Remember, you've got one of the best to teach you.' Luke would have to go to medical school to pass his exams but that would be a foregone conclusion by the time Peter had finished.

Luke grinned and nodded. 'I've got the very best,

sir,' he told him. 'You just wait, Doc, by next Christmas I'll know how to treat all kinds of things, because I'm going to grab the opportunity with both hands.'

'I know you will, Luke, and I'm very proud of you. I love you – as does Rose. You'll always be special to us. You came to us in time for Christmas, just like the best present we've ever had and, as far as we're concerned, we want you to stay forever.'

Luke nodded. Christmas had been a mixed one for him thanks to Red, but Rose and Doctor Peter had made it up to him and now he had everything he'd ever wanted.

'Yes, sir,' he said and grinned. 'I'll be here for next Christmas and all the ones that follow for the rest of my life.'

Luke had found his home, and though one day he might have a wife and family of his own, as Doctor Peter suggested, he and Rose would always be special and wherever they were would still be home to him.

Read more about Cathy Sharp's orphans whose compelling stories will tug at your heartstrings.

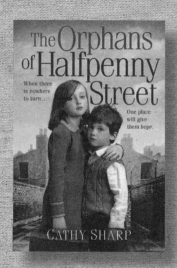

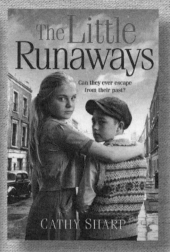

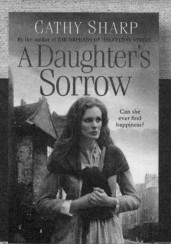

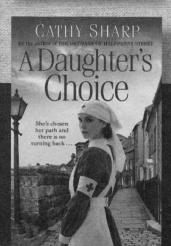

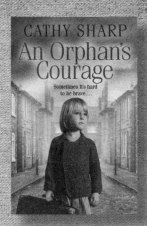

CATHY SHARP
An Orphan's Courage
Sometimes it's hard to be brave...

CATHY SHARP
The Girl in the Ragged Shawl
All she wants is a mother's love

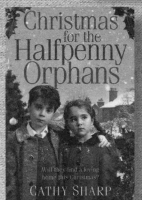

Christmas for the Halfpenny Orphans
Will they find a loving home this Christmas?
CATHY SHARP

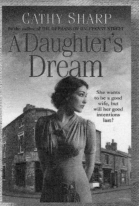

CATHY SHARP
By the author of THE ORPHANS OF HALFPENNY STREET
A Daughter's Dream
She wants to be a good wife, but will her good intentions last?

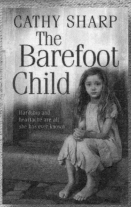

CATHY SHARP
THE Barefoot Child
Hardship and heartache are all she has ever known

CATHY SHARP
THE Winter Orphan
Will she ever find a loving home?

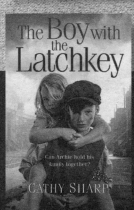

THE BOY with the Latchkey
Can Archie hold his family together?
CATHY SHARP

All available now.